The Tape Job

Elite Hockey Book 2

ALYS J. CLARKE

Cover Art by Tom Drake
Additional Art by Caroline Taylor
Editors: Ken Nicottii, AGM
Editing support: Lucy Lanceley
Proofreading: Stacey's Bookcorner Editing Service and Open Eye Editing
ISBN: 978-1-7384632-0-6
Independently Published First Edition: March 2024

Dedication

For JP, fans of British Ice Hockey, and the OG TIS Fans—you mean the world to me.

A Few Notes from the Author

This is a work of fiction. I have done my utmost to align the content with real British hockey; however, there may be differences, and this is intentional.

I purposefully haven't given the team a name. This is because I wanted any of my UK readers who are also hockey fans, to imagine it is their team, if they so wish.

I know not everyone will like Vicky, but just understand that we all handle death differently, and her reaction is akin to my own. Please forgive those of us who want to run away and hide.

As always, #justiceforBettsy.

This book is written in British English, however, I have used terminology more aligned to Canadian English (e.g. Mom instead of Mum/Mam).

Definitions

Home Grown:

The definition of a "homegrown" player is a player, who irrespective of their nationality or age, has been registered with either:

1. Their current club (who is a member of the EIHL); and/or

2. A club and/or any other Ice Hockey club affiliated with Ice Hockey UK ("IHUK"), English Ice Hockey Association ("EIHA") or Scottish Ice Hockey ("SIH") for a period, continuous or non-continuous, of two seasons or 24 months prior to his 18th birthday (or the end of the season during which they turn 18).

A non home grown player is usually classified as an import. A team is allowed a maximum number of imports as decided by the league. The roster spots for imports to consume are known as 'import slots'.

Tape Job (or, TJ,);

Act of applying tape to a hockey stick to:
   a) Protect the stick from wear and tear
   b) Change the way the stick feels

Alternatively:
A job involving a tape

Chapter 1

8 months ago: Christmas

I've drunk too much. I don't know why I let myself get this wasted. I feel worse when I step onto the balcony and the cold air hits me. Why did I open that extra bottle of wine?

It's fucking freezing out here, and my teeth chatter. I'm regretting not bringing the blanket from the back of the couch, but it'll be awkward if I go back in now. I've already attracted too much attention this evening, thanks to my inability to tone down my voice.

The door creaks open, and I glance back, locking eyes with Liam. He looks surprisingly fresh for someone who's just arrived from Toronto.

Pulling his hoodie over his head, he hands it to me without saying a word. I allow myself a second to inhale his delicious scent. It's familiar and comforting.

He nods at the chairs against the wall, and we sit down. Moving in close, he wraps his arm around my shoulder, and I lean my head into him.

I don't know why we're doing this. We should be so angry with each other now, not snuggling up on the balcony of his twin brothers' apartment, but here we are—freezing cold and cuddled together.

"You good?" he asks.

I've missed his voice. I've missed him. It's been weird between us for a few months, and all the built-up emotions flooded out as soon as he walked in today. He wasn't due to arrive until tomorrow, by all accounts, and I didn't even know he was coming. I wanted to shout, kick, scream, but I just hugged him when he walked into Ryan's apartment. It was a hug that probably lasted too long, a hug I didn't even realise I needed until we were in the moment.

I take a deep breath before replying. "Sure."

It's me that should be asking how he is. If he's good. I know it's all my fault. The past few months have been tough. Just like the first time we split up, he went on a tangent again after I called off our wedding. His Instagram blew up with new photos of him, and his hookups. He'd utterly detached from me. Nothing less than I deserved, though. Did I actually expect us to be on friendly terms?

I turn to face him. "I can't believe you're here. I thought you were done speaking to me."

He says nothing, becoming very interested in his calloused hands.

"I'm sorry," I say.

Still, he says nothing, he just nibbles at his thumbnail.

I can tell he's thinking now, and as soon as he drops his hand, he spits out a question which hits me hard in the chest.

"Was there someone else?" he asks, pausing momentarily before following up. "Is there someone else? Did you meet someone else, Vic?" He spins his head to gaze at me, his beautiful hazel eyes full of sorrow.

My heart sinks, but anger bubbles in my veins. How dare he put me in the same category as my dad. He was a serial cheat. I'd never do such a thing.

"No. There's never been anyone else," I answer.

It's the truth, and I doubt there will ever be anyone else. Yeah, I'd come close to sleeping with a few other guys when we'd split up the first time, after college, but I could never go through with it. It wasn't even their fault—it was mine. I'd freeze up and shrug them off because no one came close to Liam. Instead, I ended up falling back on my private videos of him from his first year of college when I was back in Abbotsford for my last year of school.

"What was it then? I want to hear it," he says.

I get to my feet, slightly unsteady. "I got scared."

"Scared? Scared of what?" His voice raises, but he stays seated.

I gulp, ready to expose myself. "Scared of you realising I'm not worth sticking around for and having you leave me just like everyone else does."

As soon as the words are out, I feel embarrassed at my admission. When my dad decided he wanted to fuck around instead of work on his marriage to my mom, my brother Johnny and I became accessories in whatever game they were playing. Johnny would be at hockey practice with Liam and his twin, Ryan, and I would be forced to sit in the rink's diner, waiting for the handover from Dad to Mom. It was one massive inconvenience to my dad, who was keen to get rid of me, or so it felt.

Liam is quiet, probably processing what I just said. Tears stream down my cheeks–God knows what fucking state I'm in. Am I wearing waterproof? I can't remember.

"Vic," he swallows, starts to talk but cuts himself off a couple of times. I keep quiet, giving him time to get his words out. "The only time I ever left you was for college, but that was temporary. It was in the plan. You left me, remember? You broke my heart."

I know for a fact that I've broken his heart twice. The first time, when he got signed to Toronto, I told him to forget about me. I told him I didn't want him anymore. This was also around the same time we knew his mom was close to passing away, and I still haven't got over that either. I felt closer to his mom than I ever did to mine. I'd watched his dad crash and burn when his mom was ill, and I didn't want the same for us.

"And I still couldn't let you go, letting you break my heart all over again when you called off our wedding," he says. "If anything, this should prove I won't fucking leave you."

He's right, but there's no such thing as a happy ending, is there?

"It didn't take you long to move on," I snap, referring to his social media. "You couldn't have been that broken-hearted."

That was not the right thing to say. Liam's nostrils flair, and he stands up, moving towards the balcony railing where his hands grip the bar, turning his knuckles white.

He's still for a moment before scoffing. "Yeah, right. What do you think happened, Vic?" He releases his grip and walks towards me. "I couldn't have you thinking I sat at home wallowing between games and training. It was all a fucking show."

"A show? Do you realise how that makes me feel?"

"You've broken my heart twice. Twice, Vicky." He glares at me, sadness in his eyes. "How do you think that makes me feel?"

I can't answer him. It will become a battle of broken hearts with neither of us willing to back down. Liam is too stubborn, and I'm too much of a control freak.

I half expect him to start yelling at me, telling me he doesn't want to see me, that he despises me, or whatever—but he doesn't. He's looking at his runners, deep in thought.

"I'm sorry—" He sniffs loudly, cutting me off. And I think for a moment, wondering if I can do something to show him how sorry I am. I lean in and press my lips softly against his cheek. I expect him to push me away, but his arms clamp around me, pinning me into him.

"See, even now I want to push you away, but I can't. You're like a fucking drug, Vic. I can't get enough, but I can't let you do that to me again. One minute you want to get married, the next, it's off. Then, you're calling me for phone sex. It's messed up."

Yes, shit. The phone sex. He's right again. It is messed up, but he's the only person I've ever wanted. Selfishly, I didn't even think about how he would be feeling. Now he's holding me close, and it's another reminder that I've missed this. The safety and security of Liam James Preston. The only person who's ever looked at me as a complete person, apart from his mom. I wasn't seen as an extension of Johnny or an inconvenience, as my parents saw me.

I've been a complete fucking idiot.

"You've given me a fucking boner, you know," he scoffs. "That damn perfume of yours and your hair—" I swear he sniffs my hair.

But the sound of the balcony door creaking open causes Liam's head to turn, spotting my brother, Johnny, as he pokes his head out of the apartment. "You guys, okay?" he's looking at Liam, not me.

Liam nods, and I tell him we're fine.

"Everyone's leaving now. Jen and Ryan have already gone to bed," Johnny adds. I'd forgotten we were supposed to be at a Christmas Eve-Eve party with the rest of Johnny and Ryan's hockey team.

"We'll be in soon," Liam says, his arms still wrapped around me.

Johnny slips back inside, and the door closes with a light thud. The thought of Liam leaving me now is too much to bear. I need to talk to him, to make him understand my thought process.

Liam's supposed to be staying at Johnny's place, but I can't help myself. "Come to mine?" I ask, and he nods, squeezing me.

"Told you, you're like a fucking drug, baby girl."

He takes a step back and holds his hand out to me. I take it, letting him lead the way.

It's Christmas Eve and I've somehow convinced Vicky to come skating. Seeing the look on her face—a look of pure joy as she glides across the smooth surface—I know I'm in trouble because I shouldn't be here. I shouldn't be socialising with her. I shouldn't be enjoying her.

We were meant to talk last night. I know that was the plan for both of us, but as far as I'm concerned, we can talk any time—you can't cuddle over a video call.

She's soaring towards me, her beautiful blonde hair rippling behind her and my Marlies toque pulled over her ears. She stops right before me, her palms resting on my chest.

"Why aren't you skating?" she asks, moving her hands to grab onto my biceps.

I get a whiff of her Chanel perfume and the sweetness of her shampoo, and it makes my stomach clench with excitement. I'll be taking that toque home because it'll smell like her.

"I was watching you," I say, because when Vicky is around she's all I can focus on. It's always been the same. Since I first laid eyes on her, I've known deep down that she'll either make or break me—and right now, she's fucking breaking me.

The first time I saw her, I almost landed flat on my ass because I wasn't watching where I was skating and bumped into her brother, Johnny. She's had the same effect on me ever since.

"Come on," she says, pulling my arm lightly, and I follow like the lovesick fool that I am.

Vicky told me she hasn't skated since I last took her, which was too long ago for me to recount when. She had a fall a few years back and is adamant that she'll only skate with me. This makes me feel like I'm a fucking hero or something.

I skate a lot faster than her, but I slow my pace right down so she's next to me. Our hands link automatically, just like when we were kids. We watch my brother and his girlfriend, Jenna, skating like a couple of kids too, giggling and chasing each other, similar to how Vicky and I were, always horsing around.

I take a chance and reach down, putting my right arm at the back of her knees and my left arm at the small of her back. I lift her up, and she squeals and kicks. But as soon as I've slung her over my shoulder, she lets up and giggles.

"You're a doofus," she chuckles, like the past year never happened.

I do a few laps at speed this time, and Vicky squeals with joy. It's my favourite sound, and it breaks my heart that this temporary bubble we're in will soon fucking pop and leave a horrible stain in its place. I skate over to the benches and sit her down.

"What the hell are we going to do, Vic?" I look down at her. I've got my serious face on. I'm not messing around this time.

"Pretend like I wasn't a complete idiot? And the past, however many years, never happened?" she offers, her white teeth glinting like they're out of a commercial.

"We could," I lean into her, "but then I wouldn't know all your dirty secrets."

I'm not helping myself here. As soon as I've said it, I realise I'm approaching flirting territory, which has only intensified today after sleeping in Vicky's bed last night. We only spooned, her body pressed against mine, but that made things a lot worse, in my opinion, because it was nice.

"What dirty secrets?" Vicky's eyes widen. She'll know by now that I'm horny for her. She's like a fucking pill to me, and I can't get enough.

I wink at her. "Don't play dumb—"

"Do you still have the videos?" she asks, and I can feel my blood rush south.

"Maybe." Of course I do. All of them. They're locked away, but I have them.

"Do you still watch them?" She stands up and wobbles on her skates a bit, and our eyes lock—a glint of something naughty in her gaze.

"Maybe," I choke.

"Are you done, love?"

That's a word I haven't heard in a long time, but it sends a ripple of something through my body. Lust? No, it's a lot more than lust.

She eyes me, biting her lip, still waiting for me to respond.

I clear my throat. "Sure."

She sits back down, and I flop next to her, our knees touching, and then she reaches out and puts her manicured hand on my leg. Fuck.

She knows what she's doing as her hand runs up and down my quad. She leans her head in, her breath catching directly on that golden spot on my neck. She wants me as much as I want her.

"Take your skates off and follow me," she says, undoing her laces quickly. She works in silence like she's in a race with herself, and I make headway with mine, pulling them off and reaching for my shoes underneath the bench.

I'm too weak to resist, even though I know it's a terrible idea and I should be putting an end to all the heartbreak, but I want her too. I don't think I'll ever stop. My judgement is clouded by how turned on I am.

We put our shoes on and abandon the skates. Vicky pulls me, heading to the tunnels unfamiliar to me. Still, she clearly knows where she's going as she rounds the corner, heading to the end of the last corridor we come to. She pushes open the door labelled 'Equipment Storage' and pulls me inside. The only light in the room is from an emergency sign overhead, but it's enough for her to see what she's doing as she grabs an equipment box and pushes it against the door.

I pull her towards me, wanting to taste her, to feel her pressed up against me. Her mouth is on mine, and her hand reaches for my belt buckle. My cock is hard already, and she knows it's her doing. It doesn't take her long to pull the zip down, pop the button and slide her hand into my boxers.

"I've missed you," she breathes, touching my neck with her lips.

She's doing all the right things; I'll give her that. She hasn't forgotten. Nor have I.

She tugs at my jeans, pulls them down and then follows with my boxers. Her hands grip my shaft, and the long strokes drive me crazy with want.

"You gonna be a good girl and get your panties off for me?" I whisper. A voice in the back of my mind tells me this is a bad idea, but the thought of missing out, and with how delicious she smells—I can't stop myself.

She's quick. She loses the hat, slips her shoes off and wriggles out of her leggings, her creamy skin making my mouth water. Her panties come off next, and she looks deep into my eyes, her teeth tugging at her bottom lip again.

"You're so hard for me," she says, leaning in and kissing my jaw, peppering her way down to my neck.

"I'm always fucking hard for you, Vic." It's true. She doesn't need to work to get me in the mood. I'm impatient, though. Desperate for her. "Panties. Now." I rasp.

She hands them over to me, and I bring them to my nose. Fuck. She's intoxicating.

She snatches them away from me and wraps them around my cock. Big strokes but painfully slow, all while she finds that sweet spot on my neck, knowing exactly how to kiss me and how much I can take.

But I can't take it. I'm already on the edge of coming in her hand, probably all over her panties, but I don't think that's where she wants it.

"You look fucking beautiful with your hand wrapped around my dick, baby," I pant, encouraging her.

She beams at me, her hand working quicker, and she leans in so I can feel her breath on my cheek.

"Where do you want to come, love?" Her lips trail over my throat, and I clench my whole body to stop myself from coming.

Everywhere is the honest answer. I want to claim her.

I think it over briefly, my immediate choices at the forefront of my mind. Her face? No, not right now. Over her panties? While it's a good option, I decide quickly.

"Get on your knees and open your mouth," I say. She drops in front of me, the tip of her tongue poking out and running under my shaft for a beat before she leans back and looks up at me, eyes wide with expectation.

I take my cock in my fist and pump for my release. A groan escapes me. It doesn't take me long to coat her tongue. Mine.

"You're so good at taking my load, baby. You look so fucking sexy." She looks incredible; I don't have enough words.

I watch her tongue disappear back into her mouth, and she swallows before showing me a clean display.

"Good girl," I breathe, pulling her to her feet and bringing her face to mine. Tasting the remnants of myself on her lips drives me crazy.

I pull my zip-up off and place it on the storage case, gently pushing Vicky to sit on top.

I drop to my knees. She knows what to do, parting her legs for me, letting me kiss my way along the smooth skin of the thighs.

She's fucking soaking; I can see her glistening, despite the poor lighting. A few days after a fresh wax, but I never care. The landing strip she leaves is perfect, and her pussy is flawless.

My cock is hard again, but I ignore it, burying my face in Vicky's pussy instead.

My beard scratches her, but she yelps and grabs my head, pushing me in closer. I know exactly how much pressure to apply and that she likes it just above her clit.

I slip a finger into her wetness, the walls of her pussy tight around my finger.

I always forget how good she tastes. It's like I've been starved, and she's offering respite. I lap at her, sucking gently and teasing the spot just above, knowing it won't take her long.

Her breathing is steady, and her moans are erotic—like she's saved them all up for me.

"I'm close," she breathes, and I curl my finger upwards, finding her sweet spot.

Her thighs clamp around my head as she comes, her breathing jagged, her fingers clutching at my hair. It takes her a while to let me go, relaxing her thighs and releasing her grip.

"You did real good baby," I say, moving towards her face so I can kiss her.

She wraps her arms around my neck and pulls me close, kissing me like it's our last. I want to bury my cock inside her, feel her against me, but the door behind her rattles and then vibrates as someone bangs on it from the other side.

"Lee, are you in there?"

Fuck. It's my brother.

Vicky's eyes meet mine and we scramble to get ourselves dressed, only shouting back when he calls through the door again.

Vicky gets her shoes on, moves the equipment box out of the way, and pulls the door handle.

"Oh, hey, Vicky," Jen smirks, her eyes bouncing between us.

Fuck. I bet my beard is still glistening with Vicky all over my face.

Vicky pulls the toque back on. "Don't you dare say anything, Jenna!"

There's silence for a moment while everyone waits for someone else to speak. Anything. Ryan gives in, thank fuck.

"We're heading out. We spent a while looking for you." I know he's trying not to laugh; his cheeks are puffed out.

My post-orgasm fog is clearing, and there's a knot of dread at the pit of my stomach. What the fuck are we doing? Heading back to heartbreak hotel?

Vicky squeezes through the gap in the door, and I follow with the others, heading back towards the ice.

"We've got too much to do, Vic. Are you okay with helping us carry things to Ryan and Danny's place?" Jen asks. My brother shares an apartment with another forward from the team, who is Jen's best friend Danny.

Jen, Vicky, and Becca—Danny's girlfriend—are prepping for Christmas lunch at my brother's apartment tomorrow. Jen is taking it seriously and, from what I've heard, Johnny is on turkey duty.

I nod and give Ryan a look. He knows what to do, thank fuck.

"Come and look at the dressing room, bro," he says, jerking his head towards the door up ahead. "You go ahead, ladies. We'll catch you up."

As soon as we're in through the door and the coast is clear, Ryan rounds on me.

"Did you fuck Vicky in the Equipment Store?" he snarls.

"Not exactly—"

"Fuck, Lee. Does she know what your plan is?"

"Not exactly—"

"I thought you were going to talk to her? You said that you were going to talk to her," Ryan rages. I don't know why he's getting so bent out of shape. "You can't let her lead you on and break your fucking heart again, man. What were you thinking?"

I sit down at Ryan's cubby and lean back, contemplating all my life choices up until now.

Yeah, I was planning on coming to play in the UK with Johnny and Ryan next season since I'm just chasing another call-up, but I don't know how Vicky will react to me not wanting to start anything up again. I can't put myself through another heartbreak.

"I—"

The door to the dressing room swings open slightly, and Vicky's head comes into view, still wearing my hat.

Fuck, she's cute. Her blonde hair is in loose curls over her shoulders and her bright white smile gleaming below her ocean-blue eyes. How did I wind up with her, anyway? She's too good for me. Maybe it's for the best that we go our separate ways for good this time—I just need the balls to tell her.

"Are you guys coming? Jen is—" she halts, gazing at my face, "What's going on?"

"Vic. I think we need to talk."

That's Ryan's cue. He slips past Vicky, and she steps in, closing the door behind her.

"What?" she says, her eyes darkening.

There's silence for a moment before I gather every ounce of valour. "I can't do this anymore."

And this is when I break Vicky's heart right back.

Chapter 2

Her eyes widen. She's staring at me, confused—if I recognise her expression correctly.

"What do you mean 'I can't do this anymore?' I don't understand," she says.

The dressing room is large and square, and she's standing near the door. But where Ryan's cubby is, it's only a few strides away. I debate for a moment if I should step towards her, or prompt her to sit down next to me. But she paces, and that tells me her mind is working overdrive and she could decide to do absolutely anything, so I stay where I am.

"This, Vic. Whatever the fuck it is we're doing. You want me, you don't want me, you want me, you don't want me, you flirt with me, you don't talk to me for months. I can't cope with it anymore. I can't—"

She halts and looks at me. "And you didn't want to mention this before you came with me into the equipment storage room. I can still taste your come!" She raises her voice at the last part, then she blinks, tears forming in her eyes.

Shit. Right. That's on me, but she did that thing she does to my neck and hell—I can't be held responsible for my own actions when I'm that worked up. But I get it. I'm a dick. A huge one.

"Or is this your way of getting back at me? Getting me to feel like you felt? Because I suppose it's what I deserve," she says.

"I didn't plan on doing that," I offer. "I'm sorry, I—"

"What happened this morning, Lee?" she cuts me off. I take a deep breath which prompts her into a rant. "What happened? Did Johnny say something? Or was it Ryan? Because I thought things were fine last night. I thought..." She halts and steps towards me. A single step.

"Look, I've been thinking about it for a while, Vic. We can't keep doing this, and you can't keep doing it either. I mean, why the hell did you have a complete meltdown at Ryan? He said you were convinced he was me or something."

She wipes her eyes with the sleeve of her jacket and looks down at the nails on her left hand. "I just... I had a moment, I said I was sorry. Oh, my God!" Fresh tears fall down her cheeks and seeing her like this is breaking my heart, too. I can't see her like this. I don't know what else to do but stride towards her and pull her into me. I'm not sure what I was expecting, but she pushes me away with all her strength, causing me to stumble backwards.

"Don't you fucking touch me," she snarls.

She turns and flings open the dressing room door, and she's gone in a flash before I can react.

I take a few moments to figure out what to do next. But I decide to take off after her, entering a completely empty corridor. Where the fuck did she go? I look around, craning my neck—left, right, left, right, but she's gone. Only the smell of Chanel lingering in the area.

I hear my brother's footsteps growing louder. I can always tell it's him.

"What's going on?" Ryan paces towards me.

"Have you seen Vicky?"

"No."

"She couldn't have gone far."

"What happened?"

I sigh, then I compose myself before giving him a brief run-down of the conversation I had with her. I run my hands through my hair and pace in a small circle before letting out a growl.

"Did you tell her you're coming here next season?"

"I didn't get a chance."

"Yeah, but you had time to take a trip into the equipment cupboard. I'm sure you didn't go in there for a look around, did you?"

"Whose side are you on?" I growl.

"Yours, obviously. But all I'm saying is, you shouldn't have gone and done whatever you did, knowing that you were going to call it off. It's a dick move. Any guy knows that, especially when you've got history. You could be seen as—"

"Shut the fuck up, Ryan. There wasn't anything to call off!" I know he's right, but who wants to be kicked while they're down?

"Vicky didn't think that!" Ryan raises his voice too.

"Fuck!" I let out a breath, trying to clear my thoughts. I'm feeling fidgety and anxious because all I want to do is talk to Vicky and figure out how we can fix things. My mind is working overdrive, set on considering what I can do next. Then a whole wave of fresh anger courses through me. "This is all your fault."

I round on him, but he puts his hand out, which I grab, but he spins around and grapples me. We're standing in the tunnels fighting like kids, but I don't care how childish it looks. I'm pissed.

More footsteps sound, but I don't recognise them. It's only when Jen's voice floats through the air that we stop dead.

"Oh my god, what are you doing? Where's Vicky?" She says, coming to a stop next to us.

Ryan steps back and fixes his eyes on mine.

"She ran off," we say together.

"Give us a moment please, babe," he says, his tone as soft as shit. "Could you try to find Vicky?"

She hesitates for a moment before nodding and walking away.

Ryan moves in close. "Don't you dare put this on me. You fucked up. You promised Johnny. I did you a fucking favour."

"What about that favour I did you, huh?" I say. Our faces are inches apart now, and if he wasn't that little bit stronger than me, I'd take him out.

My words hit though because his shoulders sink, and he steps back just a small amount. It's something that hasn't been brought up for a long ass time but now twice in two days.

"Figure out what you're going to do, but you have to tell Vicky if you decide you're coming here next season."

"I'll be here," I shrug, but as soon as I've said it, I know it's going to be a terrible decision.

His face relaxes, and I figure now's as good a time as any to break the news.

"It'll be my last season, bro. With you and Johnny—for old times' sake—then I'm done."

"You're kidding?" he scoffs, half-grinning.

"Nope."

Ryan's face drops into a frown. "You're retiring? Why?"

"I'm just exhausted with it all." I look down at my runners.

"Because of Vicky?" he asks.

I nod. He knows. Everything in the goddamn eco-system of hockey is just a reminder of Vicky. Everything. The smell, the noise, the feel of my hands on my stick, the stick she would have taped before.

Every time my skates hit the ice—Vicky. Every time I pull my sweater on—Vicky. Every time I look up at the jumbotron—Vicky. God only knows why, but she's there. I can't even look at Johnny sometimes, if I'm honest.

But I'll play out my last season here. Mainly because of Johnny, but I know Vicky needs a friend. She doesn't know it yet, but she does.

"Fuck. This isn't what I was expecting. Have you told Dad?"

"I haven't told anyone, except you. Yeah, this season with the Marlies' has been fine, and I got the call-up, you know, but I think I need to set myself free. We always said we'd play a season together if we could and this is our chance. Besides, something tells me you're not going back."

Ryan raises his eyebrows and opens his mouth to reply, but Jen comes into view again and stops next to him. "Did you see which way she went, Liam?"

I shake my head.

"Should I call Johnny?" she asks, looking between us.

"I'll call Johnny," I say, pulling my phone out, but he's already beat me to it; there's a text waiting for me.

Johnny

> Vicky's with me. Leave her to calm
> down. See you tomorrow.

"At least Johnny's not pissed." I flash my phone towards Ryan and Jen.

"What happened?" Jen presses, so I give her a rundown and watch her frown.

"Oh. Tomorrow will be awkward."

"No, it won't. I'll be going home tonight. In fact, I'll get my stuff and I'll head out now, even if I have to wait in the airport."

"You can't go. It's Christmas."

"Yeah, and the last thing Vicky needs is another ruined Christmas. It's settled. I'll be back in August, and we'll figure it out then."

I've never seen Ryan look so desperate as he does right now, but he nods and holds his hand out to shake mine, more of a habit than anything. I take it and pull him in, letting him squeeze me before letting go.

"We're going to make it one hell of a season, Lee. You make sure you keep the training up. And make sure you hydrate. Oh, and fucking eat right. Food is—"

"Fuel. Yes, I know." I roll my eyes at him. "But first, I'll stop off and speak with Vicky; if she's not cool with it—"

"I'll give you a ride," Ryan says, and we head towards the back doors.

I'm in this weird in-between state where I don't want to be on my own, but I don't want to be with anyone either. It's like the night I first saw Liam playing for the Toronto Maple Leafs. So obviously, coming to Johnny's is the only choice.

"Ryan just called me," Johnny says as he sits next to me on the sofa. "Lee's going back to Toronto, but he needs to swing back and pick up his things."

My stomach twists in knots. I don't want Liam to go, but I don't want him to stay either. I could scream.

"Vic, do you want to go back to yours so you don't have to see him?"

I haven't told Johnny the full story, only that we'd agreed to call it a day for good this time. Annoyingly, he had spent the past twenty minutes going on and on about how much he thought it was a good idea and how much better off I'd be.

"No. It'll be fine." I pull the blanket draped over me up higher and hug my knees. I fix my attention on a Christmas movie Johnny put on to 'get us in the spirit,' but I couldn't be further from the spirit if I tried.

We don't talk for what feels like an eternity. Johnny fidgets with his phone before tossing it aside, and when the doorbell chimes he springs to his feet, rushing over to let Liam in.

I try my hardest to concentrate on anything other than the muffled conversation. But then there's movement, and Liam's voice drifts over to me.

"Vic, can I talk to you for a moment?"

He sounds sad. Like really fucking sad. My chest heaves with the effort to stop myself from crying as the inner battle begins. I wonder if hearing him out would be best, but he takes in a breath and speaks again.

"You don't have to talk. Just listen, please."

He sounds desperate, so I nod and switch off the movie. But I keep my focus on the blank screen, hoping it'll stop me from crying. It's funny really. Not funny 'ha-ha' but funny that it's me who's got the broken heart.

He strides further into the room and moves around the sofa, coming to a stop at the side where I'm sitting before crouching; a groan slipping from his mouth. I glance over to him and then shuffle up, making room for him to sit.

"Thanks. My knee has been causing me a few issues," he says, collapsing down next to me. "I'm sorry, Vic. I'm sorry about the cupboard, and... well, I just wanted to let you know I'm thinking of retiring. But I was planning on playing one more season here with Johnny. And let's face it, Ryan is likely going to stay anyway, so it's an ideal opportunity for us to play pro together."

"You're quitting?" Johnny bursts from his bedroom as if he was waiting for an opportunity.

"Retiring, but I'm not going into that right now. I just wanted to make sure that whatever the hell is going on between me and Vic..." His eyes dart back towards me and I can't help but meet his gaze.

"Are you asking my permission to come and play here next season?" I ask, but Johnny interrupts, and thunders into the room.

"What the hell? What are you going to do instead? Why—"

"Fuck's sake, John. I'm not going into it right now. I told you that. All you need to know is that if I can get a spot next season with—"

"Is this because of Vicky?" Johnny gives me a look that could kill, but Liam jumps to his feet, as if to ward him off. I jump up too, because I don't trust Johnny's fury.

I try to shove Johnny away, he stumbles backwards and regains his footing, acting as if nothing has happened.

"Lee. Is this because of Vicky?" Johnny asks again.

"No. I told you. It's my knee," Liam says, and Johnny glances between him and me. "It's my knee, John. My knee."

"Fuck. I didn't realise it was that bad," Johnny says, finally giving in.

There's a flash of something in Liam's eyes that tells me there is more to this than his knee, and I think Johnny has hit the nail on the head.

"John, please can you give us a moment?" I say.

He doesn't want to, I can tell, but he walks backwards and sinks into the darkness of his bedroom, not even bothering to turn the light on before slamming the door.

"Johnny's pissed," I say, nonchalantly. "And I'd wager that he was right when he asked if it was because of me. Liam? Are you quitting because of me?"

His eyebrows do a weird twitch, standard for him, and his silence tells me what I suspect is true, but he doesn't answer me.

"I'm not quitting, I'm retiring. But I don't want to come here next season and have any awkwardness or whatever. I also don't want you to be in a position where you're not comfortable with me being here. This is your home now after all."

He shifts on the spot and plays with the coins he's got in his pocket, and I know he's not going to give me any more information right now.

"Do what you need to do, Lee. But don't quit hockey for my sake."

We just stare at each other for a moment, and then he lifts his arm up, as if to touch my cheek. His hand hangs in the air and I want to reach out and take it in my own, but I back away. I should be so pissed at him right now, but he looks so sad and I don't have any energy left to argue.

I don't have anywhere to storm off to, so I mutter about needing to use the bathroom, and I slip inside, locking the door behind me. I sit on the edge of the bath as I wait for him to leave, listening to every single sound that seeps under the tiny gap in between the door and its frame.

Finally, there's shuffling and mumbled speech and then a faint knock on the door.

"Vic, I'm going now, but I'll call you, okay?"

I hesitate for a moment before throwing back a weak, "Okay." And then he's gone.

Chapter 3

Liam

Present Day

I sit across from Ryan, picking at a bagel I don't really want; my stomach is tight with nerves.

"It won't be that bad," I say, trying to trick myself into thinking that because I say it, it must be true. I pop a chunk of bagel into my mouth and chew, trying to get something in me since I don't know how long it'll be until they serve food on the flight to Heathrow.

"I promise I'll try not to be so bossy. We'll be back on form in no time, bro. Trust me."

I give Ryan a line I know he wants to hear. Since we've not played together properly in a long-ass time, I know he's feeling anxious about how things will work out for us once we hit the ice. I'm confident, and I know he worked hard with the winger I'm replacing, Scott McCoy. Knowing Ryan, it probably feels like he's starting over.

"Johnny seems to think we've got a chance at the Challenge Cup with the team we'll have," Ryan says, but a flash of blonde hair from a crowd of people behind him shifts my mind to Vicky. Panic sets in. Shit. Maybe going to the UK isn't such a good idea after all.

"Do you think I'm making a mistake?" I ask. It comes out before I can properly consider my words.

"Is this about Vicky?" he asks, his left brow twitching.

I have so much to say, but I hesitate, my thoughts spinning. Thankfully, Jen appears from the washrooms and sits down next to Ryan, causing a distraction. He wraps his arm around her shoulders, and the whole scene makes me miss Vicky even more.

After Christmas, the rest of the season dragged, and the brief contact I had with her was frustrating as hell. She texted me back, but her messages were short, leaving me irritated and ruined my mood for the rest of my time in Toronto.

"Why is this so complicated?" I breathe, stretching in my seat.

"What did I miss?" Jen asks.

"Vicky," Ryan and I respond.

Jen gives me some bullshit about how excited Vicky is to see me, but Ryan does me a favour, shifting the conversation to my living arrangements. I'll be sharing with Danny, who Ryan shared with last season before he moved into Jen's room at Vicky's place.

"How're you feeling about living with Danny?" he asks.

"Fine. He seems like a nice guy," I say.

I only met him briefly at Christmas, but he seems easy going enough to share with. At least I'm not rooming with Johnny because fuck that—he's a neat freak and hates anyone using his kitchen. Even though he has his moments, he's still my best bud, aside from my brother.

Jen advises me to keep away from Danny's computer, which is fine by me considering I don't want anyone coming near mine. The brief talk of his laptop reminds me of the page I saw open on Jen's laptop earlier that day.

"We're viewing a few places when we get back, but there's one Jen is really keen on," Ryan says. He's referring to the house shopping they've been obsessing over during their summer in Canada. They're looking to buy a house close to the rink and everyone knows buying a house means big things in a relationship.

"Christ, you two are getting really serious. Next, you'll be married," I say, half-joking.

"About that—"

A loud 'ding-dong' from a speaker to our left catches my attention, and my head snaps up to the screen.

"That's our flight," Jen says as she gathers her things.

I fix my eyes back on Ryan, waiting for him to carry on. "You were saying?" I prompt.

"We've looked into this house buying stuff, and they do things a bit different to us. It sounds like a complete ball-ache if you ask me, but ultimately, things would be easier if Jen and I were married. We're not sure if that's what we're doing yet, but it's something we need to talk about."

"Are you kidding?" My face drops into a frown. "You said you never wanted to get married."

"Yeah, well, things change," Ryan shrugs.

My face is showing my concern as I look between Ryan and Jen.

"I'm not adding any pressure, Lee, just in case that's what you were thinking. If I'm honest, I didn't want to get married either, but we've not decided yet," Jen says.

I'm completely dumbfounded as to what I'm hearing. "So let me get this straight. Neither of you want to get married, so you're getting married?"

"It's purely for the legal side of things. I just don't want Jen to be in a situation where she gets tired of me but feels like she has to stick around because of the house. At least this way, it's legally half hers. I don't want to see her in any financial difficulty."

"Ry, I've already said—" Jen starts, but Ryan stops her by holding his hand out in a halt signal.

"And I've already said I'd feel better about it. If something happens, I know you'll be okay." He leans in and kisses her.

I know where his thinking is going, and it's something in the back of my mind, too: Mom. You can't be sure about the amount of time you have.

I distract myself from their moment by mindlessly checking my phone, part of me hoping that Vicky has decided to message me back—she hasn't. I put my phone in the back pocket of my jeans and pull on my sweater.

Ryan grabs his backpack and cap, flipping it backwards and sinking it onto his head before he leans in close to talk to me. "Besides, I think it's because I haven't really loved anyone before. I just don't want her to think I'm getting sappy or whatever." We all know she's got him sappy. There's no second guessing that, but his attempt at discreet conversation is poor considering Jen is standing right there, pulling her jacket on. She must be pretending she can't hear since her facial expression stays the same. "But when you know, you know, right?" he says.

I did know. At least, I thought I knew. But all I know now is that marriage is off my agenda. I can't imagine marrying anyone other than Vicky, and since I'm set on not going back there, it looks like I'm destined to stay single forever. Ryan, on the other hand, looks like he'll never be single again.

"You've really done it, Jen." I say with a smirk, grabbing my cap. "He's a goner for you."

"Anyway, we've still not decided," Ryan says.

"Yeah, well, keep me the hell out of it," I say. "If I never hear the 'M' word again, it'll be too soon."

If I had to guess right now, I'd say they'll be married by the end of next season, but I let it drop. The last thing I want is to spend nine hours sat next to the happiest couple in the world talking about their goddamn wedding plans.

We make our way to the gate and join the queue. I hang back behind Ryan and Jen, feeling like a third-wheel, which only pulls thoughts of Vicky into my head.

I pull my phone out again and do the usual sweep of her socials; some part of me hoping that she's posted something within the past few minutes, but she hasn't. I quickly abandon the scrolling and shove my phone away again, waiting for the line to move.

"Sorry, everyone. Please can you take a seat? We'll be with you as quickly as we can." A woman dressed in the get-up for Air Transat waves everyone away, causing the line to disperse with a load of groans.

I slump down into the nearest seat and drop my head into my hands. This only prolongs the inevitable for Vicky and me. Figuring out how to be friends might be difficult for us, as our relationship has never been purely platonic.

I'd spent a few years trying not to look at Vicky. Johnny had done the classic thing of warning everyone off even looking at his sister when she first started hanging around at the barn. He wasn't the only one on the team with a sister, and he wasn't the only one to stipulate that his sister was off limits. But then she kept coming over to my house after practices; not that she really wanted to, but my mom always offered for her to come along with Johnny. It's only recently that I realised it was likely for Vicky's benefit since her dad was always keen to get away. Tuesday evening practices were 'hand-over' days. Vicky's mom would pick her and Johnny up after practice, but she wasn't always on time. My mom would always invite both of them back with us for dinner or whatever.

It took my mom a year to find out about my crush on Vicky. I made the mistake of asking for a haircut, much to Ryan's disgust, and my mom immediately knew there was a girl involved.

"Who is it?" Ryan had asked from the front seat of our mom's truck.

"No one," I'd lied.

But he didn't drop it. "Is it Candice Knowles?" He'd thrown out random names of girls from school, but every single time I said no. I half debated throwing him a false lead, terrified that he'd finally say Vicky's name and my face would betray me, but I figured that'd make things worse. It was only when my brother had jumped out of the truck to get us some water from a service station that mom turned in her seat and came out with it.

"I won't tell him. I don't want to embarrass you."

I tried to deny it at first. "I don't know what you're talking about, Mom."

She gave me a knowing look. "Vicky's very special, sweetie. But she's fragile. She needs someone to look out for her and I sure as heck know that could be you."

I remember feeling the blood rush to my face, turning my cheeks hot with embarrassment. "Please don't tell Ryan or Johnny," I squeaked.

She said nothing after that, just winked at me via the rear-view mirror. We drove off in silence after Ryan got back in.

"Are you okay, Lee?" Jen's soft voice is quiet, but it's enough to rouse me and bring my focus back.

"Yes," I lie, but Jen clearly knows this. My eyes sweep over Ryan who's pacing with his phone pressed up against his ear.

"How's your dad? Did the visit go okay?" Jen asks, and I fill her in. It was uneventful but it was good to see him.

"Did you see Vicky when you were in Abbotsford? Did she reach out to meet up?"

"What? She's been in Canada?"

"Yeah. I think she went to Abbotsford for a bit."

"You're joking, right?"

"No," Jen says. "She went to spend some time with her mum, but she said it wasn't all that successful."

I don't know how much Jen knows about Vicky's parents, so I don't offer any further information.

I pull out my phone and bring up my text window with Vicky, I want to message her and ask her about her trip back home. I type out three different messages before deleting them all. Instead, I message my buds from the Marlies before pocketing my phone, feeling completely deflated. I wonder why she didn't tell me she was going home. I guess it's none of my damn business, really.

The 'ding-dong' sounds again, and we line up to board. Anxiety sits heavy in my chest because I want to ask Vicky all the questions. What did she do in Abby? Did she get to spend any time with her mom? Is she looking to move back to Canada? I'm not sure why I want to ask her these questions, but I know that I'll be spending the next nine hours worrying about her.

If someone had told me last Christmas that I'd be standing here taking photos of my ex-boyfriend's—no, ex-fiancé's—jersey, I wouldn't have believed them. The last person I want to see every day is Liam Preston, so, of course, I have to see him every fucking day.

I reach out and touch the lettering on his sweater: L. Preston, 46. It's the first time I've had to photograph it in this way, and it feels surreal. It's like I need to pinch myself to check I'm not dreaming. The way the fabric feels in my hands reminds me it's all so very real, because my nipples harden, and memories of all the jerseys he's worn over the years—that I've worn over the years—come flooding back. I drop my hand as if the material is too hot to touch.

I take a hanger from the corner of the room and slip the jersey onto it before setting it to hang from the hook of his cubby. The nameplate on the shelf above gleaming with his name.

I've been dreading this shoot. Since I found out he was coming here for the season, I've been dreading it. I even considered faking my death, or getting a new job, but none of those plans came to anything.

When my brother heard the official news, he told me, "We always said we'd love to play pro together, Vic. You can't blame him for wanting to come."

I stand back from Liam's jersey and check that it's as central as it can be before moving towards the tripod I've set up.

Mr Lopez, the team's General Manager, stands behind me. "That looks great, Vicky. Do you think you can get these on the website today?" He and Coach Adams are watching me work.

I never in a million years thought I'd be photographing Liam's jersey like this. Not in a dressing room and not playing for the team I work for. I just can't get my head around it.

"Vicky?"

Shit. That's me.

"Sure, we'll make it work." I fake a smile.

"Just let me know as soon as this goes live. I know the fans are waiting to find out more about Liam," Mr Lopez grins, nudging Coach, but when I glance back, Coach looks only half-interested.

The announcement that he'd signed went out weeks ago, but we've been phasing the teasers, and this is the last one. A shot of his jersey in his cubby, next to his brother's.

"You must be excited, Vicky? Johnny tells us this is like old times for you. When did you get into photography?" Mr Lopez had nothing to do with my recruitment, and I'm genuinely surprised he cares enough to ask.

"I was fourteen when I started. Hockey photos mainly, because of Johnny, and it was something to do to pass the time when I had to watch him practise."

"Oh right, that's great," he says, but it's clear that even though he asked, he doesn't want to listen to the answer.

"The guys are still on the ice, Vicky. If you get a chance, can you get some shots of the practice before they're done? If not, just set up for next practice." He looks at his watch. "I don't think they have long, actually."

"There won't be time today, Justin," Coach Adams cuts in.

"Right. You finish up here then, Vicky, and come see me when you're done. We need to spend some time on the social media strategy for this year. I'll get Bella to help more, it won't hurt her."

A knot of disappointment sits in my stomach. I don't know why, but I find Bella irritating as hell, and not to mention, what Jen calls 'a busy-body'.

I nod and turn my attention back to my camera as Mr. Lopez exits with Coach tagging along.

Seeing Liam's jersey hanging up like this, right in front of me, has brought home the reality of our situation because this sure as hell is going to be a long season.

I take longer than I usually would with these photos, and I'm not sure if it's because I'm trying to spend my time with the idea of Liam, but the real Liam startles me when the door to the dressing room swings open.

"... it's not even close to being as good," he says to Danny.

Danny smiles and waves, while Liam nods but doesn't make eye contact.

"I'm almost done here, Lee," I snap, feeling his impatience in the air.

"Take your time," he says, sitting down in Ryan's cubby. Knowing Ryan, he'll be last off the ice, so Liam will probably be showered and dressed by the time Ryan rocks up.

Liam's gloves come off, and he tosses them with his helmet on the floor between his knees, then he loosens his skates. He stops abruptly to pull off his practice jersey, exposing his abs since he doesn't wear an undershirt beneath his shoulder pads. I can't help stealing a glance. I know he knows that I'm looking, but I can't help myself. The tension feels thick in the air, and as soon as he finishes unlacing his skates, he pulls them off and stands up. He reaches past me for his bag, pulling out a towel and wiping the moisture from his face. I get a whiff of his sweat and cologne, and I know I need to get the fuck out of here because it's delicious, and makes me want to scream with frustration.

I take one last shot as the dressing room fills around me. Once I'm done, I put all my concentration into packing up, then organising Liam's cubby to be just as he left it.

"Vic?" He stands behind me, and my head swims with lust. "Can we talk?"

I ignore him. Despite knowing we have a lot to talk about, I'm doing the 'Vicky thing' of burying my head in the sand, and thinking it'll all go away.

He tries again.

"Vic, we can be friends, right?" he whispers close to my ear so no one else can hear.

Friends? Is he serious? I don't answer him. I grab my things, and even though I'm overloaded, there's no way I'm coming back in here.

"Let me help you," he offers, reaching for one of my bags, but I fight him for it. Our hands touching briefly before he recoils as if I've burnt him. We're both still for an instant, but I risk a glance at him, his eyes meeting mine for a moment.

"I've got it," I say, turning and heading out, careful not to wobble on my heels under the burden of my bags. I'm grateful to get out of the dressing room and into the tunnel.

"Do you need some help?" Jenna is leaning against the wall outside, talking to Ryan. I've never been so glad to see her.

I smile appreciatively because I would like the help, just not from Liam. Liam can go fuck himself.

"How's it going, Vic?" Ryan asks, shooting me a warm smile. I don't know why, but he's suddenly got a face I'd love to punch.

"Yeah, fine." I shoot him my best false smile.

Jen leans up and kisses Ryan goodbye, I turn and start walking, because watching a happy couple is not high on my list of things to do right now.

Jen catches up to me and pulls one of my bags off my shoulder, and I sigh in relief.

"Thanks, Jen. I'm just going to put my lights in the equipment storage room for now since I need them tomorrow." I lead the way towards the far end of the tunnels.

"I won't ask," she says.

"Good."

"Not yet, anyway."

I push open the door and flick on the light switch. It takes a few seconds for light to flood the room, but only about half a second for the memory of the last time I was in here to flood into my head.

We put my equipment, bar my camera, over in the far corner in silence and head back towards the ice. The tunnels are now filling with the support team, but thankfully, no one stops us to chat.

"I just need to take a few shots of the Zam," I tell Jen, pulling my camera back out.

"Things will be fine, you know, Vic."

I take a couple of shots of the Zam circling the ice, with the plan to add a caption: 'Preparing for a new season.' The illuminations above make the freshly painted surface look brighter than usual. I flick through the photos I've got, cycling back and forth between some of the one's of Liam's cubby.

"The GM wants these up on the website today," I say, flashing Jen a look at the photos. "Will you have time?"

"Sure. I can do it now," she says. "Are you okay, Vic?"

"I'm fine," I lie.

"Things will be weird at first, I know, but it won't be long and maybe you guys can be friends?"

"Not you too!"

"What?"

"That's what Liam just asked me. If we could be friends!"

"Would it be such a bad thing?" Jen asks.

"We've never really just been friends, though. We didn't start off like you and Ryan. We went from full blown avoidance, to sneaking about, to being inseparable. I don't know how to be just his friend."

"Well, maybe that's what you need to do. Be friends. It may be an excellent opportunity for you to grow without the pressure of a romantic relationship."

"For the love of Christ, Jen!" I almost yell, without thinking about how it comes across.

"What?" she raises a brow at me.

"I'm sorry—that didn't come across well. But you really need to stop being such a damn know it all."

She laughs, nudging my shoulder. "You are the one who told me you needed to grow, so grow! And, you said your mom mentioned—"

The door to the dressing room flings open in the distance and I take that as our cue to leave. The last thing I need now is another glimpse at Liam. But Jen is right, I know she is. I probably need to be friends with Liam, but this time, forget that we have a past.

Chapter 4

I can smell Coco Chanel in the air, and wonder if anyone else can. It's making me woozy with lust. Not even the copious amount of sweat lingering in the air is squashing my desire. Now I'm more sure than ever that coming here was the worst idea I've ever had in my entire life.

"Things are still awkward then, I take it," Ryan says, sitting down in his cubby.

"What do you think?"

He gives me a side eye which I recognise. "I didn't expect things to be as frosty as that," he says.

Nor did I, but if this season is my last, I want it to be a season with my brother and my best friend; that's what I need to keep telling myself, anyway. I foolishly thought I could come here and just go about my business and get over Vicky. But now I'm thinking about all the promo shoots and crap that she'll be doing soon.

I pull off my shoulder pads and toss them aside.

"What's the deal with you two, then?" Danny asks as I continue with the rest of my gear.

Even though I'm sharing an apartment with Danny, and we've become buds, we haven't spoken about Vicky at all—which has been fine by me. I haven't brought her up, and he hasn't asked. He's the perfect roommate. Or at least I thought he was. What would I even say? That I'm still in love with her? Because I can't even admit that to myself.

"I don't want to talk about it," I say, feeling Johnny's eyes on me. I'm convinced he's ready to throw a punch. He's her big brother—I'm sure he does not want to hear what is going on between me and Vicky.

But Johnny, being Johnny, has something to say about it.

"It's for the best, you know. You and Vicky being done. I mean, it must exhaust you both. Off and on and off and on—"

"Leave it, Johnny," Ryan says, but that only serves to wind Johnny up giving his reaction.

"Hey, how do you think this is for me? I'm stuck in the middle, feeling like I have to choose between one of my best friends and my sister. Honestly, it's goddamn stressful."

I swear to God, he doesn't even know the meaning of the word stressful. He has an easy life. No fucking women to stress over, that's for sure.

"We're not doing this now, Johnny," I say, giving him a piercing look because the last thing I want is a heated discussion with Johnny while everyone looks on. Luckily, he shrugs.

I already tainted the dressing room with the conversation I had last Christmas Eve, so I'm keen to get cleaned up for a temporary change of scenery.

I'm the first one to the showers, so I move around the room, getting them all going to heat the water. I step into the shower stall furthest from the door and hang my towel on the hook.

Ryan enters the stall next to me moments later, then Johnny occupies the stall opposite; it's as if they're ganging up on me, but to my relief, the conversation isn't about Vicky.

"What are we thinking of our chances for the Challenge Cup this year?" Ryan asks no one in particular.

"Hopefully, now that Lee is here, we'll have an even better top line than last season. Let's see how Jani works with both of you," Johnny says, his voice taking on a captain-like tone.

Jani is the first line centre and, from what I understand, is a pretty good match to play alongside my brother. I doubt it'll take us long to get into a rhythm.

"Remind me of your face-off percentage last season, Lee," Johnny asks.

"Fifty-eight per cent, something like that," I say.

Ryan frowns. He knows all his stats by heart, but I don't pay all that much attention to mine. I just like to get the job done.

"Impressive. Big things are going to happen, big things," Johnny says. "The first cup game is the season opener, so at least we can get off to a good start. I think Coach will put you in the power play unit."

"We're a forward down. Any news on who's going to fill the spot, Cap?"

I can't make out who asks, but I do know that there's a roster spot open for a home-grown player. Someone retired last season and for once, Johnny doesn't know shit about it.

"No news yet," Johnny replies, but uses this moment to take his leave.

"I still can't believe we've got two ex-NHL players on our team. Are you ever going to tell us what made you commit career suicide, Prez?" Bettsy says from the shower across from Ryan.

"It's not important," Ryan snaps.

"I just don't get it. It's completely outrageous," Bettsy says. He chirps on and on about it, using different variations of phrases.

"He had his reasons," I say, but the look I get from Ryan tells me I should have shut my damn mouth.

"For Christ's sake," he snaps before grabbing his towel and stalking out. I follow him.

"Did you not tell them?" I say in a strained whisper as close as I can get to his left ear.

"No. And they don't need to know."

He pops his earbud in, and I put my effort into getting dressed, trying to ignore the fact that Johnny's eyes are burning into the back of my head.

"What is it?" I glance around to him and stare.

"You need to focus, Lee. Coach isn't overly impressed you bailed on your contract last year, so my guess is, you have zero room for fuck ups," he says. He's right. Agreeing to play here last season, then bailing out and sending Ryan in my place—that wasn't cool.

"I will focus," I say, but hearing the words aloud gives me a knot of doubt in the pit of my stomach. How can I focus when Vicky is everywhere? Fuck! I feel like such a fucking idiot, and catching sight of my game jersey in my cubby only makes me feel worse.

The white lettering gleams off the overhead lights, and the first thing that pops into my head is what Vicky would look like wearing nothing but that jersey. Maybe in a pair of those heels she has too.

I try to shake the image away because getting involved with Vicky again is not an option, even if every fibre in my body is telling me otherwise. We need to keep things platonic. But the dumb thing is, I don't even know how to be her friend. We were everything, but never just friends.

"Any plans for the rest of the day?" Ryan asks, popping a bud out of his ear.

"Video games with Danny," I say, because that has already become something of a habit.

"You're coming to the junior game with me," he says. "They have an exhibition match, and I could do with the help."

Jen's uncle used to coach the juniors, but now Ryan has taken over until they find a replacement.

"I have plans," I say.

"Video games with Danny are not plans," he says. Then he leans in. "Besides, I need to keep you out of trouble. How else can I keep you from scrolling Vic's socials?"

"Fine. But you're coming for a beer afterwards," I say.

When I say beer, I mean tap water, because Ryan can be a fucking bore at times. He takes himself too seriously.

"What's this about beers?" Bettsy's standing there in his boxers, fighting with the legs of his pants.

"Beers tonight, Betts. May as well make a thing," I shrug at Ryan.

"If that's the case, everyone is coming to support the juniors. No exceptions. I want you guys cheering and shit," he says. But I already know it's a bad idea.

I know Liam's here before I see him. I can hear Ryan talking, and there's a familiar tone of laughter that floats through the air in response. His eyes meet mine as I round the corner, and my world stops for a moment. He's wearing a zip-up jacket with the team logo, a matching baseball cap with the peak backwards and he's trimmed his beard right down to almost stubble—my absolute favourite. What a prick.

"There you are!" Jenna says, bouncing into my line of sight. "Are you okay?"

"Sure," I flash her a fake smile, which she sees right through.

"I'm sorry. I didn't know he was going to be here." She glances over to Liam. "Ryan's invited the whole bloody team, by the looks of it. Apparently, he needs all the help he can get."

"Well, I'm here now, it's fine," I say, returning Danny's wave from where he stands with a few of the guys.

"Do you want to hear the latest with Danny and Becca? Because there's trouble in paradise." She flicks her eyes to Danny.

"Was it really all that paradise-y?" I say, lowering my voice to a whisper.

"Well, no. He didn't go into detail, but he said things aren't great." She pauses for a moment. "Becca was supposed to be coming along tonight, but she can't make it now. But just in case she shows up, don't mention it."

"Don't mention what? You haven't told me anything. You're a terrible gossip!"

"You know as much as I do," she says.

"I'm sorry, but that was the worst tea I've ever heard. What did he actually say? I want details." She definitely owes me details.

I guess it's always awkward when you're best friends with both parties of a couple and have been since you were all kids. It takes a few seconds for me to realise this is perhaps how Johnny is feeling. He's been stuck in the middle between Liam and me, but I know if he had to pick sides, he wouldn't pick me.

"Come on, I need the distraction." I nudge her in the ribs.

"Still thinking about Liam, huh?"

"You're changing the subject."

Jen frowns. "He basically just said that he and Becca aren't hanging out much anymore. He said she's always busy with something, making excuses not to see him—or that's what he thinks, anyway." She chews her lip. "Between us, I don't think they're right for each other."

"I can't say I've paid a lot of thought to it." I really haven't. In fact, the only thing I've been thinking about is how much I hate Liam.

Danny bellows and waves at Jen, giving her a beckoning signal. I watch her go, then I set my bag down, surveying the area, looking for Johnny because I need to talk with him. I squat down to get my things out, my fingers skimming the wool of a Marlies toque I've got stowed in the pocket, memories of the last time I wore it come flooding back.

Liam's laughter sounds out again. I stand up and risk a glance over to where he's standing. He catches my eye, and he excuses himself before walking towards me. He's quick to skirt past the line of junior skaters waiting to step onto the ice. Fuck.

"Vicster! How's it going?" he asks. He only calls me Vicster when he's trying hard to show that he's 'just a friend.' But to my surprise, he reaches down and grabs the toque from my bag. Then he holds it out to me. "It's cold, Vic. You should put it on."

What I should do is set fire to it, but he's right. I'm annoyed at myself because I didn't grab my other hat before heading out. And he knows I don't like the cold.

I drop my camera strap around my neck and reach for the hat, all while avoiding his eyes. I run my hands over my hair, setting it over my shoulders before pulling the wool over my head.

Then he does that thing that all guys do in movies, or books or whatever. He reaches out and tucks a loose strand of my hair away, and his hand lingers for longer than necessary. It only confirms what we both know; the spark between us is still there. I can hear my heartbeat in my eardrums, the thud, thud, thud, not even close to serving as a distraction, and I don't know how, but I croak out a thanks.

"Are you going to talk to me, then? Because you've usually got a lot to say." His tone is teasing, but it pisses me off because he's right. I gape at him, raking my brain for some quick-fire cocky response, but nothing comes. So, I just go with the first thing that pops into my head.

"No."

I slide past him, mindful that my ass definitely rubbed across his thigh, and make my way to the bench, feeling his eyes on me as I go.

At least I know where Johnny is, though. He's sitting at the far end where I was destined; his head snaps away from the ice when he hears me approach.

"Vic, I wondered where you were," he says as I take a seat next to him. "Nice hat." His tone is bitter, but I ignore him.

"You're in my way, John. I need to lean there to get my shots." I indicate towards the corner.

"How are things going with Lee? Are you being civil?"

"Yes."

"Really?"

"I'm doing my job. That's it."

He lets out a breath and straightens his cap.

"I do know how to be professional, you know," I say, but Johnny shakes his head and looks directly at me.

"You've been different since you came back," he says.

"Where did that come from?" I ask.

"Just thinking out loud." He stands up anyway to make room for me to squeeze into the corner.

Before I ready my camera, I turn to look at Johnny, and there's a moment where it feels like we're both kids again and I feel like sharing.

"Going home was a complete mess," I start. "And it just made me realise that mom and dad probably won't care if they never saw me ever again."

"That's not true," he says, digging his hands into the pockets of his jacket. The same team jacket that Liam is wearing, except this one is marked with a 'C.'

"Isn't it? Because I've always been a spare part—actually, it doesn't matter. Everything was perfect for you."

"Is that what you think?" he scoffs and looks out onto the ice.

"I don't even think they wanted me." It's the first time I've ever said it out loud, and I wait for something to come—tears, anger—I don't know, something. But it doesn't.

"You're being ridiculous." There it is, typical Johnny.

"Am I? Because that's how I feel." That's how I've always felt, even before our parents got divorced.

I don't resent Johnny, but I was envious of the attention he got from our dad. It was always all about Johnny. Even more so when he made a Triple-A team, and the focus was entirely on him. What we did on weekends, what we ate, how we spent any time as a family; it always revolved around hockey. And it was horrible. That was until Liam came into the picture. He made things more bearable, even if he ignored me for a long time. I used to count down the days until I'd see him next. And that first time his mom, Lois, invited me over for dinner along with Johnny, I thought I was going to explode.

"Well, they don't feel that way," Johnny says, staring at me for a moment before he nods and walks away.

I can't say I'm surprised since Johnny's immediate go-to reactions are to punch a wall or run away. Unless he's dishing out advice. I know he'll avoid this conversation for a while, and I'll let him since I'm exhausted with it myself. It's all I've been thinking about. But now, I need to concentrate on what I'm supposed to be doing.

I busy myself with my camera. As soon as the junior team file onto the bench next to me, I get a few shots of them setting up. Ryan paces behind them, giving them a pep-talk. Then Liam is there, leaning against the wall next to where Ryan stands. I can feel his eyes burning into me.

I spend the first half of the period taking shots from the corner, building up the courage to squeeze past them to change my angle. But I'm forced into action when I hear my name called.

"Vic, can you get some from centre ice?" Ryan waves me towards him and pushes himself up against the wall to let me pass, but I swear Liam keeps himself as jutted as possible, forcing me to touch him.

Just as I think I'm clear, I feel a hand settle on my shoulder, causing me to halt. "Can we talk?"

"Use your legs, boys. Let me see those feet moving!" Ryan shouts at the top of his lungs, and the bustle of the kids moving on the bench forces me to step away. I get into position and finish up my shots there for the rest of the period. Ryan's juniors score the opening goal, and I capture the all-important celly in action.

Stepping aside to let the juniors pass as the buzzer goes, I'm convinced Liam's waiting to pounce again. Instead, he disappears into the secondary dressing room with Ryan. I slump down onto the bench and flick through the shots I've got so far, the slushy water under my feet causing me to regret my choice of footwear.

I don't even notice Liam sit down next to me until he says hello and it's like he's transported me back in time. To a time when I thought we were okay, just before we went into that equipment room. My mind is working overtime, and I'm replaying Christmas Eve morning all over again. I'd woken up in bed with Liam, his arms wrapped around me, and I thought there was nowhere else I'd ever want to be. I liked it, and I got emotional and called Jen, all good. Then Liam went to the gym with Johnny and Ryan.

"What did Johnny say to you on Christmas Eve at the gym?" I blurt it out before I can fully think about what I'm asking him.

"What?"

"The morning before we went skating. We were fine and then you went to the gym. And then—what did Johnny say?" I look down at my camera as I talk, afraid of crying if I look directly at him.

"Oh, so you're talking to me now?"

"No." I stand up and slip past him, making my way over to where Johnny leans against the boards. He's facing away from me, but I catch the conversation he's in the middle of.

"Matt Rodgers? Are you serious?" Danny says from his spot opposite Johnny. "Does Bettsy know?"

"Johnny! What did you say to Lee on Christmas Eve?" I step between him and Danny, blocking off their discussion just as Liam strides over. It's rude, I know, but I need answers.

"What?" Johnny narrows his eyes.

"What did you say to Lee on Christmas Eve?" I say again.

"Nothing!"

"Vic—it's got nothing to do with Johnny," Liam says, moving towards me, but I'm scanning the area for Ryan now, since if it wasn't Johnny...

"Where's Ryan?" I say. But I don't wait for a response. I march towards the secondary dressing room with no thought of what I'm doing. The juniors stare in awe at me as I burst through the door. Ryan's standing at a marker board, drawing circles and lines and shit, but his attention flicks to me.

"Are you—"

"What did you say to Liam on Christmas Eve?"

Ryan glares at me, and then his eyes flick past me through the open door.

"Vicky, come here," Johnny tries, but I'm still fixed on Ryan.

"What did you say?" I try again, but then there's a familiar hand on my shoulder, creating a warmth that spreads down through my body, an unwanted warmth. I wriggle away, not to let myself get distracted and step back out into the tunnels.

I can hear Jen saying my name, but Bettsy comes thundering past as if someone has taped the blades of his skates and he's seeking revenge.

"Matt Rodgers?" Bettsy's shouts. His face matches the colour of his hair, a deep red that spreads across his cheeks. "What the fuck, Johnny? Why didn't you mention that Matt Rodgers is joining the team?"

All the guys, except Liam, crowd Johnny just outside the door to the dressing room. Liam is standing behind me, tugging at my arm.

"Vic, we need to talk," he says, my name slipping through his lips in such a way that I know I don't want to hear what he has to say. I'm afraid to listen to him. Then it hits me. This must be how he was feeling, and my heart feels like it's going to burst open. But I'm not ready.

I shake him away and step aside.

"Vicky—" Jen this time. My saving grace because I need to get out of here. She reaches for my hand. "Let's go home."

Chapter 5

I poise my finger on the shutter-release button, and my eye tracks his every move like I've done thousands of times. Following Liam as he skates around on the ice is simple work for me. I've seen him skate so many times I can time his every move.

He slows his pace and taps his stick on the ice, calling his brother for a pass. "Don't be a fucking show-off," he shouts, and Ryan eventually sails the puck across the neutral zone towards him.

"Do better, then!" Ryan retorts.

Liam sends it back and again, Ryan uses the opportunity to have a little fun and keep the puck to himself.

"Just saucer it across!" Liam yells at Ryan, and I can tell by his voice that he's getting irritated.

Liam receives the puck from Ryan and picks it up on the toe of his stick, the same stick I taped a few nights ago—I couldn't help myself. I snap a shot of him battling the puck like it's a fly he's been chasing just as he gives me a sideways glance. My heart leaps.

"If you want to play, bro, we can play." Liam bats the puck through the air and Ryan skates towards it, hitting it back, just like they're playing tennis or something.

"Will you guys stop fucking around and do your drills?" my brother shouts from the blue line where he's come to a stop. But Liam shouts something back, and Johnny's head snaps in my direction.

"Vic, you remember there's an entire roster to capture, and you'll have to get some shots of Matt Rodgers. Make it look like we're glad to have him here." He comes to a stop at the boards where I'm standing.

"I am," I say, peering back into the viewfinder.

"Have you spoken to him yet?"

"No."

Johnny sighs, and then he pokes at the ice with his stick. "Look, that morning at the gym, neither Ryan nor I said anything about you. In fact, I don't even think you came up in conversation." Johnny grabs a water bottle from the ledge and squirts it towards his mouth. "I know nothing, Vic."

"Fine," I snap. I don't buy it.

"Just grow a pair and speak to him." He slams the bottle down and draws his attention back to where Liam and Ryan are. "That shit you pulled the other night can't happen again. You're embarrassing yourself."

"Or am I embarrassing you?" I flash him a scowl.

"Vic—"

"I'll talk to him when I'm ready."

He sighs before throwing his attention back to Matt Rodgers who signed with us after his contract lapsed, and apparently, the club made him an offer he couldn't refuse. He's skating with a few of the other guys from the third line, but it all looks peculiar. Forced, even.

"What's the deal with him?" I whisper to Johnny.

He takes his helmet off and leans over the boards for a towel. "Don't you remember that shit last season? It's mainly some crap between him and Bettsy, but the tension in the dressing room is crazy. I didn't even know he was starting officially until I saw his goddamn name plate."

"Oh, yeah," I didn't really know a lot about it, only what I overheard, and Johnny has always been terrible at relaying information.

I remember when he first told me that Ryan was coming over to play. I almost choked on my coffee. Why the hell would Ryan give up his career? Because everyone knows a year out of the NHL makes it almost impossible to get back. It was the craziest thing I'd ever heard. When I pressed him for info, he merely shrugged and said he knew no more about it, other than he was coming since Liam couldn't anymore. I couldn't let on that it was all my fault, but it disappointed me that Johnny didn't bother to ask how Liam had convinced Ryan. It was the most infuriating thing ever, and I couldn't call up Liam and ask him myself.

Johnny tosses the towel on to the bench after scouring his head one last time. He plops his helmet back on and skates back towards Bettsy.

I cycle through the photos I've got so far before opting for one of the earlier shots I got of Liam. That's enough. I'm wondering how much longer I can stand here, anyway. I'm tracking him still, making sure he's busy. Anytime he looks in my direction, I occupy myself with my notepad, or my phone, or my camera, trying my best to avoid eye contact because he can read me like a book.

I make the mistake of taking my attention away for a second, and I can smell his sweat and the remnants of his cologne before I've set eyes on him. My body responds instantly, every part of me tensing and aching with need. Dammit, even my anatomy is out to get me.

"Thanks, by the way," he says, referring to the tape job on his stick.

"You're crap at it, so why not?" I jibe, still looking down at my camera.

"Yeah, but I appreciate it. It's not the same when I do it myself."

"Nothing's the same when you do it yourself." I regret saying it immediately.

"You're right. I've never been able to get the same result with my own hands." Even though I'm not directly looking at him, I can see him in the corner of my eye as he wiggles his eyebrows, and I can't help but smirk. But then I snap myself back.

"Photos are done, thanks. You're free to go," I say.

"Will you please just talk with me?" he asks.

I shake my head and look down at my camera.

"Hey?" I hear the clatter of a stick hitting the ice, and then I feel his index finger under my chin, pulling my head upward. "Look at me?"

I risk a glance directly at his eyes, and my breath catches in my throat. Bad idea, Vicky. Bad idea. Don't look directly at him.

I've got to give it to him. There's a way he looks at me which I've never seen from anyone else. It's as if I'm the only girl in the world. My entire body prickles with electricity.

"Don't," I rasp, batting his hand away. "I need to go." I walk away, desperate to get some space, afraid I'll try to kiss him or something because my brain is cloudy with desire.

But he's fast. I can hear him hopping over the boards, and he's blocking my way before I can get off the rubber matting, my heels pressing into the smooth surface.

"Are we going to try being friends?" he asks.

"Are you kidding?"

"No. Why would I be? We can't just throw everything away."

"You did that, Lee," I snap.

"No, actually, you did. But I want to move past it. We're going to have to spend a lot of time together, so we need to make it work."

"Well, just avoid me all the times you don't have to work with me, please."

"Vic—" Liam's voice is soft.

"Don't," I say, looking down at my feet, right at the shoes I'm wearing that Liam bought me. I remember when he gave them to me. It's as if he had read my mind and knew that I'd been looking lovingly at them for weeks—either that or he'd checked my search history and stalked my Insta. But as a general fact, Liam always seems to know what I like, what I need, and when I seem to need it. Just like I know exactly what he wants and likes too. And wearing only these heels and stockings is high on the list. Sometimes his jersey, too—nothing underneath, the rough material scratching at my skin, my nipples in particular.

"What's going on, Vicster?" There's that attempt at friendly again. He crouches down and looks up, forcing me to lock eyes with him. My skin ripples with goosebumps. I want him. I want him to take me into that equipment room and—I bite my lip. How can he even ask me that? He knows exactly what's going on. "Talk to me. Please." There's a flicker of something in that yellowy-green paradise of his eyes that I've lost myself in so many times.

"I'm not ready yet," I say, swerving around him as I hop to the unmatted area, quick on my feet, knowing he won't chase me without guards.

What did he expect? To turn up here and be friends? No way. There's too much between us to be friends.

I hate being frustrated. I just don't know how to deal with it and the more I try to figure it out, the more frustrated I get. It's a vicious circle and the object of my frustration is myself. I know now that I clearly wasn't thinking. Being apart from Vicky made me forget how she can overwhelm my senses and ignite uncontrollable emotions.

The way she smells, the way she looks at me, the sound of her voice, her laugh. I'm now in a state of desperation to touch her, feel her underneath me, hold her hand in mine, and not to mention the need I have to taste her. Because, fuck me, the taste of her lips and her pussy are enough to make me feral at the mere thought. The emotional connection we have, coupled with the sexual pull, is a dangerous combination. But feeling the way I do now, I just need something from her. Anything.

I head back into the dressing room, dropping my stick in the rack as I pass, eager to get the fuck away from here because everything about this place screams Vicky. And I need a damn shower. I get to my cubby just as the rest of the guys file in, bar Johnny and Matt Rodgers. As everyone removes their gear, the air fills with conversation about practice, but I don't feel like joining in.

"Has Johnny said anything to you, Betts?" Hutch, one of the other forwards, asks.

But before Bettsy can answer, the door to the dressing room creaks open, and Johnny, Matt, and Coach stride in.

They stop just before they reach the logo dominating the centre of the room.

"Listen in, fellas," Coach says after clearing his throat. He rocks back and forth on his feet as if he's waiting to pounce. "I know there's been some history, but please remember: you're all on the same team, and I expect you to behave like it, on and off the ice. I won't take any of that shit. And I have no problem benching any troublemakers. This isn't juniors. Professional hockey means professional hockey. Any problems, see me." Coach sweeps his gaze around the room twice before nodding. He whispers something to Johnny before turning and heading out, back through the half-open dressing room door.

"Any issues, guys?" Johnny says, using his best authoritative voice. At first, he's not looking at anyone in particular, but his gaze lays to rest on Bettsy, who's wriggling out of his underlayer.

"Betts? Matt? Do you guys need to talk anything through?" he asks.

"No," they chime.

I'd like to say that the air was clear, but it feels thicker than ever.

"Where're you living then, mate?" Hutch asks Matt from his cubby.

"I'm waiting for them to allocate me a place. I'm in a hotel for a few weeks, by the look of it," Matt replies.

Ryan grins at me. "Worst case, Jen and I will move out of Vicky's soon. I guess she'll be looking for someone to share with."

I have to bite my tongue not to show how I really feel about that idea, but he can see right through me. I have given little thought to their move. Real estate is slow here, and they haven't made any formal offers yet, so he's just messing with me.

"There'll be no need for that," Johnny says. "I think there's something coming up in our building soon."

"Why doesn't Matt live with you?" I ask Johnny.

"Because there's no need." He stomps off towards the showers. I wonder what's got him so fucking tetchy.

"Sorry, I couldn't resist," Ryan says, leaning in when the immediate area around us has cleared. "What was all that about with Vicky?"

"Nothing."

"Didn't look like nothing."

"Drop it, Ryan."

"Fine," he snaps. "Decided what you're going to do with your life after hockey, then?"

"Christ, will you quit it?"

I swear to God he's just set on pissing me off now. I told him last night that I was going to come up with a plan about my future, but unfortunately for me, Vicky has taken over my every waking thought.

"I'm just asking," he shrugs, but I've heard enough, heading to the showers before he can quiz me further.

I know what he's doing. He's trying to get me in a state of flux where I have no other option but to carry on playing, but I'm so damn wound up right now I can't think straight.

The shower room is loud from singing and chit-chat. There's no space to think. I need to relieve the tension that's building up inside me, but that'll have to wait until I get home, so I make quick work of getting myself washed before heading back to the dressing room.

There's a small knock on the door just as I'm putting my shirt on, and Ffordey, our starting goalie, heads over and pulls it open a crack, enough to stick his head out. He peers outside and I can hear Vicky.

"I need to see Liam and Matt," she says to him. He glances back, checking the state of dress everyone is in, then nods for her to enter.

"Hey guys, could you come up to the media room when you're done here, please? The GM wants me to do a quick meet and greet thing with you both. And I need to find some time to photograph your cubby, Matt."

"No problem," Matt grins at her, and it pisses me off.

Vicky says she'll see us soon before turning to leave. This is exactly what I don't need, but I finish getting ready and take Matt's lead.

"How's it going?" I say, before asking him about his career so far.

He's frosty at first, but then once he starts talking about himself, he doesn't shut up. I let him ramble on.

"Look, the other guys may be pissed at you for whatever reason, but I speak as I find. So unless I've got reason to be chippy, I won't be."

I don't think he's expecting this. His eyes widen slightly, but we don't speak to each other again.

It doesn't take me long to form an opinion of him, though.

"Hey Vicky, you're looking beautiful today," he grins at her as we walk into the media room. Who knew a sentence could take me from zero to a hundred?

Her face breaks out in a grin aimed at Matt. "Thanks!"

Vicky indicates for us to sit down. There are two chairs set up in front of the white screen. Matt takes the chair closest to Vicky, and jealousy courses through me quicker than I could have ever expected. Even though this is all my making, I'm pissed.

"Sorry to drag you up here. I'm sure you just want to get going," she says. "Hope the guys are helping you to settle in, Matt." She flashes him a grin.

"Fine, thanks. I've only just met most of the team, but everyone's been welcoming so far. Happy to help with the PR and social media stuff anytime you need. Just give me a shout."

I said I speak as I find, and I find this guy to be a fucking douche.

"I won't keep you long," she says. "Lee, can you sit down, please?" She nods towards the empty chair next to Matt and I slump down, turning my cap backwards and then forwards again before taking it off entirely.

I watch as she moves around the room. She stands behind the tripod in front of our chairs and peers into the viewfinder.

"Big smiles!" she says, pressing the shutter release button a few times. We've both done this a million times before, so it doesn't take Vicky long to check she's got a shot she can work with before sitting down herself.

"So, Matt. What's it like joining a team full of guys you've spent a long time playing against?"

He gives some bullshit answer that I tune out. She follows up with a question to me about how I'm feeling about playing with my brother and Johnny.

"I guess it's a vast difference from what you're used to," she says, but I'm not paying attention; I'm watching her perfect lips instead.

I get nudged in the ribs by Matt, and he nods towards Vicky, pulling me back into the room. The format turns to quick fire, Vicky obviously keen to get this over with. After a few more questions each, she consults her notepad and smiles to herself.

"Cool. Thank you both, we're done here. Thanks for your time." Her tone is dismissive, and I can tell by the way she's standing that she's eager to get us gone, but Matt walks straight over to her. He turns on the charm, and I can't do anything about it except watch and let the anger bubble inside me.

He doesn't get much flirting in—which is a shame for him, but not for me—before Vicky's phone rings. She frowns at the screen before bringing it to her ear.

"I need to take this. Sorry, guys. Thanks again for your time," she says, covering the speaker with her hand. She nods at the door, giving us the hint that we need to leave.

Matt follows me out and pounces on me with a question I can tell he's been waiting to ask.

"What's the deal with you and Preston, then? NHL paying you too much?" He forces a laugh.

As much as I want to tell him all about my reasons for calling it a day, I don't. And Ryan's business is Ryan's business—well, partly his business considering the circumstance of him coming here in the first place. If he wants to tell him, he can.

"I'll tell you about it another time," I lie, keen to get away from him.

As we walk past the door to the main office space, luck has it that Ryan is leaning against Jen's desk. I use that as my excuse to say my goodbyes, slipping through the open door towards him.

"How was it?" Ryan asks as I approach.

I take a seat at Vicky's empty desk and adjust the chair so it reclines fully. I grab a stress ball from an open PR box sitting at the end of her desk and start tossing it in the air.

"Oh, Vicky will be fuming," Jen says, eyeing the chair.

"She's already pissed at me, so why not make myself comfortable," I say, still working with the stress ball.

"How was it then?" Ryan asks again.

"That Matt guy is a douche."

"Well, that's what the consensus is. I take it you went in with an open mind, though. What happened?"

"It doesn't matter."

"Did he flirt with Vicky?" Ryan asks.

"He did nothing but flirt with Vicky."

Ryan moves from Jen's desk and stands about ten feet away, giving me the opportunity to toss the stress ball to him. Back and forth, back and forth. Then the sound of

Vicky's heels on the tiles of the hallway echo. She comes to a stop at the door.

I jerk my head around to look, missing my turn to catch the ball, and it hits the side of my head.

Her eyes meet mine for a split second and she hesitates for a moment before turning on the spot and leaving.

"You need to sort this shit out," Ryan says.

"She won't talk to me," I say, twisting my head back to look at him.

"Make her. Because like it or not, you're going to be working together, and the last thing we need is any drama off the ice."

"Are you expecting any drama on the ice?" I ask, raising a brow. "Because there's always room for drama."

"Figure it out," Ryan says, grabbing another ball from the box and tossing it at me—harder this time. It catches me off-guard, and it drops to the floor, rolling under Vicky's desk.

I stick my head under, spying a pair of heels which I fight to ignore. I spot the ball, too. And as I reach for it, I notice a letter sticking out of Vicky's wastepaper bin marked 'Private and Confidential'. Since I'm a nosey fuck, I want to pluck it out, but Ryan grabs the back of the chair and shakes it back and forth, forcing me to resurface.

"Come on, let's head out and let Jen work in peace," he says. I have no choice but to abandon both the ball and my curiosity.

Chapter 6

Liam

Unluckily for me, opening night means lots of media attention. And lots of media attention means lots of Vicky. I've been here a month and Vicky still hasn't spoken to me properly. She's doing her best to avoid me, and I've been in a constant state of frustration. It's simmering under my skin, ready to erupt at any minute.

She's got this black fitted dress on, and I swear she's wearing those damn heels to wind me up because I can't stop looking at her legs. She has legs for days, and her stockings make them look all shimmery. I love it.

I bought her a pair of Prada's for her twenty-first birthday, and what a fucking treat they were; especially the close up view I got when they were at eye level while her legs rested on my chest. Cost wasn't an issue, and neither was having to pay my brother back weekly. Lucky for me, he didn't ask what I needed a loan for. I'm not even sure if I would have told him because he wouldn't have understood. I don't know what it is with Vicky and heels. Anyone else can wear heels and I don't bat an eye, but when Vicky does, it drives me wild. My dick stirs, and I can't even smell her perfume yet.

I'm with the team in the tunnels waiting for warmups to start. Some guys are stretching, some are singing to the music, some are play-fighting like kids—but I'm watching Vicky.

She chats with the support team, and when she laughs, I suppress a smile. There's a mumbling next to me, then I'm jabbed in the ribs.

"I said, what's the latest with you and Vicky then, mate?" Bettsy says, his eyes following mine.

"Nothing at all. I guess it's complicated," I offer.

"It's not though, is it? Both Vicky and Lee need to sort their shit out and get away from whatever toxic environment they've created for themselves," Ryan butts in.

I glare at him. He's not wrong, of course, but I'm taken aback by his bluntness.

"Christ!" Bettsy scoffs.

"Just leave it for now, guys," Danny says, attempting to smooth the air.

Vicky spins on her heels and starts walking towards us. I'm watching the way her hips sway and images pop into my head of my hands gripping them as she bounces up and down on my dick. And suddenly, it feels a hundred degrees in the barn.

She's got her phone out and that tiny mic plugged in, ready to record a social media video, no doubt. And she begins by giving the group a wide smile, never quite looking directly at me, but I'm fixed on her as if she's keeping me alive. I want to look away, but I can't.

"Right guys, first, Danny, you're tonight's 'Shirt off his back,' so be prepared." There's a few wolf-whistles before Vicky continues. "Second, today's question is, 'who in the team would you choose as your partner in a three-legged race?'"

Christ, where does she come up with this shit? We get the signal to head towards the ice. Parker Fforde, the goalie, steps forward and wades towards the front. "Jonesy," he says without stopping. He doesn't even look in Vicky's direction; he's a fucking keener for the ice.

Jonesy is another local guy, and he's next, throwing Ffordey's name back at Vicky.

Danny's next. "Anyone bar Bettsy," he says, twirling his stick.

Bettsy steps forward. "The Captain," he says, nodding in Johnny's direction.

To my surprise, Johnny reciprocates Bettsy as he makes his way to the ice. Probably because they're super coordinated.

"Who are you going to pick?" I whisper to Ryan as we make our way forward, albeit last in the line. I don't know why I'm asking because I know he's going to pick me—at least, he better pick me.

"You, dumbass," he whispers back before stepping up to Vicky's tiny microphone and grinning at her.

"My brother, because no one else would pick him."

Vicky bites her lip, and her eyes fix on mine. Her perfume fills my nose, and I muster all the strength I have to not push her up against the wall and show her what she's been missing. Or remind myself what I've given up.

"Liam?" she says, softly. I have to shake my head to clear the fog.

"Yeah, my brother, too," I say, then I decide to use the opportunity to my advantage. "Hey, Vic, can we talk? I think I've given you enough time."

She stops recording and lowers her phone. My stomach churns with butterflies as I wait for her to reply, but she says something about me sticking around after the game to sign autographs instead. She is so damn frustrating.

"No," I say.

"What do you mean, no? You have to!" she says, pouting, and I can't help but stare at her lips, immediately thinking about pulling at her bottom lip with my teeth. She's still glaring at me, waiting for me to answer, but I have an idea.

"I will, but only if you agree to talk to me. You can't avoid me forever."

"Fine," she snaps and just in time too. Springy, the assistant coach, calls me to the ice and I could use the cool down. I shuffle past her and grab my stick from the rack. A brief warmth flows through me as I glance at the fresh tape job on the blade of my stick. It's just how I like it.

I step onto the smooth surface to a round of applause, and I lap our end of the ice a few times before swiping a puck with my stick and firing it at Ffordey. I skate behind the net and then replay the drill again. Ryan comes to skate next to me, and I slow down as if on cue.

"What was that about?" he asks, shooting at the net.

"Nothing. Literally, nothing. I've had to bribe her to speak to me," I say. I tell Ryan about the signing after the game. "All I want to do is clear the air, make things as civil as possible, considering we can't avoid each other." I don't tell him I just need something from her. Anything. Any sort of communication. That'd make me sound desperate—which I am—but he doesn't need to know this.

"When did you become such a pushover?" he asks. For fuck's sake, he's right. I shouldn't have to bribe her into speaking with me. This is ridiculous.

We fire a few more pucks towards the net before we skate over to stretch at the blue line. I focus on the bench where Vicky and Jen stand, the pair of them looking down at Vicky's camera. Then two things happen in quick succession: Vicky giggles as she glances towards me and something in me snaps.

I get to my skates and glide back to the bench, taking my helmet off as I step onto the matting. I prop my stick up against the boards and slide my gloves off, tossing all my gear on to the floor.

Vicky and Jen are watching me, brows knitted together. "Come with me," I say, as I take Vicky by the hand and pull her towards the tunnels, giving her no time to think of an excuse not to. She trails behind me, our hands linked for a moment, sending a familiar jolt of heat shooting up my arm.

We halt at the dressing room entrance, and I gently pull her hand, pinning her against the wall as I box her in with my hands on either side of her head. She's five-nine in heels, but I tower over her with my skates on.

"Vic." I move my face towards hers and she opens her mouth. "I'm not letting you go until you talk to me. I'm not dumb enough to expect you to make a declaration of lifelong friendship, but I don't expect to be ghosted. Not after everything we've been through."

I lean towards her, my eyes locked on the ocean blue of her own, and every delicious scent she's wearing fills my nose. My heart sounds in my ears, and my mouth waters in anticipation. I can hear her breathing deepen, and it's as if there's nothing else in the world happening outside of this moment.

I'm waiting for her to say something, but to my complete surprise, she closes the gap by stretching up and she kisses me. Excitement zips through my entire body. The soft brush of her lips and the warmth of her body against mine are perfect, just like they always are. Try as I might, I can't resist her because it's like the sizzling frustration has cooled, sated by Vicky's lips.

Between her perfume, her shampoo, the sweetness of whatever she's wearing on her lips—I can't help but kiss her back. My eyes close as she intoxicates me. I forget that we're supposed to be talking, or that I'm trying to repair my broken heart. Her lips, plump and delicious and soft, are too much to resist—and she opens her mouth slightly, inviting me in. She moans as my tongue meets with hers. Fuck. I'm still kissing her back and my dick is hard despite my inner monologue screaming at me to step back and be rational.

Suddenly, she retreats and my eyes snap open. She stares at me. Her face frozen in the kissing pose. Then she shakes her head as she looks.

"Damn it," she says.

"What was...?" I ask, but our eyes meet again, and my guess is that she didn't mean to do that. The way she's looking at me gives me a front-row seat to what's on her mind. Our kiss was just the way she remembered it to be, and she wants me as much as I want her, even though I've told her where we stand. I don't want to want her anymore, but I do.

"I can't," she says.

My eyes are still on hers; I take a breath. "Can't what?" I say. "I didn't—"

"Be your friend," she says, but I think I know where her mind has shifted. I need to hear it from her to be sure.

"Tell me you want nothing to do with me, and I'll leave you alone. I promise. I won't try to talk to you. I won't make things difficult. It'll be strictly work stuff."

She looks down at her shoes for what feels like the longest time, then she takes a breath, eyes still at her feet. "I want nothing to do with you," she says.

"At least fucking look at me and say it," I rasp, hammering my fist into the wall.

The crowd starts up, and I hear the sounds that accompany a team of hockey players on the move.

"I want nothing to do with you." She still doesn't look at me, but she ducks low under my arm, freeing herself, and her heels emit a dull thud on the rubber matting as she hurries away.

Frustration courses through my veins. I want to yell—so I do, the crowd drowning out my cries. My heart feels like she's crammed it into a mincer on high speed, tiny pieces of it flying all over the place, making it seem impossible to put back together. The worst bit? I know she's lying to me.

"Where've you been?" Ryan comes to a stop next to me. I don't need to answer him because the look on his face says he already knows, and he likely saw Vicky rushing past on her way back to the benches.

I stand up straight and take my gloves and helmet off him. "Your stick is on the rack," he adds.

I follow him into the dressing room, my body shaking. Talk about a mixed message. What the fuck does she think she's doing? What the fuck am I doing? Because I didn't even attempt to pull away, and now I'm feeling the regret of my actions because kissing her back has only sent the message that I wanted to kiss her. I wanted to kiss her, of course, but she didn't need to know that.

My lips tingle from the kiss, but sitting in my cubby brings me back down to the harsh reality of the situation: the conversation we had in this very spot around nine months ago.

Ryan flops down next to me. "Vicky wants me to leave her alone," I admit, my voice low. I take off my sweater to get some air to my body, dripping with sweat from whatever that was. "I guess I had it coming." I grab a towel and dry myself off.

"So that's it?" he raises a brow at me.

I lean in towards him, and he angles himself so I can whisper to him with ease. I doubt anyone will overhear us since everyone else is busy chatting. "That's it. She couldn't fucking look at me and say it. I don't think she even buys it herself," I growl.

Ryan leans in further as I take a deep breath. "You feeling okay, bud? Are you going to be okay to play?" he says.

I don't answer him, instead I refocus my attention, letting my heartbreak and confusion turn into anger, which morphs into a 'fuck it' attitude. Should I tell Ryan that she kissed me? No. I should feel violated that she's gone against what I want, but I don't. I feel wanting. If I let her in again, the chances of her breaking my heart for a third time are high, given her record—and I can't live through it again. I'm still not over the previous times. I need to distance myself and move on, all the while trying to remain professional.

"Well, she's made up her mind. Time to move on, properly this time," I say casually, trying to convince myself. "No friends." Pulling a protein bar out of my bag, I tear the wrapper off and I take a bite. "Bettsy, when are we off out on the town?"

Ryan gives me a look of concern. "C'mon on, Lee. That's not the answer."

"Why?" I snarl.

"You know—"

"Whatever. I can do what I want."

I shove the rest of the bar into my mouth and chew, but there's an uneasy feeling in my stomach, and it's not from my snack. I don't believe for one minute Vicky wants me to leave her alone, and my doing so will be torture for her.

"We can sort something soon. We've got that double-header weekend, so we can have a few after the game in the hotel," Bettsy says.

"That sounds like a fantastic plan," I say stiffly, but I know it sounds like the worst idea I've ever heard. Drinking the night before a game is never a good idea, but fuck it.

We're given a five-minute warning, and everyone settles down, ready for Johnny to give his pre-game speech. I don't listen. I don't even pretend to look at him. It's only when he gets Hutch to call out the starters that I swivel my head away from the spot I've been staring at.

"Heks, Prez, Lee, Cap, Bettsy," Hutch says in quick fire.

Everyone cheers and whoops. I pull my sweater back on and ready myself.

"Hey, Lee, can I borrow you?" Johnny asks me quietly before we head out.

I tilt my head to show him I'm listening.

"Are you okay? You look a bit flushed. Is it the knee?"

"My knee's fine. I'm fine," I say.

"Right, because we can switch things up, if need be," he offers.

I appreciate his concern; I really do. But no way is he benching me with the prospect of three measly shifts. Not that it's Johnny's decision, but he's got influence, of course.

Johnny hasn't always been the bossy defenceman that he is today. I remember back in juniors. We had a practice where Coach had a quick word with him after the session, telling him he was getting switched from centre to defence. Johnny wasn't happy, but Ryan was adamant that it was a good move. But it took me a while to agree with him. That had been the same practice he'd forgotten his skates, and his dad made him play with a pair from skate hire; no kid wants that embarrassment. Oddly enough, that was the same day that I first spoke with Vicky. Fucking Vicky.

"I'm good, John. Honest."

Before following Ffordey into the tunnels, we all bump shoulders and head towards the ice. And when Vicky comes into view, it's me who's avoiding eye contact with her.

What the fuck have I done? What the actual fuck have I done? My whole body is screaming at me to run away, but I can't even escape anywhere since I absolutely have to be here. I'm shaking as I make my way to my work area, and my knees hardly keep me upright. I've set up in a small space next to the penalty box which I've convinced management to let me use this season. I've also convinced Jen to support me. Updating socials and taking pictures is easier with her help.

I fall into my chair, then a second later, Jen appears.

"Are you okay, Vic?" She sits next to me.

"I just kissed Liam."

She gapes at me, then breaks into a smile. I busy myself getting my laptop ready with trembling hands.

"What? How?" she asks, leaning in. She's wearing Ryan's sweater. It's huge around her shoulders, and I feel a pang of envy. 'WAGs' don't traditionally wear their guy's jersey, but I love that Jen just doesn't give a shit about that and does what she wants. It's cute. And I'd be lying if I said I didn't want to be wearing Liam's.

But I'm saved by the bell, or the lights in this case, as the rink is plunged into darkness and the intro music starts. I get into position. A lucky escape, really, because I don't think I can relive the moment. Not yet anyway.

I hurry back to the benches where I get a few shots of the guys skating out, glad to have got my timing right despite my inability to think straight. My face burns with embarrassment as Liam skates past, and I thank the stars that it's dark.

Once the team is out, and the introductions are done, they roll a red carpet out onto the ice. I'm given the thumbs up to rush forward, positioning myself ready to capture the ceremonial puck-drop. I'm used to feeling like all eyes are on me at these moments, but I'm painfully aware that number forty-six is watching me.

Johnny skates forward, along with the opposing captain, and our charity partner representative makes his way onto the ice to present the puck. My brother smiles and poses, making it easy for me to do my job. Mr Opposition—a guy I've seen quite a few times before—makes no effort to look remotely happy to be alive, so I do my thing, then back off before taking a few shots of the guys on the blue line. Liam's eyes meet mine for a split second before he looks away again, then I'm off the ice just in time for the anthem to start.

As soon as the music ends, a dance tune blasts out of the speakers, and the guys do a quick lap before heading to the bench or readying themselves for puck-drop. It's my signal to rush back to the penalty box side of the ice.

I pause at the boards, and can't resist zooming in on Liam, capturing him as he prepares for the face-off. The concentration on his face, captured for an eternity, before I take a wider shot of centre ice.

The moment the game starts, I rush back to my laptop, trying to ignore Jen's eyes boring into the side of my head.

"Are you going to tell me what happened?" she probes, her knee jiggling on the spot.

"There's not a lot to tell. He wanted to talk, so instead of coming up with anything decent to say, I kissed him."

Jen opens her mouth at least twice before she says anything, "So are you two—?"

"No. I told him I didn't want to be friends with him, and I want nothing to do with him," I admit.

"After you kissed him?" she says, before adding, "Shot on goal, our #12." She taps it into the browser window and sends it out as an update across the multiple socials.

"Yeah. But it was a mistake. I didn't mean to kiss him."

"So you tripped and fell?" Jen laughs.

"Obviously, I—"

"You did it because you wanted to, correct?"

"He doesn't want me, Jen. He made that clear at Christmas," I say.

"He does want you; he just doesn't want to have his heart broken again," she says.

"Who says I'm going to break his heart again?"

"Well, he doesn't know that—away shot on goal, #91. He's trying to protect himself which is why he wants to be friends with you. My guess is that he'd rather be your friend than not have you in his life at all," she says, her eyes not leaving the ice.

"I can't be his friend, Jen."

"Well yeah, so that's why you've told him to keep away?" she asks, and I nod.

Jen drops it there, and we work in silence for a few moments before I'm back on my feet. I capture an action shot of Ryan's attempt to chip one in past the tendy's blocker, and a mid-ice check that gets a two-minute interference call, which I spot Jen noting from the corner of my eye.

I'm looking through the viewfinder when a play is made directly in front of me, Liam getting boarded by an opposing forward; his name and number pressing right up against the glass. He pushes the opposition away, which causes a retaliation, and they shove each other back and forth before the opposition shoves Liam hard enough to cause a yard-sale hit, gear flying into the air.

The crowd is loud, shouting and jeering, and it all happens so fast, but Liam's getting pulled by the shoulders and he throws a punch. He probably hits his target a little firmer than he expected because he falls forward, bringing his partner with him. They're both rolling around on the ice, gloves, and helmets idle on the surface, skates in the air. My heart is in my mouth the entire time. I just stand there in complete shock because of all the years I've watched Liam play, he's never been the one to throw a punch. Yeah, he'll shove and charge or whatever, but never throw a punch.

He gets escorted away by the stripes. Ryan, and Jani Heikkinen, a Finnish forward on Liam's line, pick up his gear and pass it over as he's stuffed into the box.

Liam glances around, grabs a water bottle and squirts it over his face; his expression one of fury. What is he thinking? This is probably because of me. As it's his first game here, too, he's now given himself a reputation early, setting the expectation that he's a fighter.

I return to Jen and my laptop, anxiously awaiting the officials' decision, hoping that she remains quiet.

I can feel Liam's eyes on me, and I risk a glance in his direction. There's a mix of emotion in his eyes. He's pissed off, and I'm now fully convinced that it's my fault, but I can't blame him. I crossed a line and made things a lot worse by going against his wishes. But when I think about it, as he stares at me, he kissed me back, didn't he?

Chapter 7

The season opener victory has lifted everyone's spirits. Even Ryan is joining in the social event planned for this evening. But my head is in a different place. Despite my stinging knuckles, all I can think about is Vicky and that kiss.

"Is that going to become a habit?" Ryan says, tossing his jersey in the laundry bin. He's referring to the fight, because despite what the crowd now think, I'm not a fighter.

"It depends," I shrug. I don't need to tell him what it depends on because he knows.

I'm just about to unlace my skates when the dressing room door creaks open and Vicky's blonde hair comes into view, causing my stomach to flip into my mouth.

"Everyone decent?" she calls and waits for grunts of approval before striding in.

"Lee, you're needed," she says, her cheeks pink.

It takes me a moment to remember what I'm needed for. "Shit, yeah. The signing. I'm on my way."

She disappears with the turn of her heel, and I take a deep breath, needing to compose myself before having to face her again. Ryan winks at me, and I put my guards on before I head out to the tunnels, spotting Vicky waiting at the barrier with Hal, the security guy.

Her teeth gleam bright as she laughs at something he says, and it irks me—what the fuck is so funny?

"Ah, there he is," Hal says as I approach them.

Vicky doesn't meet my eyes; instead she mumbles for me to follow her and starts walking towards the bar. I want to ask her what the fuck she's playing at, but in an attempt to stay professional, I follow her in silence. She leads me through the double doors to the bar area where there's a table set up with a chair behind it.

A crowd of fans queue to the right of the table and a stack of photos that I recognise to be ones of me from pre-season. I sit myself down, my knees uncomfortably crammed underneath the table, and wait for Vicky to do whatever the hell it is she does.

"Thanks for coming along, everyone!" She smiles at the crowd, and warmth spreads through my body. "I'm sure I don't need to introduce you to Liam Preston, our newest forward, who had a fantastic season opener for the club! Scoring a goal and finishing the night with four points is a great way to introduce himself to you."

There's a few cheers, claps and whoops. I grin appreciatively at the crowd.

"Please try to stick to one signature and one quick picture each. I do have some photos here for sale, if you'd like to get those autographed," Vicky indicates towards the pile on the table.

I pick up the Sharpie and un-cap it, readying myself. Vicky stands near the table, and I can feel the tension. I have to put all my concentration into focusing on the signing, trying my best to ignore her perfume floating towards me.

I'm asked to sign a mix of things, from team sweaters to pucks to photos—even someone with a 'Preston' Leafs jersey, which was a surprise. But I work my way through the line, taking selfies and a few group shots before the line thins out.

Vicky has loitered the whole time, taking a few photos here and there, probably for the socials.

"Thanks, Lee," she says finally, once the last of the fans have left.

Since we're alone, I want to ask her why the fuck she's lying to me. I also want to ask her how we can move past this and get to a point of tolerating each other and learning to live in each other's space. But I don't because I'm so furious and I know I'll end up saying something I regret or pushing her against the nearest wall and giving her a taste of her own medicine.

I take my leave and head back to the locker room, feeling Vicky's eyes watching me go.

Danny and Jani are finishing up as I push the door to the dressing room open. They make idle conversation while I undress.

"We'll meet the boys at the bar," Danny says, sitting back in his cubby and looking in my direction.

"No ladies tonight?" Jani says to him, wiggling his eyebrows.

Jani must be referring to Becca, but Danny ignores him, busying himself with packing his bag instead.

"Nah, just us boys. Cept Jen, most likely, since her and Prez are glued together. Oh, and Vicky is probably coming too."

Vicky.

As I head into the shower, I try not to think about her. Her kiss set me up for an evening of extra wanting, and I wasn't prepared for that. I'm supposed to be keeping things platonic and civil, but all I actually want to do is pin her to the wall and fuck some sense into her since she's being a fucking brat.

By the time I'm dressed and ready to go, I've composed myself enough.

When we get to the bar, I spot the rest of the team at some tables towards the back. Ryan's got Jen sitting on his lap. She has her lips pressed right up to his ear and she's whispering something that he's glad to be hearing because he's beaming.

I slide into the seat next to Jani and help myself to some beer from a pitcher in the middle of the table, swigging from my glass while I people watch.

"You okay?" Ryan says, coming to sit on the other side of me.

"Surprised you could pry yourself away," I flash.

"Be careful tonight, Lee. Last thing you want is to feel like shit tomorrow," he warns.

But he knows I'm not really paying attention. I'm on edge, waiting to see if Vicky shows up. Every single hint of blonde hair has my heart skipping until I realise it's not her.

"Can you let me out? I need a stronger drink," I say, nudging him with my leg.

He follows me over to the bar, and it doesn't take long for us to get some attention.

"You're the hockey players!" A blonde, who's definitely not Vicky, says.

She's wearing a teal-coloured miniskirt and a black tank top that makes her boobs look huge, but all it does is make me think of Vicky's tits.

"Sure," I say dismissively before giving my order to the barkeep.

"Can I get a selfie?"

Neither Ryan nor I reply, but she calls her friend over and they're whispering excitedly about us being twins. It's all stuff we've heard before albeit not in a very long time. But before I know it, she's pulling my arm around her shoulder, pressing herself into me and snapping a photo. I snatch my arm away and look around for Ryan, who appears to be fighting a similar battle.

The girl is chirping on at me, and I'm not really listening to what she's saying. There's a bit of a crowd forming. All women with the aspiration to touch my arm and slide close for a photo. I bet half of them don't even know why they're swarming around.

I make eyes with Bettsy, who saunters over, smiling widely and showing off his false teeth.

"Someone's popular," he says. Then he makes a show of trying to join in whatever the hell this is.

"Come and dance with me," one woman says, pulling at Ryan's sleeve, but he slinks away behind a fresh wave of bar revellers, leaving me to fend for myself. The woman's attention shifts to me.

"I don't dance," I say bluntly, taking a sip of the whiskey that's placed on the bar in front of me. But she's all over me, and it makes me feel damn uncomfortable.

"Come on!" she says, toying with my jacket.

"Come and dance, mate," Bettsy says, nudging me into the crowd.

I don't know how he manages it, but I find myself in the middle of a crowd of dancing women, trying their hardest to grind themselves against me. The blonde from earlier pushes her back into me and leans forward to rub her ass into my crotch. It's so crowded I can't pull away enough. She spins around and wraps her arms around my neck. I don't know if she is moving into kiss me, but I can't move away quickly enough, as a precaution, because the thought of kissing anyone that's not Vicky turns my stomach. I'm not proud to admit that I've never been able to kiss anyone else. When I've slept with other girls, it's been strictly no kissing, like something out of Pretty-fucking-Woman.

I wriggle free and head back towards the bar, ordering a fresh drink before making my way back to where Ryan and Jen sit. Then I'm back on Vicky watch, my eyes glued to the door like a love-sick puppy. But she's not here, and as much as I don't want to care, I find myself completely invested in her whereabouts.

I glance around for Johnny, half tempted to ask him if he knows where she is, but he's nowhere to be seen either.

"Where did Johnny go?" I lean over and shout at Ryan, but he shrugs, clearly too loved-up to give a shit.

I pull my phone out and check my messages, but it's only the usual group chat stuff and the odd message from a few of the guys back home.

"Hey, mate, do you want to skip going to Johnny's and go to that place across the street with my new friends?" Bettsy's crouching down to talk into my ear, some brunette pulling on his arm, but I'm not even a little tempted.

"Aww, Vicky just texted to say she's not coming," Jen says to Ryan; I catch it on the edge of my hearing, the music drowning out most of the other conversation, and I've never felt so disappointed in my life.

My first thought is to go home and dig out my clips of Vicky, but I down my drink and stand up, putting my arm around Bettsy's shoulders.

"Let's go," I say, and we make our way out of the bar.

I'll always remember the first time I saw Liam.

I knew Johnny was on a team with a set of twins, but I hadn't met them. He'd spoken about them a lot, but I wasn't all that interested—not until my parents forced me to sit in on his practices. Then I saw him.

He was undertaking skating drills with Johnny and his brother, and I don't even think I knew his name. But his number, '18,' was etched in my mind.

My first actual encounter with him was when my dad sent me to the ice just after Coach dismissed the team. I was supposed to tell Johnny to hurry up and not to take his sweet-ass time like he usually did. But by the time I made it to the tunnels, he'd disappeared out of sight.

"Can I help you?" Liam's voice drifted through the air. "Koenig's sister, right?"

"Yeah. Vicky," I replied.

He was looking right at me in a way I'd never seen anyone look at me before. I could feel the heat in my cheeks, and I'd wager that my ears were pink too. Thankfully, my toque was pulled down enough to cover them.

"Nice to meet you, Vicster. I'm Liam," he'd grinned. Then he went to hold out his hand but realised his glove was still on, retracting it awkwardly.

It was at that moment Ryan came bounding off the ice to join his brother, almost pushing him into me.

"Ryan, this is Johnny's sister. Vicky," Liam said, steadying himself.

Ryan greeted me brightly, then gave his brother a shove, trying to edge him towards the dressing room.

"Did you want Johnny?" Liam had asked me. He was tall, and on his skates, he made me feel tiny. I wanted him to pick me up and engulf me in a hug. I don't know why, since I'd never even spoken to him before, but I felt safe around him—it was odd. "Do you want me to pass on a message?" He was twisting his stick in his hands, hopping between his skates.

"Thanks. Can you tell him that Dad is waiting, and he needs to be quick? Also, he needs to return the skates to the hire desk." I must have sounded like such a loser.

He smiled, telling me he'd be sure to pass the message on, and then he and Ryan went towards the dressing room. I watched him until he reached the threshold where he stopped and turned back, locking eyes with me. With a slight smile, he'd glanced at me one last time before disappearing.

Even now, all these years later, that feeling I get when he looks at me—the feeling of being safe and noticed—is still strong. As I walk into the bar after the season opening, I spot him straight away. It's like a sixth sense. My heart leaps in my chest. He's surrounded by girls. They are draping themselves all over him, and there are selfies and touching—jealousy bubbles in my stomach.

I'm about to make my way further into the bar, but I start a mental battle with myself. I don't think I want to stay to watch Liam getting swarmed by women all night. Especially when I made a complete fool of myself by kissing him, then telling him I wanted nothing to do with him. I hesitate for a moment before creeping backwards and out on to the street where I call a taxi to take me home.

I spend my Saturday night wearing one of Liam's old hockey t-shirts and eating ice cream from the tub while I watch old episodes of 'Grey's Anatomy.' Jen has texted me four times asking where I am and if I'm okay; but I brush her off, not wanting her to feel compelled to ruin her evening for my sake. Besides, I've taken my contact lenses out now, and I'm giving my eyes a rest so I couldn't change my mind if I wanted to.

After the ice cream, I lay on the sofa, only half interested in the TV. I navigate to Liam's Insta and have a look through. Again. To my surprise, he's had a huge clear-out. He deleted or untagged lots of posts that were there before and changed his profile picture to one I took during pre-season.

As I scroll through, I feel a mix of disappointment and confusion because I feel like crying tonight, but he's giving me nothing to go off. Not one picture from tonight has made it. If I didn't know any better, I'd swear I was looking at Ryan's Insta instead—though his page has turned into a love-dovey display of affection for Jenna.

I toss my phone on the sofa and concentrate back on the TV. 'Grey's Anatomy' always reminds me of my mom.

Mom is a surgeon who runs a department specialising in cardio, and she spent so much time at work it drove her and my dad apart—or at least that's what Johnny and I were led to believe.

I think deep down that's the reason I didn't want to commit to going to Toronto with Liam. I didn't want to be a new version of my parents: myself playing the role my dad did, forever waiting at home for my mom to come home. But once she did, finding her exhausted, snappy, and not in the mood to do anything.

I always thought that's what it would be like for Liam and me, considering the environment. I could imagine him coming home tired, irritated because he'd not played his best, or they'd lost or whatever, and going straight to bed—leaving me to a long evening alone, just like my dad went through.

I can't say I blame him for having many affairs sometimes, because he clearly needed some sort of affection and connection with someone—not that he went about it the right way. But I didn't want that for me and Liam. I wanted us to have our happily-ever-after, and the idea of marrying him only to end up divorcing him later wasn't something I could agree with.

Reaching for my phone, I text my mom and ask how she is. She doesn't reply because she's probably in surgery, so I just lie here and muse. Mainly about the unsuccessful trip back home during the off-season, and how I was expecting to show up at the airport to be greeted by one of my parents, looking at least a little excited to see me. Much to my disappointment, my dad sent a cab and told the driver to drop me off at mom's place where he'd be over for dinner that evening.

When he eventually showed up, he brought in some takeout and spent the whole time swiping and tapping away on his phone like a teenager. And when he finally spoke to me, it was to ask about Johnny.

I admit, I could have tried to make conversation, but what's the point when you know someone isn't at all interested?

"Fine," I'd replied.

"Is he dating, yet?"

"No."

"How's Liam? Too bad his call-up didn't last long,"

"I'm fine actually, Dad. I appreciate you asking." The look on his face is forever etched into my mind. He doesn't care how I am. And I shouldn't be surprised. "How are things with you?" I'd thrown it out there, but it did not surprise me when he ignored me.

"I need to head out, Victoria. Your mom should be home by midnight."

He left then, without even looking back. I'd never felt lonelier in my entire life.

My mom had kept my room the same, which I was grateful for. I crawled into bed and stared at the photo of Lois, Liam's mom, that was visible via a ray of moonlight creeping through a gap in the curtains.

My phone had vibrated next to me on my bed.

Liam

Hope you're doing okay?

And that same text message brings me back to the TV; Liam again asking if I'm doing okay. I type out a few replies before deleting every single one of them. Lying back to think, I must have drifted off because I awake to see Jen draping a blanket over me.

"Hey, Vic," she says, moving around the sofa. "He spent all night watching the door, you know. Like he was waiting for you to walk in. When are you going to talk to him?"

I don't know what to say, so I give her a weak smile.

"You should talk to him. You both have a lot to say."

"I can't."

"Why not?"

Because I'm scared. "Look what happened earlier."

"Well, that was a hiccup."

"A fuck-up, Jen. It was a fuck-up. Now, please go back to your perfect lovey-dovey life and leave me to wallow."

She frowns before plucking an envelope from the side table.

"This came for you, by the way. It's been there for a few days now."

I thank her and slip it under the cushion my head is resting on. Another thing I'm not ready to face.

Chapter 8

Vicky

Johnny and I endeavour to have brunch together every Sunday. I thought we'd both be dreading this occasion after our last full interaction, but he strides in through the door as if he's floating on air. Completely un-Johnny-like.

"What's made you so happy?"

"Nothing," he says, but I don't buy it. I don't get to press him either, because a fan interrupts us. We're in the coffee place closest to our apartments today, which is also the one closest to the rink. Soon enough, a fan shoves a pen under his nose. He loves it, though—I know he does.

He signs the last napkin and looks at me with wonder. "You stayed out of sight last night." He picks his phone up and scans the QR code to bring up the menu. "I was wondering what crap you'd be asking us."

I shrug. I did my best to stay out of sight last night. I kept focused on my job; and luckily, I can get photos from a distance when I need to.

"At least you did nothing to annoy Liam," he says.

"I didn't come here to talk about Liam," I reply.

Johnny stops scrolling the menu and looks at me.

"I know Liam. I can tell when he's pissed. He wasn't himself during the opening game, nor at the bar last week, and he's been snappy ever since he got here. He's been fighting for Christ's sake. We're talking about Liam. What's going on with you two? Please enlighten me, Victoria."

I hate it when he 'Victoria's' me.

"What's it got to do with you?" I ask.

Johnny's cheeks turn pink, and he sucks in a breath through his teeth. "It's frustrating when my best face-off guy is constantly in the penalty box and not taking any face-offs."

He has been spending a lot of time in the box recently. Is that my fault? Probably. And I feel terrible about it. But what can I do? Liam's a winger but has always been exceptional at face-offs, much to Ryan's frustration. But come on, he's got to give him something. According to Johnny, the plan included maximizing Liam's participation in face-offs, even if he was substituted right after the draw.

"Fine. We briefly spoke last week. I told him I wanted him to keep away, and he obviously didn't take it very well."

He didn't handle it well. Liam got a five-minute major for fighting and a few two-minute minors sprinkled on top, which is why Johnny is pissed.

"Oh. Well, I'm not surprised. I understand you two are no longer a thing, and I've told you before, it's probably for the best, but you need to remain professional, Vic. What the fuck are you playing at?" Johnny snaps.

Wow. That's the first time I've actually heard him admit, out loud, that we were dating. Johnny ignored it before now. Even when Liam and I went to the same college, he pretended like it wasn't happening.

"Nothing. I tried to keep away last night. I—"

Johnny interrupts me. "When is this going to stop? When will you stop throwing your toys out of your crib and get your fucking act together?"

He raises his voice and people snap their heads towards our table. Blood floods to my face; I must be the colour of a damn beet. I can't bring myself to look at Johnny, so I busy myself with the menu on my phone instead.

"Someday, Vic, he'll move on for good and you'll have to cope."

Liam move on? He wouldn't, would he? "He can do what he wants. He's a single guy." As soon as I say it, I feel sick. Because it's always been us.

I remember the first time it became us.

I'd spent a full year thinking he wasn't all that keen on me; he'd hardly said two words to me—apart from that first time I went to his house. He told me how good of a cook his mom was. This was after my dad was having his usual fight with my mom about what time she was picking us up from the barn.

There was one evening in particular: my mom was stuck in surgery; she was undertaking a ten-hour operation which she could hardly just up and leave. But my dad, well, he wasn't happy that his plans were being stomped on—his plans to see his latest girlfriend, no doubt. Liam's mom, Lois, had invited Johnny to have dinner with Liam and Ryan, but my dad would only let him go on the condition that I go with him. I was being forced to tag along with Johnny. I felt like a spare part or an unwanted puppy that someone had been gifted for Christmas but didn't really want. But Lois had made me feel so welcome. She had told me she loved having a girl around because she was sick of boys. She had said it to make me feel better, but it helped.

It was a full year before Liam spoke to me properly, despite seeing him twice a week, every week by that point—even sometimes on weekends too.

It all started subtly. He'd sit next to me in the back of his mom's truck, our knees touching. Occasionally, his hand brushed against mine, but we hardly spoke. I found it odd that I had the impression of knowing everything about him. He'd always linger when I was at his place, often just hanging back a little when Johnny and Ryan had gone into the yard to play hockey or something—as if he was going to talk—but he never did.

Until one day.

I had a Canucks game on in the background, but I wasn't really watching it. Johnny and Ryan were goofing around in the yard with mini sticks, while Liam grabbed a drink in the kitchen. Lois always made sure I had the couch opposite the doors to the yard to myself when I visited, and I sort of camped there with my schoolbooks and a novel I was reading.

"Do you genuinely like hockey?" he asked me, then he did something he'd never done before. He slumped down next to me.

His leg was touching mine just the slightest amount; I could feel the tickle of his leg brushing against my skin.

"No," I shrugged, looking over at him. I remember feeling self-conscious that day because I'd got glasses for reading, and I was worried about how they would look.

"Really?"

"I don't mind it, in all honesty. It is what it is," I said.

"You sure as hell know a lot about it for someone who doesn't mind it," Liam grinned and reached across the sofa to where his guitar sat on a stand next to it. He picked it up and began strumming gently.

How did he know I knew a lot about hockey? My mind was racing, trying to figure it out. But then it clicked—he listened to me. "Well, I have to watch it a lot."

I stared at him, watching how his fingers moved, and I wondered how rough his hands were. I pushed my glasses up my nose, and he shot me a look before putting his attention back on the fretboard of his guitar.

"Those are cute, by the way. I like them." He paused for a moment, then looked at me again. "Uh, Vic?" he'd cleared his throat and shifted funny behind his guitar. I later found out he'd been sporting a boner he was trying to hide, but I hadn't noticed.

"Yeah?"

He set down his guitar and stood up. Then he held out his hand. I stared at it before realising he was offering it to me. I reached out, and his grasp engulfed mine. He asked me to follow him, pulling me behind him after I agreed.

We slipped in the backyard and past Johnny and Ryan undetected as he led me towards the back of the yard where the summerhouse was. He nudged me so I was leaning against the side wall where we couldn't be seen. He leaned in close. I could smell the mint on his breath.

"There's something I need to tell you," he said.

But he said nothing. He looked at me, his eyes locked on mine. I remember the feeling in my chest—it was like my heart was going to explode. My stomach was in knots, the anticipation almost killing me. Despite that, he didn't budge.

After a few minutes, I leaned further forward. "Are you going to kiss me?"

Our noses bumped and there was a bit of fumbling. But as soon as his lips met mine, I knew that there was no one else I ever wanted to kiss. I'd looked at his lips enough to guess what they'd feel like, but I was wrong. They were soft, and his left hand came to rest on my cheek, his thumb gently stroking my face. His mouth opened slightly, so I did the same, not really knowing how to kiss, but I followed his lead.

He'd told me later it had been his first kiss, too, but I couldn't tell. It was perfect. It was all over in a matter of seconds because his mom called us in to eat, so he pulled himself away.

"I like you, Vicster," he said before heading towards the house. Vicster. The 'friendly' name he used for me before we officially became Liam and Vicky, which was pretty much from that moment onwards.

"Could you bear the thought of him properly moving on?" Johnny interrupts my thoughts. When I hear what he says, my appetite disappears. I can't even imagine what being hungry feels like. Johnny lets out an exasperated sigh. "Thought so," he mutters under his breath.

Despite all of Johnny's faults, I love him to death. Even if he pisses me off and talks down to me. He's the only one who will ever fully understand growing up with our parents. But all of this, whatever it is, is Johnny's fault. If he hadn't played hockey as a kid, I'd never have met Liam Preston.

"None of this is easy, Johnny," I say.

I order a coffee.

"I don't get it. You were going to marry the guy and then suddenly, poof! Nothing. Not to mention that stunt you pulled just before Lois passed away." I wondered how long it would take him to bring this up.

I chew on my bottom lip and fumble in my purse for my lip balm as a distraction, but Johnny's glare is burning a hole in my head.

"If you must know, I didn't want to end up like Mom and Dad," I admit, finally. "Or Mr and Mrs Preston."

It's like the coin drops into the slot because Johnny's face changes. He understands. I probably don't need to elaborate, but I do. And once I start, I can't stop myself.

"Fuck," he says, "I didn't realise that hit you so hard, Sis."

"You can't tell Liam!" I wag my finger at him. "Promise me!"

"Why not?" Johnny asks.

"He'll want to be the hero and try to fix it, but he can't. It is what it is. He can't fix it." He can't fix me. I need to do that by myself.

The server sets a mug of coffee down in front of me, and I give a smile of thanks. She returns with a plate of food for Johnny.

"Aren't you eating?" he asks, eyeing the empty stretch of table in front of me.

"Not hungry," I mumble, taking a sip of my coffee.

This, too, is Johnny's fault. I can't say it enough. If he'd never gone to hockey, we'd never have met Liam Preston. I would be here now enjoying a delicious brunch—well, I wouldn't be here because Johnny wouldn't be playing hockey.

"Well, God knows I can't force you to eat," he says, bringing his fork to his mouth.

"What would you do if you didn't play hockey?" I ask. I fix my mind on this alternative universe I'm creating where everything is amazing.

Johnny pauses, knife and fork in the air. "Huh. Random, but I'd probably be a vet."

I almost choke on my coffee. There's been no sign that Johnny liked animals enough to become a vet. Yeah, he likes dogs and stuff but a vet?! The look on my face must be of pure confusion because Johnny sniggers.

"Nah, probably a chef," he says, resuming his meal.

I can see that, actually. The turkey Johnny cooked last Christmas was incredible and made Christmas slightly bearable—and I usually hate Christmas. I walked in on my dad getting head from some random woman one Christmas. No one wants to see their father engaged in any sex act, but surely it's worse when it's part of an affair.

Johnny knows how to add to my turmoil, however. "Did Dad call you? He said he's thinking about flying out here with Jayne."

Fucking Jayne. My dad's latest 'friend.' The latest in a long line of wonderful matches he subjects us to, only for them to disappear a few weeks later.

"When is he coming?" I ask.

"Not sure yet," Johnny shrugs, setting his cutlery down.

"Excuse me, can I—" a voice to the left of us says.

"Sure, do you have a pen?" Johnny flashes a grin.

"What?" the woman asks, looking between Johnny and me. "Sorry, I was after the salt, may I?" She reaches over and grabs the shaker from the centre of the table. Now is the time I really wish I had my camera. Johnny's face is one to capture and frame.

"Are you done?" he asks, pushing his chair back with his legs. He's in a hurry to get out of here.

I stand up, trying to suppress a laugh. And as soon as we step onto the street, Johnny asks me not to mention it to anyone. That sort of stuff is comedy gold in the dressing room, I'm sure.

"Fine, you keep quiet to Liam, and I'll keep quiet to everyone about that," I reassure him, but Johnny's embarrassment is the least of my worries. I'm dreading my dad coming to visit, and I'm dreading meeting this Jayne, but I'm dreading this season with Liam more than anything.

Liam

I have no choice but to walk past Vicky when I board the coach. She's wearing a red dress that shows a bit of cleavage, reminding me of her fantastic tits. By the time I'm sitting next to Ryan, I'm thinking about the first time I saw her naked. It's etched into my mind, that vision of perfection and, embarrassingly, I came as soon as she touched me.

Vicky's nipples are pink and pert. The perfect size to roll between my thumb and index finger. Her breasts themselves fit perfectly in the palms of my hands. I let myself slip into the thought of playing with her nipples. She loves that, and the moans she made always made my dick ache. And I loved pushing them together and sliding—

"How's the car?" Ryan nudges me in the ribs. He's referring to the branded Ford which I've landed this season. It's got an obnoxious number of team decals covering the black paint work and I can't say I'm a fan, but it's part of the job.

"Fine. When are you getting the Jeep?" I ask.

He's been talking about it like it's his firstborn or something. I've heard it all before, so I'm not really listening when he replies. My concentration is directed towards the front of the bus where Vicky sits. And now I'm thinking about the last time we kissed.

"Still trying to move on?" His eyes follow mine just as Vicky stands up and reaches for the overhead locker. Her eyes dart towards us and lock with mine for a split second before she looks away.

I lean slightly to the side to glimpse her legs, looking particularly long and shimmery today; a pair of black patent leather stilettos on her feet. This will be a long-ass coach ride. I shift in my seat, hoping that Ryan doesn't notice the situation I've allowed myself to get into.

"I'm over her," I say.

He bursts out laughing, but then, thankfully, he takes his phone out and starts doing whatever the hell he's doing, leaving me in peace. Peace to keep ogling Vicky.

I don't know how I played it cool during those early days. Ever since I laid eyes on her, I knew she was my kind of flavour, but I was a kid. I didn't want to let on that I liked a girl, especially my best friend's sister. Even now, I know she holds some sort of power over me. And I'm trying my fucking hardest to forget about her and move on, because fool me once and all that crap. I can't let her break my heart for a third time—but I'm struggling to let go. Is it just the sexual attraction that has a hold on me? Probably at the moment, anyway, because I'm horny as fuck and my dick hasn't worked properly since Christmas. My attempts to jerk off have been pathetic, and the only thing that gets me off is watching those videos I have from Vicky when we were long distance.

"Lee, please tell me you're going for fewer penalties tonight?" Johnny leans across the aisle, interrupting me.

Right, yes. I'll focus on my game and not be so fucking chippy tonight. "Sure," I offer Johnny, and out comes his goddamn notebook. I never used to be one for fighting, but I've been feeling high levels of angst recently. Fighting has been an excellent opportunity to release some of that pent up aggression.

Johnny continues his captain's speech—at least until his phone rings. He excuses himself to answer it. It's not as if we can ignore the conversation. The coach is a small, open space and Johnny does not keep his voice down.

"She'll come around... yeah... I know, but it's hard for her... uh-huh, sure... okay..." He hangs up, but I know the 'she' he is referring to is Vicky.

"Everything okay?" I ask, my head turned towards Johnny. I can feel Ryan adjusting himself as he looks over to the captain, too.

"My dad has this new girlfriend, and he's coming over soon. He wants to introduce us to her. She wants to meet me and Vicky," he says, his eyes darting to towards the front of the coach.

"How does Vicky feel about this?" I ask before I can stop myself.

I know I shouldn't care, but I do. I know Vicky's found it difficult adjusting to his new girlfriends in the past. They don't stick around for long, and as soon as a new one arrives, Vicky finds herself pushed aside again. She's never told me any of this, but I know. I see her.

Johnny shrugs. "Overreacting as usual. But he called me last night, and I told him he should talk to Vicky. He said he's been trying to call her for the past hour, but she's not picking up," Johnny adds, looking at his watch.

I follow his line of sight again, but this time, she's laughing at something Coach Adams has said, and something boils under my skin. I sure as hell know Coach isn't that funny.

Johnny drops the conversation and brings out his notebook again, leaning over to Bettsy for a short while. Then he gets up and moves a couple of rows back to the next available seat. Bettsy scoots into Johnny's seat and leans over the aisle.

I was worried Bettsy would be pissed at me for bailing at the bar last week, but he didn't even mention it when I next saw him. And thankfully, he hasn't chosen now to bring it up either.

"What do you think of Matt?" he whispers under his breath.

"He needs to work on his wrist shot," Ryan says, still scrolling through his phone.

"I don't mean that," Bettsy says. "I heard from Hutch that he's back with Rochelle."

Jenna told me all about Rochelle. Well, she gave me half the information I needed, so I asked Danny for the full story.

"You weren't gonna go there again, were you?" Ryan leans forward in his seat and looks at Bettsy.

"No, but it's awkward. Knowing that someone else on the team knows what your girlfriend looks like naked. It must be weird for you, right, Prez?"

A grin sneaks onto Bettsy's face and I see that vein in Ryan's neck pop as he asks what Bettsy's talking about.

"He's messing with you. I've never seen Jen naked," Danny says from between the gap in our seats.

"Who said I meant you?" Bettsy says.

"Quit it," Ryan scolds.

"Is it you, Betts?" I smirk, but I'm only doing it to wind Ryan up. It's a pastime of mine I've always enjoyed.

Ryan knows how to return the favour, though. "Have you decided what you're doing after hockey, yet?" I feel my face drop because, of course, I haven't paid it any thought—but I know I should be.

Johnny forces Bettsy to move along as he climbs back into his seat, asking the same question as Ryan. Fortunately, the coach's slowdown and exit from the freeway deters everyone from asking anymore questions. Johnny slides his notebook away and steps into the aisle.

Ryan and I stay seated until everyone has filed off.

"Do you think Vicky will be okay?" Ryan asks me.

"Well, I don't think she's over-reacting, that's for sure. She's always refused to meet any of her dad's new girlfriends or whatever. It wouldn't surprise me if she's flying out of the country as her dad lands here," I say as we disembark.

At the rest stop entrance, Johnny stands to the left of the doorway, appearing to talk at Vicky instead of with her. He's animated, gesturing with his hands, and Vicky looks like she's trying to hold back tears. Shall I intervene? Tell Johnny to back the fuck off? Probably not, actually. I promised Vicky I'd keep my distance, but I have to fight with myself not to lay into Johnny.

We head towards the Costa Coffee, joining the queue.

"Do you think I'm doing the right thing?" I ask Ryan. "Keeping my distance. Because I know that's what she says she wants, but—"

"It was you who decided that you were done."

"Yeah, but—"

I get cut off when Ryan's phone rings. I see Jen's name flash up on the screen, and he ducks out of the queue, giving a signal to order for him. I step forward, next in line to talk to the barista when I spot Vicky striding towards the washrooms. And if I'm not mistaken, she's crying.

My stomach drops. One thing I can't handle is Vicky crying, not like that anyway. It's the silent cry she does that's worse than hysterical tears. She's hurt. I just want to put my arms around her and tell her everything's going to be alright, even though I don't know what's going on—or if it will be alright.

I dash out of the queue and break into a jog, catching up with her just before she turns the corner to the ladies' room. I reach out and catch her hand. And when she spins around, locking eyes with me, she lets out a breath and wraps her arms around my waist. I engulf her. Wrapping myself tight around her shoulders while she sobs into my chest, I close my eyes for a moment.

Familiar tones cause me to open them, seeing Bettsy, Danny, and Hutch about ten feet away, gaping at us. They're quickly joined by a few of the other guys, and it's becoming a bit of a show, so I gently break away and look at Vicky.

"You okay, Vic?" I say, almost in a whisper.

"Yeah, just some shit with my dad," she says, wiping her tears away with her hand.

I don't even have a fucking tissue to offer her.

"Let me know if you wanna talk about it, yeah?" I completely ignore the fact that I'm supposed to be leaving her alone. But she nods and heads into the washroom.

I head over to the guys, giving them a look which tells them to not ask questions.

"Yo, where's my coffee, bud?" Ryan asks, coming to a stop beside me.

"Shit. Sorry. Don't ask," I say, heading back to the queue.

This time, I order our drinks, and a blueberry muffin for Vicky. I drop it onto her lap as I walk past her on the coach. I don't make eye contact or anything, not wanting to make it into a big deal. But as soon as I get to my seat, my phone vibrates.

Vicky

Blueberry is my favourite, thanks.

I know it's her favourite. I remember all her favourites because it's hard to forget when someone is so much in your head.

By the time we get to the rink, I revert to plan 'A' and stick to my word and keep my distance again. I'm careful to avoid any eye contact, but when we're playing that evening, it's difficult not to notice Vicky's camera stuck on me the entire time.

Chapter 9

I'm hiding out in my bedroom, my laptop open on my bed while I wait for all the pictures from last night's game to load. I couldn't face going into the office and risk seeing Liam, even though there's no practice today. I'm not up for socialising. It's the perfect day to work from home.

Today's main task is releasing the game night report written by Springy, the assistant coach. After adding some photos, I have to share it on social media by noon.

Over three-hundred photos pop up on my screen, and I pull my laptop towards me, sliding my finger along the touchpad to scroll down. An audible gasp escapes from my throat; I can't believe I took so many photos of Liam. I double click on the first in the list and quickly skim through the slideshow, searching for a shot of my brother Johnny who was the expected 'Man of the Match.' His plus-minus of plus five and impressive blocks made him an easy choice. I consider using the worst photo of him, but then I remember he could easily embarrass me, too—so I decide against it.

As soon as the first close-up of Liam pops onto my screen, my stomach does a somersault. His face is a picture of concentration, he looks, well ... I probably spend longer than necessary admiring the view before moving on. I've captured a good action shot of him firing at the net, so I pick that to use halfway down the report. I eventually find a decent image of Johnny checking someone into the boards to use as the primary image.

Editing the photos is quick, and by eleven-thirty, everything is ready. I ping an email to Jen with the content so she can get it on the website, and I wait for a link back so I can post it on our social media accounts. I'm just about to reply to an email when my phone rings. It's my dad trying me for the first time today, and I surprise myself by answering.

"Victoria, I didn't expect you to answer," he says, his tone bright. I didn't anticipate him calling during the middle of the night, but here we are.

"What can I help you with?" I try to sound passive to get a reaction, but he doesn't bite.

"How's Johnny? And Liam?"

My dad loves Liam, which makes my whole situation even more frustrating because I guarantee he'd pick Liam as a son any day over me as his actual daughter.

"Fine," I sigh, not bothering to give him an update on my wellbeing this time.

"Has your brother told you about my plans to visit?" he asks.

"Yep."

"Will you be happy to meet Jayne? She's really excited to meet you both."

"Yep," I say again, because I know there's no escaping it.

I honestly believe that I'd be more accepting of my dad's girlfriends if he'd gone about the whole thing differently. He had been secretly having affairs for years. My mom knew things were heading towards a dead-end for them, but it was still painful, and my dad continued to lie.

He'd made a point of choosing to spend time with his girlfriend over Johnny and me. I felt shoved aside. I felt like an annoying fly that my dad couldn't swat away. While Johnny focused on hockey, it took me years to discover joy in photography.

"Please, can you be nice?" he asks. "Johnny's going to make reservations for dinner."

"Yep." Third time's a charm.

This seems to appease him, and he says goodbye before hanging up.

A text comes through from Johnny a few moments later, thanking me for speaking to Dad—as if I've done him a favour. Then I get a message from Jen, giving me the link to the match report she's uploaded onto the team's website.

Once I've updated the socials, I look through more photos of Liam. He looks so familiar to me, yet seeing him in the same sweater as Johnny is alien. It's been a lifetime since they wore the same jersey. But it's the same Liam. His stick grip, slight lean during face-offs, even the way he chews his mouthguard—all familiar, as if he's always been here.

The longer I spend looking at him, the more desire creeps in. My core tugs with a yearning to see more of him. Because there's one shot I took where he's using his jersey to mop his brow and his stomach glistens with sweat and ... it's not long before I've moved on to my private collection: photos and videos I've taken of Liam. Private moments. Moments for us. My mind wanders to my very private collection. A warming ripple courses through my body, settling between my legs. I can feel my whole body prickle with excitement. I shouldn't, right? No, I really shouldn't. I know it will not end well. The more I resist the idea, the stronger my desire becomes. I toss my phone aside and roll over, trying to get the idea of Liam out of my head. But the more I try to fight it, the more frustrated I get.

Without further hesitation, I grab my phone and go straight to the 'other' videos folder, tapping in the PIN before scrolling down to the end—right to my favourite video. My mouth waters as it loads. He's holding his phone in his left hand, and his right hand rubs over his boxer shorts. The outline of his dick is visible. I let out an involuntary moan.

"I've been thinking about you all day, Vic," he says gruffly. "Look what you fucking do to me." He rubs himself. Even though I know what's coming next, I can't help but stare at the screen, unblinking. I hang on his every move. I'm waiting for him to slip his hand inside his underwear, and he does—obviously, because I've seen this so many times before.

In one firm motion, he pushes them down and grips his dick, pushing it upward. "This is what you do to me. Fuck. I wish you were here right now." He gives it a stroke and my state of arousal clouds my brain. All I can think about is sinking down onto it, feeling how full it makes me. What I'd give right now to be rocking back and forth on top of him as he grips my hips. The feeling of him hitting that spot inside me that he can always seem to find.

I'm wet. Really wet. And my clit is screaming for attention as I watch. He does a few seconds of frantic pumping with his fist before stopping and letting his dick fall onto his abs. Oh my God, I miss him. A bead of pre-come trickles from his dick. He leans forward and spits on himself, spreading the moisture over his length.

"I wish it was your pretty mouth doing that for me, Vic." His breath catches as he strokes himself again, slow and controlled, then quickly on the tip before he lets go again. "Fuck, I'm ready to explode." I'm in a trance, and I feel like it'll only take a single swipe over my clit to send me into oblivion.

"I loved seeing you touch that perfect pussy, Vic. And that beautiful look on your face when you came for me—" He cuts off, and starts jerking himself again, only to stop again. I watch the motion of his wrist as he teases himself, then he lets out a breath. "You're fucking incredible, Vic. You know I can't get enough. And since you were such a good girl in the last video you sent me, I'm going to make myself come for you, baby girl."

I don't know why, but I love it when he says that, and him knowing this adds to the whole eroticism of the video. I slide my hand into my panties to find my clit. I'm desperate to relieve myself from the ache.

The thought and the sight of him getting himself off over me turns me on beyond measure. I know he's not just jacking off to some random porn he's found online, but he's putting on a show for me. He teases himself, jerking himself, then stopping, then whispering something into the speaker. He tenses himself up a few times, trying to hold off.

"I can't hold off any longer, Vic. I wish this was going right down your throat."

I've seen this clip so many times before that I can time my orgasm with his. So I do, my breath catching in my throat as he lets out a groan, his come shooting onto his stomach. I watch in awe as his dick tenses and relaxes in time with the hard muscles of his stomach. My mouth waters at the thought of swallowing his load. But as soon as I fall back down, shame washes over me.

I launch my phone towards the end of my bed, annoyed at myself for giving in and watching the clip. But in my haste to get rid of my phone, I forgot to turn off the video. His beautiful voice trickles through the speaker, and I can't help but skip back and listen after I retrieve it. He's flicked the camera around so I can see his face and he gives me a special look before signing off.

"I love you. I can't wait to see you this weekend. I want to hear about your week. Then I want you in my bed." He winks, then the video ends.

I re-watch that last bit three or four times before eventually switching it off. Then I grab my pillow and put it over my head so I can scream into my pillowcase. Despite a pretty decent orgasm, that ache deep inside of me is persisting. It's like having an ache only Liam can soothe.

I roll over and hug the pillow to me, eventually dropping off to sleep, Liam's face floating through a dream I have. I'm startled awake when I hear the front door slam, bringing me around with a pounding headache.

I need to get some fresh air.

Johnny taps away on his phone, leaving me to set up the weights for the next set. The team has exclusive use of the gym in the apartment building, but this is the first time I've had a session with Johnny since I've been here. The equipment is black, grey, and purple, and the mirrors make the room look huge despite it being the same size as the living area of our apartments.

"Figured out what you're doing after hockey yet?" he says, tossing his phone next to his gym bag.

"Why does everyone keep asking me that?" I add the second dumbbell clamp and step up to the long bar.

"Because you should have a plan. Simon Pearce had a side hustle for years before he retired."

"I don't know who that is, but he can kiss my ass."

"He was the guy Rodgers replaced. A benchwarmer, but he had his shit together. He had a plan."

It wouldn't surprise me if this Simon Pearce guy had other skills, but what have I got? Nothing I can think of. I mean, I can play the guitar but I'm no rockstar. But then I remember that renovation project Ryan has planned.

"Actually, I do have a plan—Ryan and I are going to flip houses." I blurt it out and it's so random, I surprise myself. I pick the bar up and check my form before starting my set. Johnny watches me, his lips quivering in an attempt to reply, but his eyes flick down to his phone which is lighting up with notifications.

I finish my set and make room for Johnny. He steps up to the bar and squats down to position himself ready for his first set. Just as his hands touch the bar, his phone rings.

"Want me to get that for you?" I ask.

"No! No—just leave it." He almost drops the bar but keeps his form to continue his set.

His phone rings off and then again.

"Shut that fucking thing up!" Danny shouts. He's spotting Ryan, and they both look over at us. Johnny lets out a huff before stepping away from the bar and retrieving his phone. He skims the screen for a bit and his face drops into a frown.

"You okay, bud?" I ask.

"Um, yeah. Look, I've got to head off," he says, grabbing his towel. He slings his gym bag over his shoulder and hurries out of the door. I don't know what's happening with Johnny, but something feels off. I'm not one to press, and I know he'll tell me if there was anything really troubling him, but I'm still worried.

I glance at the clock on the far wall, then stop the workout setting on my watch, signalling to Ryan that time's up. He nods. We clean down the equipment before putting it away, then take showers before saying goodbye to Danny.

"I have been thinking about future plans, you know," I say as we head towards the building's lobby. "I mentioned something about flipping houses to Johnny but I think I'll get one of those qualifications in personal training."

Ryan holds the door open after him, and we step outside. "Huh—now that's an idea I've been considering, too."

"Personal training?"

"Nah, flipping houses."

"The personal training thing sounds like hell."

"Well, since you'll still have hockey..." I trail off, not wanting to admit that I don't really want to give it up; it just feels like I have to.

He pulls out his fob and buzzes us into his building. "Well, rather you than me. You could always coach." I have considered coaching, but it's a bit of a cliche—though I guess I shouldn't completely discount it, but personal training feels like a good way to keep fit. "You could always take over from me. I'm only filling in after all."

We enter his apartment after he's reassured me we'll have the place to ourselves for the third time.

"Come and pick what you want in your shake," Ryan says, moving into the kitchen.

I wait for him to move away from the larder cupboard when I spot Vicky's keys on the counter, the unmistakable 'Boston U Hockey' keyring dangling off her house key. I move towards my brother, using my loudest whisper.

"You said she wouldn't be home!"

He follows my eyes, his own landing on the keys.

"Fuck. I didn't think she was. She's usually at the rink now." He steps towards the open plan area to eye Vicky's bedroom door which swings open at that very moment.

"Oh, hey," Vicky says, her eyes wide. She turns her head, spotting me. Her cheeks, already pink, flash red.

"Everything okay?" Ryan asks her, moving back into the kitchen.

Vicky follows him, her bare feet padding along the floor. She's wearing a Boston U Hockey t-shirt that I know used to belong to me and some shorts which make her legs look as delightful as ever. She doesn't have any makeup on, and she's tied her hair up in a loose pony. It's one of my favourite sights: relaxed Vicky. Except she doesn't look relaxed at all.

"I just spoke to my dad. He's visiting soon, with his new girlfriend," she says, flicking the coffee machine on.

"Johnny said something about it. Let us know if we can help or whatever," Ryan offers.

Vicky keeps looking at me, and I'm thinking maybe I should bail because I promised to stay away, and now I'm in her kitchen.

"I best get going," I say, making my decision and eyeing Ryan.

"You don't have to, Lee," she says. "I won't stop you hanging out with your brother." She looks at me, and the way her lips quiver makes me want to pull her bottom one between my teeth.

"Are you sure?"

She nods and pours herself a coffee, grabbing another mug and pouring one for me, too. And before I know it, we're sitting on the sofa acting like we're old friends or something, watching some crap called 'Homes Under the Hammer' that Ryan stumbled upon. It's about home renovation, and it's got corny theme music that ends up stuck in my head. The BBC knows what it's doing because after the second run-down house, I'm hooked—curious to find out what happened with the one-bed-flat in Durham.

"This is good inspiration," Ryan says during the first commercial break.

"Inspiration for what?" Vicky says.

"Lee and I are thinking about flipping houses."

"Do you think we could actually do it, though?" I say, fixed on the damn TV.

"I think we could," Ryan says. "We've got the money to do it, bro. If we could get Johnny involved too, he's good with tools, and you did that woodwork stuff in college."

Shit, I'd forgotten about the woodwork stuff. It's been a long time.

"I've been talking to Danny, and he's interested in running a gym. I was considering if that'd be something worth pursuing," I say.

As soon as the words are out, I realise what I'm implying—that I'm staying, too. I mumble something about us perhaps doing it back home to cover my ass.

"Maybe," Ryan says, a worry on his face because I know he's not planning on going back. But when the scene changes to the flat in Durham, we're quiet again.

"I need to speak to Danny," he says. "We can look at buying a building suitable for a gym and renovate it first. It can be exactly as we want it then. You can do your PT thing there?"

With excitement in his eyes, he quickly disappears into the room he shares with Jen.

"What PT thing?" Vicky asks.

"Just an idea I've got for when I retire. But the house flipping thing is something I'm really keen on."

"You know these things don't happen overnight, right? The season will be almost over by the time you buy a place," she says.

"Well, I haven't figured out all the details."

She adjusts herself to sit cross-legged. My eyes immediately dash to her crotch, knowing what fucking joy lies within. I want to get up and walk away, but I've got a semi now and she'll one hundred per cent notice. Everyone knows grey sweatpants are unforgiving.

She moves again, stretching a leg out, but all I see is a vision of that leg slung over my shoulder while I—

"Lee, are you coming? I've got to swing by the realtor's office before I pick Jen up," Ryan says as he wanders back out of his room with a laptop under his arm.

To my relief, Vicky stands up and excuses herself. I must be staring at the space she's left because Ryan throws a cushion at my head, startling me.

"Right, yes. I'm coming."

I wish I was.

Chapter 10

I rest my cheek on the cold surface of my desk. Jen pops an earbud out and looks at me. "How did it go?"

"How did what go?" I ask.

"Your meeting with the GM? That's where you've been, right?"

"Oh, Fuck!"

I sit back up in a panic, glancing at the clock. I'm ten minutes late. I'm never late, but since the season opener, I've been all over the place. I'm not sleeping properly, I'm hardly eating, and I feel like I'm being followed around by a black cloud.

"Vicky, you've got a Post-It note stuck to your face," Bella, the marketing assistant, says as I walk past her desk.

I run my hands over my face briefly before tugging the note from my cheek. "Thanks, Bella."

'Can we push back by 15? Justin'

Thank fuck for that. I make a detour into the washroom, checking my face in the mirror. Thank the lord for makeup because the dark circles under my eyes are getting more difficult to hide. I give my hair a quick fluff and head to the GM's office, knocking briefly on the open door.

"Vicky, come on in. Take a seat. Sorry to push you back." The GM beckons me with his hand.

"Oh, that's no problem, Sir," I smile.

He drums his fingers on his desk. "I've been coordinating with Lisa, and we've scheduled another 'Meet the Players' night. Can you call her and arrange?"

Lisa helps us with big events. We worked with her to organise last year's Ladies' Night, but I think the last 'Meet the Players' night was before I joined the club.

I nod and Mr. Lopez smiles. We agree to meet up in a few days for me to update him.

"Oh, Vicky, the focus is on our new signing, remember? Preferrable Liam over Matthew, though. The fans are loving the 'twin thing.' I want you to do a social media drive. One of those Tok things, an interview on YouTube and a Facebook live, I think. Consider putting a mic on Liam or something while they practice." I give him my best fake smile while he finishes briefing me. "Before I forget, get Bella to help you out."

"Oh, sure," I reply.

He chats further, then waves me off. I head back to my desk, disappointed that Bella needs to help. I drop Lisa an email before turning to Jen. She's looking down at the ice, her earbuds still in, but I slide over to her and nudge her.

"The guys are coming in," she says, and I lean over, my heart pulls in my chest when I spot Liam. I told him to stay away, but I watched daytime TV with him like it was nothing. Now I have to do a media drive with him? My stomach flips.

I fill Jen in on the ask from the GM. She doesn't need me to explain: it means hours of one-on-one time together.

"Sounds like something you can easily manage," she says.

"I don't think I can," I confess.

"What? Why not? I thought you were being civil."

"I don't want to talk about it right now, Jen."

"Fine," she says, putting the earbud back in, but the way I'm staring at her must give her the impression that I do want to talk about it. "Right …" She glances at Bella's empty desk before sliding over to me. "What's going on, Vic?"

I've been asking myself the same thing. Why did I tell Liam I wanted nothing to do with him? It's the opposite of what I want, but I can't bear the thought of only being his friend. We've never been just friends, really. We were always pining after one another, waiting for someone to break.

First, I don't want to end up like my parents; second, I don't want to end up like his parents; and third, there's no such thing as a happy ending, is there? My parents left a massive black hole in my heart, and so did Liam's parents. They were so in love, and then Mrs Preston had to get sick and leave Mr. Preston all alone forever, and I'll never forgive her for that.

"Okay, we won't talk about it." Jen lets out a sigh. "This will cheer you up… remember when Ry and I did that 10K? Well, they e-mailed me some 'finisher' photos the other day, and you should see my face." She pulls out her phone and taps a few times before handing it over. "Look at Ryan, though! He looks like he's just stepped out of an episode of Baywatch. He's not even sweating! He makes me sick!" she scoffs.

We cycle through the photos, and I congratulate her on her effort. I hand her back her phone, grateful for the few minutes of distraction she provided, but there really is no escaping the social media drive. How am I going to get through it? I need to think of something. Because I really can't be doing one-on-one time with him, knowing he can practically read my mind. Potentially knowing that I've been getting off to those old videos I have of him. I feel pathetic.

I browse the internet for a short while before an idea pops into my head, but I need to start the ball rolling now.

"I think I'm coming down with something, you know. It's warm in here. Are you warm?" I say to Jen, overdramatically fanning myself.

"What's wrong?"

"I just don't feel right. Maybe I should head home." I start grabbing my things, throwing them into my bag. "I'll work from home. In my room. To keep the germs at bay."

Jen's about to say something, but I give her a wave and grab my coat before making tracks. On my way out, I narrowly avoid bumping into Kirsty from HR.

"Are you okay, Vicky?" she asks, taking a step backwards.

"Yeah, but—" I start.

"Great, I've just been down to the ice to see Johnny about some sponsorship, and the GM wanted me to run the media stuff by Liam. I've given him the heads up."

Fuck. My. Life. He'll be expecting me to get in touch now. "I'm not feeling great, so I'm going home to rest."

"Oh no! Well, I hope you feel better soon. I'm sure we can push the media stuff right up to the wire if you're not better in a few days," Kirsty says.

I give her a shaky smile and head towards the double doors and down the stairs into the main lobby. The girls on the front desk give me a wave as I head towards the main exit.

"It's not unlocked yet, Vicky. We don't unlock those doors until public skate is due to start." I rattle the door handle, willing it to open, but of course, it's locked as promised. "You'll need to exit through the back." Fuck. This is all I need. I thank them as I walk past, heading to the bar area where I stop to pull on my coat. Taking a breath, I reluctantly slip through the next set of double doors leading to the ice.

I'm greeted by the chatter of twenty or so guys, the sound of sticks slapping pucks and the unmistakable sound of skates slicing through the ice. A few heads turn in my direction when I close in on the benches and that familiar hockey-player smell fills my nose. I see Liam straight away, but he's one of the few skaters not looking at me; a pang of disappointment hits me in the chest.

I make a quick glance at Johnny and give him a wave before picking up my pace towards the back exit. Just as I'm about to reach the double doors, a breathy call that I know to be Liam stops me in my tracks. But I keep walking because one clear look at me and he'll know I'm not sick.

My brother is standing in my kitchen when I get home from the gym. He's batch cooking and Danny is lounging on the sofa as if it's completely acceptable for someone to use your kitchen for meal prep when they don't live there anymore.

"What the fuck are you doing?" I ask him, glowering at his plastic containers. They're all over the goddamn place.

"What does it look like I'm doing?"

"But why?" My voice cracks in disbelief.

"Vicky's sick. I'm not wanting to catch whatever it is she's got. I can't afford to be sick right now," he says.

"Sick? What do you mean, sick? How sick is she?" I ask as worry creeps through me. Maybe that's why she avoided me after practice yesterday.

"She told Jen it's the flu, but we can't be sure. It could be COVID." He spoons some broccoli into his containers. "I've not seen her. She's kept to her room, but she's been using the kitchen, obviously. Until she's well again, I'm not risking it."

"The flu? Vicky has the flu?" Alarm bells start ringing.

"That's what Jen told me that Vicky told her," Ryan replies.

I'm not buying it. Vicky is one of these weird people who doesn't get sick. At least, hardly ever. She's never late, and she doesn't get sick.

"Can you call her and ask if she's really sick?" I pace next to the counter.

"You're joking, right?" Ryan says, raising an eyebrow at me.

"No, I'm not joking. Just call her and ask!"

"Call her yourself," Ryan shrugs.

"Dude, do you not listen to me? I told her I'd leave her alone. I can't be calling her asking about her health."

"I'm not calling her," he says firmly.

"Please?" I put my hands together as if I'm praying. "Please? Give her a call and put her on speakerphone, then ask about 'Meet the Players.' Make something up." I know if I can just hear her voice, I'll be able to tell if she's actually sick or not.

My eyes bore into Ryan, I don't let up. I'm stubborn, I can do this all day. I know he'll eventually give in.

"Christ's sake, fine." Ryan pulls his phone out of his pocket and unlocks it before setting it on the counter. He taps the screen a few times and dials Vicky, pressing the speaker phone button while we listen to it ring.

"Hello?"

"Oh, hey, Vic. It's Ryan," he says, hesitating. He looks at me with a pitiful expression.

"Yeah, I know... I have you saved."

"Yeah, sorry, so... um... 'Meet the Players.' Just wondering if you knew when it was?" Ryan looks at me and shrugs. He's fucking terrible at this. Note to self: next time, ask Danny.

"Didn't you get the email?" Vicky pauses. "Actually, you replied to the email. All the information is on there."

I'm concentrating, listening hard, and give Ryan the signal to keep her talking.

"Oh, yeah, sorry. I'm a dumbass. How're you feeling, anyway?"

I scowl at him. He mouths an angry 'What?' as Vicky replies.

"Still sick. I think Bella will have to do the media stuff that's planned."

I've heard enough. She's not sick, and she's not even pretending to do her fake sick voice. I signal with my hand that Ryan can cut the call. He makes pleasantries and hangs up.

"Happy?" Ryan asks.

"No. She's not sick, so you can do your meal prep in your own goddamn kitchen. I bet she's faking to avoid the media stuff she's got to do with me, so someone else has to do it."

"Bro, she literally just said that Bella is going to do it," he says.

"Who the fuck is Bella?" I hadn't been listening to what she was saying, but how she was saying it. Before Ryan can respond, my phone vibrates in my pocket.

"It's Vicky!" I yell as I glance at the screen.

"Are you going to answer it?" Ryan asks.

"Can you keep the noise down, mate? I'm trying to watch something here," Danny calls from the sofa.

I shake my head. She's forgetting that I agreed to leave her alone aside from when it comes to her doing her job. I guess I'll have to communicate with her—I'm not that much of a dick, but I can't answer the phone as if I'm waiting for her to call me. I let it ring off and wait a solid fifteen minutes before calling her back because I'm as fake busy as she's fake sick.

"Hi, Liam," she says after it rings a few times. Now this is Vicky's fake sick voice, I'm sure of it. I've heard it at least a dozen times when she used to call in sick to her Saturday job so we could spend the day in bed.

"Hey, I missed a call from you?" I ask, trying to sound formal.

"Oh, yeah. Thanks for calling back. I just need to let you know the plan for your social media drive: I'm sick, so Bella is going to cover for me."

"Oh, sorry to hear that. Hope you feel better soon," I say, but I realise I need to be more meh. "Can you text it to me? I'm kind of swamped right now."

"Oh, sure," she mumbles.

This is the hardest thing I've ever had to do, but I round the call up before we can talk any further. Just speaking to her brings so much emotion. I want to ask her how her day has gone. I want to ask her if she slept well. I want to just talk to her. I already feel like hugging her at the rest stop was a step out of line, so making idle conversation now isn't a good idea.

I can feel Danny and Ryan watching me, so I get up and head to my room, locking the door behind me. I lay on my bed and try to block out all thoughts of Vicky. But it doesn't take me long to stray. Soon enough, I cycle through my Google drive of all the photos I've got of Vicky, with Vicky, some of them by Vicky too. It's hard for my heart, but I can't help myself.

As I'm flicking through the photos, my thumb scrolling, I come to a stop on the media folder—and one file in particular. It's a file that I haven't forgotten about, but I've not actively thought of either. I wonder if I should open it, but it feels … wrong? I'm not sure. My heart is beating fiercely in my chest. I make a split-second decision and tap on the video to start the download.

"Lee, are you eating?" The bang on my door comes before the video even downloads, snapping me back. "Jen's cooking," my brother shouts. I lay there for a moment, wondering if I can watch just a few seconds of it, but he bangs again. "She's doing potatoes."

I guess that's the universe telling me I shouldn't watch the damn clip.

Chapter 11

I've been 'fake-sick' for a few days now, and I'm wondering how long I can keep up the façade. Jen must know I'm not actually sick. Ryan's been acting like I'm a leper, whereas she's still happy to use the same kitchen as me, which is where I am when she gets home from work. She's carrying groceries and sets them down on the white marble effect counter before turning to me.

"I've got you a few things. You know, to keep your strength up." She searches through the bags. I can smell freshly baked bread and crane my neck to see what else she has.

She lines a few items out on the counter: the bread, some fresh soup, a bar of Galaxy chocolate. She rummages through the bags and pulls out a magazine and bubble bath.

"I appreciate it, Jen, thanks." I don't offer her a hug, but I gave her my warmest smile because she's so considerate—even when I'm faking it.

"Ryan said he'll eat at Johnny's, and if he asks, you were in your room the whole time, and I disinfected all the surfaces before even stepping foot in here. Sit down and I'll bring you a drink." She waves me past the threshold between the kitchen and the living area.

The kettle turns on as I settle in front of the TV with TSN playing in the background. It's one of those things that I appreciate as a comfort blanket. It reminds me of home, it feels such a normal thing to have on. Jen set it up with a VPN, and I pretended to know what she was talking about when she talked me through it.

The Maple Leafs quickly make an appearance. The highlights remind me of last season.

"Remember when we saw Liam on TV as a Leaf for the first time?" I ask Jen as she makes her way towards me with a mug of something hot.

"Yeah, it was exciting!" She hands me a mug and casts her eyes to the TV.

"Seeing him then, Jen, I knew we were in a place that we likely couldn't return from. I was so proud of him, though." I'm filled with regret about what I should have said or done before Liam's call-up. "I should have been there. I made the biggest mistake of my life, Jen."

Jen sits near me on the sofa and turns to face me. "I'm still rooting for you," she smiles. "Something's not right if you rely on a guy to make you happy. You need to be happy for you. Completely. And the rest will follow."

Jen. Perpetually optimistic and increasingly wise. I honestly don't know where I'd be without her these days. Thanks to Liam, I have a roommate I get along with, otherwise I'd probably be stuck with a random person I wouldn't get along with. Or worse—I'd be sharing with Johnny.

"Has he said anything to Ryan?" I ask, sipping my coffee. Ryan avoiding me right now might be a good thing since he's always with Jen, leaving no time for us to talk properly.

"Not really. According to Ryan, it's probably for the best that you two are done. But I think that's coming from a place of love for his brother. He doesn't want to see him hurting anymore."

My heart sinks. I did that. I'm the one who's causing him that pain. If Johnny and Ryan believe it's for the best, then it probably is—right? Telling Liam to keep his distance was the right decision. I sigh, unsure of what to say, but Jen offers her thoughts.

"I think it's still all to play for. Do you want him to leave you alone?" I concentrate on the TV, afraid to answer, and Jen sips her tea. She doesn't press me further, but we both know I don't.

Every flick of a blue sweater on TV makes me think of Liam. I'm proud of him, even if it was brief. I always knew he'd make it deep down. During his last year in college, he was adamant that he'd hold out and see if Boston wanted to sign him, given that I was staying there for another year. He met with their General Manager, but his preference was clear to me. I insisted he take the offer from Toronto. It was a fantastic offer.

"You'll finish up here, and then come up to Toronto, right, baby girl? We've done the long-distance thing before. We can do it again. It's only for a short time." I remember him saying this as if he'd already planned it out, and I was excited. That changed when Liam's mom, Lois called.

She'd started with the pleasantries. She asked about school, my part-time job, and various other topics. Then she asked about Liam, of course, and if I'd seen Johnny recently. It was all the usual things that she'd call me to talk about. Every single week without fail, on a Thursday afternoon when she knew I had a few hours free, she would call. I would tell her all about my week, and she would listen. She'd even listen to my rambling about the girls in my classes sometimes and how much I was enjoying Liam's hockey season—or not. But she always listened.

"Sweetie, I know it's a big ask, but do you think you could fly home this weekend? I know Liam's going to see Ryan, and I wouldn't usually ask but—"

"I'd love to," I said, not even waiting for her to finish. The thought of seeing her and having a weekend for just us girls was exactly what I needed, considering I spent most of my time in the hockey house full of boys.

So, we figured it all out, and I told Liam I was going home for the weekend and I'd see him on Sunday. I didn't know it then, but he knew exactly why his mom had called me. He'd been doing a great job at hiding his heartache.

Lois made a show of picking me up at the airport. She even stood there with a sign: my name in huge pink letters. It'd make me cringe now, but Lois made it endearing and I loved it. She took us out for dinner, and I didn't have a single suspicion that something was off. She looked well; she looked happy. We spent the rest of the evening watching sappy movies and eating popcorn. But the world stopped turning on the Saturday morning.

I slept in Liam's room. It still smelt like him, even though there were fresh sheets on the bed. Liam had covered his walls with photos of us, hockey memories and various memorabilia; it was still the same as I remember it. I remember feeling at ease and happy. Until I got downstairs.

Lois was sitting in the kitchen with her brother, Liam's Uncle G, who gave me a hug before abruptly leaving.

"What's going on?" I asked, knowing that Uncle G never came over this early.

"Vicky, come and sit with me." She patted the seat Uncle G had vacated, and I walked over and tentatively sat down.

"This is bad news, isn't it? I can tell."

"No, no, not bad news, sweetie. Just news that I need you to process and understand." She slid over a mug of coffee and smiled warmly at me.

"Not bad news? Then what is it? You're worrying me, Lois."

She paused for a moment. The smile she was wearing dropped slightly just before she spoke. "Several months ago, I found a lump. I thought nothing of it, but you know what Jack is like." She rolled her eyes at this. Liam's dad was a stickler for any sign of sickness, even a cough. I knew it all too well. "So, I got it checked out, and it came back as cancer." She talked about it as if she was telling me about her day at work. So nonchalant and carefree that I didn't really understand what she was saying. My mouth had dropped open, but she continued. "So anyway, they ran more tests, and it turned out that it has spread quite a lot and—" Her eyes watered at this point. It was the kick I needed to say something.

"But it'll be okay, right? They can operate. I'll call my mom. She'll know someone." I remember fumbling for my phone, then dropping it. Lois put her hand out and rested it on my arm. The warmth of her touch seeping into my skin, a warmth that I know no one will ever be able to replicate: a mother's love.

"Oh, sweetie—" She blinked a few times and dabbed the corner of her eye with her sleeve. "Jack called her straight away, and she got us in with a colleague of hers who's a specialist in all these things I've never even heard of, but..."

My eyes had prickled with the threat of tears, and her next words set me off into an oblivion of tears, turning me hysterical.

"... there's nothing they can do."

"I thought you said it wasn't bad news?" I remember yelping these words, surprised she could even understand me.

"Well, I've had a good life. I've got a wonderful husband, two boys that I love more than life itself, and you. A daughter I didn't know I needed until... there you were. I'm counting that as an excellent life, and nothing close to being bad news. We all have our time, and now is mine."

I don't remember what happened next, apart from the familiar smell of Liam engulfing me and cradling me in his arms as I sobbed. He wasn't even supposed to be there, but he was, and I'd never been more grateful to see him in my entire life.

I had so many questions I wanted to ask, so many things I knew I needed to say to her; but I couldn't stop the tears, even for a moment. I remember thinking how selfish I was acting because she wasn't even my mom. I should be the one consoling Liam, not the other way around. But I was beside myself, and I completely shut down.

It took me hours to calm down. Liam and I laid on his bed, holding each other for what felt like forever. Just like when his Gramps passed away, he'd acted like he was invincible.

What hit me the most was the look on Jack's face when I gave Lois the final hug goodbye before Liam drove us back to the airport. His usual gaze towards his wife resembled the one I recognised from Liam's expression towards me. Complete, undisputed, true love. However, it took me a few days to realise that something was different this time. And it broke me. It shouldn't have, but it did. And I'll never forgive myself for my actions.

Returning to Liam's room on campus, I waited for him to leave for the gym before I packed up my things. As I shoved things into my bag, a scenario played out in my head. I didn't want Liam to feel the way Jack was feeling right now: helpless, scared, lonely. Leaving seemed like the only solution. A way to spare him from future turmoil.

Except when he got back, I told him we were done. And he looked at me exactly the same way I'd seen his dad look at his mom. Heartbroken. I felt lost and helpless, my world crumbling around me. Looking back, I realise how dumb it was; but in the moment, I genuinely thought I was doing what was best for us. For Liam.

I got a call later that week from Jack to say she'd gone. I got on the first flight I could to Toronto, and this time, it was me holding Liam as he sobbed into my chest.

"I wonder if he brought his Leafs jersey with him," Jen muses as something else flicks onto the screen. "Ryan has packed all his Jets stuff up. Would you believe it?"

I highly doubt he came without his Leafs jersey. Just like he's probably brought his Marlies jersey, too, and his Boston U sweater—then I remember that's what I have in my closet: both home and away. I was always so proud to wear it. If he was home, I was wearing his away jersey, and vice versa. And I loved that after every game, even with the swarm of girls outside the dressing rooms, he'd come straight to me.

"We used to have sex in his Boston U sweaters all the time," I tell Jen. I'm usually against kissing and telling, or even any talk of sex outside of Liam, but now I feel like I want to share.

"What?" she says, eyes wide.

"Yeah, always me wearing just the sweaters. Never him," I grin, allowing myself a giggle, too.

I leave the bit out about the heels, though.

"Speaking of wearing sweaters, I've not seen Becca down the rink in a while."

"Yeah, I think they're done with each other, but she's not even talking to me about it. And Danny doesn't seem overly bothered this time."

We cut the conversation short when my phone vibrates on the counter. I rush over to it, disappointed that it's Bella's name—not that I'm expecting to hear from anyone else.

I let it ring off and then text her instead, making out like my voice is too horse to chat.

Bella

> Liam is avoiding my calls. I need to sort out some dates for the live mic session. Help!!

"Did you tell Ryan how I feel about Bella?" I frown at Jen, walking back over to the sofa with my phone.

"It may have slipped out, yes," she says. "Sorry."

Between Ryan and Liam, news travels fast.

"I'm guessing Liam's avoiding her because he feels like he's doing me a service," I say, showing Jen the message I had from Bella.

"Oh, shit."

"I guess I'll have to call him and square things away. It's the least I can do considering Bella is pretty much doing my job for me at the moment." I pull Liam's contact information onto the screen. "I'm going to call him here if that's okay? I need the moral support."

Jen nods, and I hit dial. My heart is thudding in my chest.

My first year of college felt like the longest year of my life. Vicky was over 2,500 miles away in B.C., and I was in Boston, trying my hardest to get through my first year without her. Yeah, we video called every single day, and my college buddies always ripped into me. It wasn't cool to start college as a taken man, apparently, but Vicky was it for me and we made it work.

Every other month, she would visit so we could maximise our time together, often spending it in bed when I wasn't playing hockey. Not always fucking—often just talking, watching crappy movies, just being together. It was bliss. We were so happy for that entire weekend, and we were even happier when she started at Boston U a year after me.

One thing that kept us going during our time apart was exchanging videos in response to each other. It had started as phone sex, but then she surprised me by sending me a video I could watch over and over again—it was only fair that I returned the favour. I still have the videos, and I believe she still has mine as well.

I'm lying in bed, horny and frustrated. I've spent all morning at the gym picturing Vicky in those yoga pants she used to wear, working out alongside me just like she used to do. It's as if she used to bend over on purpose, trying to get a reaction. And now all I want is for her to sink down onto my dick and ride me, but I'll have to make do with one of those old videos.

I navigate to my special Vicky folder and tap the password in before that voice in my head tells me I'm a complete chump for even going there. So, instead, I pull up some site Danny sent me the link to and flick through, aimlessly looking for something to catch my eye, but nothing does. I've never been big into porn since I didn't need it, and I can't help but think of how different these women are from Vicky. I end up tossing my phone down on the bed and screaming into a pillow as I hold it over my face.

Deep breath.

I go for a run around the block to calm myself down, but when I'm taking a shower afterward, my mind is running over a memory I have of Vicky in my damn shower in Toronto. She sunk to her knees, and the rest was a fog. And now my brain is working into overdrive, trying to remember the scene as if it was happening again right in front of me. But all that's actually in front of me is my throbbing dick; and there's nothing else for it.

I grab a towel and step back into my bedroom, drying off quickly before collapsing down on my bed. I grab my phone and navigate to that folder, searching through the files for my favourite clip. The file downloads from the cloud and I tap it, giving it a few seconds to load, but the anticipation causes my dick to leak pre-come. I give it a squeeze, then a few strokes as Vicky fills the screen of my phone.

I watch as she moves the camera, showing me her beautiful pink nipples and giving them a pinch, before she pans down, flashing me a view of some red lace panties, her hand rubbing herself over the material. I know which panties those are because they're tucked away in the back of my closet. I briefly contemplate fetching them, but I'm too captivated by the video to break away.

She's still teasing herself over the fabric, and I can definitely spot a damp patch. Then she slips them to the side, showing me her pussy, bare bar a landing strip that she knows I love. It's fucking glorious and my mouth waters. She's glistening with wetness. She slips her middle finger into herself, pumping a few times before retracting it and spreading herself to show me her clit.

What I'd give to bury my face in there, right now.

I grasp my dick and watch Vicky circle around her clit with her middle finger. I grip my shaft and give myself big, long strokes, trying to imagine that it's her doing it. Only a few, before I get the lube out and add a few squirts of that, trying to imagine that smoothness is the feel of her pussy, not my own fist.

She keeps circling, never directly touching her clit, and she's whispering about the video she's watching—it's one of me jerking off. She's talking about how much she wants to be giving my balls a gentle tug as she strokes the head of my dick and how much she wants me to unload over her pussy. Before long, she's telling me she's getting close.

Video Vicky immediately stops and waits a moment before resuming her play. She's teasing herself just like I like her too, so she's begging me to let her come, not that I ever stop her.

She does this twice more before she tells me she can't hold back. She's panting as she comes, moans rippling through the audio, matching my own as I come over my stomach. It's erotic as fuck, and I can't take my eyes off the clip as she sucks her fingers clean. I watch as she blows me a kiss before turning the camera off.

The post-orgasm fog clears, and embarrassment sets in. I feel like such a loser, jacking off to old videos of my ex-girlfriend. But in my defence, nothing else seems to get me there, and I was desperate for release. I may not want my heart broken again, but that doesn't stop me from being intoxicated by her. And not to mention, incredibly turned on by everything she does. That's going to be difficult to shake.

My phone rings as I'm cleaning up, and it's a number I don't recognise—I let it ring off. The entire sequence happens twice more before Vicky's name flashes up on the screen. But my heart hammers: does she know what I've been doing? Fuck, I didn't think this through. Would she detect it just from my voice? I pause briefly before answering.

"Hello?"

"Hi, Lee. Sorry to bother you. Bella's trying to get in touch with you about arranging a good time to mic you up." Vicky coughs for impact.

"Right. Whenever," I say bluntly, attempting not to give anything away.

"I'll put it down for next practice, then."

I can tell by her voice she's not sounding good. Nothing to do with fake illness, though, and I make a split-second decision to press her.

"You okay, Vic? Aside from your, um, flu."

"Yeah, fine," she lies.

"How are things with your dad?" I ask.

She sighs. "He's due out here in a few weeks. He's pushing it back, thankfully, but he's bringing his new girlfriend."

"Johnny mentioned something about it," I tell her, "Vic, I know you said you wanted me to keep my distance, but I'm always here for you, okay?" I curse myself as soon as I've said it. I don't want her assuming I'll always rush to her aid, even though I would—I just don't want her aware of it.

"Thanks, Lee," she says, "and thanks again for the muffin."

We're silent for a moment, then I hear whispering on the other end of the line before Vicky's voice hits my ear again.

"Jen asked if Ryan is there or if he's still at Johnny's?"

"I'm not his keeper," I hiss, but I don't know why I'm being so mean. "Sorry, yeah, he's still at Johnny's."

We end the call and I slump down on my bed, wondering what the fuck I'm going to do about Vicky.

Chapter 12

I'm really dragging out the fake-sick thing. It's time for me to give up and go back to the office. But since today's the day Bella is running with the Facebook Live and Liam's mic'd-up session, I decide to stay at home for one more day.

Bella and I have spent a lot of time planning over video calls and emails, so I'm not surprised when her name flashes up on my phone.

Bella

> It's not going well. He's hardly talking!

Bella

> And we're supposed to go live in twenty!

I had a feeling Liam would do this. He's literally the chattiest guy ever, so why is he being a douche about it and making things difficult? I fire a message back to Bella, telling her to pull him aside and give him a talking to—but she calls me.

"Vic, he's quite intimidating," she says after explaining the current situation in detail.

"You have one job right now, Bella. ONE. JOB."

"I know, but he doesn't acknowledge me when I talk to him. It's as if he's not listening," she says.

I feel like I have no choice but to tell Bella I'm on my way. I grab my coat and slip into my favourite shoes before heading out. And when I get the rink, ten minutes later, she's as white as Johnny's practice sweater.

"I'm not cut out for this, Vicky," she says, explaining that Bettsy has been in full flirt mode, and Johnny has been in full on yell mode. She usually just sits up in the office, sheltered from the crap that goes on down here —definitely sheltered from the 'lad banter' as Bettsy calls it.

"I'm so sorry, Vicky, I know you're sick—"

"It's fine. I'm actually feeling loads better." I lean over the edge of the home bench. "Liam!" I bang my fist on the boards to get his attention.

The whole team swivel their heads in my direction, and Liam's eyes widen when he spots me. He skates over with little determination and comes to a stop, letting his skates bump into the boards.

"Yeah?" he asks, no emotion on his face.

His forehead is sweaty, and I spot the mic cable snaking around the back of his neck. I lean forward and grab the mic pack taped to his waist, sliding the power switch to 'off.' I glance behind me to make sure Bella's out of earshot before continuing. "Lee, what the fuck is going on? Why aren't you complying?"

"I've got nothing to say," he shrugs.

Is he kidding? He's always got something to say.

"Why are you making this difficult? We need two and a half minutes of something to post online that isn't limited to the sound of your skates on the ice."

"There'll be a few puck noises too," he says. "ASMR. People love it."

I glare at him. And as he stares right back, his face drops into a frown.

"Why did you lie about being sick? We agreed to keep things strictly work related, but you can't even do that!" he says.

"Oh," I frown. "I don't know. I—"

"Turn the goddamn mic back on, but you're doing the other media shit. No Bella," Liam says, angling himself so I can reach the mic control. "I don't like the way she fucking looks at me."

I flick the switch, and he skates away.

I approach Bella, who's seated at a fold-up table with the office laptop.

"Vicky, I'm sorry," she offers.

"Don't worry. He can be a goddamn pest when he wants to be." I pull up a chair and sit next to her, focusing on the laptop while we wait for the mic playback to come through.

"So, I was thinking about the questions to ask," Bella offers. "I've been looking at the other team's social media streams. A good one would be to ask how they picked their number."

"No," I snap. It comes out a lot harsher than I intended. Bella's eyes widen. "Sorry, but no. Leave the questions up to me." That's the last question I wanted to ask. But I wonder what he would say. "Are you ready to start the live stream, Bella?" I ask, eyeing the time.

She nods and reaches for the work phone.

"Try and focus on Liam when you can but be mindful that he'll still be doing his usual routine. No interview from him today, but you will need to pull Johnny into the live for a quick segment. Free talking, no planned questions—but Johnny knows what he's doing. Just give him a wave and ask him how training is going, and he'll take care of the rest."

"Right," Bella says, her hands visibly shaking.

I give her a winning smile before she heads off to stand at the Zamboni entrance. Someone has already opened the doors for her, and there's a small bit of rubber matting set out on the ice for her to stand on.

I put the headphones on, flicking through the social media screens while I wait for Liam to talk. There's a muffle of conversation before I hear Liam reply, "—season three? Yeah, I liked the first two seasons." His voice is loud and clear through the mic.

He's talking to Hutch about a television show as Jen snaps the right headphone off my ear and sits next to me on a folding chair she's brought with her.

"Feeling better?" she grins, glancing towards where Liam is. "I hope he's more exciting than Ryan was."

Ryan spent his whole-time mic'd up explaining to Scotty, a winger from last season, about his pre-game routine. It was horrible and obviously scripted, but Ryan's not good with media stuff.

"Only talk about a TV show so far," I reply.

I listen for a few more moments. Liam is now telling Hutch about his thoughts on the season finale. Yawn. I give Jen a dejected look. She stands up and makes her way to the boards, eyeing Bella to make sure she stays out of the shot. Jen waves at Ryan; he glides over straight away.

They're whispering and giggling before Ryan nods and skates back towards Liam.

"Just told Ry to make it more exciting," Jen says, sitting back down.

I watch and listen as Ryan closes in on Liam, challenging him to a 'keepy-uppy' with the puck. I must admit, the content does become a bit more interesting. A few minutes pass and Liam is appearing more relaxed. Then, I hear the usual boyish banter of hockey players and realise that what I get, is what I get. I pass the headphones to Jen to give myself a break.

Twenty minutes later, Bella shouts that the live has ended and everyone can go back to normal, but no one pays any attention. The microphone Liam is wearing causes a crackling through the headphones, and Jen takes them off and puts them down on the table.

"I'm going to get a drink. I'll grab you a coffee." She heads off, and I automatically put on the headphones as I flick through the socials. I expected to hear things in the 'NSFW' category, but what followed surpassed all expectations.

"—and the only thing I can jerk off to are those videos of Vicky. From when we did long distance—"

I hastily glance at the ice where Liam and Ryan stand near the now empty net. My stomach is in my mouth, and the blood rushes away from my head; dizziness washes over me. He's been doing what I've been doing, then. Fuck.

"Are you okay, Vic? You look like you've seen a ghost." Jen places a cup in front of me.

Thank fuck, Jen wasn't listening in on this. Not that she won't find out anyway since Ryan is a blabbermouth. I take a breath and take the headphones off, knowing I'll one hundred per cent be listening to that last bit again.

"Either Liam's forgotten he's being recorded, or he wanted me to hear him." I look at Jen, eyes wide and eyebrows arched.

"What did he say?"

"I'm sure you'll find out later," I tell her.

Liam and Ryan huddle close while they chat until Coach calls them in.

I feel something, but I can't put my finger on it. I take a few moments to realise that it's my arousal screaming at me. I feel really fucking horny at the thought of Liam still getting off to my videos. Crap.

"Do you want me to help tidy up?" Jen asks. "I'm hanging about, anyway. I need to chat with Danny quickly."

"Yeah, that'll be great, thanks."

"Did you know the guys are talking about flipping a house?" she asks.

"I heard something about it, yeah."

I want to chat with her, I really do, but I'm more focused on the ache between my legs that no effort from me can rid. It's becoming a permanent fixture. I wake up with it and go to sleep with it. No amount of masturbating is helping, and now it's even worse.

When the guys skate towards the benches to leave the ice, I hover by the door to stop Liam on his way past so I can remove the microphone. If he can see my hands shaking, he doesn't let on; and I'm grateful for it because they are practically vibrating.

I steel myself to thank him as I unclip the wires, the buzz of attraction still strong between us as my fingers brush his sweaty skin. He lifts his sweater up for me to get better access, and since he never wears an undershirt—opting to go straight on with his shoulder pads—I get a view of his glistening abs and a hint of the tattoos he has on his chest. There's a trail of dark hair leading down towards, and I let my mind wander. My pussy is screaming at me, and knowing that his dick is merely sheltered behind a few layers of fabric doesn't help. Nor does the mix of his sweat and cologne. I don't know how I manage it, but I get the mic fully disconnected and free from his body without: a) passing out; and/or, b) making a complete idiot of myself.

"How was that?" he asks. "Did you get what you need, or can I help you with anything else?"

Our eyes connect for the briefest of moments, and I know he can read my mind. But I need to remain professional, so

I opt for an appropriate response that doesn't involve me telling him to take me to the equipment storage room.

"Sure, thanks again," I say, swiftly putting the equipment back into a waiting box as I turn away.

I'm painfully aware that he's watching me, but I'm relieved when I hear his skates thudding on the rubber matting as he heads back to the dressing room. I need to either change my underwear or remove them completely.

I can't shake the feeling that I've fucked up as we return to the dressing room. I sit in my cubby and un-lace my skates, mirroring my brother. Sulking, Danny enters the dressing room and collapses into the cubby on my right. He reaches for his phone and taps away, making no effort to get out of his gear. But I'm thinking about our conversation earlier today.

"Hey, Dan, you've done that mic thing before, right?" I lean in and lower my voice as he sits down. He mentioned that he'd done a load of media stuff in his first season as a pro.

He nods and tilts his head towards me. "Yeah, it's shit, right? You have to be so careful about what you say—you know, in case it comes back to bite you in the arse later."

Fuck.

"Did you say something risqué?" he grins, wiggling his eyebrows.

"I definitely said something I shouldn't have said while I was talking with Ryan. That Bella chick shouted that filming was done, and I let my guard down."

"It's only Vicky that hears it anyway, so you should be fine—" He stops talking when he catches my expression. "Fuck."

"Fuck indeed."

"What did you say?" he asks, but I wave him off. I'm not ready to relive that moment yet. 'Mortified' is not a strong enough word.

I lean towards Ryan. "The goddamn mic was on the whole time!"

"Fuck," he says, adding to the ever-growing stack of 'fucks' already in the air. "I didn't even think about it, else I would have cut in." He stands up and slips his shorts off but I'm too worried to focus on anything, including getting undressed. The moment is replaying in my head. The whole conversation trickles on. What I said. What Ryan said. Bella yelling. Me talking again.

"Bella and Jen were there too," I gasp, feeling my sweat sweating. "Everyone will know." My stomach drops.

"What will everyone know?" Johnny asks from his cubby across the room, but I can't even bring myself to look at him, let alone respond. What am I supposed to say? I've been reliant on his sister's videos for jerk-off material? Nah, Johnny would not appreciate hearing about that, I'm sure.

I shake my head and stand up, engaging Danny in some phatic conversation to distract myself enough so my hands stop trembling. He probably knows I don't give a shit about the weather, but he appeases me by chatting with me. I manage to calm myself down enough to undress, then I head to the showers, planning to take my time. Part of me is hoping that Vicky would have cleared off by the time I'm done, so I can avoid any further embarrassment. But another part is hoping I can steal another look at her.

I'm replaying the scene again; but this time, my attention is on the moment she had to take the mic off me. I can still feel her touch on my stomach, her fingers leaving a trail of heat that can't be replicated by anyone else—and my dick stirs.

Johnny bangs into the shower stall next to me, killing my arousal—thank fuck. Steam erupts from his shower head—preheated by Hutch. It's standard for whoever gets to the shower room first gets all the showers going to heat the water.

He asks me again what I think everyone will know again, but this time, I tell him I don't want to talk about it. Instead of pressing the matter, he moves on—but he continues to talk about Vicky. "At least my sister's feeling better."

I grunt.

"What's got into you? Ever since you've got here—"

"I was going to ask you the same thing, John," I snap. "I've hardly seen you. You got a secret girlfriend or something?"

But he ignores my question and continues, convincing me further that he has a secret girlfriend.

"Glad to see that she's being civil, at least. I've told her you two are better off apart," he adds.

"I think I agree, actually," Ryan adds from the opposite shower stall. "It caused so much drama last year, you don't want to revisit that. Not to mention—"

"I'm keeping away," I reassure them.

I finish my shower silently, eager to get away from any more conversation with Johnny and Ryan.

Bettsy and Danny are already back in the dressing room and as soon as I walk back in, their heads snap towards me.

"Fancy a pint, Lee? I know it's only the afternoon but—" Bettsy offers.

"Fucking right, I do. Are we going straight from here?"

I towel off and get dressed as we talk through a plan. And it's not long before Johnny and Ryan are back in the dressing room, giving us disapproving stares in response to the pub talk.

Ryan has always maintained a strict 'no alcohol during the season' policy and I've only known him to pause it during the Christmas break last year. Not even our mom passing away triggered an alcohol rebellion.

"If any of you are anything other than on form tomorrow, there'll be consequences," Johnny says, pointing his finger between me, Bettsy, Danny, and Hutch.

"If I didn't know any better, I'd guess he was no fun at parties," Bettsy says. "But I know him, so I know he isn't fun at parties."

We decide to drop our gear at home before heading to the pub. I glance at the clock, hoping that Vicky will have left already. But as Danny opens the door ahead of me and Hutch, her familiar laugh glides through the air, turning my stomach to Jello.

She's standing right outside the door chatting with one of the equipment managers and makes eye contact with me straight away. I let my gaze rest on hers for longer than I should before she steps forward. Her body language is telling me she wants to talk.

"Can you give us a moment?" I ask the guys, stepping towards her.

The tunnel clears out, only the hum of cooling in our ears. She steps forward, so she's almost touching me, her face angled up towards mine; I bet she can hear my heart pounding. She extends herself so her mouth is directly next to that sweet spot on my neck. Her hair smells like coconut and her perfume sends my brain into a fog of lust.

I don't know how long she's lingering there, but her breathing changes, and I feel it warm on my earlobe as she whispers.

"If it makes you feel any better, love, I can only come watching your videos too."

My heart leaps out of my chest, and I'm stiff as a board as her hand fumbles in my pocket. It's over in a flash. She spins on her heels and walks away from me, her amazing ass in my sights as she goes.

I have a feeling I know what she's done.

I slip my hand into my pocket and caress the material of her thong, the fabric damp with her arousal. Knowing that she's walking away from me with no panties on makes me want to chase after her and bend her over the home bench—show her the consequences of her brattish behaviour. Not that I didn't provoke it somewhat. But she's got me. I'll give it to her. It's Vicky one, Liam zero. This is completely against everything in my plan. She's smart. She knows that resisting the contents of my pocket will be difficult for me.

I consider heading back into the dressing room, straight for the showers, while the crotch of these panties is still warm, but that'll involve seeing Johnny and Ryan again—not a good idea. I glance around and I consider the equipment storage cupboard for a moment before I spot one of the support team heading that way with a box. Then, to my horror, I glimpse into Coach's office, giving it consideration, before deciding against jerking off at his desk.

I shake my head, realising I have no choice but to put the knowledge that Vicky's underwear—still warm, still damp—is in my pocket as I head towards the double doors. I swing them open to find the guys waiting for me.

"What was that about?" Bettsy asks, flashing me a gappy smile.

I don't want to lie to him, but I can't tell him the truth. "She told me that today was a success. She has some great content to use." I hope that she'll at least have something she can use, so if Bettsy bothers to listen to it—which I doubt he will—it'll cover my ass.

Danny laughs knowingly, but does me a favour and says no more. And Hutch acts as if everything is normal, which, of course it is. Everything is normal.

Chapter 13

It's been a week since I slipped my panties into Liam's pocket. A week! And I've heard nothing. Nothing. Nada. Zilch. I honestly don't know what I was expecting, but I wasn't expecting a full-on silent treatment. Maybe a 'Vicky, what the fuck are you doing,' or perhaps a 'Vicky, please refrain from putting your dirty panties in my pocket,' but nothing. He hasn't so much as glanced over in my general direction during practice, and I've been down there every single time with my camera. Nor has he visited Ryan during the times I've been home.

I'm waiting for a call from Lisa regarding 'Meet the Players' which is scheduled for Thursday next week, and I pass the time thinking about Liam and the letter Jen handed me. I still have to muster the courage to open it.

I'm in another world when my phone rings, and I only remember I was expecting her call when Lisa's bright tone chimes down the receiver.

It doesn't take her long to bring up the new social content after we exchange pleasantries. "I've seen all the new content on the clubs' socials, Vicky. Liam has come across great! The interview was great too. I didn't realise you two had such a history."

Despite three failed attempts, the YouTube interview went smoothly, eventually. Bella wasn't overly useful as she was flustered and nervous, which she later admitted was because of Liam. And I'm willing to wager that she has a bit of a crush on him.

I stifle a cough. I was not expecting her to pick up on that. "Thanks, Lisa. I appreciate your feedback."

I briefly discuss the TikTok content with Lisa which was mainly a mix of footage I'd already captured with a quick-fire question round added in. The fans love that sort of thing. Now everyone knows Liam's favourite movie, hot drink, and flavour of ice cream—much to his delight. And we eventually move the conversation to 'Meet the Players.'

"I think we're good to go, Vicky. Nothing else left to sweep up. The hotel is happy to accommodate the drinks package we wanted after all," Lisa says. I express my gratitude, and I'm surprised when Lisa mentions Liam's name again. "Excuse me for being so forward, but you and Liam—"

I cut her off, telling her that there is no me and Liam. In the footage there were awkward moments where he would catch himself staring at me. And on more than one occasion, I found myself doing the same. I didn't think of it as a big deal until a few people started commenting and asking questions—Jen being one of them.

Lisa apologises and shifts the conversation, which I completely zone out of because I spot Liam's name flash up on my phone. I hesitate before unlocking my phone and tapping his name.

Liam

> I know it's been a while. I didn't know if I should text, but I've given in. I wanted to share with you the impact that your little game had last week.

Within seconds a video arrives, instantly recognizable without even opening it, causing me to yelp. The preview is a show of Liam's broad chest—and he's shirtless. I think I may have just died.

"Vicky? Is everything okay?" Lisa asks on the other end of the line. In my state of distraction, I hadn't realised she was still talking. Liam's diversion pulls me in, forcing me to abruptly cut off the conversation.

"I need to go, sorry. There's an issue with TikTok I need to resolve." It's complete trash, but it's the first thing I think of.

I'm relieved when Lisa tells me she'll speak with me soon and hangs up. But as I set the phone down, I can feel Jenna staring at me.

"What the—?"

"Gotta go!" I don't give her time to finish because I've already slipped my heels back on. I grab my phone and half-jog, half-bound into the corridor, where I check the occupancy of each meeting room in turn.

The GM catches my eye as he spots me peering into the boardroom. I give him a brief smile before moving on. An unattended laptop occupies the next meeting room, so that's a no-go, too. But the media room is next, and I thank the stars it's empty.

I slip inside, praying that Coach Adams doesn't have a review session planned. Closing the door, I take a seat in the first chair I see. I curse myself for not grabbing my earphones, but there really wasn't time to waste. I'm acting like an addict in need of my fix. My hands are shaking as I wait for the video to download. And as soon as Liam comes into view, along with the familiar pair of panties that I left in his pocket, I'm a puddle of water.

I know I shouldn't watch this at work, but I can't bear the thought of it sitting there, waiting to be played while I ignore it. This was made specifically for me to watch, and I can't resist. I glue my eyes to the screen. I know that if someone came in right now and told me the barn was on fire, I wouldn't be able to look away. The temptation to slip my fingers into my panties and rub my aching clit washes over me. But given the environment, I need to draw the line somewhere. I cross my legs instead and rock back and forth gently in my seat, trying to provide some friction.

I'm in awe of how his fist works his dick. I know his jerk-off routine now, and what pattern he goes with. It doesn't make it any less arousing. In fact, I love knowing his routine so well because I feel like I'm in control of his orgasm. My pussy is aching, and I'm close to giving in just to take the edge off. Knowing that he's close—and it wouldn't take me long to get there either—seems to be a good enough reason to sway my control the wrong way. But to my complete horror and frustration, he stops the video just before he comes.

I stare at my phone for a moment in disbelief. I pick my jaw up from the floor and rewind the clip ever so slightly to check there hasn't been a technical malfunction. But it's as clear as day: he's left out the good bit—the come-shot.

My cheeks flush and I purse my lips, thinking about what do to next. I pull his contact information up and hesitate before concluding this is exactly what he wants. What a prick. He's turning this into a game. A game that I can play, too. Or, did I start this by giving him my underwear in the first place? Whatever. All I know is he'll be expecting me to be enraged—to call or text him, demanding the rest of the clip—and of course, I want to, but I'm not going to give him the satisfaction.

Liam hates being ignored while I can't let anything go. Not the best combination in this situation. I think for a moment before an idea comes into my head. I need a distraction.

I regain composure and return to the office, pausing at Kirsty's desk. She's worked at the club for five years and deals with all the HR matters. I just love the way she does her eye makeup.

"Everything okay with TikTok?" she asks, raising a brow.

"What? Oh yeah. It's all fine." I perch myself on the edge of her desk.

"Are you okay? You look flustered," she says. She's not wrong there, but I ignore her concerns and go in with my question.

"How do you feel about going speed dating again?"

We last went speed dating before Christmas for a bit of fun. I mean, we didn't take it seriously, and I wound up meeting a guy called Gary. I took him along as my date to Jen and Ryan's Christmas drinks, but I haven't heard from him since, and I'm fine with that. He was the only guy at the event who didn't look at me like I was a piece of meat. It was refreshing, but going out with him made me realise then that I wasn't ready.

"Oh sure, that was fun! Shall I see when the next one is?" Kirsty pulls her phone out and taps the screen. She found out about it from a Facebook group she's in that promotes events for singles. It's run by a lady called ReLinda who seemed very enthusiastic about us finding true love last time. I don't know long Kirsty has been single for, but she's never talked about a boyfriend since I've known her.

"There's one on Monday night," she says, flashing me her phone screen.

"Odd night, but okay, let's do it."

"Is there no chance of you and Liam working things out?" she asks. I watch her tap through a few screens as she books the spots.

"Liam? Who's he?" I smile, but I hear a scoff from Jen in the corner.

She doesn't press me when I get back to my desk, and I try to look busy so she won't get the chance. Not that I need to pretend to be busy because I am busy fuming about Liam's video. How dare he leave out the good bit! I love nothing more than hearing him come. It's hot, which is obviously why he left it out—to get me all hot and bothered. And wanting. But one thing I do know is that one day I'll see the end of that video.

I could cut the tension in the air with my skate. I lean against the wall of the tunnel watching Vicky setting up her tiny microphone, ready to ask whatever the hell is she's going to ask us this time. She's wearing my favourite pair of heels again; but as I watch her move, all I can think about is what her reaction would have been to the video I sent her. Since I've heard nothing, I can only assume that she's ignoring me to piss me off.

It's a Sunday home game, and everyone's feeling deflated after yesterday's loss. Johnny was quick to lay the blame on me, accusing me of being distracted. I mean, I am distracted, but I'm still playing well. And I'm focused—at least, I should be. But again, I find myself looking at Vicky's shapely hips and the way her ass curves in her dress.

We get the call to move forward, and the line moves slowly after Ffordey steps onto the ice. When I'm three guys away from Vicky, I can make out her question through the noise of the crowd. She's flicking her hair and batting her eyelashes at the whole goddamn team, and my jaw hits the floor when Bettsy answers her question and Vicky giggles before touching his arm. Her eyes flash in my direction ever so subtly, but I know exactly what she's doing: she's being a brat.

I clench my jaw and grab my stick from the rack, gripping it tightly.

"How do you feel about disappointing endings?" she asks Hutch. I can't believe my ears. What the fuck is she playing at? His brows knit as he glances around for help, confused by the question.

"What, like a film or something?" he asks.

"Sure. Let's just say a video, or a movie," she offers, casting me a glance. I swear there was an emphasis on the word 'video.'

"Well, I'd give it a poor rating, I guess," Hutch says. He steps onto the ice and Bettsy shuffles forward.

He gives Vicky some crap about not appreciating anything other than a happy ending, and Jani grunts before pushing past.

Vicky bites her lip as I step towards her, and I'm trying to think fast on my feet, but I'm distracted by her perfume. She opens her mouth to speak, but I don't even give her chance to verbalise the question on the marker board she's propped up against the bench. I dive in with my answer: "Filmmakers rely on the quality of their props for success. Sometimes, they need a lot more to work with." I don't stick around for her reaction, but I can feel the hole she's burning into my head.

Okay, so I lied. I came harder than I have in a while, or at least that's what it felt like, but I didn't want to give Vicky the complete show when she's sending mixed signals and playing games. She explicitly told me to keep away, and then she's slipping her underwear into my pocket—warm and wet underwear she knows I can't resist. How can I keep away when she's pulling shit like this? I honestly don't know how long I'll be able to keep my cool.

"Vicky comes out with some crap," Ryan says, coming to a stop next to me. We drop to the ice and start stretching. "That wasn't anything to do with you, was it?"

"No," I say firmly. "No idea what she's on about. Any update on finding a house?" I quickly change the subject and get Ryan talking about house hunting.

"It's slow progress," he says.

"Something will come up."

"Heck yeah, it will! Bettsy said his dad is an electrician and knows everyone we could need. I'm just thinking we can do some bits ourselves. You've got your woodwork skills, and Johnny's handy. But he can't do plumbing, can he?" This piques Ryan's curiosity, and he gets up and skates towards Johnny, leaning in to enquire about his pipe skills, no doubt.

This gives ample opportunity for Pritch, one of the third liners, to slide in next to me. Jasper Pritchard, a centre from Michigan, is entering his third season here. He's a nice guy—chippy, sort of our enforcer—and doesn't let anything faze him. Not even Vicky, who, of course, is the topic of conversation.

"Hey Lee. Vicky's been exceptionally flirty with me tonight. I think she's interested, but I know you guys have some history. I just wondered if you'd mind if I asked her out."

I know I shouldn't be jealous, but it bubbles in my stomach, and I feel like I could throw up. I take a deep breath and spend a moment thinking before answering him.

"You know what, Pritch, I think she'd love to. We're water under the bridge," I say, knowing that I'm pretty much lying to him. Would two people who still watch clips of each other getting off consider themselves as water under the bridge? I think not. But my guess is Vicky will probably shoot him down, so I don't mind him expressing an interest. Nothing will come of it, right?

"What's the deal with you two, then?" he asks as we get to our skates. "If I'm going there, I want to prepare fully."

I honestly don't know where to start, so I start at the beginning as we fire pucks towards Ffordey.

"We started dating properly when I was sixteen, Vicky was fifteen. Then, I went off to college. She followed me out a year later. We were pretty solid until I got signed and then it went a bit off course."

As soon as I say it aloud, I realise how pathetic it sounds. Poor Liam and all that crap.

"Oh," he replies.

"After getting back together, we did long-distance for a while. The plan was that I come here too. And we'd get married, but Vicky called the wedding off."

Pritch flicks a puck towards Ffordey's glove. "So, she dumped you twice?" he says. Fuck. Like I said, pathetic. "You know what? I think I'll leave it. Seems like Vicky has some things to figure out," he comments as he skates away.

Well, that backfired. And if Vicky hears about it, she'll be angry, even though it's all true. Come to think of it, she never gave me a genuine reason for her sudden change of heart about the wedding. I know for a fact that she never fell out of love with me since she's let that nugget of information slip since. But I try to push it aside and concentrate on my warm-up. But that doesn't go to plan either. When I skate around the net and join the queue to shoot, I notice Vicky watching me from the bench through the lens of her camera. And then I replay my conversation with Pritch, wondering if I could—or should have—said something different.

My rookie year was an absolute gong show in reflection. I don't even know how I made it past camp. I was a complete and utter mess, relying on those goddamn videos of Vicky to get me by. And by the hope that one day she'd change her mind, which she did—until she didn't again.

What pisses me off the most is that it was her idea to get married. She suggested it and I jumped at it, keen to put whatever we'd been through behind us and move on. We were both excited to make that move; and Vicky confessed that she'd been planning our wedding since she first saw me, even practising writing her name on things: Mrs Victoria Preston. Funny thing was, I knew, but I liked that she did it.

I absent-mindedly play with a puck, contemplating what could have been for us. My thoughts drift to the baby Vicky miscarried after thirteen weeks of hopeful anticipation that we'd become parents. I wonder where I'd be right now if that had been different. But the British accent of Hutch hits my ears and reminds me where I am, and what I'm doing—trying to get over Vicky, not pine over her and our past.

The buzzer sounds overhead signalling the end of warm-ups, and I make my way towards the bench, taking my place in line again. I wait as the guys ahead of me step onto the rubber matting, and I listen to someone ahead of me telling Bettsy that life's too short not to take a shot. It's a cliché term, but it hits me. Vicky comes into view up ahead, and my eyes are straight at her feet, checking out her shoes again—like the loser I am. If I recall, I'd bought them when we flew out to Vegas for a long weekend, never actually seeing a casino the whole time. That was a fucking great weekend, and a great weekend of fucking, which gets me excited and gives me a bit of courage. As I close in on Vicky, I meet her eyes and make a point of looking down at her cleavage before moving my mouth close to her ear.

"I came really fucking hard into your panties, Vic," I breathe and the little shiver that courses through her is all the response I need.

Chapter 14

It should surprise me to see Gary here again, but it doesn't. He spots me straight away and heads towards me with a spring in his step. "Victoria!" he coos. "I wasn't expecting to see you here!"

"Hi Gary," I smile, praying to the stars that Kirsty comes back with the drinks sooner rather than later. "How are things?" Although I have no desire to speak with him, I try to be polite.

"Oh, fine. Yes, fine." He's fidgeting with the loose change in his pocket, and he's not making eye contact. I don't know what to say to him since he didn't leave his answer with much of an opening for conversation, but luckily, Kirsty appears at my side and passes me a glass of wine.

"You remember Gary, right? From the last time we were here?"

"Sure," she smiles, dragging out the 'r.' She has no clue who he is.

"I think I saw—oh yes, come on Vicky," she pulls me by the elbow. "Why did you go out with him?" she asks when he's out of earshot.

"I—" Her face drops. "Oh shit, I did see—"

I follow her line of sight and my jaw drops when I spot Johnny and Bettsy leaning against a wall at the back of the social club. I feel relieved knowing I can avoid admitting to Kirsty that Gary was the only guy who didn't proposition me for sex; but I feel less relieved that my brother is here—at speed dating. Johnny looks like he may pass out, but Bettsy beams and waves before beckoning us over.

"Oh, wow! Bettsy doesn't look half bad with teeth," Kirsty whispers as we close in on them. She's right. Bettsy has a full set of teeth, clearly for the occasion, and he looks good.

"Alright, or what?" he says. I don't understand him, but Kirsty acknowledges it as a mere "hello."

"Fancy seeing you here, dear brother," I smile at Johnny, who doesn't know where to look, and what's more, he's had a haircut.

"Vicky," he nods, not looking directly at me.

Then it occurs to me that these hockey boys always travel in packs. I have to resist going overboard with the head-craning as I try to spot Liam.

"He's not here, if that's what you're wondering," Bettsy says, noticing my inquisitiveness.

I'm disappointed because all I can think about is Liam and how the video would have ended if he came as hard as he said. I'm desperate to see him. The thought of it excites me—but instead I have to subject myself to a series of two-minute conversations with twenty strangers. Okay, eighteen now, considering I already know Bettsy, and Johnny is my brother.

A blonde lady with a big smile walks to the front of the room and taps the microphone.

"Hi, everyone. Thanks for coming. I'm ReLinda, and I'm happy to help in any way I can." We're told the men will rotate seats after each buzzer, allowing us two minutes per person. She points out where we can pick up a match card, where we put the name of the person and a tick or a cross between shifts. If two people have a tick for each other, contact details will be exchanged. "Remember to have fun and stay safe!"

As we head towards our seats, I decide to get Johnny sitting opposite me first to get that over and done with, and it'll give me two minutes to quiz him as to why he's here.

"You don't date," I say, before the starting buzzer has even sounded.

Johnny shrugs, "Bettsy didn't want to come alone."

ReLinda announces the start of speed-dating.

"Then why did you get a haircut?"

"Because I needed a damn haircut. Quit it."

We bicker back and forth for a bit before Johnny changes the subject to Dad.

"He's due on Friday, you remember?" he says. "He wants to catch my game on Saturday."

I scoff. "He's never cared about your games, John. Why would he care now?"

"Jayne's interested by all accounts."

"How much do we know about Jayne?" I ask him.

"I think she's younger than him—" he starts, annoyingly the buzzer sounds putting a stop to our discussion. It's now a conversation I need to follow up on.

I have a whole load of questions. How much younger is she? Is she someone who aspires to start a family? Surely Dad's too old for babies at his age.

Bettsy slides into the seat next, and I compliment him on his teeth before asking how he is. We briefly chat about nothing in particular, but then he turns the conversation to Liam.

"I don't know what happened last week, Vic, but whatever you said to Lee caused him to bail early." He's talking about the day I slipped my thong into Liam's pocket after practice. "It was pointless him coming out. He had one pint and then made his excuses. I reckon it's got something to do with your brief encounter," Bettsy grins.

At least I can surmise that it didn't take him the full week to get around to recording that video. But before I can respond to Bettsy, the buzzer sounds, and he moves on to Kirsty. Thank fuck.

But, by the time I've spoken to the next few guys, I'm wishing Bettsy was back. Or, dare I say it, Johnny.

Relief washes over me as the buzzer sounds for a longer period, signalling the half-time break. I make my way to the bar to get a fresh drink, deciding that I should be more drunk than I am for this sort of thing.

"Meet anyone you like?" Kirsty says, squeezing into a gap next to me.

"Not really, but we'll see how it goes. How about you?" I ask, not expecting Kirsty to blush as much as she does.

"Your brother is quite charming, Vic."

"Let me stop you right there," I say, holding my hand up.

"You asked," she giggles, nudging me. I recognise that look: it's the same one Jen had when she was just friends with Ryan.

I decide not to ask Kirsty any further questions, and we make our way back to our chairs to start the second round. Just before I settle into my seat, my phone vibrates in my purse. I sneak a peek.

Liam

I know I offered to be there when your dad visits, but he's just called me and invited me to have dinner with you guys. Is that cool?

I read the message at least three times to understand what he's saying. My dad rang him. He rang him. Stuart Koenig rang Liam Preston. Liam and I were together for years, and Dad never called him. What the hell does this mean?

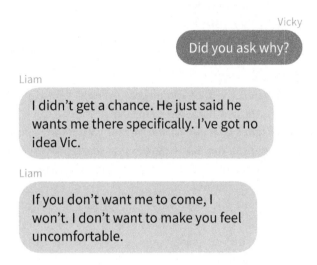

Vicky

Did you ask why?

Liam

I didn't get a chance. He just said he wants me there specifically. I've got no idea Vic.

Liam

If you don't want me to come, I won't. I don't want to make you feel uncomfortable.

I pause for a moment, reading back over my message exchange with Liam, and I decide I very much want him there.

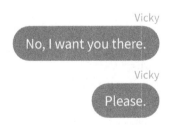

Vicky

No, I want you there.

Vicky

Please.

He sends me a 'thumbs up' emoji, and I stuff my phone back in my bag. I've never had such a weird text chat with Liam. He's never sent me a thumbs up emoji before. An eggplant emoji, yes, but never a thumbs up. And I don't know why, but it pisses me off a little.

I'm simmering with curiosity as I sit back down to speed date. I let my 'dates' talk for as much of the two minutes as possible because I'm even less in the mood now. And when Gary sits in front of me, I ask him about field hockey, and fortunately, he uses the full two-minutes on that.

When the final buzzer goes, I'm relieved to be done; I just want to go home and call my mom. I slip out of my chair and head over to the desk and join the matching queue.

"I'm sorry that things didn't work out for you and Gary, but it looks like you've had a good night!" ReLinda hands me back the completed match form. I'm in disbelief as I stare at the four phone numbers, clueless about what to do. Kirsty, on the other hand, ends up with Johnny's phone number which I suspect she already has. Bettsy manages to secure two numbers which was two more than he expected, according to him.

"Does Liam know you're here then?" Bettsy asks as we head out.

"Why would he, Mike? We're both free and single to do whatever and whomever we want."

"Really? So, why hasn't he taped his own stick yet?"

Fuck. When did Bettsy get so observant? I didn't plan to keep doing it, but when he first got here and his gear arrived, I just picked his sticks out of the pile and taped them. And I've been re-taping them ever since. Liam isn't the type of guy who re-tapes his twig after every game, anyway, opting to do it only when absolutely necessary. I've been monitoring the state of his blade between games. But we're in a different place now, and maybe it's time to cut that cord loose—after I see the end of that video, of course.

The clubs' 'Meet the Players' night takes place in a fancy hotel across the city. There are banners and live-action shots scattered around the room, and a large flat-screen plays footage of the season so far whilst the fans mingle with the team. It's a night for schmoozing and thanking the guests for their support, something Johnny is absolutely loving—the guy can't smile wide enough.

It's not even nine o'clock, but I'm ready to call it a day. I feel socially exhausted, and I've lost count of the number of selfies I've been asked for, all whilst trying to pretend I'm not looking for Vicky. Bettsy and I are at the bar waiting for her and Lisa, the events manager, to get the show on the road. They have a planned presentation; and, by the sound of it, a few of us might be called up to speak.

Bettsy's got this new set of false teeth clipped in, and they look pretty good. He's ironed his shirt and trimmed his gingery beard. And if I didn't know any better, I'd say there was a girl involved.

"Who you trying to impress, Betts?" I ask, sipping my beer.

He doesn't acknowledge me straight away because his eyes are darting around the room as if he's looking for someone. I nudge him and ask again.

"Just someone I met on Monday. She said she may stop by," he says, pulling at his collar.

"Where'd you go on Monday?" I ask. "And why wasn't I invited?"

"I went speed dating. Just a bit of fun. Didn't think it'd be your scene."

"Speed dating?" I knit my brows together.

"Yeah. I ran into Vicky and Kirsty, actually," he says.

"Vicky Koenig?" I ask just in case there's another Vicky I didn't know about.

Bettsy nods and takes a sip of his water. Another first. I've never known Bettsy to pass up an opportunity to drink. "She told me she got four matches."

"Good for her," I reply, trying to keep it cool, but that knot of dread fills my stomach.

I hate to admit it, but I feel jealous, even though it's unjustified. Vicky's always had other guys show her interest, but she's never paid them any attention. But speed dating—that just shows how keen she is to meet someone new.

I take my phone out of my pocket and open Google, typing in 'how to not be jealous.' The search results blow me away. Literally millions of pages claiming to answer my question. I skim the results, picking up a common word amongst the pages: insecurity. Am I insecure? Fuck. Who knows. I give that a Google too, and up pops: 'Are you feeling insecure? Take the quiz and find out!' Enough of that. I'm not taking a goddamn quiz. I toss my phone down on the bar and turn towards Bettsy. He's still glancing around the room while he chews his lip. He takes another drink before asking me a question.

"I hear you and Preston are getting a house to flip?"

But before I can answer, he waves at a woman with jet black hair cascading down her back. She makes her way through the crowd and beams at him. As Bettsy introduces us, I can't help but think he's punching. Then, there's movement behind me and Vicky's perfume fills my nose. She makes a grab for my phone; and before I can process what she's doing, she's weaving her way through the crowd, surprisingly quick even with those fucking stilettos on.

I take off after her, completely ignoring the looks of confusion from people in the crowd as I push my way through. I'm about to catch up with her when she turns the corner and slips into the ladies' washroom, my phone clutched in her hand.

Staring at the door, I think for a moment. Should I follow her in there? It's probably not the best idea I have, but I glance around before slipping inside. There's a corridor which leads to the washroom, and as I step into the open area, I spot Vicky leaning up against the counter near the sinks. The stalls opposite are all empty and the oddly placed green velvet couch sits unoccupied in the middle of the room.

"You really need to change your pass code, love," she says, scrolling through my phone. It's like she's not even surprised to see me here.

I rush towards her. She spins around, attempting to hold my cell out of reach. When I talk to her, I'm addressing her in the mirror. "What are you doing?"

"I want to see the rest of my video," she giggles.

"Your video?"

"You made it for me, didn't you?" Her eyes meet mine in our reflection, but I can't argue with her. "Why are you being such a tease, Lee?"

"Me being a tease? You're kidding, right?"

"Even now I can feel your dick pressed into my ass," she whispers. I don't understand why, but I push into her a little more. "You know what I want, and you're teasing me."

The smell of her hair, her perfume, and the fact that she's got this blouse on which makes her tits look incredible forces my arousal to take over. It completely voids me of any cognitive thought. And I ignore my inner voice telling me to abandon my phone and leave.

Do I know what she wants? I think so, and I'm feeling bold enough, and horny enough, to confirm my suspicions.

"What do you want, Vic?" I reach around, wrapping my arm around her and fixing my hand on her throat, forcing her to look forward and right into the mirror. I lean forward and whisper into her ear. "Do you need me to help get you off? I bet you're fucking wet for me, right, baby girl?"

Maintaining eye contact in the mirror, I slip my free hand up her skirt and reach for the heat in between her legs. Of course, she's wet. She's actually fucking soaking, and it sends me into a frenzy. I push away the flimsy fabric and swipe my finger across her clit, causing her to shiver and lean back into me.

"Someone could come in," she gasps, gazing at me via the mirror. She's abandoned my phone, and I could just make a grab for it and leave, but I don't.

"Do you want me to stop?" I ask her reflection.

She shakes her head: no.

I know I shouldn't be doing this. How would it appear if someone catches the latest signing with his hand under the photographer's skirt? But I can't help myself.

"Good girl," I say into her ear, giving her clit another caress. "Did you touch yourself watching my video? Did you make yourself come as I stroked my dick? I was so fucking hard for you—" I rub my crotch into her ass. "Can you feel how hard I am now? Because this is nothing compared to how hard I was."

"Yes," she breathes. She almost buckles under me but steadies herself, leaning against me. But with that, the washroom door creaks open and Bella's voice floats through the air. "Vic, are you in here? They're waiting for you."

Vicky reacts straight away, pulling herself away from me.

"Coming," she shouts.

"You wish," I whisper at her, and she grins back at me.

"Send me my video." She readjusts her skirt and checks herself in the mirror.

"You're being such a brat, Vic."

"We'll talk about this later," she huffs, heading to the door.

I steal a taste of her from my finger. Then I wash my hands, grab my phone, and follow her out moments later. Vicky is wading through the crowd to join Lisa at the front. She's looking visibly flustered, and all I'm thinking of now is how wet her panties are—I want them. I can't fathom the origin of this desire I have for Vicky's panties. I wouldn't want anything to do with anyone else's, just hers. It's got to be the knowledge that it's me who's got them wet in the first place, and they've been close to her perfect pussy. Besides, the knowledge that I turn her on as much as she does me has always been arousing.

I catch eyes with Ryan, seeing the confusion on his face.

"What were you doing in the ladies' room?" he says in my ear.

"Nothing. I thought it was the gents," I lie.

"With Vicky? Coincidence? I think not."

"Why did you ask then?" We're both looking forward, talking out of the corners of our mouths. But when he shifts closer, I give in. "Okay, fine. She took my phone in there. I don't know why, but she just grabbed it and ran." Another lie, but he doesn't need to know about the video.

"I don't buy it—" Ryan halts because Vicky's reached the microphone, and she breaks out into an infectious smile.

She stands next to Lisa, and they both beam at the room before starting their speech. They thank everyone for being here. Then she calls for me which catches me off-guard. Someone shoves me forward, and I make my way towards the front—through a cheering crowd, Vicky's eyes not leaving mine.

I join her and Lisa on the small platform, but Vicky keeps up the show for the crowd.

"There are high expectations for this season. Now we're blessed with the twin brother of our star forward. What have you set out to achieve this season, Liam?" she asks me, but this question is double edged.

I can play.

"I'm not here to mess around. I know this is a game, but winning is my goal," I say. It's aimed more towards Vicky than at the crowd, but it gets a round of applause.

After sharing a few more crowd-pleasing remarks, I step off the platform to a round of applause. And there's a few more words from Vicky before she lets Lisa discuss the upcoming events for the season.

"You're playing with fire, Vic," I say to her when we're out of earshot.

"What if I want to get burnt?" she says, her hand brushing my cheek. "Are you telling me you didn't want those panties? And that you don't want these?" she hitches her skirt up ever so slightly and my breath catches in my throat.

I'm hard again and my rational brain has completely disappeared because I lean in and whisper into her ear. "Give me those and you'll get your video."

And with a smirk, she turns and heads back towards the washroom.

Chapter 15

Liam Preston is true to his word. I am now the proud recipient of a delicious full-length clip. He didn't lie; he did come hard, and I've enjoyed it more times than I care to admit.

My original frustration of not having a new video, inclusive of a happy ending, is nothing compared to the frustration I feel now. The throbbing ache deep inside me which, I strongly suspect, can only be sated by Liam fucking me like he's making up for lost time. I want him—no, I need him.

I had considered texting him an eggplant and water spray emoji, because he'd know what I'm really asking for, but it needs to be his idea. Ideally, he needs to be the one to initiate because he's stubborn and won't give in if I ask him outright.

As I ponder this, the door to the restaurant swings open and in walks Liam, polished to perfection in a charcoal grey suit with an emerald-green tie. He's trimmed his beard again into the style I love, and he's swept his hair to the side like it's been freshly cut. I bite my lip and lean forward to rock on my chair, desperate for some friction.

He's shown to our table and gives Johnny a guy hug before sitting right next to me, his knee almost touching my own. My whole body tenses.

"What's going on, Vic?" he asks in a casual tone.

"Nothing really, just waiting on Dad." Obviously, I'm waiting for my dad. Why am I nervous?

Johnny stands up and excuses himself, heading to the washroom; Liam takes the opportunity to shimmy his chair in closer. He reaches his hand out and moves my hair away from my left ear and as he leans in, I can feel his breath on my cheek. I shiver.

"You look beautiful, as always," he says. "You know, I was hoping you'd return the favour with the video."

Oh my. The excitement of this suggestion goes straight to my pussy. My brain, now void of cognitive thought, has me responding in a way I'm not expecting. It's as if my arousal is talking for me.

"Wouldn't you prefer a live show?"

He clears his throat and shifts in his seat. I hear him take a breath, ready to respond; but Johnny comes back, followed by a server to take our drinks order. Liam and I stick with water, but Johnny orders a beer since there's no morning skate.

My brother, sitting opposite me, glares as if he's trying to figure out what we were talking about, but I ask him a question to shift his focus. "I'm going to regret asking, but how's Kirsty?"

"Kirsty? From human resources?" Liam asks, looking towards Johnny.

"I haven't really seen her. It's not a good idea to mix work with that sort of stuff. It can get messy." Johnny gives us a look of contempt.

"What did I miss?" Liam asks as the server brings our drinks order.

"Johnny and Bettsy went speed dating," I say.

"Yeah, so did you." Johnny adds.

"So I heard," Liam pauses.

"Vicky was popular," Johnny says; but thankfully his phone vibrates, distracting him before he can say anymore.

"Dad's running late," he says. "He'll be late and suggests that we order some appetisers."

Typical Dad. Always working on his own schedule. The only time he ever worried about being late was for Johnny's practices. I used to always ask Johnny what it was like being dad's favourite. It's funny, because Dad doesn't even like hockey, but he always pretended to show an interest for some reason. It wasn't until years later I found out it was because Dad was sleeping with one of the skate hire assistants. He'd disappear for periods of time, reappearing fifteen minutes later with a smile on his face, asking if I needed anything for school or hobbies. This is how I got my first camera. I didn't even ask for it, but it was a gift to serve as a distraction—to keep me occupied.

"How popular were you at speed dating, Vicky?" Liam asks.

I brush it off, not feeling like I need to share that I've had four guys texting me, none of whom I want to see again. But Johnny can't help giving us his opinion.

"I'm just glad you're moving on, Vic. We just need to hook you up now, Lee."

When the server returns, we order some appetisers and Johnny leans forward to talk to Liam about the plans for property flipping which Johnny has been roped into helping with.

I excuse myself when the conversation gets dry, making my way to the washrooms. There's a row of doors labelled 'Sir' or 'Ma'am,' all individually equipped with a toilet, a sink fitted into a cabinet and some fancy vases full of artificial flowers.

I slip into the first washroom and pull out my phone. I'm thinking about Liam and his comment about wanting a video sending back. Looking around, I'm grateful that this is a fancy restaurant and the place is clean because I hitch my dress up and push my panties down.

I quickly snap a photo of them around my ankles and send it with the caption: 'Want to see more?'

Liam

You've got my attention.

Next, I send him a photo of my dress hitched up, my upper thighs on display. Then, a photo of my very moist fingers.

I wait a few moments before the reply comes through.

Liam

Unlock the door.

Oh shit. I pull my panties off and shuffle my dress down before popping the lock. Liam pushes his way inside before he secures the door again.

He spots the lace in my hand and grabs my panties from me, shoving them in his pocket.

"Pull your dress up and lean against the wall." He drops to a squat in front of me. I follow the command and try to steady my breathing as he looks up at me. "You'll need to make this quick, Vic. Can you do that for me?"

I nod, my eyes fixed on his.

"Good girl," he says, leaning in and hoisting my left leg onto his shoulder.

This is not how I pictured my evening, but I'm not complaining. I can feel my clit crying out for attention, and he knows what to do straight away, his tongue flat and eager against me. No fingers today.

I have no choice but to grip on to his head as he works, changing the angle to flick his tongue quick and firm over my clit. He's not even attempting to tease me or edge me. He's just going for it, and it doesn't take long to feel my climax building.

"I'm coming!" I gasp, and he picks up the pace to see me through my orgasm.

As soon as I pant, trying to catch my breath, he's standing in front of me, smirking. He quickly washes his face and hands at the sink before exiting the washroom.

Again, I'm left wanting more than he's given me. I could scream. I get it—hardly an ideal setting with my brother waiting at the table too. But I'm frustrated. There's an ache deep inside me I know Liam could remediate. A kiss would have been nice too.

I freshen up and fix my dress before leaving the washroom. I stop at the bar to order a fresh drink, a gin this time.

My dad is sitting at the table laughing and joking with Liam and Johnny as I steer myself towards my seat. He's next to a short woman with dyed blonde hair, dark roots about an inch long. Next to her, a boy about fourteen or fifteen sits in a stiff suit that was clearly bought for the occasion.

"There you are, Victoria. I'd like to introduce you to Jayne. And Cody, Jayne's son."

I greet them before slipping back into my seat, ignoring Johnny who asks where I've been.

"I was just telling Liam about Cody's skills on the ice," Dad says.

Unsure of how to respond, I distract myself by perusing the menu, only half paying attention to the conversation. It's all Liam-hockey this, and Liam-hockey that—poor Johnny doesn't get mentioned once.

"Cody intends to follow your footsteps, Liam. Minus the distraction, of course," he chuckles to himself as he cocks his head in my direction.

"Distraction?" Liam says. "Vicky was anything but a distraction. She kept me in line. Made sure I was eating right, keeping on top of my fitness, not to mention her help with my schoolwork."

Dad scoffs. "Cody will be fine with all that. Hey, do you think you could introduce him to Ryan tomorrow?" Ah, there it is. This is a meet and greet for Cody. No genuine desire for Dad to have a meal with his children.

Jayne says nothing. She casually glances at the menu. I'm thankful for the server's arrival to give us a new focus.

"I've already eaten, so I'll just go for the steak. No potato, just the side salad," Liam grins, causing me to almost choke on my gin. "The appetisers were delicious."

The server gets to me. I order the chicken salad then Johnny orders the salmon.

"How did you two meet?" Johnny asks Dad after everyone has ordered.

"I bumped into Jayne at the store. She recognised me from an old photo at the barn with you boys. She said it surprised her I hadn't aged," he laughs, reaching to put his hand on Jayne's arm. She shifts in her seat so that Dad is slightly out of reach.

I'm just grateful she's not trying to put in a load of false effort like some of Dad's ex's have—attempting to win our favour or something.

Dad fidgets with a napkin and tries the conversation again. "Cody would love to get some ice time with you before we go home," Dad says to Liam.

"I guess I could—"

This gets Jayne's attention, and she breaks into a smile. "With Ryan too?"

Liam tilts his head, looking between Johnny and me. "I'm not—"

"Did you come here just to schmooze Liam, Dad?" I interrupt.

"No, Vicky, I came to see my children and my daughter's boyfriend since he's in the city, too."

"Boyfriend? Do you not listen to me?" I say.

But Liam jumps in with a response. A statement that puts a fresh wound in my heart. "She's not my girlfriend, Stuart. We haven't been together for over a year. That ship has well and truly sailed."

The table goes quieter than before, though I'm not sure how it's possible. I take a large gulp of gin, pretending that I wasn't elated half an hour ago with his head between my legs. I try and push away the urge to speak my mind, and I surprise myself for lasting a whole minute. I take another gulp of gin and then I take a breath.

I turn to face Liam. "Has it sailed? Has it sailed for good?" I pause. "Is that it?"

"Well, we've spoken about this, Vic—"

"Sure. I guess I just assumed that recent events would have—" I cut off. "Unless it's just been a bit of a temporary satisfaction and something to keep you occupied."

"What recent events?" Johnny asks, but we ignore him.

Then the servers bring our food, and the conversation is suspended.

"Let's tuck in," Dad says, as if things are completely normal. And to my complete horror, Liam reaches for his knife and fork and starts cutting into his steak.

"How can you sit there and eat like everything is fine?" I say.

"We'll talk about this later, Vic," says Liam.

I've done something stupid. I'm catching feelings again. Not that they really left, but this is Liam for Christ's sake. How can I keep a disconnect between my heart and my horniness when it comes to him? I'm a fool. And embarrassment sets in.

But Johnny is relentless. "What recent events, Vicky?"

"Forget it, Johnny," I say.

"Wait. Are you sleeping with him? After everything you said, Lee? What the fuck is this?" Johnny's eyes are wide, and his hands rest as fists on the table.

"No. We're not sleeping together. But apparently—" I begin.

"Vicky, just leave it. We'll talk about it later," Liam says.

"No, we'll talk about it now!" I yell, half surprised at myself for doing so.

"Vicky, stop. You're causing a scene," Johnny says.

"Shut up, Johnny," I snap.

"Vicky, that's enough," Dad says.

People are looking, but I don't care. Tears fill in my eyes. I feel even more heartbroken than I thought possible. I look over at Liam.

"Let's talk about this another time," he says softly, but at least he knows better than to tell me to pipe down.

"No," I croak.

"For fuck's sake, Vicky, leave it there," Johnny says, but my emotions are running high and the last thing I want is for Johnny to stick his ugly nose in.

"Keep out of this, Johnny."

Dad takes this opportunity to apologise to Jayne for our behaviour which only angers me further.

"You should apologise to me for inviting Liam," I say to Dad through tears.

"What's the problem? Jayne and Cody—"

"For Christ's sake, I'm done. I'm literally the last person you care about, Dad. As long as Johnny and Liam are here—that's all you care about. It's always been the same. I've always been a spare part and even now, you're not considering my feelings." I stand up and grab my purse. "No doubt you'll be at the game tomorrow, but please don't talk to me. In fact, please proceed as normal and pretend like I don't exist."

I shuffle between tables, feeling all eyes on me as I head for the exit. Liam is shouting my name, and as much as I want to turn around and run to him, seeking his comfort, his words ring through my head: 'That ship has well and truly sailed'. So, I leave without looking back.

I rush towards the restaurant door, hoping to catch Vicky before she disappears. However, Johnny catches up with me before I make it.

"I'll go after her," he says. "You've done enough, already. That entire situation was all your fault. Honestly, Lee. Stay the hell away from Vicky. The last thing she needs is further upset."

"Why don't you tell your dad that? Because he doesn't give a shit about whether Vicky is distressed or not."

"Don't bring my dad in to this," Johnny says, but his phone snatches away his focus by vibrating in his pocket. He slips his hand into his pocket and sighs when he reads the screen.

"Something more important, John?" I ask.

But he doesn't look up from his phone. All he does is frown.

"Is it Vicky?" I ask.

"No. But I mean it. Keep away from her. I'll see you tomorrow." And he's gone.

He's acting like a complete jerk, and I can't figure out why. The Johnny I know is always so focused, but he's easily distracted as of late; he hasn't been this bad since—shit. It hits me like a check to the head. When I joked about him having a secret girlfriend, that's all it was, a joke. But I'm thinking that it's not a joke at all. Why he's being so shady about it though, is anyone's guess. I find myself trying to think of how long I've known Johnny to be single. He ended things with Sarah years ago, and it wasn't a clean break from what he said. Ultimately, he's been single since then. When he first moved here, he mentioned having a few flings but never having a girlfriend.

"Come and sit back down, Liam," Stuart calls. "I was going to ask if Cody could come along to morning skate. I'm sure Coach won't mind."

Ignoring Stuart, I head to the maître d' and hand over my credit card because, moreover, I don't want anyone saying I'm cheap.

Once I've paid, I push open the door and head outside. The cool air hits my face, and I know where I'm heading. I hurry to my car, not even pausing to wince at the decals before getting in.

I try Vicky at least five times on the drive home, but she doesn't pick up. Then, I contemplate calling Ryan to see if she made it home; but as soon as I pull onto our street, I spot her light on.

I reach the entrance to the parking lot and swipe in before stopping in my usual spot, making a quick exit and heading for the front of the buildings. It has started to rain, so I duck my head to pick up my pace, not seeing anyone standing there until I thud straight into someone.

"Christ, Lee, watch where you're going!"

Johnny's standing there in his dress shirt, no jacket, sopping wet—as if he's been standing out in the rain.

"What are you doing here?" I ask.

And with that, the door to our building swings open and Bettsy comes out.

"I left my fob inside," Johnny says, pushing past Bettsy and heading for the stairs without so much of a backwards glance.

"Who pissed in his cornflakes?" Bettsy asks, but I shrug and head towards Vicky's building; I can worry about Johnny later.

Luck is on my side when the lady from the top floor rounds the corner, umbrella overhead.

"Hi Ryan, how's your day?" she smiles.

I play along because I need to tailgate. We exchange pleasantries—me doing my best impression of Ryan—then I loiter at his front door. I pretend to look through my pockets for my keys while she disappears into the elevator.

I haven't thought this through. I'm standing here, wondering if I should knock on the door and hope that Vicky answers. But if she's wallowing in her room, I'll likely get Jen—or worse, Ryan. Because Ryan will ask questions I'm not ready to answer, and then he'll probably tell Johnny I was here looking for Vicky. And since Johnny told me to keep away, it'll likely cause a rift in the locker room. What I can't understand is why Johnny suddenly cares. He never cared before; in fact, he never ever mentioned it. All those years Vicky and I were together, he never brought it up.

I feel sick. I don't know what I'll even say to her, but I can't wait around forever. I decide the best course of action is to text her, so I pull out my phone and tap a message out.

Liam

Let me in.

There's nothing for a moment, then I see she's read my message. I listen hard at the door, but there's no movement inside.

Liam

I don't care if your makeup has run. Let me in.

Then there's a whoosh of a door opening in the distance, making me jump and drop my phone. It clatters to the floor and causes an echo. As I bend down to grab it, Vicky's door swings open. When I stand up, I'm face to face with my brother. Fuck. This wasn't part of my plan.

"Christ, Lee. What are you doing creeping around here at this hour?"

I briefly debate whether to be honest and mention that I need to talk to Vicky, but Johnny's words echo in my head. Not that I'm afraid of Johnny, but I don't want the trouble. Even if I ask Ryan not to say anything, I can't risk him slipping up and causing a whole world of problems.

"I need to talk with you," I say abruptly. It's the first thing that pops into my head.

Ryan turns to Jen. "Do you mind, babe? I know..." and I chuckle to myself. This version of Ryan is hilarious.

But as I look into the apartment, I spot Vicky standing at her bedroom door, eyes wide.

"See, nothing to worry about, Vic. You can go back to bed now," Ryan says as he walks past.

After she slips into her room, I follow Ryan into the living area.

"What's up?" he sits on the sofa, and I sit next to him. I'm trying to think fast, but luckily, I spot a realtor's booklet on the coffee table, so I ask him what the latest is with the house buying venture.

"You've come here to ask me about real estate? It's—" He checks the time on his phone.

"Okay, I didn't." I change direction, thinking about Johnny. "Any thoughts on what's going on with Johnny?" I must not be making any sense. But he goes along with it.

"What do you mean? Did something happen at dinner?"

"Nah, forget about dinner. That was a fucking shit show though, but Johnny's acting... weird. I think he's seeing someone but doesn't want any of us finding out."

"Nah, Johnny wouldn't have reason to do that, would he?"

I fill him in on the evening, and then giving him my best Johnny impression, forgetting myself in the moment and neglecting to leave out the bit where he told me to keep away from Vicky.

"The thing is with Johnny, he likes to be in control," Ryan says, as if he's reading my mind.

No shit, Ryan. Johnny's been our best friend for a long time. This is not breaking news.

"He's right though. All this back and forth with Vicky—it needs to stop. You're setting yourself up for another heartbreak. It's not healthy."

Whose side is he on?

He frowns, taking in my expression. "Lee, I hate to say it, but give this some thought. The first time you broke up was hell, and the second time you didn't even mention it. But look what the outcome of that was, and now? If she does it again, what will happen? I can't predict the outcome, but I know it won't be good. Step away briefly, then assess if a friendship is possible. It sucks seeing you like this, bud."

The more Johnny and Ryan keep on at me to leave Vicky alone, the more I want to do the opposite.

"How about you start dating or something? I think Jen has a few single—"

"No," I say, cutting him off. "Let me deal with it. I don't want anyone fucking setting me up. Talk about something else."

My snappy tone has the effect I want because he clears his throat and circles back to talking about his plans for a house flip and a place he and Jen went to view. I let Ryan discuss it for a few moments longer, then I tell him I'm ready to head out.

"I'm just going to grab a water," I say, slipping into the kitchen. This is when I spot Vicky's keys. I make a split decision and grab the Boston U hockey keyring—closing my hand around it, feeling the plastic dig into my palm.

I say my goodbyes and leave, except, I don't actually leave. I loiter in the hallway while I wait for Ryan to go to bed.

Chapter 16

Vicky

I spent my first month of college making out with Liam a lot. It was our first taste of living together, even though we weren't officially living together. He lived off campus in a house share with three other guys from the hockey team. My dorm room was merely a storage space for my extra clothes and belongings. I spent every single night with Liam. We were making up for lost time. We were inseparable.

I enjoyed my classes, and I enjoyed the routine we'd gotten ourselves into. My favourite thing, however, was watching Liam play hockey. It brought forth nostalgic thoughts, yet allowed me to live in the present, and I felt like me again.

I remember the first of his hockey games which I attended in my freshman year. As soon as the final buzzer sounded, I made my way to the dressing rooms as pre-agreed with Liam. And as I stood outside waiting for him, I couldn't help but feel out of place. As a newcomer, I received contemptuous looks from some sophomore girls.

"Who are you waiting for?" one girl had asked me. I hadn't seen her around campus before, but she was clearly a veteran in dressing room loitering. I was wearing Liam's away sweater, and I caught her studying the sleeve. "Liam Preston?" I recall her jaw dropping—literally. "How did you get that jersey?"

Before I could answer, Liam cut through the crowd and dropped his gear, the dull thud catching the attention of people surrounding us. He pulled me into his arms and lifted me into the air, spinning me around. It felt like we had the tunnel all to ourselves.

It was the start of college life for us, and we were completely consumed by each other as we went about our days. He'd even get up for morning practice or dryland before coming back to bed, pulling me into him and spooning me until we absolutely had to go to class.

Things were perfect. He was perfect. We were perfect.

"I'm going to marry you one day, Vic," he'd told me one morning. He was looking into my eyes—still inside me, if I remember correctly.

Initially, I thought it was post-orgasm crap, but he repeated it a few days later while I was doing the dishes after dinner. He'd wrapped his arms around my waist and kissed my neck before whispering into my ear.

"Would you take my name? Or keep yours?" he said, his chin resting on my shoulder.

I didn't have to think twice. I'd been writing 'Mrs Victoria Preston' on all my damn notebooks ever since I met him. No scrap that—ever since I first saw him and found out his name.

"I dislike my dad, so what do you think?" I'd turned around and grinned, then I'd kissed him. The reality was, it had nothing to do with me disliking my dad, but rather everything to do with being his wife.

"I think I fucking love you," he'd replied, wrapping himself around me and planting kisses along my neck. That wasn't the first time he'd said it, but it was the first time he'd said it like that. I was completely consumed by my love for him, and I don't know what came over me, but I'd asked him to fuck me, right there and then.

He'd lifted me up and pulled my shorts off, slipping my panties to the side with no time to waste. I watched him slip his sweats down enough to free his dick.

"Look how fucking hard you make me, baby girl," he said, rubbing the tip of his cock over my clit. I gasped and bit down on my lip to stop myself crying out. I wasn't sure who else was home, so we had to keep the noise down.

Grabbing my hips and pulling me towards him, he'd pushed into me, his eyes tightening as he filled me. "Fuck, you feel good. You're so tight and it feels... fuck." He thrusted slow and steady, and as I stretched around him, he reached between us with his right hand and rubbed my clit.

The worry of being caught only served as fuel because he sped up and his thrusts became urgent and focused. My hands had trailed over his shoulders and down his back as he fucked me. He'd bulked out since playing college hockey, and I loved how his body felt right up against me.

I buried my head in his chest as I came, and I did something completely bold as I felt him tense. I pushed him away and got to my knees, letting him finish down my throat. I hoped I hadn't ruined his orgasm—luckily, I hadn't.

My phone vibrates next to me on the bed, startling me. I'd been lying in bed, replaying those moments in my head, hoping to be magically transported back in time. He used to make me feel like the only girl in the world, but tonight he brought me back to the harsh reality of our collective failures to make things right.

Liam

Let me in.

Shit. My heart hammers in my chest. Do I want to see him? I feel stuck in that midway point between wanting him to barge in here and tell me he wants me back, and never wanting to see him again. This is typical us. We are all or nothing. No in-between.

I swipe down on my notifications to read the message again, but accidentally tap the box, opening up my conversation with him. Fuck. He'll see that I've read it because he's online. I'm close to switching my phone off when it rings in my hand. I watch it, waiting for it to dial off. But the ringing persists, giving me no choice but to go outside and ask him to leave me alone.

Checking myself in the mirror, I reconsider. If I'm going to tell him to leave, I should at least look half decent while doing it. As I'm reaching for my hairbrush, another message comes through.

Liam

I don't care if your makeup has run. Let me in.

Rolling my eyes, I fumble to my bedroom door and, as I step out of my room into the hallway, Jenna is standing there with two mugs, trying to open her bedroom door with her elbow.

Her eyes widen when she sees me. "Oh, my goodness, Vic. What's happened? Are you okay?"

I don't think Jen has ever seen me in this state before: mascara smudged around my eyes. "Yeah, I'm fine," I say, just as there's a distinct 'omph' that comes from the front door, followed by an f-bomb. It sounds distinctly like someone dropping their phone.

Jenna's eyes dart towards the noise, and the door handle to her bedroom flicks up when her elbow loses traction. Ryan sticks his head out a few seconds later.

"What's going on?" he asks.

"I think there's someone out there," Jen says, eyeing the front door.

Oh, shit. Ryan swiftly unlocks and swings the door open, showing no concern for who might be on the other side. But he comes face to face with his brother.

"Christ, Lee. What are you doing creeping around here at this hour?"

"I need to talk with you," he blurts out, and he does a good job of avoiding my eyes until Ryan looks back at Jen.

"Do you mind, babe? I know…"

Jen nods. "Sure."

"Nothing to worry about, Vic. You can go back to bed now," Ryan says as he walks past, and I sink back into my bedroom, closing the door behind me.

I'm on edge, listening attentively, expecting Liam to enter any moment. I'm conflicted about whether I want him to come in or not, but there's a knock on the door.

I breathe a sigh of relief when I let Jen in.

"How was tonight?" she says, sitting down on the end of my bed. "Because that's the face of someone who didn't have a good time."

"Awful. And I've been a complete idiot, Jen. That's all you need to know." I flop down onto my bed and pull the covers up to my chin.

I want to tell her the full story, but I know she won't be able to keep it quiet from Ryan even if she wanted to. He'd pry it out of her and then, knowing my luck, Mike Betts would find out and then, the whole city, no—the whole country would know.

"I'm sure it's not that bad," she says, perching against my desk. I'm not sure if it's a good thing or not, but her eyes land on the letters I've done a crap job at hiding, and they pull her attention.

"Vic, these letters—"

"I know. I need to open them."

"What are they?" she asks, and then, to my horror, she stands up and grabs the one from the top. She flips it over and studies the return address. Her eyebrows raise slightly and then she looks over to my bed. "Vic, are you in some kind of trouble?"

"Yes, and no." I hide my face, completely ashamed that as a grown woman, I've failed at being a responsible adult.

"Which one?"

"Okay, yes. But I can fix it."

"How much do you owe?"

A bucket full of pucks has just dropped into my stomach. "I don't actually know."

"Can I open them? Just so we're aware of what we're dealing with."

This coaxes me out of bed. "No, I guess I need to do it."

She takes a step back, and I feel a fresh wave of tears prickling behind my eyes. The paper rips easy and I slide the letter out, unfolding it before taking another breath.

"How much are we talking?" Jen says after I've had a beat to skim over. I cuss under my breath and hand her the letter.

"Well, there's nothing we can't handle. I'll sort it and you can pay me back," she shrugs.

"Oh my God, I can't ask you to do that! I can't owe you three grand!"

"Sure, you can. Besides, you're not asking, I'm offering. It's fine. I've got savings. I've still got my redundancy money."

I burst into tears and Jen crowds me, giving me the warmest hug I've ever had since Lois.

"I got you. It'll be fine," she says, rubbing my back, soothing me.

But I can't bring myself to tell her that there are multiple letters.

I wait at least thirty minutes after Ryan sees me out, loitering outside in the hallway like a creep, listening out for any movement from inside the apartment. When I'm convinced everyone's in bed, I slip the key into the lock, holding my breath as the latch clicks.

As soon as I reach the door to Vicky's room, I wonder if I'm doing the right thing. But Ryan and Johnny's advice to keep away rings through my brain, and then I remember the look on Vicky's face earlier, and I know I need to talk to her. Besides, this is like a middle finger to Johnny and Ryan.

I open Vicky's door just enough for me to squeeze through. The room is in complete darkness. But I can hear the fan she insists on, whirring away in the corner. I can just make out her breathing. I consider for a moment how to play it. I can't jump onto the bed and startle her because Vicky would scream, and Ryan would run in here. So, I edge around to where she's laying and start whispering her name, elevating my voice a little and then reaching out to stroke her arm.

"Vic? Vic, it's me," I whisper. She stirs, then realises I'm standing over her and starts with a yelp. "Shh! It's Liam."

"Oh, my fucking Christ!" She sits up and there's a scramble before the lamp next to the bed comes to life. "You almost gave me a fucking heart attack! What the hell are you doing?"

"I needed to talk with you."

"How did you—"

"I stole your key."

"You stole my key?" She's acting like this is the first time I've snuck into her bedroom; but I guess it's fair, considering how things are between us. I've not seen the inside of Vicky's room properly, only ever half-exposed during the video calls we've had in the past. It's full of memories, most of which we share, and it doesn't take long for me to spot a photo of my mom on the wall.

"Lee?"

"Sorry, yeah." Without paying it much thought, I kick my shoes off and take my jacket off before laying on the bed next to Vicky.

"What's happening?" she exclaims.

"I fucked up." I briefly gaze at the ceiling before turning to look at her. "I'm sorry. I shouldn't have..." I pause to compose myself, unsure of what I am apologizing for. "Look, I don't know why I was so blunt earlier, but fuck, Vic. What the hell are we doing?"

"I don't know," she says weakly, slipping down the headboard, so she's laying down, then she turns towards me. We lock eyes in silence, only the fan breaking the stillness. "Where do we go from here?" she finally says.

"Nowhere. Johnny told me to keep away from you, and Ryan agrees that's the best plan. I know it's not their decision but..."

"Do you want to keep away?" she whispers.

I swallow hard. "No. But I have to. I can't go through that again."

"I'm sorry. I'm so sorry. I never wanted to—"

But I lean in towards her and press my finger to her lips. "Please, don't." I know as soon as she starts, she'll cry, and then I'll cry. She understands, nodding and silencing herself.

I originally came here wanting to have it out with her, to demand answers. But it doesn't feel like that's the right thing to do anymore. We continue to stare at each other. And afraid I may want to lean forward and kiss her, I change the subject drastically. "Hey, do you think Johnny has a secret girlfriend?"

"A secret girlfriend? What?" Vicky laughs—the hushed, silent sort of laugh that she perfected back when we were kids, and it's like fucking music to my ears.

"He's acting shady. Holding his phone close, dropping everything and disappearing as soon as it goes off. I made a joke about it the other day, and he stonewalled me."

"Johnny's too much of a douche to have a girlfriend," Vicky says, taking a deep breath in to stop herself from sniggering.

And before I know it, we're here, right in each other's space, whispering back and forth. The light from her lamp is enough for me to get lost in her eyes. It's just like old times. It's dangerous territory.

"So, why didn't you tell me you were back in Canada?" I ask her when we pause again.

"I just needed some time to think."

"Did you see your folks?"

"Yes, but I shouldn't have bothered." Sadness fills her eyes as she tells me about her dad sending a taxi to pick her up, and then the shit attempt at a nice father-daughter dinner. "Going back made me question where I belong, Lee. Like, I was excited to go home, but it didn't really feel like home anymore. Do you know what I mean?"

Sadly, I did. "I don't really know where home is either, Vic," I say, but then I realise I do because I feel at home right now. Part of me wants to tell her, but I'm already crossing the line by still being here. "I guess, if I had to pick where to go next, I'd go to Vancouver. But I don't know." I really didn't know. I haven't decided what I'm going to do with myself when I retire, and I hadn't paid any thought to where I'd end up.

Vicky reads my mind. "Have you decided on your post-season plans?"

"No." I roll onto my back. "And I'm supposed to figure it out soon. I need a plan."

"Why are you putting so much pressure on yourself? You don't have to figure anything out immediately. If you wanted, you could take a year off and do whatever you liked. But it seems obvious to me," Vicky says, and I feel the bed shift as she rolls over, too. "You shouldn't quit. Think about it," she says. We fall silent again.

"What's your plan once your visa expires? Are you planning to renew it?" I ask.

"I guess it depends on what Johnny's doing. It's weird, Lee, because Johnny's Johnny, but I've sort of gotten used to him being around, and I—" she stops and shifts on the bed again.

"What?" I prompt.

"I don't know. But I think I'm going to estrange myself from my parents. So, Johnny is all I've got." I roll over, locking eyes with her once again. "Neither my dad nor my mom makes me feel very good about myself. When I spoke briefly with a counsellor back home, she made me realize that I have control over these things and can take action," she says.

"You have me too, you know," I say, and before I know it, I've pulled her into me. I'm holding her to my chest, and it feels so normal.

I wake up hours later with Vicky wrapped around me. I have no choice but to wriggle free and tuck her in because I can't risk Ryan catching me in the morning.

She stirs slightly as I lean down and kiss her forehead. "See you tomorrow."

"Lee?"

"Yeah?"

"Thank you."

Chapter 17

My head is pounding. It's one of those headaches you get when you haven't had enough sleep and you're thrown back into consciousness before you're ready.

After Liam left, I laid there reflecting on our encounter and wishing I had said different things. And it wasn't long before my mind jumped to the conversation I'd had with Jen earlier that evening. There's no way in hell I can let her pay for my fuck up, so I did the only thing I could think of. I got out of bed, put the light on and went rummaging through my wardrobe. I picked out the most valuable items I own.

As I lay them out on the floor, I realised I didn't even know what sort of number I was working towards. Gathering the letters that had steadily piled up, I took a deep breath and opened them all, one by one. Some of them were reminders, so could be discarded; but once I got the unique ones picked out, I grabbed my phone and opened the calculator app.

It was one of the hardest things I've ever had to face—but I did it. Then I burst into tears. I carried on sorting through my things and listed a load of them online. Finally, I added a post to my Instagram account, making out that I was clearing my collection of previous seasonal wear to make space for new. I fired out a message to Jen anyway, hoping that her phone was on silent, telling her not to pay anything.

I pop two paracetamol pills in my mouth and take a gulp of water, willing my headache to disappear. It's loud as fuck in the rink today, and the GM is floating around so I can't duck out early. He's invited some reporters in from the local newspaper, and I'm tasked with hosting them. They want to interview Liam and Ryan about the current season and their experience playing here.

As I wander around, I try to ignore the fact that my dad, Jayne, and Cody are here, watching from the stands. What I can't ignore, however, is the smugness I feel upon hearing that Coach Adams has given Johnny a big fat 'no' to Cody joining in morning skate; an idea my dad probably concocted last night.

"We're not insured, anyway," Coach Adams had said when I overheard Johnny asking him for his permission. I felt ecstatic, knowing how angry my dad would probably be. Then I saw Johnny talking on his phone with his brow furrowed.

My elation is short lived when the GM brings Dean, the journalist, over to stand with me. Dean has written for us in the past but hasn't visited the rink recently. He usually goes off the match night reports for his write-ups.

Dean and I exchange greetings briefly before he asks about Liam and Ryan. "Where are the twins, Vicky?" He cranes his neck towards the ice before looking at his watch. "I need to get an interview. Could you snap a few pictures of them together, too? There is a shortage of photographers at the paper."

"I'll see if I can find them." I give him my signature smile and take my leave.

Tapping on the dressing room door, I don't have to wait long before it swings open and Danny steps past, nodding in greeting. Ryan is standing at his cubby, and Liam sitting at his, taping his stick. His practice jersey is still hanging up behind him. The sight takes me back to when he first taught me how to do it.

"Can you teach me?" I'd asked him, reaching for the roll of white tape he'd placed on the kitchen counter.

"To do what exactly?" He'd wiggled his eyebrows at me and moved his hand along the shaft of his stick.

"Cut it out," I laughed, swatting him with my hand then he spun me around so I pressed my back up against his chest. I was painfully aware of how much I was shaking, but he handed me his stick, flipping it so the blade was in the air.

"Here. Just do it how you think it should be done. Because I'm pretty sure you watch me every time."

"What if I don't do it the way you like?"

"I'm sure I'll like how you do it." I heard him suck in a breath and then, he tugged the tape away from my palm and found the end. "Just give it a go," he whispered.

Placing the first strip of tape on, I bent the loose end over the heel of the blade. Then I placed the roll over my index and middle finger and begin. Up, down, up, down, up, down, like I'd seen Liam do so many times.

"See, you're a natural."

When given the opportunity, I'd tape Liam's stick from then onwards.

I swallow hard, still watching him work the white tape back and forth. I told myself no more stick taping, and I've stuck to it. I should probably tell myself no staring too, but I can't help it.

"What's going on, Vic?" Ryan says, his tone friendly. "I hear you were successful at speed-dating."

It's impossible not to notice Liam's eyes on mine as he shifts his concentration away from the heel of his stick. He's watching me, waiting for my reply. Trying to shake it off, I mention that there's a journalist waiting to do a quick interview.

"Really? Christ." Ryan looks at his brother and wrinkles his nose.

"I've got you." Liam places the last bit of tape on his blade and snips it with some scissors.

"I guess we better get this over with," says Ryan.

Liam stands up and reaches for his sweater, but his eyes don't leave me. My skin prickles with excitement and I'm desperate for him to be close again. I wanted to kiss him. No, scrap that, I wanted him to kiss me.

Even as I walk away, I feel him watching me. It's only when I get back to the bench that I afford myself a deep breath.

Ryan and Liam are here moments later. Liam has his sweater half tucked in as usual, and I introduce them to Dean who instructs me to get the photos before he starts his interview.

Dean leans in to check out my shots after a while. "These are great, Vicky. Listen, I'm starting something on the side, a bit of freelance work, and I'd love for you to help me out with the photography. Would you be interested? There's no immediate need for an answer. Here's my details. Call me." Dean hands me a square business card, and I slip it into my camera case before excusing myself.

Johnny skates over as soon as he spots me standing at the boards.

"Has Dad apologised yet?" he asks.

"No."

"What did that journalist want?"

"He's interviewing the guys."

"Have you spoken with Lee?" Johnny asks.

"Christ, Johnny. Please leave it." I kept quiet about Liam sneaking into my room last night.

"Just wondering, because I've told him he needs to leave you alone," Johnny says. "I'm sick of seeing you in this mess, Vic. You need to snap out of it. Move on. Instead of obsessing over Liam, focus on living your life."

"I wish you'd just keep out of my damn business," I yell.

I don't even bother excusing myself from Johnny; I turn on my heel and walk away.

It's all fake smiles and shit while we talk to this Dean guy. Despite my mood, I deliver a speech about how happy we are to be here, praising the city and the fans. It's not not true, but I couldn't care less right now.

I take the lead with Ryan chiming in only when necessary, as usual. He hates talking to the media. It's an easy interview anyway. Dean's questions primarily revolve around our NHL careers and upbringing in B.C., before he shifts the topic to Johnny.

"Word is that you two grew up with our humble captain, Jonathan Koenig. What was that like?" Dean holds his phone out, a recording app live on the screen.

I grin. "Johnny is brilliant. He's always been a role model and a fantastic leader."

Speaking of Johnny, he's in my peripheral vision talking with Vicky. I'm watching the interaction intently, and it's not long until she's marching away from him as if he's pissed her off.

"Liam, your socials are a lot quieter this season. Is there any reason for this?"

"I'm sorry, what?" I snap back to the conversation. Dean holds the tail end of his phone up to my mouth and curls his lips into a smile as he asks again.

Fuck. What am I supposed to say to that? That I'm done showing off a life I pretended to live? I think for a moment, then he prompts me again.

"Should we assume that you're seeing someone?"

"No," I say. "I mean, yes. I mean, it's complicated."

I feel Ryan go rigid next to me, but I know better than to look at him. The media recognise it as a cry for help and will only start asking more questions.

"Oh, so you're single and looking to mingle or?" He elongates the 'r' sound.

I open my mouth to reply, but Coach Adams yells across the ice. I'm unsure how he can project his voice so well. It never fails to land on the correct ears.

"Not single. Not seeing anyone," I say, which makes no sense at all.

"We need to get going," Ryan suggests.

"Right. We'll leave it there," Dean says.

As soon as he slides his phone away, he changes the tone of his voice.

"Thanks, both. I really appreciate it."

"No problem," I shrug, and Ryan and I edge closer to the ice.

I can hear Dean at the edge of my hearing mention Vicky and her blog to one of the other media reps, and it piques my interest, but Coach's snappy words grab my attention.

"Nice of you to join us," he says, gliding over. He's dressed in a team tracksuit zipped up right to his chin and a baseball cap pulled low over his eyes. You can never really tell what mood he's in.

"Right, guys. I don't know why any of you have your sticks because we're bag skating today."

I glance down at the tape job I whizzed through, now a pointless effort.

"You're so slow today! Come the fuck on!" Coach shouts at everyone. He grabs my stick from my hands and bangs it against the ice before tossing it back towards me.

We all shuffle to the bench and lay our sticks on the rack, then make our way to the red line and line up. We only manage a couple of lines before Coach screams at us again.

"Christ. We need to do this more often. You guys are an embarrassment." Coach blows his whistle and resets us on the red line. "This time, I want you to make an effort."

The whistle sounds, and we take off again—back and forth between the red line and the goal line. My legs start to burn, but I push through. In times like these, you can easily spot who's on top of their fitness. Ryan and I easily match each other's pace, driven by our competitive streak. We work hard to out-skate the other, resulting in us skating faster.

Danny is surprisingly quick. He keeps up with Ryan and me, while Hutch, who was fast as hell according to Ryan, slows down after a few minutes. It's only when Bettsy trips over himself that Coach blows his whistle and gives us a five-minute breather.

"So that's them, huh?" Ryan asks, as we grab a couple of water bottles from the boards. He's eyeing the stands where Vicky's dad and his new family sit.

"Yep."

"Well, it won't be long until he's announcing their engagement," Ryan says.

He's not wrong. Vicky's dad, Stuart, has been engaged at least twice since his divorce from Vicky's mom.

"I think Vicky's sick of it," I say. "Or maybe she just hates weddings in general." I don't know why I say it, but bitterness courses through me.

"I can't believe you were going to get married, bud." Ryan shakes his head. "I can't imagine you married."

"Why not? I guess I always thought I'd marry Vicky," I reply. "And she always said the same thing. A part of me still wonders why she called it all off." I think about those times in college I used to tell her I'd marry her one day. I'd never meant anything more.

"She hasn't told you?" Bettsy's voice sails through the air as he comes to a stop behind us. "It's because she doesn't want to end up like your parents or her parents. Something like that anyway." He says it as if I'm asking him to explain how to shoot a puck.

"What?" Ryan and I say together.

After all this time, and all this bullshit, that's the reason? Surely not.

"Johnny told me but he—ah, shit." Bettsy's face drops.

I bet Johnny told him not to say anything. Before I think about the consequences, I charge over to Johnny and check him mid-ice, causing him to keel over. Then I toss my gloves, ready to go.

"What the fuck, man?" he says, looking up at me, his ass firmly planted on the ice.

"Get up!" I yell, grabbing at his sweater and pulling him to his skates. I let him balance himself before taking a swing for him. He ducks and then backs away.

"Fucking fight back, you fucking ..."

I want an even fight, at least. But then the air changes, and the rest of the guys gather around, trying to break up whatever this is. The next voice I hear belongs to Coach.

"STOP!"

I don't know what's more frustrating: Johnny refusing to fight back, or my brother pulling at my sweater, prying me from Johnny.

"What the fuck are you doing?" Coach Adams is between Johnny and me, acting as a barrier. "Get him off the damn ice. Now," he says, directing Ryan to lead me off.

As I head back to the bench, I spot Vicky. Her eyes are on me—staring, mouth agape. And the look I give her, I'm sure, does not emphasise how pissed I am.

"What the hell was that about?" she asks as I walk past, but Ryan keeps pushing me onward.

I'm sick of all of this. Games. Secrets. Lies. It's exhausting. I'm exhausted. And I thought we were getting somewhere after our talk last night, and now this.

Ryan pushes open the dressing room door and shoves me back into my cubby.

"Sort your shit out," he says, before he backs away, exiting as quickly as we came in.

The door swings open a few moments later, and I'm half expecting Coach to be the one walking through, ready to ream my ass, but it's Johnny.

"What the fuck was that?" he asks.

"Sorry. I didn't get a punch in. You're supposed to be bleeding."

He scrunches his face up and whips his helmet off. "What the fuck is going on, Lee?"

"Why wouldn't you tell me you knew why Vicky called off our wedding?" I keep my eyes on the floor. I can't even bear to look at Johnny. He's enraging.

"Oh. That."

"What do you mean 'Oh, that?'" I'm ready to take another go at him.

"How—"

"Bettsy."

"Fucking, Bettsy," Johnny says.

"No. Atta boy, Bettsy. You should have told me if you knew because Vicky wasn't going to. I deserve to know!"

"It's not for me to tell. Besides, I promised her I wouldn't." He shrugs. It's like he doesn't even care.

"It didn't stop you telling Bettsy, though, did it? You're supposed to be my best friend. You know what?" I stand up. "Don't speak to me."

I undress, completely blanking out whatever shit is coming from Johnny's mouth. I head for the showers with a towel wrapped around my waist, leaving him standing there, desperate for acknowledgement; he hates being ignored as much as I do. I hear the door to the dressing room open and slam shut; minutes later, it opens and closes again. But I carry on showering, and then I can feel someone standing near the door.

"Leave me alone, John—"

"What was that about?" Vicky asks.

She takes me by surprise, and it doesn't exactly help that I'm standing here naked.

"Fuck, Vic. You shouldn't be in here."

"You just went for Johnny mid-practice. I think I deserve to know what's going on. I have a feeling it's got something to do with me."

I can hardly believe what she's saying. She deserves to know what's going on? I feel angrier than I have in a long time, so I take a few deep breaths before turning towards her.

"And I didn't deserve to find out why my fiancée called off our wedding from Bettsy." I switch off the water and swing open the saloon style door to the shower. Vicky's gaze lands straight on my dick. She opens her mouth to speak, her eyes darting between my face and my crotch. "Christ, it's nothing you haven't seen before." I grab my towel and wrap it around my waist.

"How did Bettsy—"

"Johnny can't keep his fucking mouth shut."

"Oh." She pauses and straightens up. "Why does it matter now, anyway? That ship has sailed, remember." There's a hint of venom in her voice.

"Don't you fucking dare. You broke my heart. Twice, remember? You owe me an explanation. I've been putting off asking you, you know. I didn't want to cause any more upset or whatever, but I'm done now, Vic. I want to hear it from you. Not Johnny, not Bettsy, not Ryan, because I wouldn't be surprised if he fucking knows. Actually, I bet the entire team knows." I'm almost shouting at this point, my blood boiling.

"They don't. Lee, they don't. Look, I didn't want to end up like my parents. Or your parents for that matter. My parent's relationship was a fucking mess, and when your mom told me she was..."

"Don't," I say, pushing past her.

I don't want to listen to Vicky talk about my mom because right now, I'm already re-living enough heartbreak as it is.

Chapter 18

It had been Vicky's idea to get married. It was January, and we were spending every single night on the phone: video calling, sexting, whatever. It was like we were reliving our college days.

We were on a video call one Friday evening. Evening for me anyway, middle of the night for Vicky. She had her iPad propped up against a pillow next to her on her bed. I tried to insist that she sleep, but she refused, and there was no point arguing with her because, despite my stubbornness, she always won.

I'd lost count of how many times she'd fallen asleep while talking with me, and I didn't mind. I just enjoyed knowing that she was there. But this particular night, she was wide awake.

"You had a good game," she said, and we talked about it for a short while. Vicky knew hockey, even though sometimes she'd pretend she hated it. But the conversation always led in the same direction: her poking fun about my sweater. "I don't understand how you can wear it half-tucked!"

"I don't know why it bothers you so much. Remember, I thought of you before going out onto the ice."

"You're such a dick," she laughed. Then she watched me toss some rolls of tape into my hockey bag. "Do you miss me taping your stick?"

"I wish you'd do something to my other stick." Vicky scoffed at my terrible attempt at flirting, but I genuinely loved her reaction. "Well, that's something else that always reminds me of you," I'd said, on a serious note. "Honestly, it seems like everything reminds me of you these days."

"Well, ditto. I miss you," she said. Then she went into a speech about all the things she missed the most. I waited for her to finish before asking about her plans to stay in the UK with Johnny.

"I don't know. I mean, what are your plans?"

"I'll go wherever you want to go," I said.

She chewed her lip then looked directly into the camera. "Let's get married," she said. "I mean, we always said we'd end up married, so why not?"

No need for contemplation on my part. "I've already got you a ring, baby girl. I don't think it'll do it justice for me to show you now, so I guess you'll have to wait."

Her face lit up. "Were you going to ask me, then?"

"Always," I said. "I love you. I've only ever loved you. Besides, who else would put up with you?" I winked at her, and her smile was contagious.

After lengthy discussions, we devised a plan. I'd play out the rest of the season for the Marlies, then go over to the UK, marrying Vicky and playing hockey on Johnny's team.

Johnny had smoothed it over with the GM, and I had spoken with Ronnie, my agent. She wasn't happy. In fact, I'd say she was on the verge of un-signing me, but I persuaded her to help me out.

It was meant to be our happily ever after. All I had to do was inform my brother that Vicky and I had gotten back together, and we were engaged.

That was until Vicky decided she wasn't keen after all.

I remember the day like it was yesterday; and to make matters worse, I was worrying about an ongoing issue with my knee. With the season on pause for All-Star week, I was packing up to fly to the UK and spend a week with Vicky. I had my suitcase laid out on my bed. I tossed things in whilst listening to a playlist Vicky and I had put together—completely oblivious to what was about to happen.

Then she called me.

"How's the knee?" she asked as soon as I picked up.

I can't say it was out of character because she always asked about stuff like that. She knew I was having trouble with it. We talked for around twenty minutes before her tone changed. I guess she was building up the courage.

"I've changed my mind," she'd blurted out, finally.

"About the venue?" I'd naively asked, thinking back when she mentioned her uncertainty.

"No. The wedding."

We were planning a very small affair, with the aspiration to do a bit of travelling when we could, and then have a party afterwards with our friends and family.

"You want to have a big showy one, instead? We can do that. It's not a problem—"

"No, Liam. I don't want to marry you."

It was obvious that it was her first time saying it out loud. Her voice cracked and broke, as if holding back tears.

"You don't want to marry me?" I asked her.

"No."

"Why not?"

"Because I don't. I've changed my mind. I'm allowed to change my mind," she snapped.

But I hung up at that point. I couldn't listen to her anymore. And I cried. I'm not even ashamed to admit I cried. I sobbed uncontrollably, as if a lifetime's worth of withheld tears were pouring out of me. I don't even think I cried that much when my mom died. Probably because we knew it was coming, so we had time to mentally prepare.

My initial instinct was to fly over and demand answers. Then, I remembered the heartbreak from the first time and how I needed to heal myself all over again. It was at this point the dread set in. I'd crawled into bed and shut the world out, turning my phone off. I didn't even go to the gym. I hardly ate. I hardly slept. I just lay there in complete nothingness.

On the afternoon of the third day, Ryan arrived at my place. He'd used his key to let himself in, and he groaned in disgust when he made it into my bedroom.

"What the hell happened?" he asked, pulling back the curtains in an overly dramatic fashion. "You haven't been answering your phone."

I covered my head with my blankets, then I lied to him. "Just some issues with my knee, and I had a few heavy nights."

He called bullshit straight away. "Is this about a girl?"

It's about the girl, I had wanted to say, but I busied myself by rolling out of bed and reaching for a pair of sweatpants.

I hadn't told Ryan that Vicky and I were back on, in fear of a moment like this. It was embarrassing to have your heart broken by your high-school sweetheart once, and now for a second time—I was a chump.

He opened the windows and started clearing up some trash I'd left lying around. Then just as he went to reach for a stack of papers, I intercepted.

"Alright, chill. I'll go get something to drink." Ryan walked through to the kitchen.

I skimmed over the papers, bile rising in my throat. I'd signed the dotted line. Fuck. Shit. Bitch. I'd agreed to play in the UK. The idea of going there immediately was unbearable, and I threw up in the trash can.

After I'd cleaned myself up, I sat next to Ryan on the sofa and took a long drink of water. He didn't press me any further; instead, he handed me my Xbox controller. My mind was racing, and all I could think about was that fucking contract I'd signed. What the hell was I going to do? I mean, I could probably get Ronnie to make some calls, but I was already on thin ice.

I looked at Ryan and back at the TV a couple of times before taking a lung-full of air. "Hey, bud. Have you signed your renewal yet?"

"Nah, I'm meeting with Ronnie next week." Ronnie, always made sure to meet in person before a signing.

"Are you still weighing up your options?" I asked, testing the waters. He mentioned a few weeks ago that he was questioning if there was more to life than his NHL career. He'd said it in a state of thinking aloud; and when I pressed him, he'd shaken it off fairly quickly. That was until a week later when he mentioned Germany in passing. In all honesty, that wasn't the first time he'd mentioned it either, but he could never set his mind on a plan, always defaulting to carrying on as normal.

"I'll just see what Ronnie has to say," he shrugged, reaching for the TV remote and switching the games console off.

I watch him flick through the channels for a while, building up the courage to come out and ask him the million-dollar question.

"I need to cash in on that favour," I asked. Ryan froze in his seat. It's something that I never thought I'd actually want to be repaid. But right then, I couldn't think of anything else.

"What do you need?" he replied, but little did he know I was about to change the course of his future entirely.

"How'd you feel about playing with Johnny next season?"

I'd kept my focus on the TV, doing my utmost to avoid eye contact.

"Ha. You're kidding, right? He's in—"

"I'm not kidding." The TV flicked off, and Ryan leaned forward, giving me this look that I'd only seen a few times before: serious mode activated. "I wouldn't ask unless I absolutely had to. Please." I swivelled my head towards him, and his expression matched mine. "Please, Ryan."

"What's going on?" he asked.

"I made a bet with Johnny, so I'm sort of fixed on it. I can't let Johnny down now and since you—"

"A bet? What kind of bet?"

I didn't have an answer, so I came up with some crap and prayed it would be enough. I threw the word 'playoff' in there and said I'd been tipped off that I was likely to get called-up. All crap but I said it—and then I waited.

As a family, we have this thing about bets, and I knew Ryan would have a hard time saying no. Besides, if anyone could take a year out of the NHL and go back, it's him. He works ten times harder than me, and I remember thinking that it might humble him. Maybe he would discover that there's more to life than hockey. And he did.

Now I'm sharing a dressing room with my brother and Johnny again, like we did when we were kids; and Vicky Koenig is still driving me fucking crazy. All because of the fucking plan I made up on the fly.

She's standing there with her hands on her hips, and her chest heaving with an effort to remain calm. Her last words lingering in the air.

"Lee?" I drop my hands from my hips and glare at him.

"I shouldn't have come here. What the fuck was I thinking?" He shakes his head and droplets of water slide from his damp hair onto his neck.

"Please don't say that. You're having a great time, aren't you? Your brother is here and Johnny—"

"You've been watching. You must have noticed that my game is off. I'm under-performing. This isn't me. Fighting and... this whole fucking situation is a mess. It's probably a good thing that this is my last season."

"You don't mean that."

"I really do. You don't get it, do you?" He turns his head, so his eyes meet mine. "I can't stop myself when it comes to you. You've got this fucking hold on me, and I can't figure out how to get out. Everything I do, even hockey. I'm ..."

He raises his voice, and I can see the anger in his eyes.

I take another step towards him. If I have such a hold on him, why is he doing such a good job of keeping me at arm's length? Aside from the bathroom incident, of course, but now's not the time to mention that.

I reach out and set my hand on his arm, and he looks at my fingers, then towards the door. He breathes in as his fingers drum against the wood of his cubby.

"Lee—" I whisper, not sure of what I plan on saying.

"You broke my heart, Vicky!" It's almost a yell. "You broke my heart, and why? What the hell for?" He shifts his concentration to my face, and he's looking at me as if his life depends on it. He's waiting for an answer.

"I was scared," I say.

He scoffs. "Of what?"

He's right. I had nothing to be scared of. He's always been there for me. Through everything—and how did I repay him? Breaking his heart. Twice. Tears start to well in my eyes.

"You've seen that shit show my parents passed off as a marriage. I didn't want us to end up like them. And then your parents—"

"Stop. I get it." He looks away again, but I see the tears welling in his eyes. "But we're not our parents."

"No, but I saw the way your dad was when—"

"Vicky, please stop."

"I need to get it out, Lee. You need to hear it." I pause for a moment, and he flicks his gaze to land on me again. "I did want to marry you. I mean, I do. But the way I saw your dad's heartbreak, I can't put you through that!"

"That's ridiculous. Because you've already put me through something similar, except I've had to look at you every single day. And that's fucking worse." We're silent for a moment, and I know I have no choice but to switch things up—to look at the positives.

"But everything worked out okay, didn't it? You stayed in Toronto and had your shot and it paid off. You made it."

He hisses. "What else was I supposed to do? I focused all my energy on last season when you called off our wedding. I had no choice."

"But you made it!" I say.

He turns to face me this time. "It means nothing. NHL? That was Ryan's dream, not mine. Yeah, it was great and all that, but it meant fuck all without you. You were everything to me, Vic. Fuck. You are everything to me. But you didn't trust us to make it."

"I'm sorry. I'm so sorry. I can't tell you how sorry I am. I love you, Liam." I step towards him tentatively, and he engulfs me in a hug. I clutch onto his damp skin as if this were the last ever hug in the world. "I'm sorry, Lee. I really am. I'm a coward, and I've been struggling for as long as I remember to deal with my emotions. Not that I'm making excuses, because I was a complete—"

"Please, stop talking," he says, and his grip around me tightens.

"Where do we go from here?" I ask. Then there's a clattering outside and a rumble of skates hitting the rubber matting.

"You have to leave," he says, quickly retreating into the showers. All I can do is nod as I spin around and walk away.

Seconds later, the dressing room door springs open and Ffordey, the goalie, wades in, followed by Danny and Hutch.

"Alright, Vic?" Danny says, flopping down at his cubby.

"Yeah, just thought I left my tripod in here," I lie. "Oh, Parker, before I forget, I need to arrange a signing with you."

I briefly speak with Ffordey and make a plan while Liam exits the shower room and prepares to get dressed—as if he's just got out of the shower.

Liam doesn't look at me, and I make a quick move to leave just as Coach pushes through, not paying me any attention—thank God. He makes a beeline for Liam.

"My office. Now."

Liam follows him out of the dressing room, just about dressed. I'm left surrounded by half the hockey team as they file in. My presence goes unnoticed by all of them, even though I shouldn't be here. It's only when Johnny enters that things turn sour.

"What are you doing in here?" he growls.

"My tri—"

"Were you talking with Liam? Because you need to keep away. You're fucking his game up. Listen to me. I've told him, and now I'm telling you."

I want to tell him he can't dictate what I do, but I'm so ready to leave. I stride to the door and exit into the corridor.

Coach Adams has left his door slightly ajar, and I can hear a mumble of voices. I can't help myself. I approach his door quietly, focusing on listening while doing my best to ignore the loud noise from the dressing room. Even with the door closed I can still hear Bettsy.

"...the way I see it, Preston, they promised me a winger who is a sharp skater and can deliver on face offs. Both are true, yeah, but you're lacking discipline. Your brother vouched for you, career history aside. He's put his neck on the line for you after that stunt you pulled last year with your contract. The GM wasn't impressed and, frankly, nor am I. You're in and out of the damn box, not even having the opportunity to take face offs, then attacking the captain? What on earth was that about?"

"I can only apologise, Coach. I'd like to promise you it won't happen again, but right now I can't. I'm struggling with a personal situation that's affecting my game. I'm working on it. Johnny and I had a disagreement, and I let my emotions get the better of me. I'll try harder."

There's a pause. I can hear shuffling feet, as if Coach is pacing. Then a drawer opens and closes.

"I appreciate your honesty but I've got no choice. I'm sitting you out of the game tonight. Use the time to figure your shit out. You're on a very thin line, do you understand me? Now, if the GM asks, you've got a lower body injury that we're taking a precaution on."

That's my signal to leave, so I head back towards the ice, and then I spot my dad waiting at the benches. For fuck's sake.

"Vicky, can we talk?" Dad says. He's on his own, no sign of Jayne or Cody.

"I'm really not feeling up to it."

"I'm sorry about last night. I don't mean to make everything about your brother, or Liam for that matter."

"Right."

"And I want to apologise for my behaviour overall. I haven't been a very good role model to you, nor Johnny. I need to do better."

I can't bring myself to look at him. All the years of him being emotionally absent have taken a toll on me. I firmly believe that things would be a lot worse if it weren't for Liam and Lois.

"Vicky, at least look at me," Dad says. "You haven't withdrawn your allowance." I wondered if he would mention it.

"I think I need some space, Dad."

"Really? So you don't want my help?"

It's not a secret that my job isn't all that well paid. I mean, it's okay. My bills are paid, but it doesn't allow much room for luxuries such as nice shoes. But if I truly want to move on and heal, I need to look after myself and estrange completely. Time to grow up. Time to rid the demons.

"I don't want your help," I say.

I spot Johnny coming out of the dressing room.

"There you are, Vic—"

"Not now, Johnny," I say, and I push past him.

I go back to the office to gather my things, wondering what the fuck I do next.

Chapter 19

The longer I stare at the ceiling, the more I'm convinced that it's not white—it's more of an off-white. And it's really starting to bug me.

I'd usually be napping but there's no point since I'm benched. Aside from that, I doubt I'd be able to fall asleep anyway. My brain is working overtime, thinking of Vicky. And Johnny. And how pissed my brother's going to be when he reads my text.

I replay the conversation I had with Vicky, wondering what the fuck we do next. Despite everything, I can't stay mad at her. She said she loved me too.

I want to call her and tell her about the conversation with Coach, but she beats me to it; my phone vibrates softly on the mattress. I answer it and place her on speakerphone.

"Did I wake you? I heard what Coach said. I was eavesdropping," she says.

"Yeah, well, I probably got off lightly. He put me down as a lower-body injury."

She sighs, and I can practically hear her thinking. "This is all my fault, Lee. I'm sorry. I know I've got a lot to be sorry for, but I really am."

"Forget about it. Johnny was a complete douche, so it's not like he didn't deserve a punch."

She chuckles, and it sends a jolt of pleasure through me; I really miss making her laugh. And just like when I was in her room, the conversation switches to chatter.

The more we talk, the more I realise how much I've missed her. And not just the sex. I miss her. And I miss us goofing around together. I miss finding something funny and needing to tell her about it. And I miss doing this; just hanging out, even if it's via the phone. Before I know it, we've been talking shit for half an hour.

Just before we hang up, she softens her voice. "Lee? Is it too late to try this friends' thing? Because I know I don't deserve the chance, but—"

"Sure. Friends."

We hang up and I can't help smiling. I feel like we're finally moving forward. But the next challenge I face is Ryan, and I wince when his name pops up on the screen. I know he's livid.

Sitting on the bench instead of playing is every hockey player's worst nightmare. Having an injury is frustrating as hell, but when you're benched for your own shortcomings—it's a fucking travesty.

To make matters worse, I've got to sit here in a suit and smile and pretend to be happy. I'm all for showing support, but it's difficult while I watch my teammates struggle to cover my spot. Of course, Ryan isn't struggling, but the overall effort has increased. And they've switched Matt Rodgers to play wing aside my brother, and it's a complete gong show.

Do I regret it? Yes. Would I do it again? Without a doubt.

I'm pissed I didn't get a clean hit on Johnny, but I don't want to miss out on ice time, so I need to rein it in. But this isn't the first time I've had to sit out with a fake lower-body injury.

While playing a road game, Ryan got into a fight outside when he went to grab something from the bus. He witnessed a confrontation between one of the opposing forwards and a girl—with raised voices and heated exchanges. Next thing Ryan knew, the guy threw a punch, missed, and Ryan retaliated. One thing led to another, and the opposition coach was pulling our coach to the side to have a word, telling him that Ryan Preston had been seen beating the shit out of one of his boys.

Miraculously, Ryan escaped without a scratch, bar some swelling on his right hand. And when he was whispering frantically about his fuck up, I couldn't help but tell Coach it was me, not Ryan.

That road game wasn't just any road game. Scouts from the WHL were there, and I knew Ryan had been building up to this moment for a long-ass time. I was lucky that I had a good record, and once Coach knew the score, he cleared it with the opposition. And they agreed to leave it lay and not get the cops involved—probably to save their reputation more than anything.

"Because you're a good kid, I'll put you down as a lower-body injury," Coach had whispered before sweeping out of the room.

Three games I had to miss, and three games Ryan impressed enough to get an offer. And then he spent the rest of the season expressing his gratitude, saying he'd make it up to me someday—which he did. And now he's planning the rest of his life around that repaid favour.

I shuffle left as I see him skating towards my end of the bench. He swings his legs over and slides in next to me.

"What did Vicky want earlier?" he pops his mouthguard out as he leans forward. Despite him looking ahead, I know he's waiting for a reply.

"Nothing," I lie.

"She seemed to have something to say." He glances at me, and I swear to God he can read my mind sometimes. "You need closure." He mops a towel over his forehead then wipes down his visor before tossing it aside. "You can't continue as you are. You've not been yourself since you got here, and it's starting to piss me off."

As he takes his next shift, guilt floods through me—all this because I couldn't exercise any self-control.

There's shuffling on the bench, and Bettsy slides down, followed by Johnny. I do my best to ignore them both, putting my concentration on the game.

The next time I speak is when Ryan's next to me again.

"Did she tell you the full story? Why she called it off?"

"Sort of," I reply.

"I thought you said she had nothing to say," he snaps.

Well, shit. He got me there. And now he's really pissed.

I think for a moment then decide to tell him what the current situation is. "I think we're going to try this friends' thing,"

But then he's gone again. I watch him closely this time, leaning over the boards, my elbows on the edge.

"Come on, bud, move your feet," I yell, encouraging him to skate harder out of a turn he's aiming for. I know how he plays, and I can tell he's not playing his best.

He sails around and receives a pass from Rodgers, sneaking it past the opposition's defence before he fires it at the net, where it narrowly misses with a 'clink'. An audible groan from the crowd emulates the frustration on my brothers' face. I can't make it out, but he shouts something at Matt. An angry something.

Fortunately, we're up by two at the end of the first, so it's not as bad as it could be. But I still feel terrible; I'm replaying Ryan's clanger. And when we're heading back to the dressing room, I walk beside him.

"I could have gotten that rebound if I had been there. That would have been an easy goal," I say, but I swiftly realise I should shut my damn mouth.

"Well, you weren't there, were you? When will you quit messing up and be present? I'm getting sick of the half-assed effort, Lee. There's always something that gives you an excuse to lose your concentration. Either you're in and out of the box or—" He pauses. "You need to sort your shit out." The dressing room door slams behind him.

I don't follow him, knowing that at times like this, it's best to give him space. Instead, I loiter outside. I've fucked up. I know he's right. I need to fix things and stay out of my own mind. I hear a camera shutter to my left. My head snaps towards Vicky, her beautiful blue eyes twinkling at me as she smiles and it feels like everything has changed between us.

"Hey Lee, could you grab Ryan for a sec, please?" Jen asks.

I didn't even notice Jen standing next to Vicky because, as always, Vicky takes up my entire concentration. I slip into the dressing room and look around for Ryan and find him sitting next to Jani.

"Jen's looking for you," I say.

At first, I don't think he heard me, but then he stands up and walks towards the door.

"He'll come around," Jani shrugs. "Has Coach spoken with you yet?"

"About what?"

As if by summons, Coach makes his way over and with a commanding nod, he beckons me to a quiet corner of the dressing room. "Preston. I've been talking with Jani, and I've decided you'll wear his 'A.' It's not up for discussion, but I think it'll push you to consider your actions. I'm giving you a shot at leading by example. Don't fuck it up."

He's gone in a flash, before I can respond.

"Good idea, yes?" Jani says, putting his arm around my shoulder.

I'm speechless. But there's something bubbling inside me, and I know exactly what it is. I want to share the news with Vicky.

As if on cue, my phone vibrates in my pocket.

Vicky

> Coach just told me the news.
> Photoshoot on Monday. Congrats!

I smile, but it fades quickly because I don't deserve it.

I think about it through the next two periods. What will I say to Ryan? It sort of feels like I've been rewarded for bad behaviour.

Ryan tries to avoid my end of the bench for the next two periods. Even during the second intermission, he busies himself chatting to anyone who will listen, which is out of character for him.

I'm feeling deflated when the final buzzer goes. I shake hands with everyone and, to my relief, when I get to Ryan, he fist-bumps me as he walks past. I follow him into the dressing room where we both sit in our cubby's.

"I don't want to argue with you, Lee but you seriously need to sort your shit out. Should I rephrase it to make it easier to understand?" Ryan says, as we wait for Coach to debrief us.

"Coach has given me Jani's 'A.'"

"I thought he would. Jani mentioned it earlier, it was his idea. And I think it'll be good for you. Give you something to focus your attention on."

Coach bursts into the room, grinning, pausing my conversation with Ryan.

"Great win, guys, but we can do better." He pops a piece of gum into his mouth and chews before continuing. "Liam Preston will wear the 'A' that Heikkinen wore, just so everyone knows. It's all been squared away, but please give him your support. Oh, and I'm switching the lines up. Betts will stay first pair, and I'm putting Koenig with Jones."

There's confusion and mumbling. Everyone looks towards Johnny, who's fiddling with the end of his skate lace.

"Did you know about this?" I hear Bettsy ask Johnny. However, Johnny is not forthcoming with a response. But when Ryan catches my eye, I know we're both thinking the same thing. It wasn't Coach's decision—it was an ask from Johnny.

I'm hovering next to the players' benches, and as soon as I hear the double doors at the very end of the corridor open, a jolt of excitement runs through me. Once Liam's jersey had been fixed with an 'A' I planned a photoshoot at the rink. I invited Johnny, Danny and Pritch too, because I need a shot of the captain with the three alternates for the website.

I only saw Liam yesterday on the away trip, but we're talking again, and it feels good. I've been looking forward to seeing him again but my elation quickly dies when Johnny's stupid face comes into view. He's walking quickly, as if he's in a hurry, and he's coming in my direction.

"Vic, I wanted to talk to you before the others get here," he says, dropping his gear on the floor.

"Well, I don't want to talk to you." I busy myself by rummaging aimlessly through my camera bag.

"How long are you going to keep this up?"

"How long are you going to be an ass?"

He huffs. "I'm sorry that I told Bettsy."

"That's not why I'm pissed at you. Honestly, it was probably a favour to me because everything is out in the open now. The real reason I'm pissed is that I thought you were on my side. But I'm wondering if you're just another version of Dad."

"You don't mean that," he snaps. But after I scoff loudly, his tone changes. "Look, I'm going through some shit right now, and I'm not in the right headspace."

"What shit?" I ask.

"Nothing. It doesn't matter."

"Does this have anything to do with your secret girlfriend?"

Johnny's eyes widen. "I don't have a secret girlfriend."

I hear the double doors swing open, followed by the echo of talk from three familiar voices. Johnny sighs before grabbing his bag.

"Dad said you're not accepting any help from him anymore."

"Nope. Don't need it," I say, half lying to him because I really do need it. At least to put myself in a good position, anyway. Behind Johnny, I lock eyes with Liam for a second before he slips out of view, Danny and Pritch on his tail. "You better suit up," I say, flicking my head towards the dressing room.

Johnny takes his leave, and I ready myself for the shots I have planned while I wait for them to come to the ice. Johnny is the first out. He does laps while he waits, saving me from any interaction.

Pritch and Danny are out next. They join Johnny, grouping together for a few rounds. Then Liam finally makes his way out and grabs his stick on the way past. I've redone his tape, and I can see him inspecting his blade as he twists the shaft of his stick in his hands.

"Let's get this over with," I call to the guys as I step gingerly onto the ice.

I round them up into position and get started, only having to pause a few times for Danny to compose himself.

Danny asks what everyone wants to know. "Are you going to tell us anymore about the defensive pairings, John?" All eyes are on Johnny.

"There's nothing to tell," he says, smiling. His expression drops to a frown after I've taken my shot.

"Well Bettsy said—"

"Leave it, please, Danny," Johnny snaps. "Vic, are we done here?"

"Yes, but I need Lee's jersey. I'll come get it in fifteen minutes," I say.

Johnny's away before I can blink.

"I don't know what's gotten into him, but I hope he snaps out of it soon," Danny says to Pritch and Liam as they head towards the bench.

I can't say I disagree with him. If I was in a better mood, I'd be turning up at his place demanding answers. Johnny has never been this bad before.

I leave the ice and start packing up my things when I receive a phone call from an unknown number. My brain works overtime as I try and decipher who it could be. The bank? My credit card company? Fuck it. Time to grow up.

"Hello?"

My whole body relaxes when a familiar voice sounds through the earpiece. It's Dean, the journalist. He makes small talk, complains about the weather—then tells me he's got a proposition for me.

"How do you feel about rugby?"

"Rugby? The place or the sport?"

"Would my answer change your answer?"

It's amusing since I've never been to the place or watched the sport. "What're you getting at?" I ask.

"I wanted to talk to you about some photoshoots," he says. "I need to find a photographer to take pictures of the boys. They've got a big game coming up, and I thought I'd ask you."

"I've only ever shot hockey."

"How different can it be? It'll be cold. There'll be guys chasing a common object. I'd pay you, of course," Dean says.

Pay me for it? I guess it could definitely come in handy since I've not had any success winning the lottery, and my stuff isn't selling as quickly as I'd hoped. I agree, and Dean tells me that he'll text me the details before hanging up.

I head down to the dressing room. It sounds quiet inside, but I knock on the door. Liam's voice beckons me inside. He's sitting in his cubby wearing only his boxers, tapping away at his phone. He lifts his head as soon as I walk in.

"Oh, is everyone else gone?" I say, looking around.

"Why are you selling a load of your stuff?"

Shit.

"I'm just having a clear out," I shrug, pretending to still survey the room.

"Some of those were gifts. Why are you selling gifts?" Tossing his phone down, he stands up and moves towards me, towering over me. I stare at his solid chest, taking in his tattoos before mapping each muscle with my eyes. I'm desperate to reach out and touch him. "Vicky? Answer me, please."

"Check again. None of my listings were gifts."

"I remember everything I've ever gifted you, and there's a pair of Jimmy whatevers listed that look like the ones I bought you."

"They're at least three seasons later. Trust me," I say.

"Right, fine, whatever." He gives me a straight-faced look. His eyebrows almost forming a straight line. It's adorable, but he's angry. "What's going on?"

"I ... okay, fine. My dad was sort of helping me out with money and he's not anymore, so I need to re-jig a few things. They are the only things I have that hold any value. Except for my car, that could also be an option."

As soon as I say it, I sound pathetic, and I can feel the tears prickling behind my eyes.

"Fuck, Vic. Why didn't you just come to me?" He runs his hand through his hair.

"Ask my ex for money? No, thanks. I can look after myself," I say, furrowing my brow because that's another lie.

"You're not selling your damn shoes." He steps back towards his cubby and reaches for his phone. "Or your car."

"What are you doing?" I make a grab for it as he taps away, but he holds it out of reach.

I could start jumping up and down, waving my arms to reach it, but what good would that actually do? Apart from adding to the pitiful display of the situation.

"Buying the shoes," he says, edging away further.

"You can't!" I protest.

"Fucking watch me."

I try to reach for his phone in desperation, but he's quick, and steps around me, wrapping his arms around my shoulders, locking me in.

"Let me go!" I try to wiggle free, but he's too strong.

"Vic, let me help you. I can. I want to."

I hear him breathing me in, and I swear to God, his dick is pressing into me.

"Are you hard?!" I half-yell.

He leans in and whispers into my ear. "Your ass is rubbing my dick. What do you expect?"

Fuck! That ignites something inside me. Well, let's be honest. It was already ignited, but he's just thrown gas on the fire, and now it's burning wildly, waiting to be extinguished.

"There. Done," he says, releasing his grip. But I stay where I am, enjoying the contact.

I don't know what to say. I'm ashamed and beyond grateful, but this wasn't part of my plan. "You didn't have to do that." A single tear trickles down my cheek.

"I know. But I don't want you selling your stuff."

"It's only stuff," I say.

"Yeah, that means a lot to you."

"Thank you," I croak out. Then before I know it, I'm bawling. Liam's arms tighten around me again, and he spins me around, so I bury my head in his chest. He smells incredible, and I want to breathe him in forever. But he pulls back abruptly and looks at me.

"Your dad was helping you out... was that a long-term thing? What's the deal, Vic?"

I sit in his cubby, ignoring the fact that he's standing there in his boxers, his crotch practically level with my eyes. "Well, this job doesn't pay great. I mean, it's fine, but I've been living beyond my means, and—"

"Are you in debt?"

The tears return, and I nod without making eye contact. "But I should be okay now, thanks to you."

"Should be? How much debt, Vic?" He crouches down so his eyes are level with mine. I can't lie to him.

"Seven thousand."

"Dollars or pounds?"

"Pounds."

"Christ, Vic."

"I know. I've been such an idiot. And now I'm having a panic about how I'll manage when Jen and Ryan move out because I can't afford to pay the whole rent on my own. Not on that place. I'll probably have to move." I can't bring myself to admit that I've thought about asking Johnny if I can stay with him.

"But we can fix it. I can—"

"No. I told Jen the same. She offered to pay off one of my credit cards, but I told her no. Which is why I put the stuff up for sale."

He sits down next to me. "I know you don't want my help, but—"

"I can't keep relying on other people, Liam. I need to grow up and figure this out for myself."

"At least let me pay what you owe. Then you can start with a clean slate."

"No. Thank you, but no." I stand up and hastily wipe the tears away with the back of my hand. I glance at my watch and press Liam to move aside for me to get the shots of his sweater.

"I'm here for you, though," he says, kissing my cheek before moving to get dressed. But I'm crying behind my camera and can't even look at him. "I'm always here for you, Vic."

Chapter 20

Liam

I have to time it perfectly. Because finding an opportunity to slip into Vicky's room is difficult when you have the same schedule as one of her roommates. I've been thinking about her situation non-stop, and I can't help but feel like I need to swoop in and fix things. Probably because I always want to be the hero in Vicky's eyes.

She'll be pissed off when she finds out I've been in her room. It's her safe space and I'm invading. But I'm willing to risk it because I know she won't let me help any more than I have done already.

I wait until Ryan has left to pick up Jen from work. I know I have a small window, because it's a Wednesday and they stop at the store on the way home. On the other hand, Vicky is working late at a photo shoot for that Dean guy. I have about forty minutes, but my plan is to finish in twenty, leaving time for any major mistakes.

Letting myself into their apartment, I call out into the empty space, just to be sure I'm alone. When no one replies, I make my way to Vicky's bedroom door and pause to take a breath, before reaching for the handle.

Once I'm in her room, that familiar scent of Chanel fills my lungs, and I can't help but take a deep breath. Her room, seeped in darkness the last time I was here, looks so Vicky with the light on. It's painted white with accents in rose gold and, of course, aqua. Ever since I've known Vicky, she's been obsessed with anything sitting between green and blue hues.

I take my phone out and snap a few pictures, to make sure I can set everything to how it was when I got here. I don't know how much digging I'll need to do. Vicky isn't likely to notice if something has moved a few centimetres, but she will know if something is hugely out of place.

I take my shoes off and leave them next to the shoe rack to the left of her door, allowing myself just a moment to picture her wearing a pair of the heels she's got lined up.

Glancing around, I check her desk first. Primarily used for makeup, she has a box open at the end of the counter full of various colour pallets and brushes. Her hairdryer sits next to a mirror propped against the wall, and there's a stack of papers towards the far end of the desk. I carefully skim through them. There're various bits of junk mail mainly, however, at the very bottom I find two notices for payment. I toss the papers on top of my shoes to take home.

I try her drawers next. Though, would she put mail in her underwear drawer? It's unlikely, but it doesn't hurt to check. I tug on a handle, and Vicky's collection of personal items come into view. I can't help but reach in and feel the material of a few familiar pairs, the fabric feeling incredible against the roughness of my fingers. I search for the teal panties she has, which has a certain effect on me that I can't describe. I'm disappointed when I don't find them, but I do find something that causes my heart to pound loudly. Blood pumps through my ears when I find a whole wad of ticket stubs—Marlies ticket stubs. Flicking through them confirms she attended a lot of my games. There's even one as recent as the April just gone. Well, more than one. In fact, there's stubs for all the games directly after the season ended here. As I look through them, I realise after everything we've been through—fucking around with our feelings, her calling things off, me calling things off, Vicky still came to see me. A bitter taste fills my mouth. Why wouldn't she tell me she was there? If I'd known she was there... I guess I don't know what I'd have done, but still.

I place the stubs back where I found them and push the drawer shut. I rummage through the rest of the unit but nothing of interest is to be found. Moving on to her closet, I'm not surprised to see a long row of shoes along the floor. I need to clear some pairs to reach a box of what appears to be papers, hidden at the back. I carefully rearrange them and reach for the container, sliding it out gently. Bingo. I look through and see a few bills and statements. I scoop them all up, putting them with the others to sort through later in the comfort of my bedroom. But when I push the box back in place, I spot a more familiar container labelled 'Memories,' in Vicky's cursive handwriting on the front. I know I shouldn't, but I can't help but pull the box towards me.

Taking the lid off, I glance inside tentatively, as if something is going to jump out at me. But I break into a smile because the box is full of photos and random objects, which may be considered crap to anyone else, but to Vicky and me, they're priceless. My eyes cloud with the danger of tears as I rummage through the box as if I'm looking for a lost item. There's photo after photo of me and Vicky and a fair few of Vicky and my mom. Lots of me playing hockey, and even more candid shots of me living my life, with Vicky right by my side. There are photos I didn't even realise existed. Photos of us, and recollections that were just fragments in my mind until now.

At the very bottom of the box, there's the puck from the first goal I scored with Vicky as my girlfriend. The rubber, partially worn on one side. A roll of tape: white. A broken stick blade, taped in true Vicky style with some doodles I did; her head resting on the shoulder of my sweaty jersey as I drew. All in this one box, lives a showcase of my life with Vicky.

My phone vibrates in my pocket, throwing me back to the here and now. I ignore it, using it as a sign to hurry the fuck up. I put the boxes back and line the shoes up, just like I found them. But as I stand up, and start to close the door to her closet, I spot a row of my old hockey sweaters.

I reach out and touch the first of the Boston-U jerseys. It's probably been worn by Vicky more than me, but in a single moment, it's as if a mini-movie of my college years plays back in quick-time. Mostly of Vicky beaming at me, or her cheeks red from the cold as we skated together, or her body pressed up against mine, sometimes naked, sometimes not. But there's no denying that she's in my head. No scratch that, my soul.

Tears fill my eyes as I realise there's no one else I'd rather share these moments with. Even in difficult times, things felt perfect. It didn't matter because I had Vicky and Vicky had me.

But now? Vicky's decisions and her inability to let me love her fully has got us to this point. Friends. And heartbreak. Heartbreak: something else of mine reserved just for Vicky. Because there's no one else I'd ever let in enough to break my heart and I'd let Vicky break my heart a million times over if necessary. Because, I loved her then, and I love her now. I can't imagine a time when I wouldn't love her.

I don't know what to do with this revelation but I'm sobbing as I hurry to put my runners back on before collecting all the papers. I take a moment to compose myself, using the sleeve of my hoodie to wipe away the tears. I'm just about to leave when I spot Vicky's laundry basket right next to her desk. There's a pair of teal panties right on top and the image of Vicky wearing them pops into my head, just as I feel my dick swell in my jeans.

Shoving them into my back pocket, I'm out of there with a plan to go straight home, pay Vicky's bills, then get acquainted with her panties again.

Cold weather is fine, but rain that feels like needles hitting your face is not. Especially when I'm supposed to be standing outside for eighty whole minutes. And in bad lighting.

Dean met us in the rugby clubhouse and introduced me to the guy organising the evening. I naively thought I could stand inside, taking advantage of whatever shelter I could. But I quickly realised the building was about three hundred yards from the rugby pitch.

Johnny and I stand out in the cold, our winter coats zipped up to our throats as I hope to catch a good enough shot.

"Do you even know the rules, Vic?" Johnny asks, hopping on the spot.

"Do you?"

"I'm not the one getting involved," he says. He didn't have to come but he changed his mind at the last minute.

"I'm hardly getting involved. I'm just taking some pictures. It's paid work."

"Have you thought anymore about what you're going to do after Ryan moves out?" he asks as I make a tactical choice and switch lenses.

"Start an 'OnlyFans'" I joke, but looking at Johnny's face tells me he doesn't find it funny at all. "I am kidding, you know. No need to be so serious."

"Well, I've told you. You're welcome to stay at my place. I know you probably don't want to, but it'll buy you some time to figure it out."

"Thanks, John."

He seems overly chirpy tonight, but it's short-lived. His mood changes pretty much straight away when he pulls his phone out of his pocket and glances down at the screen.

"Right, Johnny, are you going to tell me what the hell is going on? Because—"

"It's nothing. Dad has been asking me if you've begged me for money yet. I think he's expecting you to lean on me since you're refusing his help."

"I hope you told him I'm doing absolutely fine?" Johnny knew I had to list some of my things for sale, but I didn't tell him that the buyer of my shoe collection was Liam.

"Are you sure? You could always ask Mom for money if things get that bad."

"All of Dad's money is Mom's anyway. Where do you think he got it?"

He doesn't respond to that question.

"How did you get yourself into financial trouble, Vic? Because I'm pretty sure your salary can cover your half of your rent and stuff."

"I've been living outside of my means, Johnny. So, I need to cut back on the shoes, makeup and stuff." I keep quiet about the fact that the majority of it was used for flights and hockey tickets. He wouldn't understand. I needed to fly to Toronto at short notice, and they had only had first class left, so I put it on my credit card. Okay, needed is a strong word, but I couldn't help myself. I try and change the subject although it's a poor choice. "How's Dad?" I ask. It's weird—I don't want to care, but I do.

"He split up with Jayne. But he'll get over it, I'm sure."

I can't help but laugh out loud. She used him to get to Ryan and Liam and since Dad didn't deliver, it makes sense that she'd call it off.

Johnny tucks his phone away. "Speaking of Lee, I need to fix that, too. I've been such a shit friend."

You've been a shit brother, too, I think.

"Well, yes and no. I'm grateful you didn't tell him, but you shouldn't have told Bettsy," I say.

"I'm sorry. I wasn't thinking. My mind has been all over the place lately."

I don't press him any further. He clears his throat, looking ahead at the pitch, and asks if Liam and I are speaking again.

"We're going to try being friends," I say.

"Well, keep it that way because he's got a shot at making something good from this season. I don't want his mind wandering or his heart getting broken again. Or your heart, for that matter. I say this as a friend to Liam and a brother to you. You're better off apart." I concentrate on my job before I'm tempted to start another argument with Johnny. "Right, Vic, this is called a line-up, and you should be able to get some good shots from over there." He points to our right and I shuffle along.

"How do you even know this?"

"Kirsty likes Rugby," he shrugs.

"Is Kirsty your secret girlfriend?" I practically squeal at him, but he shakes his head.

"Nah, but we've been hanging out a bit as friends. We got on well at speed-dating and, if I'm honest, I was hoping for a connection but we just didn't spark. She said the same thing, so it's all good."

Damn it. As much as I was hoping I'd just cracked the secret, I believe him. Even as the night goes on and Johnny mentions Kirsty a few more times, I become even more convinced he's telling me the truth.

During half-time we make our way into the clubhouse to get some hot drinks. When Johnny excuses himself, I find myself scrolling through my socials.

"Hey, Vicky," a deep voice calls out behind me. I whip my head around, coming chest-to-face with a guy about Liam's height with broad shoulders. He's got what looks like day-old stubble, and he's wearing a polo shirt that stretches across his chest.

"Yes?" I look at him, with a tiny feeling that I recognise him.

"Neil," he says, holding out a hand. "Remember? We met at that speed-dating event."

"Oh, Neil. Of course."

I didn't remember. And now I feel shit for not remembering.

"I'm disappointed we didn't match, but I guess fate brought us together again." I stare at him, willing myself to say something. "Sorry, I should have said I'm the captain, but I'm not playing tonight. Got an injury I'm working through, but I hear you're going to be a regular with the photography?"

His hand is oddly smooth for a sportsman; I smile politely as I shake it.

"I remember you saying that you usually photograph ice hockey?"

"Yeah, that's right. I have no clue about rugby," I say.

"I'll have to teach you the rules at some point. How about going out for a drink sometime? Unless you really weren't keen on matching."

"I didn't match with anyone that night. I just went along to keep a friend company." I don't know why I lie to him, but it feels like the nicer thing to do. Shit. Is this me indicating that I do want to go for a drink with him?

"Maybe," I smile, unsure of what else to say. I stand there, waiting for the feelings to come, but they don't. No butterflies or sparks of arousal creeping through me. Nothing.

Then, as if he's planned it, Johnny appears behind me.

"We best get back, Vic," he says, ushering me to the door of the clubhouse. "Who was that?" He flicks his head towards where Neil is still standing.

"Apparently, he was at speed-dating. Says he's the captain but isn't playing because of an injury."

"Huh? I don't remember him."

"Were you looking for guys? Is that the reason you changed your mind about tonight?" I prod Johnny in the arm, but the look he gives me tells me I'm seriously wrong.

"Be careful," he says, leading me back towards the pitch. But Johnny doesn't realise that even if I did find Neil attractive, I'm too hung up on Liam to act on it, even if it means I'm destined to stay single forever. I think I'm coming to terms with the fact that it's Liam or nothing for me. Except I have no idea how to tell him.

Chapter 21

Liam

"How's the house-hunting going?" I ask Ryan as we move to the squat rack. "Jen still refusing to pick somewhere?" We're in the gym in our building, the usual time, the usual day.

"Yeah, and I don't understand it. One minute she's super keen and the next, she's saying she can wait and there's no hurry. But Vicky walked in on me getting head yesterday. I'm ready to move out."

I spit out the water I just chugged. "What the hell?"

"She didn't see anything," Ryan shrugs. "But I want us to have our own space."

"I can appreciate that." Dropping my voice, I lean in closer. "I learnt Vicky is having some money troubles. Jen probably wants to stay until she knows Vicky is okay financially."

Johnny is on the other side of the gym; and even though I'm not actively avoiding him, I'm not seeking him out, either. I don't know if he knows, so it's best to assume not.

"How do you know?" Ryan asks, loading a cross bar with weights. I fill him in on the events of the photoshoot, his eyebrows shooting up when I tell him about the shoes she listed for sale. "Oh, shit. Does she need some help?"

"Obviously she needs help. But I think she's fine now." I look down at my runners.

"Have you paid it off?"

"Well, sort of, yeah. But it's just to reset things for her. Once things settle, I'll see if she needs help to budget." I don't tell him about taking her key or that I used it to let myself in and find whatever bills I could. And I definitely leave out of the bit about me snooping through her underwear drawer. "Please don't mention it though, bud. You know she's proud about stuff, but there's shit going on with her dad—"

"Yeah, Johnny said she's cutting him out or something. I can't say I blame her. If I was Johnny, I'd do the same." He's quiet for a moment then he shifts on his feet. He looks serious, as if he's about to say something important, but my phone rings and interrupts the moment.

Danny's name flashes across the screen, and I reach down to pick it up. It stops ringing and immediately starts back up again.

"You better get that. Danny never rings twice."

He's not wrong, so I hit accept.

"Mate, Vicky's here and she's fuming. She literally pushed me out of the way to get into your room. She's fucking strong for such a—"

"Where is she now?"

"In your room! Going through your wardrobe. She said she's looking for something," Danny says.

I stop breathing for a second as panic sets in. I don't even grab my things before turning and jogging towards the door. I take the stairs two at a time because I absolutely cannot have Vicky going through my closet.

I reach the door to my and Danny's apartment and fling it open. Danny's standing awkwardly on the threshold of my bedroom. "I'm sorry, Lee. I tried to stop her." He steps away.

Vicky is sitting on my bed, surrounded by the contents of my closet. The presentation box that my Maple Leafs jersey came in is open on her lap. I feel sick. I scan the area first, then focus on the box. My jersey looks untouched—thankfully.

"What the hell is going on? Why are you going through my stuff?" I say.

"You told me you got rid of it." I swallow hard. She holds up a plastic wallet containing a CD. "You told me you got rid of it," she says again, raising her voice.

It takes a few seconds for her words to sink in. "Well, I almost did."

"But you didn't." She pushes the presentation box aside and stands up. "Where's your laptop?"

"Vic—" I make a grab for her, trying to reach for the disk, but she loses her balance, landing on the bed with a flop. I take the opportunity to grab it from her.

"Give that back to me!" she says, reaching for my hand.

"Were you looking for this?" I wave the disk in the air.

"I was looking for my key—and my panties! If you can go through my closet, I can go through yours. Now give that back to me!"

"Wait—how did you know?" But she stands on my bed and charges at me, practically piggy backing me as she tries to reach for the disk. But I manage to grab onto her and send her back onto my bed, pinning her down.

"What are you doing?" she demands, but I'm hovering over her.

"Vic, you don't know what you're doing," I say.

"Get off me!" she squeals.

"Stop being such a brat and fucking listen to me!"

I try to get her to keep still, so I can explain, but she keeps wriggling underneath me, and all I can think of doing is leaning down and kissing her. So, I do.

A few things happen at once. Vicky stops moving, then she relaxes. Then she wraps her legs around my waist, clamping me down on top of her.

My heart pounds hard, sending all the blood I have to spare down to my dick. Vicky must feel it too because she lifts her hips up to push against me.

I interrupt the kiss to lock eyes with her, hoping to understand what she's thinking.

"Kiss me again, Lee," she whispers. I do. This time softly, parting my lips and she does the same. As if we're in sync again, my tongue finds hers, and she lets out a moan, sending a shiver through my body. And as she leans her head back, I know exactly what she's asking for. I kiss my way down to her neck, and she squirms underneath me—only for a brief moment before she pushes at my chest.

"Stop. You're trying to distract me, and it's working!" she yells. She pushes at my chest again and I let up, moving off her.

"Now give me the disk, Lee!" she says, getting off the bed.

"Sorry, did you say disk or dick?" I can't help myself, and I chuckle when a smile sneaks across her lips.

"Stop it!"

She's ignited that goddamn fire again, and I stoke it. Willing it to burn brighter despite knowing it's definitely a bad idea. "Wouldn't you rather just re-enact it instead?" I wiggle my eyebrows. I can tell she's thinking about it briefly, just as Jen's voice sails through the partially open door.

"What the hell is going on? Danny said—"

"Liam has something that belongs to me," Vicky says.

"No, I don't." But I forget my position and relax my arm. She makes a grab for the disk and hurries out through the open door. "Move!" I yell at Danny as he dodges Vicky, blocking my exit. But the front door slams, and I know I've lost this battle.

"What the hell was that about?" Ryan asks, coming from the bathroom. But I'm not interested, deciding instead to make a run for it, grabbing my keys on the way out. If she's putting that disk into her laptop, I need to be there when she does.

By the time I reach the bottom of the stairs, she is stepping out of the elevator.

"What the fuck are you playing at?" I ask.

"I could ask you the same thing! You told me you'd gotten rid of it!" Her cheeks pink up, and she keeps her eyes to the ground. "Have you—?"

"No. Well, not in a long time." I can't help but grin. The thought of what we recorded back in college makes my dick hard.

"Oh."

"I've considered it," I say. "But before you get any ideas, there's no way you're watching that without me."

"I'm not going to watch it. I'm going to get rid of it." She looks at her fingernails.

"You're totally going to watch it, aren't you?"

"No! I just said I'm getting rid of it." But she doesn't look at me.

"Vic—do you think that's the only copy?"

"You did not!"

"Didn't I?" I step forward as she steps back, and she comes to a stop against the wall next to the elevator. I lean in, putting my left hand next to her head. I angle in closer and ask, "Wouldn't you be disappointed to find out that I got rid of it?"

She stumbles over her words for a moment, then lets out a sigh. "Fine. Yes. But only because I'm intrigued."

"About what?" I raise a brow.

"Nothing. It doesn't matter." She stumbles over her words. "Kiss me, Lee." She shakes her head. "I mean, give me my key. And I want my panties back!"

"Your key is at the barn, but you can have it back. The panties, on the other hand, I'm pretty sure you wouldn't want those back after the mess I made." I live to see her reaction to comments like this. I know what I'm doing and I love it.

"I—" I edge closer to her, and my eyes meet hers. "Fuck," she breathes out, almost inaudible.

"Vic, do you want to see the mess I made?"

This time, she kisses me. It's only a short one, but it's a moment where my dick is harder than ever. But she pulls away and turns her head so she's not looking directly at me. "Do you really have a copy?"

"What do you think?" I tap my temple and give her a wink. Her cheeks flush red, and I'm horny enough to brave it. "If I ever need an extra special party for one, it's my go to—"

She gasps and then spins around, making a quick exit towards the door. Once she's out of sight, I drop her a text.

Liam

> I'll know when you've watched it, don't worry.

"You made a sex tape?" Quinn, my classmate and roommate in college, said when I told her.

We sat in the library, and I had to tell her to use her indoor voice.

"It's not a sex tape, per se," I replied. "More of an oral sex tape."

"A blow job? Wow! This brings a whole new meaning to the phrase 'tape job,'" she giggled. I had to give her that because it made me laugh too. "Who's idea was it? I bet it was Liam's, wasn't it?"

"Well, it wasn't anyone's idea. It just came about and neither of us really stopped it from happening. My new camera came in the mail, and we were testing out the video recording feature. One thing led to another."

"This is brilliant!" Quinn said.

"So now we're even," I told her, because I already had a secret of hers, so I thought it was only fair that she held one of mine—besides, I was dying to tell someone.

"Did you put it online?"

"Uh, no! Liam's got it, but he's going to destroy it."

"What's the point of making it if you're going to get rid of it? That's no fun. I say put it online. Make sure you blur your face out."

"It's not going online," I reminded her.

"It's probably already on there. You can't trust guys with this sort of stuff. I bet the entire hockey team has seen it too."

My stomach turned—I felt sick. Would Liam really do that?

"Why are you saying these things?" I asked her, packing up my things as quickly as I could.

I jogged down the steps of the library, almost falling on my ass, narrowly avoiding someone carrying a Styrofoam cup. I threw an apology behind me as I made my way to my car.

I raced over to Liam's place, completely disregarding the speed limit. I parked illegally outside, putting the worry of a ticket to the back of my mind. I didn't bother knocking when I arrived since they kept the door unlocked during the day. I burst in to find him lounging on the sofa with a teammate, watching the Boston game from the previous night.

"Hey, baby girl," he said, snapping his head towards me. "I thought I was seeing you after practice. Do you want to watch the game with us?"

"Lee, can I talk with you, please?"

I practically dragged him up to his room, closing and locking the door behind us.

"Are you okay?" he asked.

"Shh, this is important!" I hissed at him. "You wouldn't put that tape online, would you?"

"Well, it's a CD but ... where's this come from?"

"You wouldn't, would you? Or show the guys. Oh my God, or Johnny!" Panic had set in.

"You think I'd show your brother a clip of his sister—" I put my hands over his mouth because I couldn't bear to hear him mutter the words aloud. Knowing my luck, the entire team was standing on the other side of his door listening in like their lives depended on it. Then they'd know what we'd done. What we'd made. What he'd made me do.

"No one else is going to see it, don't worry." He paused and looked at me, grinning. "I wouldn't mind rewatching it to pick up some tips on doing it again. I've been thinking about it non-stop and—"

"Shh!" I was more than embarrassed. I thought I'd peed myself but we realised later that's not what it was.

"Look," he lowered his voice, "It's for us and us only. If you want me to get rid of it, I will. I don't want to, but I will. I mean—it was fucking hot, wasn't it?"

He wasn't wrong. It was, and I'd felt nothing like it before. We both found being filmed exciting, but I had worried about it falling into the wrong hands.

"But—"

"Relax, Vic. Relax. I'll get rid of it. Trust me." He wrapped his arms around me and kissed the top of my head.

And I did trust him. I still do. I think he's the only person I've ever really trusted, apart from his mom.

"Okay, fine," I said, sitting down on his bed.

"Fine, you want me to get rid of it?"

"Yes. I mean, no. I mean, keep it. But—"

Liam sighed, running his hands through his hair. "I'll do whatever you want. Just let me know."

For weeks afterward, we played a game of 'keep or bin' which involved me asking for him to get rid of it before quickly changing my mind again.

A month later, we were in his room after a game.

"Look, do you want to keep it?" he got the disk out of the designated hiding place and offered it to me. "That way, you can decide what you want to do with it."

"No. You keep it," I said.

"Fine." Liam moved to put the disk back.

"Actually, Lee, pass it here," I snatched it from him, then made a grab for his laptop. "Let's watch it. It'll help me make my decision," I lied.

He laughed, but as soon as I pressed play, the humour quickly died down. And before long, we were undertaking a re-enactment.

And now here it is.

I remember when we broke up the first time, Liam told me he'd got rid of it, and I was more disappointed than I thought I'd be. I thought about it, though. About how it made me feel and how much I wanted to re-live the moment.

I re-read his latest message, asking me if I've given in yet, but I know he's just teasing me. Just like he was teasing me when he kissed me. I touch my lips absentmindedly as I dial his number because it's been playing on my mind that I never thanked him for paying my cards off. My heart races when it starts ringing.

"Did you watch it yet?" he laughs as he answers his phone. The way he says it makes me rock back and forth on my bed, desperate for any sort of friction ... friction that never materialises.

"No. I just called to say thank you. For paying my cards. I can't tell you how grateful I am and I want to pay you back."

"No way. I don't want anything."

"Liam, why are you being so nice to me? I put you through hell."

"Do you really need to ask me that? End of conversation." He goes quiet before I hear him take a breath. "Look, I know I shouldn't have gone through your room. I know it was a breach of privacy."

"Are you sorry for stealing my panties?" I smirk.

"Er—"

"I wish I could have seen what you did with them." The words come out before I can stop myself.

"Vic—"

"Forget it. Anyway, I guess Danny, Jen, and Ryan had a lot to say when you went back upstairs?"

"I couldn't think of a decent cover story. I told them you had some embarrassing footage of me falling over the boards onto the bench."

"Well, that works."

"No, Danny wants to see it now," Liam says.

"Just tell him the disk is damaged," I offer.

"I'll figure it out. Don't worry."

But then a horrifying thought pops into my head. "Lee, does Ryan know?"

"No, he doesn't. Nor does Johnny, because I know that's what you're going to ask next."

The anxiety creeps away. And after I hang up, I put the disk in my closet, hoping to forget all about it. But over the next few weeks, it seems to take over my every waking thought. I even start pulling it out of the plastic case and turning it over in my hands before shoving it away again.

In fact, Liam seems to take over my mind completely. From the disk, to that kiss, to the constant wondering what he did with my favourite pair of panties—well, I can guess what he did, but I wanted to see. Instead, I had to settle for closing my eyes, working through a mental image of a scenario. Liam, with my panties wrapped around his cock as he stroked himself to orgasm. Liam, perhaps enjoying the scent of my pussy. That thought is enough to give me a shaking orgasm. I'm pretty sure most people do not think of their 'friends' like this.

Having to see him every single day doesn't help either because he finds opportunities to flirt. Morning skate, pre-game photos, warm-ups. Every time we're in the same space, he either winks at me or leans in really close and whispers something.

And I can't help but seek him out more and more. In true Liam style, he embraces the attention that I give him. He even mouthed something as he caught my camera lens pointed at him; it was just before he leant in to take a face-off during yesterday's game. I'm pretty sure it involved my panties, but I can't be sure.

But the depth of mine and Liam's relationship is on full display shortly after the face-off 'mouthing' incident. Bella bounces towards my desk just before the team's mid-week practice.

"I need your help, Vicky. I pitched a marketing strategy to Mr. Lopez, and he loves it. But first, I need to get some footage of the guys telling the camera why they chose their number."

My heart sinks. I'm not sure why, but I feel vulnerable—exposed, even. Bella explains what she wants help with, and I have no choice but to agree.

I wait in the tunnels with my camcorder just before the guys are supposed to leave the dressing room. I've written the question on a marker board and placed it next to the tripod I've set up. I did it this way as to avoid actually speaking to Liam because I'm so nervous and embarrassed, I can't even think straight.

It's just my luck that the guys trickle out of the dressing room today, and time seems to pass at a snail's pace. I feel like I may pass out when he finally enters the tunnel to the ice after Ryan.

I don't even hear Ryan's response to the question, but I spot him raise an eyebrow at Liam before stepping onto the ice. Liam reads the sign, then looks at me, then looks back at the sign. His eyes flick to the camcorder, and he answers as if it's the most natural thing in the world.

"Number forty-six. April sixth. It's her birthday."

My birthday.

And he skates away.

Chapter 22

Liam

The walls in this damn hotel are paper thin. If I didn't know any better, I'd swear there was a snore-off going on between the two rooms on either side of me. And shoving a spare pillow around my neck, trying to cover my ears does nothing. So, after half an hour, I give in. I pull my sweats on, throw on a t-shirt and slip on my runners.

I take the stairs down to the front desk. The whole place is deserted, bar a lonely receptionist sitting behind a polished counter, flicking through a desk calendar with cars on it. I overheard someone saying earlier that the whole place is almost booked out, so I'm taking a shot here, but I'm willing to try anything at this point. It's eleven o'clock, and I'm exhausted from the game earlier. If we hadn't won, I'd be feeling a hell of a lot worse.

I approach the desk and psyche myself up; it's time to turn on the charm. I glance at the receptionist's name tag and muster my most alluring smile.

"Hey there, Shannon. How's your evening going?"

She sets the calendar down and flicks her eyes to mine, a pink flush warming her cheeks.

"Good, thank you. How's yours?" Her Scottish accent is a surprise, considering we're not in Scotland, and I consider paying it a compliment, but I don't want to overplay it.

"Well, it could be better." I pause before continuing. "I appreciate you're busy here, but I'm having a few issues with my room."

"I'm sorry to hear that. What's the problem?"

I tell her all about my wonderful neighbours and my failed attempt at slumber, but all she does is frown.

"I apologise, but there's nothing I can do. We're fully booked. I can offer you complimentary ear plugs?"

"Would you be able to double-check the room availability, please?"

A few taps away on her keyboard confirm what we already know. The next thing I know, I'm heading back up to my room, clutching the complimentary ear plugs as if they hold the power of sleep. But low and behold, a further twenty minutes later, I'm frustrated.

Right now, the only thing I can think of is finding somewhere else to sleep. I grab my bag and throw on my cap, making my way down to room 332 where I know Ryan is sleeping, but as soon as I hear Jen giggling from inside, I keep walking. I don't want to experience my brother getting head any more than Vicky did.

I'm still pissed at Johnny, or I'd be knocking on his door next. But I try my chances and knock on Danny's door, the next corridor along, but of course, it's not Danny's room. Vicky opens the door in her button up nightshirt, bare feet, and her hair loose around her face.

"Shit, did I wake you?" I stare at her, completely caught off-guard. She looks hot, and now I'm wondering what panties she's wearing.

"No, I was just—" She looks at my bag and back to my face. "Is this a booty call?"

"Do you want it to be a booty call?" I lean against the door frame. That got her sweating, and I'd be lying if I said I hadn't been waiting for her to call and invite me over. But I don't press things; I don't want her thinking I'm desperate for the chance. "I was looking for Danny, actually. But I can't remember what room he's in. Do you know?"

"No idea, sorry. Is Danny your booty call?" she sniggers.

"Nah, I'm having an issue with my room, and Jen's in with Ryan, so I figured I'd ask Danny if I could crash on his sofa."

"What's the issue?" she asks.

"Snoring neighbours."

"Did you go down to the front desk? They could move you."

"Yes, but they're booked up. They gave me some earplugs. Complimentary."

Vicky winches. "I'm sorry. You're welcome to come and use my sofa if you can't find anyone else. I know how crap you'll feel tomorrow if you don't sleep."

She's not wrong. We've got another road game tomorrow and I need to get some sleep.

"Nah, I'll figure it out. Sorry to bother you, Vic."

She nods and closes the door, leaving me with a dilemma. I pull my phone out, thinking I'll drop Danny a text, but my phone has no reception. I pull up the settings and see if they have Wi-Fi; but when I tap to connect, it gives me some shit about being connected but with no internet connection.

I pace the corridor a few more times before returning to Vicky's door and stopping. Thinking it's a bad idea, I talk myself out of knocking a couple of times before finally giving in. She swings open the door and holds her arm out before I can finish knocking.

"Get your ass in here." I dump my bag on the luggage rack and take my cap off. "I'm almost done watching something. It doesn't have long left."

Vicky hops back on the bed and pulls her laptop towards her, pressing play once she's settled in.

"Wait, is your internet working?" I pull my phone out of my pocket in hope.

She hits pause. "No. I downloaded it to watch later."

"Right."

She presses play again, and I take a seat on the sofa. I'm not a genius, but it's clear that it's only about four and a half feet long. I misjudged the one in my room in desperation, apparently.

Unsure of what to do with myself, I strike up conversation by saying the first thing that pops into my head. "How's your evening been? Thought anymore about what I did with your panties?"

Vicky taps a button on the keyboard, pausing the playback before she looks at me. Her cheeks are visibly flushed, but she shakes it off. "Just give me like twenty minutes. I just want to watch the end."

Back on it goes, but I can't help myself. "What's got you so invested?"

She taps the keyboard again. "Lee, you can sleep in the hallway if you like. I don't care. Just give me twenty damn minutes."

She hits play again, and I shuffle over to the bed and lean in to look.

"Oh. Is this that wedding show? Where they don't see each other before getting hitched?"

"Yes. Either sit and watch or shut up. This is the most exciting part."

She leans back against the headboard, her legs stretched out. I kick my shoes off and hop onto the mattress next to her.

"Who's the guy? He looks like he loves himself a bit too much," I say.

She taps pause. "So, he's married to that girl in the green dress, and she's really into him, but he literally doesn't give a shit. I feel terrible for her because she's trying, but he's only got eyes for the one in red." She presses play and points at different people on the screen.

"Who's the one in red married to?"

A further rundown of who's who followed by Vicky's opinions on the matter. And before I know it, I'm just as invested.

"So, they're saying if they want to stay or leave?" I ask.

"Yeah. I can't believe you've never seen this before."

"I can't believe you watch this crap."

"Yeah, well, I like it."

"I didn't think you gave a crap about weddings."

"What's that supposed to mean?"

"Nothing. Forget I said anything."

"Look, Lee. I've apologised and regretted my actions every day since. I'm not sure what else I can do."

"Fine," I say, moving back over to the sofa. "You're right. Let's just forget about it."

The show keeps on playing, but she's not even watching it. She's looking down at her hands. I feel frustrated, and there's a question right on the tip of my tongue. I briefly hold on to it before it bursts out of me.

"Did you want to marry me, Vic? Because I play the whole thing over and over in my head. Some nights I can't even sleep."

She doesn't look at me, but she turns her head slightly in my direction. "I wanted nothing more."

When she says stuff like this, it really makes me wonder why the hell we aren't married and why she let her opinions of our parents get the better of her.

"So why aren't we? I mean, I know you've told me why, but I can't get my head around it. We had a good thing going on. Were you happy?"

The question hangs in the air for what feels like a full minute. "Yes. I was happy." She snaps her laptop shut, and the room goes silent "You should get some sleep, Lee. You've got morning skate in like, seven hours."

"Fine. We'll say no more about it."

But knowing that she was happy, and I was happy, makes things a hell of a lot more frustrating.

I brush my teeth in the adjoining bathroom and finish getting ready for bed. By the time I return to the bedroom, Liam has grabbed the extra pillow and blanket from the top of the closet and is lying on the sofa. His legs hang off the arm, his head tilted awkwardly; he looks completely ridiculous. It's as if someone is trying to cram an action figure into a box half its size.

I wonder if I should offer him the bed. The sofa doesn't look that bad, and it's only for one night. But the sigh he lets out gives me motivation to let him simmer. I know he's pissed, and I know it's because of me. He won't want to talk about it anymore, given his last words to me. I switch the light off, switch the fan on, and climb into bed, the cold sheets making me shiver.

"Are you cold?" Liam's voice floats across the room. "I can hear your teeth chattering, Vic. Do you want this extra blanket?"

My heart practically explodes. He's always been the same, putting everyone else ahead of himself, and it makes me feel even guiltier.

"No. Thanks, though." I can hear him shifting on the sofa and the rustling of the blanket. "Are you cold?"

"No."

"Oh."

"What?"

I hate the feeling between us. I want us to go back a few hours—back to the harmless flirting. What if...

"If you were feeling cold, you could just come and sleep here. It's not as if we've not shared a bed before."

"I'm fine," he says. I know he's being a gentleman and a stubborn one at that.

"Lee, just get in the damn bed, you don't even fit on the sofa. You're going to ache tomorrow otherwise."

There's fumbling, and then I feel a whoosh of air as the bed gives under Liam's weight. It doesn't take long for the usual antics that come with sharing a bed with Liam to resume. He pulls the duvet towards himself, coaxing it away from me.

"Stop stealing the duvet!" I pull it back.

"You're joking, right? You're using it as a cocoon!"

"No, I'm not," I say, and he rolls over slightly, taking a chunk of duvet with him.

Naturally, this starts a game of tug-of-war; back and forth, back and forth. It's like I'm sharing a bed with a child.

"Why are you being a brat, Vic?" he says. "Because you invite me to share the bed, but you don't want to share the bed."

"It's fucking cold. Did you bring the extra blanket?"

"If you turned off the fan, you wouldn't be cold."

I scoff. He knows I can't sleep without it. Even in the middle of a Canadian winter, I have to have it on.

I tuck the duvet underneath my body and when Liam pulls it next, he pulls me along with it. We're sandwiched together and the heat of his body makes my skin tingle.

I expect him to retreat but he doesn't and I find myself rolling over so I can rest my head on his chest, basking in his warmth, and he accepts me. I can hear his heart beating, the gentle rhythm soothing every cell of me. His fingers trace circles on my back, I feel safe, warm and completely whole. Everything feels perfect. Fuck.

"The last time we cuddled like this was last Christmas," I whisper into the darkness, partially wondering if he's still awake. But he answers me almost instantly.

"I know, and I loved it then too."

I wasn't expecting him to say that. That night was the last night we spent together. The night before he told me he couldn't do this anymore. I wonder if I said that aloud as he turns his head to speak to me.

"I know you regret a lot of things, Vic, and I know you're sorry. I feel the same about Christmas Eve. I'm sorry too. But you have to understand. I didn't know what else to do."

"I know."

We lay there in each other's arms as if nothing has happened since last Christmas.

"You said you loved me," he says, after a period of complete silence.

"What?"

"Right before I was benched a few weeks ago. In the dressing room."

"Oh, yeah."

"You know, I'll never not love you either, Vic. You've got this hold on me, and I can't help having this pull towards you."

"I believe everything happens for a reason, and it's led us to where we are now. Ryan wouldn't have met Jenna, He's so happy. You did that," I say. "I have a question for you," I angle my head towards him. "How did you convince him to take your spot?" It's something I've always wondered but never really asked. I expect Liam to shoot me down, tell me it's none of my business, but then he starts telling me about a road trip that him and Ryan were on.

"Coach was making a big deal about the scouts, and I just couldn't let Ryan miss it. Right before Mom died, she forced us to confess because she had a strong suspicion that we lied about it."

"Oh, my god! What did she say when you told her?"

"She just said she understood and then said that he clearly owed me a favour. I know she said it as a joke, but Ryan took it seriously. For years afterwards, he'd ask me what he could do. And then what happened with us happened, and I asked him. I knew he toyed with the idea of exploring his options but couldn't commit, so I took a shot. And the rest is history.

Do me a favour, though, Vic? Please don't mention it to anyone. It's Ryan's business, and I don't want him in a tight spot with gossip or whatever. I know he would never admit to anyone that he was tiring of his life in the NHL."

"Of course," I say.

"Besides, he roped me in to helping with the juniors yesterday, and they think I pried him away from the NHL kicking and screaming. I mean, he laid it on that he was full on pissed, and he probably played that card when he first came here too. Deep down, he needed the kick; I know my brother. He was chasing the next thing, and he didn't know it at the time, but that was Jenna."

"What's next for you, Lee?" I prop myself up on my elbow, straining to see his face in the darkness.

"I guess I need to figure some stuff out."

I listen to him talk for what feels like hours, and I must have drifted off to sleep because I wake up cold. A note sits on the pillow saying he's gone to morning skate. A pang of excitement fills me as I read his handwriting; so familiarly untidy:

Chapter 23

Liam

The home crowd cheers as Bettsy gets slammed into the boards near the trapezoid. For a moment, I think he's going to hit the ice, but he stumbles sideways and regains his balance before dropping his stick.

"You wanna go?" I hear him yelling at the opponent who checked him, and suddenly they're pulling at each other's sweaters.

"Right, right, that's enough," the ref says, trying to control the situation. But as soon as Bettsy relaxes his grip, he gets a fist to the face which knocks him straight on his ass.

I help him to his feet and skate him over to the penalty box, but he's shouting back over his shoulder. "What the fuck is your problem? That was a dirty check!"

"Have a word with him," the ref tells me, since Johnny's not on the ice. "His temper is leaving a lot to be desired but it's two for roughing since I'm feeling generous."

I nod. "You need to calm down, bud. What's going on with you?"

"It was just a dirty check." He sits down as the penalty box door slams shut.

"You've never reacted that way before," I say.

He shrugs. "I guess I'm in the mood for a fight."

Before I skate off, I make eye contact with Vicky who peeks around her camera. She's standing directly to the right of the away penalty box with my old Marlies toque pulled over her head. She looks fucking cute, so I wink at her, and I'm almost certain I see her cheeks flush pink.

I have had little time to speak with her today. We had morning skate, then a team brunch, then Coach had us watching previous games. By the time we were released to rest up, Vicky was busy prepping for tonight and building up the hype on socials. I caught her briefly before warmups, but there were too many listening ears to have a proper conversation.

I thought she would have mentioned the note I left her—but nothing. Now I'm left wondering if I made a huge mistake, but a little voice in my head tells me that Vicky would have definitely made a point of telling me where to stick it if it was the wrong move.

I skate back to the bench, swinging my legs over the boards, and I sit down next to Ryan.

"Are you going to tell me where you slept last night?" he asks, popping his mouthguard out.

"I think I prefer Johnny and Bettsy as a pair," I say, ignoring his question.

"I've been thinking about asking you all day, but I figured you'd tell me if you had anything to share."

"Nothing happened," I say, knowing that he absolutely knows exactly where I was last night. "I had snoring neighbours. I thought I was knocking on Danny's door to sleep on his couch, but ... well, you know."

"Do you think it's a good idea?" Play starts again. I lean forward and rest my stick against the boards. I lock my eyes on Danny's position to the left of the face-off, pretending Ryan's question isn't hanging in the air. "Lee?" he nudges my arm, but I focus forward.

We win the draw, and the puck slides back towards Danny who receives it and sends it across to Hutch before powering towards the offensive zone. Ryan and I switch with Hutch and Danny and enter the play in the neutral zone. I poke the puck away from an opposing forward and it has enough momentum to land on the blade of Jani's stick who fires it in Ryan's direction.

My eyes follow Ryan's movement, and I can tell he's going to line up a pass to me as soon as he's passed the blue line. We're faster than the opposition forwards, and I can hear Johnny who's now standing at the point calling for a pass. I sail the puck back to him, and he one-times it into the top left of the net. There's only a small cheer from our fans, since the away section is tiny and not everyone makes the trip, but every goal should be celebrated. We gather around Johnny then skate back in a single line to bump hands with the rest of the guys and return to centre ice for the face-off.

Leaning down, I risk a quick glance over to the boards and spot Vicky. Knowing that she's watching me intently makes me want to show-off a little—which is odd considering I know she's technically always watching me. Has something shifted between us? Maybe it has for me. The ref gives us a heads-up and drops the puck. I win and flick it to my left where Ryan's waiting. As I skate backwards, I make a bit of a show by doing some fancy footwork, playing on Vicky's attention. I feel like I'm back in juniors again, but I'm focused. When Jani receives a pass from Ryan, taking us into the offensive zone, I'm ready. I skate to his right and accept a saucer pass that sails nicely over the stick of an opposing forward. I flick it towards Ryan, who's placed himself just outside the tendy's crease. He's waiting, but there's a scramble. A rebound opportunity comes my way, so I bat the puck mid-air as it sails towards me, down into the net on the blocker side.

I skate around the edge of the ice, then sink down onto one knee. Locking eyes with Vicky, who definitely mouths something that looks suspiciously like 'show-off'.

"Nice work," Ryan says after we sit back down on the bench. "If showing off is going to score us goals like that, keep doing it."

I thought that would be the last he'd mention of my situation with Vicky, but he doesn't waste any time when we're alone in the showers after the game.

"Do you think it's a good idea?" he says from the next stall.

"I told you, nothing happened."

"I've seen the way you're looking at her."

"Nah," I shake it off.

"Look, Johnny and I have been talking," he stops the water and grabs his towel. "You guys seem to do much better as friends."

"I'm sorry for my bluntness, but you've never really seen how good we are together. You both buried your heads in the sand like it wasn't happening."

"But we saw the drama and the headache it caused. According to Johnny, Vicky was a mess when she called off the wedding, so it sounds like you both need to take a step back." He pauses and clicks his tongue. "And I'm not trying to be a dick, but it seems like she treats you like crap."

"You don't know the full story!" I yell.

"Please explain then. Because I know how broken you were that day you asked me to take your place."

"She broke my fucking heart! What else did you expect me to do?"

"Exactly, Lee. She broke your heart. And here you are, acting as if she's the new girl in school and you're trying to win her attention. Grow the fuck up and think about what you're getting yourself in for."

He looks at me for a moment then turns on the spot and strides out of the shower room.

Well, that escalated quickly. One minute we're fine, the next he blows his top at me. But how can I possibly explain how I feel? I don't even know how to explain it myself. I'll always love Vicky, and I have a strong feeling that she feels the same. It's as if it's in our blood. I'm not sure I can handle Ryan being angry with me though. He's my brother. Is this me having to choose between him and Vicky? I hope to God not because I don't think I could.

It's been years since I've seen Liam play like he did tonight. It was all fancy moves and the crap that came with his attempt at impressing me when we were kids. He didn't need to impress me, but I never told him that. I always found his attempts endearing and warming. But I keep playing last night over in my mind and what it means for us now. I must be staring into the abyss because I jump out of my skin when my phone vibrates in my pocket.

I recognise Dean's number straight away, and I answer in my usual chirpy tone which he reciprocates.

"I'm calling to check your availability for the next few weeks," he says.

Pacing up and down the tunnel outside the dressing room, I consider my schedule whilst giving silent nods of goodbye to the guys that are heading towards the exit. I also make a mental note to check with the GM that he won't mind me taking the extra work on. I'm positive he won't mind if it doesn't get in the way of my day job. I agree to help Dean, letting slip that I find the extra money useful.

"Are you in a tight spot with money, Vicky?" As soon as I've ended the call, Matt Rodgers springs up from behind me, and I wonder how long he's been loitering.

"I'm fine," I say casually, slipping my phone back into my pocket.

"Are you sure? It sounds like you agreed to do extra work on the side for cash." He looks me up and down which makes me involuntarily shiver with disgust.

"I said I'm fine. Thanks." I try my hardest to remain polite, but he steps forward and blocks my path.

"What are you willing to do for a hundred quid?" he asks.

"What?"

"Do you have a price list? I'm curious."

Unsure of what to say, I hesitate briefly, but he notices my camera and smiles. "I'm not talking about photography here, Vicky. But we can take pictures if you like."

I'm usually quite forward and confident, but this guy has me feeling uncomfortable. And dare I say it, a little afraid. As I try to glance around him, he subtly moves, blocking my view of the dressing room door. Where the fuck is everyone else?

"I won't tell anyone if you don't want me to but I can help you out. You scratch an itch, and I'll help you out with your rent or whatever."

"I thought you had a girlfriend?" I have no idea why I say it, but it's the only thing that comes to mind.

"Sometimes we don't get what we need, do we? And if we can come to an arrangement, we'll both be happy, won't we? It can be our little secret."

He leans in further, and I can feel his breath on my hair. My brain is screaming at my legs to side-step him; however, I take a full second to actually do it. But he grabs my arm and grips it tight.

"You're hurting me," I say, trying to shake his hand away, but he doesn't let up.

"Just think about it, Vicky. Is it more than money you want?" He pauses for a moment. "What is it that women seem to want these days ..." He muses to himself. "A new car? No. A baby? Do you want me to put a baby in you, Vicky?"

A sickness rises from my stomach. Who even says stuff like that?

"You're not into that kind of thing?" he asks. But I just stare at him, completely disbelieving. A distant door creaks causing him to quickly let go of my arm and step back.

"You know where to find me if you change your mind," he says, and then he's gone.

I stand here completely stunned by what just happened. I'm willing myself to move just as Jen's voice lands in my ear. "Are you okay, Vicky? You look as white as the ice."

"Yes, I'm fine," I say, trying to shake it off. I double-check I have everything before we head towards the rink's back door. We reach the exit and Jen pushes the handle, letting the cold air from the outside hit us briefly before we step outside. The team gathers around the coach while Johnny stands by the storage area, ready to take my bag.

"Thanks," I say.

"Are you alright?" he asks, turning back towards me. But I throw my arms around him and squeeze.

"What's going on?" he says, returning the hug. I'll admit, it's rare that I offer him a hug, but I feel like I could do with the comfort. "Is this about Liam? Because I'll kill him."

"No, it's nothing. I just wanted to give you a hug," I say, pulling away quickly, hoping that he can't see the tears forming in my eyes. I don't wait for him to answer before I step on the coach behind Jen but my eyes lock with Matt's from where he's sitting. He smiles at me, making my skin crawl with disgust.

Sitting down, I put my earphones in, shutting out the world. I feel sick and anxious because there's no way I can avoid Matt permanently. He's going to be around for the rest of the season at a minimum. My mind reels, and I only notice Liam boarding when he waves his hand in front of my face.

"You okay, Vic?" he asks. But when I don't answer, he slides into the seat next to me and puts his arm around me. "What's going on?" he presses, but I feel no shame in laying my head on his shoulder and lacing my fingers with his as we set off.

"I'm just really tried," I say, popping an earbud out.

I'm replaying my encounter with Matt, and I know I can't ever tell Liam what he said to me because I'd likely end up trying to bail him out of jail or something. Snuggling into Liam, I think of what could have been for us. Our baby. Our future.

"Hey, are you going to tell me?"

"I told you, I'm just tired," I say. "You've still got my apartment key, right?"

"Want me to keep you warm again later?" he whispers, taking the earbud from me.

I nod.

"I may need to wait until Ryan's gone to bed," he says. "I'll explain later."

And instead of giving me back my earbud, he puts it in his own ear. And it's like we're kids again, sharing the same moment with music we both love.

He chuckles. "I love this one."

And I love you, Liam.

Chapter 24

I climb into the back of Ryan's Jeep and pretend to play on my phone as he drives Jen and me home from the rink. Johnny and Vicky are in the car behind us, and I can see Ryan's eyes flicking between the rear-view mirror and me.

"You and Vicky looked cosy on the coach," he says, his face hardening.

"Yeah, well, she was upset," I say defensively.

"Right. And she wanted comfort from you specifically, did she?"

"Ry, come on. You're being ridiculous." Jen turns in her seat and gives me a warm smile before continuing to address Ryan. "She was upset. I'm not sure what happened, but she wasn't herself when I found her outside the dressing room after the game. Liam was just helping a friend out."

Ryan's grunt suggests he'll remain sour with me for a few days before the haze lifts but at least he says goodnight to me before we part ways. I have to head up to the eighth floor with Johnny and Danny, pretending to head home like everyone else. But deep down, I'm desperate to rush over to Vicky's and warm her up again. Completely innocently, of course. Because lots of people, I assume, keep their ex-girlfriend warm whenever she asks. Besides, Jen confirmed that she really was upset, so it'd be a dick move for me not to comfort her.

"Lee, mind if I come in for a moment?" Johnny asks as Danny unlocks the door. I'm too tired to have a serious conversation with Johnny right now, and I'm desperate to get away. But I think we're at the point where we need to clear the air, so I nod and he follows me inside. We loiter near the front door while Danny heads straight to his room. He doesn't even bother to shut his bedroom door behind him as he falls face first onto his mattress.

"I won't keep you long," Johnny says. For a moment, I expect him to have the same complaint about me sitting with Vicky on the coach but he doesn't mention it. "I just wanted to apologise for letting you down."

He looks at me with genuine sorrow in his eyes. Something that Johnny rarely has reason to show, if I'm honest. I don't want to argue with him or have an ongoing feud any more than he does, so I accept his apology so we can both get on with our lives.

"Thanks, I appreciate it."

"I should have asked Vicky to tell you herself," he says. "I get why she didn't want to share, but secrets rarely end well, and I should know."

"What's that supposed to mean?"

"Nothing." He shakes his head, but I press him again.

"You got a secret, John?"

"No, no. Nothing like that. Just speaking figuratively, you know."

But I can't say I do. "Is this about your secret girlfriend?"

He lets out an exasperated breath. "I don't have a secret girlfriend."

"Boyfriend?" I try.

"No. I'm not seeing anyone. Quit it."

It's like old times again: me bugging Johnny about his love life and Johnny being his usual closed-book self. But I drop it there. Because as much as I want to find out what Johnny's talking about—being a nosey fuck—I'm more interested in finding out what's going on with Vicky.

"Well, I appreciate the apology. And I accept it."

"Thanks." He's playing with his keys in his pocket while he rocks back and forth between his feet. Judging by the look of it, this isn't over.

"Spit it out, John. What else is on your mind?"

Now I'm being a douche—but I'm tired and I'm pretty sure Johnny is keen to get some sleep, too.

"It's nothing," he says, but then he quickly backtracks. "Okay, but I want you to know that I didn't apologise just for this reason, and I really wouldn't ask unless I absolutely had to." He meets my eyes. "I'm hoping you would be able to lend me three grand." The way he looks at me, I know for sure he wouldn't be asking unless there really was no other way. Suddenly, I feel sorry for him.

"You don't want it for anything illegal, do you?" I ask.

"No, no. Nothing like that, but I'd appreciate you keeping this between us. I know it's a big ask. But—"

"Yeah, sure," I say cutting him off. "I'll fix it tomorrow. I'm wiped."

I see him out, probably appearing too keen to get rid of him. But when I hear his front door close down the hallway, I shut Danny's bedroom door and drop Vicky a text, asking if Ryan and Jen are out of the way yet. She replies almost instantly, as if she was watching her phone.

Vicky

They're still drinking tea in the living
room!!

Liam

Can you come here instead?

Vicky

They'll see me leave.

Shit. As I pause to think of a plan, another message arrives.

Vicky

Maybe the universe is telling us we
should stay apart tonight.

My heart drops in my chest. Because I've been reminded of
how much I love sharing a bed with Vicky, and just like the
drug she is, I want more.

Liam

Do you want us to stay apart tonight?

Vicky

No. Do you?

Liam

No.

Liam

Just text me when they go to bed.

I definitely don't want to lie down while I wait, because I feel completely exhausted. Instead, I make myself a coffee and hope to Christ that Ryan and Jen turn in soon.

I consider tomorrow morning. Ryan will expect me to go for a run in the morning. With no practice or training scheduled, I can go back to bed in the afternoon for some extra sleep if I need it. But the more I run through my intent to stay with Vicky, I realise I don't feel bad about it. I mean, Vicky and I are both single—free to do what we please—but the thought of telling my brother that I'm back in her bed fills me with dread. What if he disowns me?

Perhaps I'll have just one last night with Vicky wrapped in my arms—my friendly arms, that is—then call it a day.

And I wait for her text.

"Lee, what are we doing?" I climb into bed next to him and roll to face him.

"Going to sleep?" he says.

"No, I mean ... what are we doing?"

Liam and I have been sneaking between each other's rooms for a few weeks. And as much as I enjoy sharing my space with him, I'm beyond confused. Is this going to be our permanent state? Falling asleep in each other's arms, then spending the next day trying to avoid stealing glances, acting like we are the most basic of basic friends.

It's been purely platonic, and I thought I was okay with that. But I'm not naïve enough to think that Liam brings a mini hockey stick to bed to poke me in the back all night long. I'm horny. And he's horny. But we're in a state of limbo because I either want him to pin me down and fuck me into next week or leave me alone forever so I can shake the feeling.

"Do you want to watch your show? Because I'm happy with whatever, Vic. Or we could watch our tape?" He winks at me before he pulls me in closer, and I hear him inhale deeply. "Wait ...did you change your shampoo?"

"Yes."

"I don't like it. I mean, I like it, but it's not you, is it?"

"I've had to make some adjustments. I've even learnt how to do my own nails too. But you're changing the subject." I roll over to face him and he blinks at me, ever so slowly.

"What?"

"What?" I say, poking him in the chest.

"What, what?"

"Stop it," I laugh. "Just tell me what we're doing because we've been sneaking around, and I don't really know why ... oh, actually, Johnny would probably lose his shit if he knew, so I guess that's why. I'm embarrassed to admit I really enjoy sharing a bed with you, despite the duvet hogging issue, but I'm just so—"

He leans in and kisses me as if it's nothing. Soft at first, but then he nips at my lower lip and I snake my tongue out. And just like that, the muscle memory floods back. We've kissed a lot. And I know exactly what he likes, which means he knows exactly what I like too. Just before he's due to suck on my lip, he pulls away.

I stare at him, mouth still in the kissing position, and he grins.

"Well, at least that shut you up."

"You're a douche!" I give him a playful nudge. I'm smiling and he's smiling back at me—it's infectious.

"For the record, I really enjoy sharing a bed with you, too," he says after a moment. "I've been enjoying the time we've been sharing, and I guess I don't want to jinx things. Because when we are together like this, we're happy, aren't we? Are you happy? Because I don't even know—"

Now it's my turn to kiss him. It's a kiss that moves me into the clouds, floating me so high that I forget about anything else in the world—apart from the throbbing coming from my clit. That spot which feels too deep inside of me for anyone else to reach, bar Liam. His right hand is trailing along my side, down the curve under my ribs and up onto my hip. Back and forth, back and forth. But I want more.

"What do you want us to be doing, Vic? Because this could get complicated. What if we fuck things up again?" He pulls away abruptly, but I decide to play along.

"Okay, if that's what you want. Friends it is," I shrug.

"I'm not saying that's what I want!"

"Then what do you want? I mean, I don't think we have to put a label on it or anything but—"

"How about just friends that help to relieve some of the pressure?" He moves his hand to trail along my back this time, and he knows exactly what he's doing to fuel the fire.

"Are you sure that's a good idea?" I know it's literally the worst idea he's ever had. And we both know it. One taste of the pie and we'll both be coming back for more. But the idea of having that delicious feeling coursing through my veins is clouding my judgement. Is this my insatiable arousal talking? Because, at this point, I'll do whatever the hell he wants us to do if it means having him in my bed.

With that, he rolls me onto my back, and he's on top of me in a flash—his hands holding my wrists above my head and his knees on either side of my hips. I can feel him pushing against me, and I'm ready to scream with frustration.

"Is this what you want?" It's almost a growl and I bite my lip, nodding. "Let's think this through. Do you want me to go home?" he asks, looking right at me. His face is not even a centimetre away from mine; I can feel the stubble of his beard on my face.

"No," I shake my head.

"Do you want me to kiss you here?" he leans down and peppers a kiss on my neck before kissing the spot between my tits. I can feel myself quivering.

"Words, Vic."

"Yes."

"Do you want me to make you come?" he purposefully flicks his hips, pushing his dick against me, and I yelp before trying to wriggle underneath him, desperate for friction.

"Is that a no?" he relaxes his grip a bit. He knows exactly what he's doing.

"No, I ... please, Lee," I say.

"Please, what?"

"Please, I'm dying here. Please, make me come."

"That's a good girl. All you had to do was ask." He leans in closer, kissing a spot under my ear before whispering, "You don't really have to beg, baby girl, because I want it just as much as you do." My mouth forms an 'o.' "I want to taste you, I want to hear you, I want you to come while I suck your clit."

A whimper escapes my throat, and he shifts his weight so that he's lying next to me; but his lips don't leave my skin. His hand finds my left nipple through the fabric of my cami, and he pinches hard. A wave of pleasure shoots all the way through me, and I'm eager for him to travel lower—hands, tongue, dick. I don't care. I want him.

"Slide off your shorts and panties, then spread your legs," he says, and he fumbles with the fabric covering my boobs before pushing it up and out of the way.

I'm watching his tongue trailing up towards the curve of my breast instead of concentrating on getting half naked. But a further prompt gets me moving, and I feel the excitement absolutely everywhere. I wouldn't be surprised if I came with a single touch, but I wriggle out of my clothes. He takes a nipple between his teeth and sucks deeply while pushing my legs apart.

"Please, Lee," I am at the point of begging now.

"Remember when I made you come just by doing this?" He sucks and gently bites my nipple before moving to the next, making me whimper.

"Yes," I breathe. As much as I remember, I want him to touch me a lot farther south. I'm desperate for it. In fact, I make a decision to relieve a bit of the pressure. My hand sneaks downward. But of course, he grabs my wrist and pushes me away.

"No, you don't," he says, and looks up at me with a grin that half excites me, half scares me. The fear I have now is that of being too scared to come because I may just pass out. But in a flash, he's between my legs as he breathes me in.

"I fucking love your pussy. Have I ever told you that? You're already wet for me."

All I manage is a whimper. Then he spreads my legs and bends my knees, pushing my thighs back. I feel so very exposed, but I don't care. He kisses the insides of my thighs. I close my eyes, gasping when I feel him brush a finger from my clit to my pussy before sliding it inside.

"You're so fucking tight, Vic." Then I hear him suck his finger. "Fucking beautiful."

I'm almost quivering. When I feel his tongue flick my clit with the briefest of movements, I'm close to begging him. It's only when I feel his hand on my pussy again that I know he's going to give me what I want: a Liam-induced orgasm.

His tongue circles my clit and because I'm so close to coming already, I don't care about anything else. I feel like I need to put all my effort into holding off, but he keeps going. Circles, and more circles—then he abruptly stops. His tongue vibrates against me before he slips a finger into my pussy.

I let out an involuntary cry, and he has to remind me I definitely need to be quiet.

"I can't!"

"You're going to have to, or I'll have to stop."

"You better not fucking stop!"

"Put a pillow over your head, Vic. Seriously, you need to be quiet."

His tongue flicks again and I reach for a pillow and hold it close. I honestly don't know how I can be quiet. Even if I wanted to.

"I don't know how I could forget how good you feel," he says, pumping a finger in and out. He adds another, and the fullness is a feeling I've missed. "I don't know how I could forget how good you taste, either." He works his finger, then pauses. "Are you ready to let go for me, baby?"

I free up my left hand to grasp onto his hair as he returns to the circling. It's only for a moment though, because next thing I know, he's sucking on my clit. I can feel the bed gently rocking, and the motion of it all—his fingers, his tongue ... I come with a muffled cry into the pillow, and I think I might pass out.

"You're such a good girl for me," he says. Then there's the unmistakable sound of him grunting as he comes into his boxers.

"Fuck," he gasps. "That was hot."

But when he crawls up the bed and kisses me, I know it's going to be difficult for this to be a one-off.

Chapter 25

Liam

The entire team is getting fitted for suits today for the upcoming Ladies' Night, which is this week. It's an evening for the ladies of our fan-base to sit down for a fancy dinner, then dance with us players. Vicky is organising it with some help from Lisa, who arranged 'Meet the Players.'

Ryan called me earlier today and asked if I could meet him at the tailor's earlier than planned, and it's made me anxious. He's not been himself lately. Part of me wonders if he's hiding something; the other part wonders if he knows that my relations with Vicky have been getting even more personal. Most people would call what we're doing 'friends with benefits.' I'd probably refer to it as 'friends with needs,' but whatever it is, I'm worried he's figured it out before I've found an opportunity to come clean.

But when I meet up with him in town, he looks pleased to see me. We greet each other in the usual manner of a fist-bump, but he says nothing as I follow him inside, a bell ringing overhead as we enter.

The store is empty, apart from us, and it seems like they've crammed everything in to maximise the small space. Towards the back, there are rows of jackets ready to try on. I follow Ryan as he meanders towards them, passing through the shelves of shirts, ties, and waistcoats.

"I don't know how we'll all fit in here," I muse as we close in on the jackets.

Ryan completely ignores me and starts pawing at the offerings. "How do you feel about navy?"

I open my mouth to respond when an eager-looking man who looks close to seventy saunters out of a door I hadn't noticed. He stares at us before checking his watch.

"You're early," he says. "I wasn't expecting your group until four, but since you're here—"

"Actually, can you give us a moment, please?" Ryan asks. "I thought we'd come in early to browse."

Still not understanding what Ryan's wanting to browse for exactly, I smile at the tailor who nods before disappearing towards the rack of pants.

Ryan turns back to me. "So, thoughts on navy?"

"I thought Vicky had picked a colour scheme?"

"Yeah, she did. But I mean, for me. For general use."

"General use? Who buys a suit for general use? Besides, don't you have shit-tonne of suits already?" I pick one up from the rack and hold it out, examining the cut on the shoulders before putting it back.

"Yeah, but I need a new one." He stumbles over his words. I'm still confused as hell until I look over at him, then to the suits, then back to him.

"When you say 'general use,' do you mean 'wedding use?'" I say, raising an eyebrow.

"Well, yeah, no, I mean, I don't know. Maybe?"

"Which is it? Because I'm pretty sure people don't buy general suits for weddings."

"Okay, an engagement suit then," he snaps.

Now we're getting somewhere.

I select another jacket from the shelf and eye it tentatively before lowering my voice. "I'm pretty sure you have nicer suits than this already."

Ryan snatches the jacket from me and hangs it up. "Forget it."

"I'm sorry, but if you're going to propose, you should go all out. Go to Tom Ford or whatever—"

"I have three of those. I don't like the fit."

"Then why do you have three?" I ask.

Ryan scowls at me.

"Look, I'm just saying—" but I'm interrupted by the tinkling bell over the door as the rest of the team pile into the store.

As predicted, it's a matter of seconds before we're all crammed together, shoulder to shoulder. But when the door opens again, Vicky's voice sounds from the threshold.

"Oh, my God! Does no one read e-mails? I said you needed to come in groups of four from four o'clock!"

She pushes her way through the crowd, looking around before asking if anyone has seen the tailor. As if on cue, he appears from the small room at the back again, his face dropping when he looks around.

"I'm fixing it, Mr Lewis," Vicky says before listing out four names. She tells everyone else they can leave until summoned.

As people sift out, the tailor edges close to Vicky. "Since you're here, Miss Koenig, may I take the time to remind you we will charge for missing or soiled items. I mean, after last year I will have to take a larger deposit. I understand the absence of a tie or a pocket square, but a waistcoat?"

He looks pissed.

"We apologised for that, and the team have assured me they will be more considerate with the rentals this time. Thanks for giving us a second chance."

Ryan and I follow Bettsy and Hutch outside before crossing the street to join Johnny and Ffordey at the coffee place opposite.

"You never told us what happened to that pocket square, Prez," Hutch says, as we queue for drinks.

"And you're never going to find out," Ryan says.

"Why do I feel like this is a story I need to know?" I ask.

"Forget it," Ryan says, nudging me away.

We order with the barista, and then we pull up some chairs next to Johnny and Ffordey with our coffees. Bettsy launches into a story that I'm only half listening to. I'm watching the tailor's opposite, hoping to catch another glimpse of Vicky. I arranged for her to receive a gift basket with shampoo, perfume, and some other stuff I know she likes, and I'm keen to know if she got it.

"So yeah, they call it 'cat-poo-chino,'" Bettsy says, nudging me.

"They call it what?" Hutch asks, eyes wide.

"There's a coffee bean that these cat-like animals in Indonesia eat. And when they shit them out, they use the remnants to make coffee. The animal's stomach acid removes the hard shell from the beans."

"I'm done listening to anything you've got to say. Ever." Danny's mouth is wide open. "How do you know about this, anyway? You've never been to Indonesia."

"No, but someone else has—" He cuts himself off when something grabs his attention. He stands up and nearly topples the table with his legs. "Kelly! Kelly! Over here!" He's waving as if he's trying to coax a plane from the sky. A redhead, who looks like a hot version of Bettsy, walks towards us. She unwinds a scarf from her neck and pulls off a pair of gloves, shoving them in her coat pocket. "What are you doing here?" he says. "Guys, this is my sister, Kelly. Kel, I was just telling the guys about the cat-poo-chino."

Kelly smiles awkwardly and pushes her hair behind her ears.

"When did you go to Indonesia?" I ask, trying to make her feel at ease.

"Oh, I haven't been. Stacey did. My big sister."

"Yeah, Stacey," Bettsy points around the table at everyone in turn, "is off-limits, remember? And before any of you dicks try anything with Kelly, she's too young. Anyway, what are you doing here?" he spins his head to look at Kelly.

"Am I not allowed to come into town to meet a friend?"

"Well, sure, but never mind. Do you want me to introduce you? Oh wait, you know Danny and Hutch—oh, and Johnny, of course. But this is Ryan and Liam and—"

"Oh, twins?" she says, almost pleased with herself for having worked it out. We do the whole routine where we pretend to not have noticed that we're twins, and she giggles. Johnny stands up and interrupts our flow, his chair scraping across the floor tiles.

"Vicky's standing across the street like she's about to kick some ass," he says. "Come on, guys. I think it's Prez, Lee, myself, and Danny next."

"I should go," Kelly says. "But I'll be watching your game this weekend. Mike has given me his tickets."

Saying our goodbyes to Kelly, we make our way back to the tailor's. As soon as we cross the road and come within six feet of Vicky, I notice the fury on her face.

"Johnny. A word, please?"

"What?" he says.

But Vicky ushers the rest of us into the store so we can't eavesdrop. It's a full five minutes before Johnny joins us near the rail of jackets.

"What was that about?" I ask him, slipping one on.

"Vicky being Vicky," he shrugs, giving nothing away as he waits his turn.

Frustrating as Johnny is, I don't want to press him in case it provokes the beast. And I definitely don't want Johnny checking in on my situation with Vicky. We're in a pretty good place right now, and I'm happy to leave things that way.

A few jackets later, I finally try on some pants before the tailor whips out his tape measure and gets to work. He takes a few minutes to measure me up before moving on to Ryan. Then I get myself dressed again and wait for my brother.

"So, what's the plan, then?" I whisper to Ryan when he joins me to re-dress. "Are you going to propose?"

He jerks his head towards Danny and Johnny to check that they're out of earshot.

"Yeah, I am. I mean, I know I said I didn't want to get married and whatever, but it just feels right, you know?"

Sadly, I did know. I drift to the thought of my planned proposal for Vicky, and I can feel the tears prickling behind my eyes.

"You okay, bud?" Ryan says, putting his hand on my arm.

"Yeah. Yeah. I'm just stoked you've found the one, you know? I mean, for years you were lost or whatever. But, anyway, yeah. I'm happy for you." Fuck, when did I get so sappy? But all this makes me think about Vicky and how I'm going to tell Ryan about whatever the hell it is we're doing.

Typically, he knows what I'm thinking.

"Look, I know I've been tough on you about Vicky. I know you're trying to move on or whatever. But if you work it out, I won't stand in your way or anything—you know that, right?

I just want you to understand your worth, and I know how much it took for you to get over her, and I don't want you to be in that state again."

This is the ideal moment for me to confess, but all I can manage is a nod.

We bro-hug in the middle of the store just as Vicky tells us our time is up.

I'm anxious. Matt Rodgers will arrive soon, and I'm afraid the sandwich I had for lunch might make a reappearance. I decided to leave his group until last, and now we're almost at that point. I wish I'd gotten him in first to get the interaction over and done with.

I'm getting the hire paperwork finalised when my phone vibrates on the counter next to me. I'm so relieved to see Jen's name.

"There's a huge gift basket in the office for you," she says as soon as I pick up.

I stare blankly at the wall behind the counter for a moment before responding. "A gift basket?"

"Yes. It's got some fancy shampoo, Chanel perfume, some... ooo, what is this?" I hear rummaging.

"Is there a card?"

"Do I need to answer that?" she says.

"No," I reply because I know it's from Liam and my heart feels full to burst. I'm reminded of my impending doom by a fumble of movement from the back of the store. "Actually, Jen, while I've got you. Do you think you could come down to the tailor's and help me out with something?"

"What do you need help with?" she says.

What do I need her help with? Shit. I haven't thought that far ahead. I inject confidence into my voice and smile as I talk. "Do I need a reason? Just a little help would be great."

"I would Vic, but I'm busy."

I glance around the tailor's quickly before making a plea based on the first thing my eyes land on. "Pocket squares. I need help with the pocket squares."

"Is this a joke?" she says.

"Why would it be a joke?"

"No reason," she says. But then I remember the warning I had earlier regarding pocket squares.

"Whatever happened with you, Ryan, and the pocket square is all in the past. Now, please, Jen. I'm begging you."

She sighs but agrees, telling me she'll be fifteen minutes.

Shit. I wasn't sure if fifteen minutes would be soon enough, but I figure I can ask Bettsy to hang around since he's the last one here.

"I'm thinking that I prefer a longer cut on the arms," I hear him say from the back of the store. There're several exchanges of conversation before I make out the tailor dismissing him. He disappears into the fitting room to get dressed again just as the bell above the door tinkles, announcing someone's entry.

I can hear my heart pounding in my ears as I try to busy myself. Keeping my eyes on my clipboard, I lean against the counter and, as the footsteps get closer, I breathe in relief when Liam wraps his arms around me.

"Someone may see," I say, looking around.

"Nah, it's fine," he says, and he kisses my neck before breaking away. "I just wanted to do that quickly. Did you get my gift?"

"I hear it's in the office," I say. "Thank you. Did you come here to check?"

"I wanted to tell you something. Ryan said he wouldn't stand in our way or anything, you know, if we—"

But the way he says it makes it sound like we needed Ryan's permission, which is not what I signed up for. "Did we need to seek his approval?" I say, my voice flat.

"No, but—"

"Hey, Lee, do you want to grab a pint?" Bettsy calls from the back of the store. He's half-dressed, in a polo shirt with his jeans undone.

The front door opens again as Matt Rodgers slips in along with the last two guys on my list. I'd overlooked the fact that he wouldn't be coming alone, and I'm grateful for the company. I make brief conversation with the newcomers, trying to involve Liam, but Bettsy makes his way to the front and signals he's ready to leave.

"I'll see you later, yeah?" Liam whispers, and I nod.

Luckily for me, that brief conversation with Liam has put me in a sour mood. So if Matt tries anything, it's likely that my knee would meet his balls. But he says nothing. At least not at first, anyway. He simply smiles and shakes hands with the tailor before his group is ushered towards the back of the shop.

To my relief, Jen pops her head into the store next. "Did you want a brew? I'll go across the road and grab us some drinks."

"I'll come with you," I say, making a rash decision to sign the paperwork, not concerning myself with the last few fittings. I leave a note for the tailor, asking him to call me if there are any issues before I follow Jen out into the chilly December air.

"I thought you wanted my help with the pocket squares?"

"Yeah, do you think that silver-grey is a good choice of colour?"

"I like the navy," she says. "But we both know you're going to go with the silver. What did you actually need my help with?"

I usher her out of the store, and we head across the street.

"I just don't like being alone with that Matt Rodgers. He gives me the creeps," I shiver.

Jen pushes the door open to the coffee shop, and we spot Johnny in the far corner talking to a girl I've never seen before. His head snaps up, and as soon as he catches my eye, he hurries over. "Did you know Bettsy had a sister?"

"No?"

"Well, that's her. She said she was coming along to the home game this weekend. Anyway, gotta head out. See you later." He's out of the coffee shop in a cloud of smoke. As soon as the door thuds shut behind him, Jen raises her eyebrows at me.

"That was weird," she says. I agree, but Johnny can be weird, and I'm still feeling uneasy about everything. "But anyway, Matt is creepy. Have you seen his girlfriend hanging around after the games? I've tried to be friendly, but she just looks down her nose at me."

I can't say I've noticed the girlfriend; but then again, I'm usually not paying much attention to anyone other than Liam. I'm surprised Jen's not noticed this, or if she has, she's not said anything. As we queue, I debate letting her in on all the things that have been happening because I hate sneaking around, and it's becoming stressful.

"Vic, is that your phone ringing?" Jen nudges me out of a stare I didn't realise I was doing. By the time I pull my phone out, I've missed the call. A few moments later, I'm notified of a voicemail. I put the phone to my ear and listen as the queue moves.

"Oh my God," I say under my breath as I hang up. "Someone's paid a big chunk of my rent upfront. Was it—"

"Nope, it wasn't me. I mean I thought about it because there's a few places we're really interested in putting in an offer for, but I figured that after Liam—"

"Shit. Then who?"

Jen orders for us as I tap out a message to Liam. He texts back straight away.

Liam

No. But I can probably guess who did.

Vicky

My phone vibrates in my hand. I don't let it get past one ring before I answer it.

"Look, he asked me not to mention it, but whatever. Given his track record—"

"Was it Johnny?"

"Well, that'd be my guess. He asked if he could borrow three grand, and I just gave it to him. I knew he wouldn't ask unless he absolutely had no other choice." There's a mumble of conversation off the line. "Johnny's just walked in, actually. Do you want me to ask him?"

"Where are you?"

"That Wetherspoons on the corner, what's it called Betts?" There's more mumbling while he has a side conversation, but I know where it is. I tell him I'll be there soon.

"Change of plans, Jen. We're going to the pub instead."

"But—"

"Come on."

We abandon our drinks, and I use the short walk to tell Jen that Liam suspects Johnny paid it. By the time we get to the pub, we have to push our way through the cluster of people crowding the door.

It doesn't take me long to spot the team with Bettsy's laugh booming across the open space.

"Where's Johnny?" I ask no one in particular, glancing around for him.

"He was here a minute ago," Danny shrugs before taking a gulp of his drink.

I fish my phone out of my bag and dial him, but it goes straight to voicemail. I try him a few more times before I give in and send him a text, asking where he is. It sits on 'sent' rather than 'delivered.' Now I'm pissed.

"I want answers," I yell towards Jen. "Where the fuck is he?"

But no one seems to know. Even when I call by his apartment later, there's no answer. His car is gone, and now I'm starting to get worried.

"What if he's in trouble?" I ask Liam, later that evening. I'd been pacing my apartment, so I thought it was only fair to give Liam's floor equal wear.

"He's probably just hooking up or something."

"The secret girlfriend!" I gasp, but Danny tries to reassure me that there definitely isn't a secret girlfriend.

"Has he said something to you?" I question Danny, but he shrugs and goes back to watching TV.

I'm on the verge of retrieving my spare key to his place and searching for clues when a text message comes through.

Johnny

> I'm fine. Stop freaking out—I've gone to
> visit a friend. See you tomorrow.

I stare at my phone in complete awe. That's all he's got to say for himself? I try to think who Johnny's other friends are, since he's definitely not with anyone from the hockey team. And now I'm even more convinced that he definitely has a secret girlfriend.

Chapter 26

Liam

I hardly slept last night, and it wasn't from the beer I drank. I know I need to speak with Ryan, and the longer I leave it, the more difficult it'll get. Like ripping off a Band-Aid, I need to get it over and done with. My brother hates being lied to; I think most people do, really. But I've already made the mistake of keeping something from him before, and I want to be honest with him.

I get dressed and grab a baseball cap before heading over to his place, swinging by the coffee shop first to buy him a bribe. I get Vicky an iced coffee just in case she's in the mood for one.

Tailgating Mrs Upstairs on the way in, she wishes Ryan a good day before disappearing into the elevator. I take the stairs up to Vicky's floor, wondering how I'm supposed to knock on his door with no free hands. As if he can sense my being, Ryan opens the door and stares out at me in his running gear, his face still red from the cold outside.

He beckons me in and takes a coffee from me, leading me towards the kitchen.

"I already know why you're here," he says. "I haven't figured out what I'm doing about the suit yet."

"Actually, this isn't about the suit."

I take a quick look around and see that Vicky must still be in bed.

"Where's Jen?" I ask.

"Taking a shower. So, no talk about yesterday. I beg you."

"You always think the worst of me. Look, just do what you need to do. Don't worry about trying to play by the unwritten rules. Wear a suit, don't. Get married, don't. Whatever."

He thinks for a moment, then nods. "So, if it's not about the suit, it's about ..." his eyes land on the iced coffee that he must have overlooked before, "...Vicky, right?"

"Well, yeah. I don't really know what to say." I look down at my coffee cup.

"I hear you got her a fancy basket full of all her favourite things. Are you back together?" his tone is disapproving and sets a sinking feeling in my stomach.

"Shit. I don't know, Ryan." I look over at her door.

"Hm. Well, anyway, you've set an expectation now. And put me to shame." He pulls out his phone and taps a few times before scrolling. "I've started making a list of Jen's favourite things, but—"

"It's not a competition. I noticed she was using a new shampoo. A different shampoo. I'm just helping." Ryan looks at me blankly, so I change the subject. "Do you want to get to the rink early? We can skate. And talk."

He nods, and I wait for him to grab his gear before placing the coffee outside of Vicky's door and tapping on it before we head out.

I run up to my apartment and grab my gear before meeting Ryan next to his Jeep. We throw our bags in the trunk, and I hop into the passenger's side.

Ryan backs up and we roll out of the parking lot, pausing at the exit for the barrier to swing open to let us through.

"Shit, is that Johnny?" he says as we pull out onto the main road. He's not wrong. Johnny's getting out of a cab, fumbling in his pocket for his keys. Ryan pulls over and winds down the window.

"You okay, pal?"

Johnny looks completely horrified to see us, and he adjusts his cap before calling back in response. "Yeah—I'll catch you at practice." He swipes his entry fob before he hurries inside. The door swings shut behind him.

"He's definitely got a secret girlfriend," I say, pulling my phone out and dropping Vicky a text since I doubt Johnny would have thought to update her on his welfare.

"Speaking of which, tell me what's going on. You said you weren't back together but—"

"Well, we're not, but we're not not either. Fuck. I don't know." I drum my fingers against the dash as Ryan waits at a set of lights. "We're not sleeping together. If that's what you're asking. But we've been sleeping together."

"You're making absolutely zero sense," he says.

I remind him about the hotel room situation—that we spent the night together. Then I tell him I went over after the night I sat with her on the coach too.

"I fucking knew some shit was going on then!"

"All we did was sleep, honestly."

"Lucky for you, Jen is all for it, so I'm probably less pissed than I should be. I just don't want to see you get hurt, that's all."

We come to a stop in the players' parking lot and climb out, grabbing our bags from the trunk. There's no one around at this time, and the doors are locked. Ryan swipes his card to gain access, and we head towards the dressing room.

"I feel like I'm stuck, though. I mean, I want to give things a go, but I know what you're saying. I can't go through that again. I think that's probably why we haven't actually slept together. If I do, I'll be dropping every single barrier I've put up."

I wait for Ryan to come up with a solution for me, but he doesn't; he just listens.

"Jen had me read 'Men are from Mars and Women are from Venus,'" he admits when I ask him why he's not providing me the answers I so desperately need. "Honestly, it's really insightful. You should read it. Basically, women just want men to listen, but we don't. We're fixers, and we want to fix. So, the next time a woman is ranting on about something, just listen instead. They love it." Huh? I put this in the back of my mind to consider later as we lace up our skates, not bothering with our full gear. "Do you think this is why you came here in the first place? To see if you could move forward with Vicky?"

I swallow hard. "Well, I came here intending to retire next season. I wanted to make the most of my final year with you and Johnny. But I think I also wanted to fix things with Vicky because we have such a past, man. I can't just throw all that away, I've tried and I don't feel like me—I wish I could explain it properly. I know I can't rely on someone else to be happy, and you know I don't believe in soul mates. I guess what I'm saying is, I know that there are probably lots of women I'd likely be compatible with, but I'll always choose Vicky. I just can't explain why."

"You don't need to explain it," he says, turning his head towards me. "And even though I won't be happy about it, I'll always be here to help if things go sour. But you should definitely make sure you're both on the same page and there're no fucking secrets. All or nothing."

I get that.

"Bring your gloves," Ryan says as we head towards the ice. We each grab our sticks, and he takes a few pucks and shoves them into the pouch of his hoodie.

"I thought we were skating?" I say.

Ryan shrugs. "May as well have some fun while we're here."

And we do. We don't talk at all. We just play like we're kids again with nothing else to worry about except what time Mom was picking us up. It's only when we stop to get some water that Ryan asks me the question I've been turning over in my head for months.

"Are you really sure you want to give hockey up?"

"No," I answer honestly. "But I think I know what I need to do because as ridiculous as it sounds..." I pause. But he nods, because he knows exactly what I'm thinking. If, somehow, Vicky and I are in a good place, I can think about carrying on.

"Come on," he says, looking at his watch. "We've got some time to play 'Defend the Bucket.'"

We return our sticks to the bench, and Ryan leaves the ice to grab a bucket. Enjoying a moment of calm, I take the time to skate around. I complete two full laps of the ice, and on the bend of my third, a flash of blonde catches my eye. An infectious smile breaks out on my face—my heart leaping slightly as I watch Vicky's interaction with Ryan. They're both nodding in conversation, and it doesn't look as if anyone is out for blood. The whole interaction looks civil, my opinion cemented when they hug each other.

When they break apart, Vicky looks over towards me, her teeth gleaming as bright as the ice. "Thanks for my coffee," she says.

"What's going on here?" I smile, looking at her and my brother.

"I'll leave you guys to it," Ryan says before disappearing.

"I just wanted to check in with Ryan. Since you're convinced that we need his permission to see me." I open my mouth to talk, but she steps on the ice and skates towards me, smirking. "Seriously. Jen told me you and Ryan were here. I thought I'd come and see if you wanted to skate. I miss you, Lee. I don't want it to be just about the fooling around, you know? We used to have so much fun together." She pauses. "Look, I know you want Ryan to be okay with us, and I know we don't need his permission, but it's all good."

I grab her hand and pull her in. Kissing her, not giving a crap if anyone is watching—because I choose her, and hopefully that means I can choose hockey too.

Johnny looks like he's not slept properly in days, which is how long he's been avoiding me. Phone calls unanswered, text messages not returned, and he wasn't answering his door. Yesterday, I caved and found his key, but the fucker changed the lock.

He was late for practice. He's dragging his feet as he skates, and his momentum looks non-existent. I glance at the clock, figuring out how long I must wait until I can reasonably go downstairs and corner him. They have ten minutes left before they hit the showers.

"And he's not said anything to you?" I ask Kirsty from where I stand at the window. I've learnt that she and Johnny are friends and, even though it felt weird at first, it makes sense.

I'm looking down at the ice, watching Liam this time. He's bouncing a puck on the end of his stick.

"No, but you should probably talk to him if you're worried," she says.

"Of course, I'm worried! Have you seen the state of him?"

Kirsty joins me at the window next to Jen's empty desk, and we watch for a few moments. "He must have told Liam, though. Or Ryan," she says after a few moments.

Johnny now stands at the point with his stick twirling in his hand. He's wallowing his feet back and forth. I'm trying to see if he's shaved, but I can't quite make out that level of detail.

Kirsty heads back to her desk, and I carry on watching the drills on the ice. My eyes are drifting between Liam and Johnny. I need to tell Johnny about us. Even if we haven't put a label on it, I still don't feel comfortable hiding it from him.

"Vicky, are you going to answer that?"

"What?"

"Jenna's desk phone," Kirsty says. It's not until it rings off and starts trilling again that I even notice it was making a noise.

"Hello?" I lean over her desk and pick up the receiver, stretching the phone cord as far as it'll go so I can keep an eye on Johnny.

"Vicky, it's me."

"Jen? Why are you ringing your own phone? Where are you?"

"I need a favour," she says.

"Can it wait? Johnny's—"

"Vicky. Listen carefully. I'm at the registrar's office near the central library, and they have a cancellation. I need you to get Ryan and get his ass down here in half an hour. Half an hour, Vicky. Eleven-thirty. Please tell me you can do that?" I stare ahead in complete disbelief, not even sure what I'm hearing. Jen rushes me, making me realise now isn't the time to ask questions. "I don't care if you have to disrupt practice, but he needs to be here. I'll explain all later."

The line goes dead, and I slam the receiver down. Not bothering to grab my jacket, I start towards the door before turning back to pick up one thing I know I can't go without: my camera. The corridor to the stairs is empty, but unfortunately, the GM is exiting his office.

"Ah, Vicky. Just the person—I was hoping to catch you." I come to a halt right in front of him, wobbling on my heels as I stop. "Are you okay? In a hurry?"

I falter as I try to think of something to say. I can almost hear the clock ticking, taunting me.

"Um, yeah. I'm sorry… it's women's things, you know," I say. I discovered from a young age that men hate this. Random men, that is.

The GM opens his mouth as if to speak, but he stares at me completely dumbfounded. Then he nods, moving aside to let me pass. I'm off again, only slowing down to take the stairs down to the lobby.

I power walk through to the bar, then towards the doors to the ice, and I fling them open with a sense of purpose to see the ice deserted. Empty.

Fuck.

I speed towards the tunnels, but as I turn the corner, I come face to face with Coach.

"Vicky, a word," he says, as if he's been waiting for me. This is beyond frustrating.

"Could I just—"

But Coach stares at me as if I'm asking him to donate his life savings to junior hockey. I have no choice but to follow him into his office, hoping he'll make it quick.

He nods at the empty seat in the corner. The walls are full of various memorabilia, and there are bits of paper everywhere except for the space at the centre of his desk. He sits in his chair and rests his elbows on the surface, rubbing his hands through his hair before letting out a sigh.

"If I smoked, I'd be having a cigarette now," he says. "But I just wanted to check in with you. Johnny said you've been having a hard time with your father, and I know he's felt it, too—even if he doesn't talk about it. Do you know if he's looking after himself? I appreciate this is a tough question since you don't actually have to tell me anything, but that Johnny Koenig is not the same Johnny Koenig I gave the 'C' to. I have a duty of care for my guys, and I hope he takes the rest time seriously. When he comes back—"

"Rest time?" I ask, knitting my brows.

"Yeah, he requested some leave. He'll be back to play next weekend, but he'll be missing practice for the rest of the week." Coach makes small talk for a few minutes before telling me to look after myself, standard 'I'm done talking' for him.

After leaving Coach's office, I head directly to the dressing room. I knock once and peek inside.

"Where's Johnny?" I ask into the room, but I already know he's not here.

"He took off, but he said he'll call you," Ryan says, pulling a t-shirt over his head.

As soon as I lock eyes with him, I remember Jen. "Actually, Ryan, can I borrow you for a sec?"

Liam gives me a questioning look as Ryan comes to the door.

"Jenna called. You need to go. Now."

His face changes and he knows exactly what I'm talking about. "What did she say? Is there a cancellation or—"

"Yes. Go."

"Lee. Let's go," he says before turning to me. "You should come, too. We need witnesses."

***

On the way home, I get Liam to stop at a gift shop so I can buy one of those obnoxious balloons that says 'Just Married' in the shape of a car. I also get a tonne of confetti and some banners before heading home to decorate our apartment.

"I can't believe I just witnessed my brother getting married whilst wearing his runners," Liam says. He's standing on Ryan's side of the bed, holding up his side of a banner while I pin mine to Jen's side. "I'm glad things changed for us because I'd want a huge, fancy wedding. That was fucking dreadful."

"Keep your opinions to yourself. Did you see how happy they were?"

Liam frowns. I didn't realise he cared so much.

I finish putting up the banners before emptying the confetti over their bed. I leave the balloon in the corner of the room so they'll see it as soon as they come in.

When I head into the living room, my phone rings. It's Johnny.

"I'm okay, Vic. I'm just feeling exhausted, and I need a break," he says when I ask how he is.

"Where did you go after the suit fitting?"

"I just needed to get away," he says. Then I ask why he paid my rent and why he changed his locks. I feel like it's a game of twenty questions without him giving me answers.

"Look, I'll talk to you another time. Just trust me on this, will you? I know I'll miss Ladies' Night, and I'm sorry, but trust me."

Leaving me with more questions than answers, he hangs up.

"Do you want pasta or potatoes?" Liam asks as I walk into the kitchen.

"I'm not hungry," I say.

"Johnny will be fine, Vic. Just give him space. Remember when he broke up with Sarah?" Johnny's last girlfriend, Sarah, caused a huge emotional impact on Johnny, and I remember it well. But I stare ahead, deep in thought. "Pasta it is," Liam says, leaning down and kissing my forehead. "I'll bring it through when it's ready. Just be prepared to give him a lot of time," he says.

"Do you think he'll be upset that he missed Ryan's wedding?"

"Nah. It wasn't a real wedding, anyway."

"It was a real wedding, Lee. It may just be a piece of paper to you guys, but it's the real thing. It's the commitment. It's everything."

But when the front door opens and Jenna walks through, spotting the crap I've set out in her bedroom, the look on her face supports my logic that it is everything. Because even if it was just a piece of paper, today is her wedding day.

"Let's go to your place," I say to Liam. "Leave the newlyweds in peace." I hop up from the sofa and give Jenna the tightest, most genuine hug I can muster before wishing her every happiness.

Chapter 27

I lie on my bed waiting for Vicky, flicking through the channels on the TV; the one that Ryan helped me fix to the wall. I haven't even bothered to change out of my tux. I expect her to be in her lounge wear; but when my bedroom door open, she slips inside still dressed in the incredible gown she wore for Ladies' Night.

Without a word, she unzips her dress, steps out of it, picks it up, and drapes it over the chair in the corner of my room.

"What are you trying to do to me?" I groan. She's standing there in a pair of sheen stockings and her Louboutin's. A matching set of underwear made from a dark-green lacy material makes my dick instantly hard.

"What?" She steps out of her shoes and pads over to my closet, plucking a t-shirt out and dropping it over her head. Her bra comes off next. She rummages underneath the fabric of the shirt and, as if by magic, it appears out of the left sleeve.

"You could have at least let me see your tits," I say.

She sits on the edge of the bed, and I glue my eyes to her, intently watching as she rolls her stockings off.

"Fuck me," I whisper, but loud enough for her to turn her head towards me with a grin on her face.

"You okay?"

"Are you doing this on purpose?" I ask. "Because this isn't fair."

"What's not fair?" she rolls off her other stocking and then hops onto the bed, kneeling. She's looking at me, her hair loose over her right shoulder, and she bites her lip.

"You know you're a smokeshow at the best of times, but right now ..." I have to adjust my dick which has become uncomfortable underneath my slacks.

Vicky sits there for a moment as if she's thinking. She opens her mouth to speak—once, twice, and a third time before settling on keeping it closed. She turns around and looks at the TV.

"Are you okay?" I ask. In a flash, she's facing me again, her hands on her thighs as she folds her legs underneath her. "You've got that look in your eye."

The look. The look Vicky has when she wants something and I have a feeling I know what she wants.

"Well, I know we said just one time and all, but what about a friendly favour?"

This gets my attention. "A friendly favour?"

"Well, yeah, just as a one-off." She shifts to straddle my calves. "Another one-off."

"I, uh—"

"It's just an idea. We don't have to," she says, moving away, but I'm quick with my belt. As soon as I undo it, she's looking at me with those beautiful eyes of hers.

"I, uh ..." All the words I thought I knew have gone.

She leans forward, tugging at my pants, and I raise my hips. "You can say no," she says. But I'm quick with my boxers, pushing them down, forcing my dick to spring free. Undoing the buttons on my dress shirt gives it some space.

"I know I've said this before, but I love it," she says.

"What do you love?" I ask, playing the game.

"You know what!"

"Tell me, Vic. Tell me what you love."

I take my dick into my right palm and give it a squeeze.

"Your dick, I love it. I love watching you touch it, I love touching it myself, I love—"

Just watching how she stares at me, complete awe on her face, makes me harder than I thought possible. I want her to touch me.

"Since you've been a good girl this evening, why don't you come and show me how much you love it?" I coax.

She crosses her legs at her ankles and raises her hips into the air, giving me an incredible view of her ass. As soon as I reach out and touch her face, she grins. Batting my hand away from my dick, she leans in closer. She's got her cheek pressed against my shaft, and the heat of her breath is driving me to the point of wanting to take control and fuck her. I want to make her forget there was anything other than us two. But I hold off, waiting to see what she'll do next.

She kisses my thighs gently, running her nails up and down. Then she kisses lightly over my shaft before she sits up slightly and spits onto my dick.

Fuck me, I've definitely missed her in this way. I have to put all my effort into not coming at the very sight of her. Her videos don't do her justice. My minds-eye doesn't do her justice. Nothing ever prepares me for Vicky.

Is this truly another one-time thing? But that's a problem for another time because I'm leaking pre-come and all I can think about is how good I know she feels. Her mouth, her pussy—even that one time she let me put my dick in her ass. I can't get enough.

She wraps her hand around my cock, teasing the head with shallow pumps and rubbing the pre-come around the tip with the pad of her thumb. It takes my breath away, forcing me to suck in air through my teeth.

"You're perfect, you know that, right?" I ask, my voice rough with lust.

Her big blue eyes fix on mine as she pumps, occasionally snaking her tongue out to tease the underside of my dick. "I love how hard you get for me," she says. I take the cue to provide her with the reassurance I know she's craving.

"I'm so fucking hard, baby girl. That's what you do to me. Seeing you playing with my dick ... fuck! You look so pretty like that."

It's true. She's beautiful all the time, but especially when her face is like this, close to my dick. But I know she looks even prettier with her eyes watering as I hit the back of her throat. She's teasing me and it's working. The anticipation she's building is making my balls ache.

She surprises me by popping the end of my dick into her mouth. The heat of her tongue causes me to groan. Shit. I thought I remembered how good her mouth felt, but this... fuck! My dick disappearing into her mouth is a sight like no other. She's so perfect, and I tell her so. I tell her she's such a good fucking girl to me.

"Show me your tits," I say, propping myself up slightly higher. She sits back and whips her shirt over her head, and my eyes fix on her nipples—the right one is my favourite. It's small and pert, and I want to suck it.

She cups her boobs in her hands and pinches her nipples, throwing her head back in ecstasy. I want to reach out and touch her, but I'm enjoying the show too much. I reach for my dick to give it a jerk, but she bats my hand away again.

In a flash, she's straddling me, facing towards the end of the bed; her hands woven together as she strokes me; her ass is almost in my face. I can smell her, and I'm desperate to just push her panties aside and slide my tongue along her pussy.

I'm completely engrossed. I'm enjoying the show so much I can't fathom why she stops. It's abrupt, and I'm about to protest when she repositions herself so my dick rubs on the lace of her panties. And just when I think I can't take it anymore, she tugs them to the side, showing me her perfect pussy, pink and glistening.

God, I've missed her. More than she can ever know. The scene elevates the anticipation and the excitement I'm feeling. I've completely forgotten about any heartache because my cock is throbbing. As soon as she reaches back and rubs the very tip of my dick against her, teasing me with the prospect of her slipping it inside, I can't take it anymore. I come. I can't help myself. "Oh, fuck," I say, groaning as my whole body shakes.

She flips herself around, eyes wide. "Oh, Lee," she says before taking my dick into her mouth, sucking me deep until I'm almost crying. God, I've never wanted someone as much as I wanted Vicky. I always want Vicky.

"You're fucking incredible, Vic," I say, my mind still cloudy. I reach for her, pulling her up so I can kiss her. My hands fumble with the sides of her panties, and she gives me what I want, helping me get rid of them.

I'm probably rougher than I'd usually be, but I pull her up towards my chest so I have a direct sight of that beautiful pussy of hers.

"Oh my God," she whispers. "I haven't waxed."

"Shut the fuck up and sit on my face like a good girl," I say, gripping her hips and moving her into position. Everything about her turns me into a state of desperation. I'm desperate to touch her, feel her, taste her, smell her. I can't get enough.

I slip a finger inside her. "Fuck, Vic, how fucking wet are you?" I say before putting all my attention on her clit. It's practically quivering with the need to be touched. "Tell me

what you want, Vic." I flick her clit just the once, enough
to give her an idea of what I can offer.

She gasps.

"It's an imperative statement, Vicky. Tell me what you
want." I cup her ass and pull her away, teasing her.

She looks down at me impatiently. "I want you to make
me come." Let's face it, I was always going to give her what
she wants. I always have.

Pulling her pussy down onto my mouth, I take her clit
gently between my teeth. I wish I could drag this out
longer—mainly for my own personal gain—but she is
shuddering above me. I set my tongue to flick directly over
her clit. She lets out a familiar cry. I react quickly, slipping
my middle finger into her pussy. The sound she makes,
and the way her body shakes with her orgasm, gets me
rock hard again. I want to tell her I love hearing her come.
That I love the taste of her on my tongue as she does, that
I love how she reacts to me. But my mouth is busy, and I'm
in heaven.

"I can't—" she says, leaning forward, trying to hold
herself up. I grip her hips and roll her off me so she's lying
on the bed. I lower my face towards hers and kiss her. I'm
not even sure how long we're kissing for, but the gentle
nudge from Vicky's hand on my chest pushes me away.

"Your phone is ringing," she says.

"Let it ring." I lean down to kiss her again.

"It's been ringing for ages. It stops and starts again
straight away."

With a groan, I roll over and extract my phone from the
pocket of my discarded pants.

"What?" I say as soon as I answer.

"Where are you, bro? How quick can you get to the rink?"

"What the hell for?"

"Just get down here. And bring Danny with you."

"Is it important?"

"Are you really asking me that?" Ryan says, then he hangs up.

"I guess I'm going to the rink," I say. "Do you want to stay here? I don't know how long I'll be."

"It's probably best that I go," she says, grabbing for my t-shirt.

I'm more than disappointed. "Vic—"

"Just come to mine when you're done," she says, rolling her eyes at me. "My bed is more comfortable. But text me when you get there, I want to know what's so important."

When he wasn't playing hockey, Liam and I used to spend Sunday afternoons in the campus library, usually to get away from the constant noise that was the hockey house.

One particular Sunday, Liam appeared to be deeply engrossed in his screen as he worked on something last-minute. I had nothing to work on, so I pulled out a novel I was reading and occupied myself. Or tried to anyway. I glanced at Liam, watching the concentration on his face as he worked. He was handsome. I always wondered how I got so lucky. I loved the way his jaw tightened and slacked as he read, and he sporadically adjusted himself in his seat, rubbing the stubble on his face as he did so. I loved everything about him.

"I can feel you watching me," he said, grinning at me.

"I can't help it." And to my delight, he gave me a beckoning nod. I slid off my chair and straddled his lap.

His hands wrapped around my waist, pulling me close; and I distinctly remember him smelling my hair. I was wearing his hockey jacket, much to the envy of the girls on campus. I felt like I belonged to him, and I was all for it.

"Lee, can I ask you something?" I asked. I wasn't sure why I chose this time to ask him, but it felt right.

He nodded.

"I was reading something the other day, and I wondered if you felt like taking charge." I'd giggled after I said it because it sounded better in my head.

"Like, bossing you? Because you're a law unto yourself. There's no way you're listening to me," he chuckled.

"Hey!" I jabbed him in the chest.

"What? I'm just saying you can be a brat at times, Vic." I frowned at him. "But I'm not complaining!" he said.

"I am not a brat!" I protested.

"Just saying that makes you sound like one. But, hey, if you want me to be the boss and make you shut up, I can sure as hell shut you up with something." He wiggled his eyebrows and pulled me closer, dotting kisses along my jaw.

"You're a good girl, sometimes though," he whispered.

I shivered slightly before my hands found his nape, twisting my fingers into his hair.

He pulled back and looked at me. "Do you like me calling you a good girl? Because there's a look in your eye that makes me go all woozy."

Words had caught in my throat. He had shifted my position on his lap so I could feel the lump in his jeans.

"Answer me, Vicky."

I gulped. "You know how much of a control freak I am, Lee, but you ..." I kissed along his jaw. "... you can take the reins in some circumstances. You know that, right?"

He breathed deeply, and I knew I had his attention. I leaned forward and whispered into his ear. "Are you—"

"I'm always fucking hard for you, Vic."

I wriggled on his lap and leaned back slightly, surprising myself by popping the button on my jeans before sliding my hand inside. I was just as horny as he was, and I wanted him to know it.

"Vic ..." he looked around, probably checking that no one could see us. His eyes divert back to me as I pulled my hand out from my jeans and slipped my fingers into my mouth. "Vic ..." he said again.

"Are you going to make me stop?" I asked.

"Study room. Now," he growled at me, and I slid off his lap and away. Getting caught added to the excitement.

He fucked me against the door of the study room. If someone had walked past, they would have definitely seen us. And that moment was just the beginning.

But right now, we both knew that 'one more time' would turn into 'just one more time.'

As I stood in the corner of the showers after practice, my leg hitched up over Liam's shoulder as I held my hand over my mouth. I knew it wouldn't be the last time. Nor was the time I spent on my knees in the media room, Liam's back against the closed door.

And it's only getting more frequent.

All of that became apparent when I got a text from him last week.

Liam

> Meet me in the equipment storage room.

And it was oh so good. Now we've practically lost count. But there's a pressing matter that's frustrating the hell out of me. I'm mulling it over as I lie in bed after our most recent encounter.

"Why won't you have sex with me?" I ask when he returns from the bathroom. My post-orgasm fog has cleared and I'm ready to talk.

"What?"

"Why won't you have sex me?"

"We've had sex loads of times," he says, climbing into bed.

"Not recently, we haven't. I mean, we've been fooling around for weeks now, and I'm desperate for you to fuck me. There I said it."

"We're just building up to it, aren't we? Taking things slow."

"You're kidding?" I scoff.

"No?"

"Lee, I don't think we're the type of people who 'take things slow.'" I use my fingers to do the air-quotes, and he laughs. "You're just being mean!" I throw him a pouty face, hoping it'll annoy him enough so that he feels he has to teach me a lesson, but it doesn't work.

"Stop being a brat, Vic. Just let us get there. It'll be worth the wait."

"Shall we watch the video?" I ask. I'm pulling out all the stops now, hoping to encourage him. I even give him a gentle kiss along that special spot on his neck, but he turns me down.

"Nah, let's just cuddle. Isn't our show on soon?"

Now I'm mad. Mad because I want to cuddle him, and I want to watch my show—which is now, officially, our show. But I'm also mad because every single day I live with that ache inside me that cannot be sated. I'd be lying if I said it didn't enter my mind to use his morning wood to my advantage, but that would cross a major boundary.

Sulking, I turn off the light, turn on the TV and find myself in my favourite place: Liam's arms, despite my frustration. He's twisting a strand of my hair between his fingers, and he's gently kissing my head in intervals. Then I hear him take a breath.

"Hey, can I ask you something?"

"Sure," I say, adjusting myself slightly so I can look at him.

"Did you run up that debt coming to see me? Last season, with the Marlies?"

Shit. I have a feeling he already knows the answer to that.

"I found the ticket stubs when I was looking for your bills. I mean, I was also looking through your underwear drawer, but yeah," he says.

"It wasn't all on that," I admit. "I saw a counsellor too. It wasn't for very long, but I thought it would help deal with my emotional instability. It helped, but I got scared. I mean, I can blame my parents for it, but I can't rely on anyone else to help me fix it, can I?"

He says nothing, but he pulls me closer and kisses my forehead. "You know I've got you, right?"

He doesn't need to elaborate. I know exactly what he's saying, and I appreciate him so much.

"Lee. I know we've been through a lot, but I know there's one emotion ... one I've always been grateful for not being able to control. I'm not expecting you to feel the same as I do or anything ... but I love you and I don't think I'll ever stop."

Silence again. But he kisses me—and that says it all.

Chapter 28

Liam

"Has anyone seen that show where they get two strangers to get married?" Bettsy says to no one in particular. We're in the dressing room getting ready for tonight's game.

I know exactly what show he's on about, but I don't want to admit it's quickly become our show. I pretty much know all the participants by name because I watch it every night while Vicky's tucked into my chest. I wouldn't have it any other way.

"Why? Are you thinking about doing it?" Danny laughs.

"Actually, yes. But not for those reasons. They send you on an all-expenses-paid holiday," Bettsy says, pulling on his shoulder pads.

"That's called a fucking honeymoon, Betts," I say, half laughing. "And it's after you get married."

"I'm just saying it's a good idea."

"Or, you could just pay for a holiday and not have the hassle of arranging a divorce afterwards," Hutch says.

"Do they actually get married? Because I'd bet that it's all for show and they just pretend for the camera. You'd need to consummate that shit."

"Not even an all-expenses holiday could convince me to sleep with you, Betts," Danny says. "What'd you reckon, Johnny? Would you do it?"

"Do what?" Johnny says, apparently only half-listening to the conversation. Since the impromptu fun we had after Ladies' Night, dragging Johnny out for a game of friendly 3v3 hockey, he seems a little more like himself, but still not regular old Johnny.

"Get married to someone you've never met."

"Nah," he says, turning away. "I'm never getting married."

"Everyone says that, but they do. Look at Ryan here."

Since Ryan and Jen's quick wedding, everyone has been finding the opportunity to crack a joke. But it's only because everyone wants what they have. Even me. A pang of jealousy sears through me because I want to be in that position with Vicky. The thing is though, I know we're both afraid. Afraid of the judgement we'd probably get from everyone else. The speculation of when we'll be splitting up again—not that we're officially back together now or anything.

I shake the complications of my relationship, or situationship, from my mind and finish getting ready. I make my way to the ice with Danny.

"Where did you disappear to after practice yesterday?" he says as we enter the tunnel towards the rink. "I thought you were coming to the driving range?"

"I just had to take care of something," I lie, zooming off towards the net as soon as my skates touch the ice.

I want to tell Danny, I really do. Because the whole thing was hilarious. Vicky had texted me, asking me to meet her in the equipment storage room. I was half-way there when she came running towards me.

"Someone's already in there!" she said, pulling my arm towards the direction of the exit. But when I asked her who, she turned red. "I'd rather not say," she said, looking like she was about to burst into tears but she'd given the game away.

"Johnny?"

"Yes!" she squeaked. "And I know he wasn't on his own."

We didn't get a chance to hang around and see who else came out of the room because Ryan was calling me asking why I wasn't at the driving range.

"I'm not dumb, you know," Danny says. "I know about you and Vicky."

"Well, shit." I flick a puck towards the net.

"Yeah. And Johnny doesn't know?"

"Not officially. Well, Vicky's waiting for him to be in a better mental state, and I agree with her. I guess we'll see how it goes—wait, who the fuck is that?" I'm staring directly at a beefy guy leaning on the boards next to the benches. He's got this tight-fitting V-neck t-shirt on, and he looks like he's been punched in the nose recently. I'd still wager that he doesn't have a hard time getting a date. He's got a big square jaw covered in stubble, and his hair is short as if he's just had a fresh cut.

Ryan skates over and comes to a stop next to me, then his eyes follow mine.

"Who the fuck is that?" he echos.

"Hell knows. Ask him what he wants. Maybe he's lost," I say, but the puck Ryan's playing with has captured his attention, and he's not listening.

"Hey!" The guy is waving in our direction, and Danny lets out a gasp.

"Oh my God. It can't be—"

"What?" I say.

"I know who that is! That's Neil Jenkins!" Danny says.

"Who?"

"Neil Jenkins, he plays rugby for—"

"What does he want?" I cut in, but Danny skates towards the bench. I edge closer slightly so I can listen.

"Alright, mate? It is you, isn't it?" Danny asks, and the warmth coming from his cheeks is enough to melt the ice.

"I'm looking for Victoria Koenig," Neil 'whatshisface' says with a grin.

My heart stops.

"Vicky? She's not here right now, but I can pass on a message," Danny says in an ever-so-helpful tone.

But before I can hear a reply, Johnny is standing right next to me, nudging my arm and saying my name.

"What?" I say, not taking my eyes off Neil and Danny. He better not be taking a message to pass on.

Johnny looks over towards the bench. "Oh, it's—"

"Not you as well."

"Dude, everyone knows who he is. He plays for his country, for Christ's sake."

I spot a loose puck nearby and wrist it towards Danny, trying to break up his conversation, but it hits him on the ass and rebounds towards Bettsy. Danny doesn't even acknowledge it. He's too busy laughing at something Neil says.

The conversation bounces back and forth for a further minute before Danny nods and skates back towards me.

"What did he want Vicky for?" I ask.

"Oh, he didn't say. But he did say that he'd come back another time."

"He plays for that team Vicky takes photos of," Johnny says. "And he was at that speed-dating we went to a while back. I think that's where they first met."

"What?" My jaw hits the ice.

"I think she turned him down, but it doesn't matter anyway, does it? Haven't you both moved on?" Johnny says in a firm tone.

Coach's whistle blows, and he rounds us up. But I'm flustered. All the talk of Vicky and that Neil guy has got me sweating before we've even started practice. What if she's roped him in to satisfy her? I wondered how long it would take her to realise that we were doing everything except sex, and I can tell she's pissed. But she wouldn't, surely not?

Despite my best efforts, images of Vicky and Neil flood my mind and a sickness bubbles in my stomach. What the fuck am I going to do? Because in my head, everything bar sex is fine since there's less chance of us building an attachment. However, I know that logic is a complete pile of crap. I've convinced myself that refraining from sex is the key to keeping my heart taped back together. But now it feels like the worst idea I've ever had.

I get a text message from Liam as I'm setting up my camera for filming.

Liam

> Neil was looking for you earlier.

I mutter to myself, repeating the name Neil over and over until I realise whom he's talking about. Then another moment to understand why he would be looking for me.

Vicky

> Rugby player Neil?

Liam

> How many Neil's do you know? But yes, he said he'd visit you another time.

I can't decipher Liam's tone from his text message, but I can probably guess that he's leaping to conclusions. Instead of trying to plead innocence to something I have legitimately nothing to do with, I shove my phone back in my pocket and finish setting up.

My watch tells me they should be out any second, and when I hear the dressing room door creak open, I spot Liam straight away. He's quickly joined by Danny, Hutch, and Bettsy who pace towards the marker board which I've propped up against the wall. This weeks' question is about pizza toppings.

"Hey, Neil was looking for you," Danny says, wiggling his eyebrows.

"Anyone would think he came to see you. He was so excited, Vic," Bettsy says. "What did he want? Are you seeing him or something?"

I give Bettsy the response I know Liam is waiting to hear: he asked, I said no, end of story.

Luckily for me, the topic of pizza is enough of a distraction for Bettsy, and he considers it for longer than anyone should. The rest of the guy's file past without another word about Neil—Liam included.

When Johnny eventually leaves the dressing room behind Ryan, I notice the energy everyone else is feeling, with it being the last game before Christmas, has not rubbed off on Johnny, who is still moody and distant.

We had brunch this morning, and the conversation was non-existent. I still haven't been able to bring myself to tell him about me and Liam. We're not sleeping together, that's for sure, except we physically sleep together most nights. I think it's only right to tell Johnny.

With the camera set up, the queue moves slowly as each of the guys read the board.

Johnny's the last up, and he flicks his eyes over the marker board briefly. "Pineapple," he says, then leans in and lowers his voice. "I need to talk with you," he says into my ear.

"Can it wait?" I ask, but Johnny has already taken a step around me so he can look me directly in the eye.

"John, I'm filming!" I mouth at him, nodding towards the camera I've set up.

"Pause it, or edit this out, whatever—Vicky, I don't care."

"What do you want?" I ask him through gritted teeth.

"Just wanted to let you know, I've cut Dad out too. I mean, I've just come to my senses, I guess."

Pausing the recording, I try to understand his expression as I look at him, but he avoids eye contact. "What happened?"

"I don't want to go into detail now, but I'll tell you another time. I just want you to know I'm sorry for everything, and I know I've been pretty shitty. I love you, Sis."

Johnny bolts past me in a flash, and I stand there in complete shock. It's only when Jen taps my arm that I pull my attention back to here and now.

"Are you okay?" she asks.

I shake my head, then I recall where she's been all afternoon. "How did the house viewing go?" I ask her as I gather my equipment.

"I think we're going to put in an offer," she says.

We go to the home bench where she unpacks two iPads and switches them on. "It was the only place we've seen that Ryan likes and he sees enough potential in. I think he's been watching too much TV. He needs to get a daytime job because I'm worried about his sanity."

I watch her set up the iPads, and then she pulls a laptop out of her bag. Jen crouches down at the bench, resting her computer on it as if it's a desk. I'm focused completely on what she's doing which means I have no warning that Matt Rodgers has made his way over to us. He leans in through the access door, his stick stretched out in front of him.

"I would say 'while you're down there,' but I don't do fat chicks." He grins down at Jen, and my jaw drops open in both shock and disgust.

"Good thing I wasn't offering because—"

I don't know how I struggled to yell at him the other day but hearing someone insult my friend lights a fuse that starts burning away. Burning. Burning. And then it blows.

"Who the fuck do you think you are?"

"If I didn't know any better, I'd say you were feeling a bit jealous, Vicky. But my offer still stands if you wanted to reconsider."

I don't know how I manage it, but I swing for him, aiming for his nose. Jen is behind me in an instant, pulling me back; and the next moment, Johnny has his arms around Matt. Johnny is bigger than him and pushes him over the threshold between the ice and bench with ease as he drags him towards the dressing room.

The sound of skates across the ice penetrates the air. "What the hell is going on?" Ryan skids to a stop.

Jen shakes her head. "Nothing. It's fine. Nothing at all."

"It didn't look like nothing," Liam's voice this time, and they both step off the ice. "Are you both okay?"

"It wasn't nothing. That fucking shit-stain just insulted Jenna," I yell, and before I can think through a plan, I'm hurrying down the tunnel towards the dressing room with the intent to cause harm.

"Vicky, come back. It's fine." Jen tugs on my hand.

"Let me go, Jen. He's not getting away with that," I say.

"What did he say?" Ryan says.

"It's nothing, it's fine," Jen says.

"Jenna, what did he say?"

Before I can interject with an account of Matt's vile attempt at conversation, Hal, the security guard, steps over and whispers something into Ryan's ear.

It takes less than ten seconds for Ryan to go from zero to one hundred. He runs past me, followed by Liam. The door to the dressing room slams shut behind them.

"I'm sorry ladies, but that guy is a nasty piece of work, and there's no way I'm letting him get away with that," Hal says.

"Ryan will get suspended!" Jen shrieks before pushing past me towards the dressing room. I hurry along behind her.

We arrive just in time to see a fist approaching Matt, then Danny and Bettsy enter the room and nudge us out of the way.

"This is completely ridiculous," Jen says, turning towards Danny. "Get Ryan off him now, Danny. Or I'll never forgive you."

Danny swiftly drags Ryan away, and then it's Liam's turn to throw a punch. He's pulled away by Bettsy.

My heart drops in my chest because I know Liam's previous hit on Johnny was a warning, and this will definitely be a suspension if Coach finds out. Next thing I know, Johnny also swings at Matt, then Coach bursts in.

"What the hell is going on?" he bellows. Every gaze falls on Matt, who is now bleeding. His nose is streaming red, and he uses the sleeve of his jersey to control the flow.

But the next voice is Liam's.

"Touch her again, and I'll fucking kill you. That's a promise."

Coach looks like he's on fire. Even I'm terrified of him. "Everyone out, except you lot," he says, pointing at Johnny, Liam, Ryan and Matt.

I begin to protest, but I'm quickly pulled away and lined up with everyone in the tunnel.

"What the hell happened?" Danny asks, and I waste no time telling him what he said to Jen. Before continuing my recount, Coach emerges from the dressing room and stands in front of me.

"My office, now," he says, before disappearing out of sight.

I hesitate for a moment before hurrying along after him, tapping on the door that swings open immediately.

"Coach, please don't suspend Liam—" I begin, but he interrupts me.

"Did Rodgers offer you money in exchange for sexual favours?" he asks abruptly.

"I, uh, yes. But I didn't—"

"Well, it appears that he had no problem boasting about his attempt to your brother and both Preston boys. Of course, this provoked a response from everyone, but I wanted you to know that I don't tolerate such behaviour."

I'm confused for a moment, thinking he means that he doesn't tolerate the retaliation, but he goes on to say that he's suspending Matt and will look to investigate further.

I can't help myself. The next thing I know, I'm filling Coach in on what Matt said to Jen.

"Christ, no wonder they were so keen to get rid of him," Coach says under his breath before dismissing me.

I slip out of his office and into the tunnels, almost walking into Liam. It appears to be his turn to eavesdrop.

"I want to know everything he said to you," he says. Giving no warning, he pulls me into him and holds me tightly to his chest. And for some reason, I start to cry.

"It doesn't matter now anyway," I say.

He pulls back, kisses my cheek and wipes away a tear that rolls down my face. "It matters to me. You always matter to me."

As I'm beckoned by Jen towards the ice because the guys have a game to play, Liam's words ring in my head. *You always matter to me.*

But I didn't tell him. I couldn't face saying those words out loud again. I wanted to let it go.

Chapter 29

I'll always remember the first Christmas I spent with Vicky. I'd been pleading with my mom for weeks to let Vicky join us for the holidays, but she reminded me she had her own family and her own parents, who would probably want to spend time with her.

We went skating on the morning of Christmas Eve. I'd bought her a new scarf, and I was so excited to gift it to her. It was teal and fluffy and warm and perfect for winter. She still has the scarf now; it's tatty, but she refuses to get rid of it.

"Excited about tomorrow?" I'd asked her as we headed to get a hot chocolate after skating. Christmas was a huge thing in my house. My mom always went crazy with the decorations, the food, and the family time. We played games in our pyjamas all day and then watched a movie, eventually being so full that we'd fall asleep in front of the TV. But the look on her face broke my heart.

"Not really," she said. "My dad will just spend the day moping about, and my mom is working."

"Really?" I said.

"It's no big deal. It's just like another day for me and Johnny. Nothing special happens. We've tried to make it exciting, but it's not the same, is it?" She frowned and then sniffed.

"Yeah, but you get to open presents, right?"

"Not really. I mean, Johnny and I just get a cheque each. I'm not ungrateful or anything, but I'd rather they got us a pair of socks each—or something—and spent the day with us. It's not about the money or the gifts."

I didn't think I could feel anymore crushed, but I did. The thought of Vicky and Johnny sitting there on Christmas Day as if it was any other day.

"What about food?" I asked.

"What about it? Johnny and I will probably just make some grilled cheese or whatever."

That was the breaking point for me.

"How come you've never told me this before?"

"It doesn't matter," she shrugged. "I'm not bothered."

But I could tell she was. Then it clicked why she hated her birthday too. Like it was an inconvenience to her parents rather than a celebration.

She told me that one year Johnny had to remind their folks it was her birthday—on her actual birthday. That killed me. Probably because my parents made a whole fuss out of mine. Ryan and I weren't used to it being anything other than exciting.

But Christmas is supposed to be all about family, and it sounded like her parents didn't care.

When my mom pulled up outside the barn and we climbed into her truck, I wanted to come straight out with it; but I also didn't want to embarrass Vicky.

I saw Vicky to her door, kissed her, and went back to my mom with a heavy heart. It took her all of five seconds to ask me what I was so upset about.

"She doesn't even get a gift, Mom," I said. "What kind of sick parents do that? I mean, I understand that not everyone can afford it, but they have a lot of money!"

"Liam, it's not our business."

"What's that supposed to mean? She has grilled cheese on Christmas Day— as a main meal!"

That got Mom's attention.

"Maybe I'll call Stuart and invite them all over. I mean, I always go overboard, so a few extra people will be fine."

It turned out that Stuart was delighted for Johnny and Vicky to spend Christmas with us. He was hoping to visit an old friend in Vancouver and could drop them off on the way. My blood boiled at the thought of him just abandoning his kids, but I was grateful that my mom had offered. I knew both Vicky and Johnny would have a blast with us.

I got my dad to take me to the closest store that was still open late on Christmas Eve, and I bought Vicky a pair of novelty Santa socks. I wrapped them up and put them under the tree. And every year since, I buy her a pair of novelty socks, mostly ones with Santa on them when possible. Even when we haven't been in a good place, I've always made sure she had Santa socks.

"Two pairs?" she asks, beaming at me.

"One's for last year because I didn't get the chance to give them to you, did I? But we won't talk about that."

"You're so thoughtful. Thank you."

Christmas music blasts from the TV in her apartment. Ryan and Jenna, still in their newly wedded bubble, sit on the other side of the room exchanging gifts.

"You're welcome." I pull her on top of my lap and nuzzle at her neck. "Hey, do you still have that scarf I got you?"

"Which one? You've got me loads of scarves."

"That teal one," I say.

"Again, which one?" she teases.

"The one I gave you on Christmas Eve, when—"

"I'm just teasing. I know which one. I love it. Which is why I don't wear it out anymore. It looks like I've worn it to death. It's in my closet. I'm surprised you didn't see it when you were snooping."

She leans in and kisses me, and my brain turns into a fuzzy mess. We still haven't had sex, and I think we're now at the point where it may be awkward if someone tries to initiate it.

"Do you want your present now?" she says, pulling a gift bag out from behind her.

I peek into the bag and pull out a guitar pick. "I couldn't afford to get you a guitar, though, but I thought I'd see if Danny will let you borrow his. He said he doesn't use it."

"Wow! It's been a while since I've played. I doubt I'll even remember, but I appreciate it. Thanks."

I stopped playing when Vicky called the wedding off, and it's something I've put into the very back of my mind. I didn't bring a guitar with me, nor do I really know if I want to play again.

"I just want you to know that I love your playing and your singing voice. And I have no photos of you with your guitar."

"None at all?"

"No. I was always so enamoured that it never occurred to me to pause and take a photo."

"You know what? I'll get a guitar. It may be fun to play again."

Without Vicky, I sort of lost all joy for music. I thought it would be something that would keep me going, but it was just another thing that reminded me of her. Except with music, it was easily pushed aside—unlike hockey.

The day goes by in a blur of laughter and what Jen calls 'merriment.' It's not until eight in the evening when we hear from Johnny; we're still sitting here in paper crowns. He tells us he spent Christmas with his mom.

"Is Mom there?" Vicky asks Johnny via the screen of the iPad.

"Nah, she got called in. But she said hi." I know Vicky is disappointed, even if she says she isn't. "I haven't seen Dad though. I think he's in Vancouver."

Vicky scoffs, "Probably with his new family."

And then the weirdest thing happens—Johnny giggles. He actually giggles at something, or someone, off screen. "Who're you with, John?" I ask.

"Look, I've got to go," he says. And in a blink, the call ends and we're sitting here looking at an empty screen.

"That was weird," I say.

"That's probably why he wanted to go home. Knowing Mom would be at work, and Dad would do whatever the hell he's doing—I bet Johnny is still seeing someone, or he's got a hooker."

Ryan scoffs. "Johnny would rather jerk off for the rest of his life than pay for sex."

"I don't understand why he's being so secretive though," Vicky says.

"Probably the same reason you two are." Ryan looks between me and Vicky.

"We're not being secretive," Vicky says.

"Then what are you being? Are you back together, or ...?"

"We don't have to answer that," Vicky says.

"And how do you feel about that, Lee?" Ryan asks me.

"I, um, I guess we haven't decided or put a label on it. Do we need to? I mean—"

"Well, you obviously don't have to put a label on it, but would you consider seeing other people?" Ryan says.

"No, but—"

"So, what are you doing, then? This is exactly what I was referring to."

"What?" Confusion hits me now.

"Ry, keep out if it. It's none of our business," Jen says.

"It'll be my business when Vicky calls it all off again at a moment's notice."

"Excuse me—!"

"That's enough." Jen, the voice of reason, interjects, and we're saved by the bell as Danny and Hutch arrive with one of those mini keg machines. But it's bugging me. What are we doing? I don't want to be seeing anyone else. Does Vicky?

"Does it bother you? That we haven't put a label on it?" Liam says as soon as my bedroom door is closed.

Yes. Yes, it does. But the fear of scaring him off forces me to lie. "No. Does it bother you?"

"No. But just so you know, I'm not seeing anyone else."

I climb into bed and wait for Liam to get undressed. There's just something about the way he moves that just keeps me wanting to look at him. But right now, I'm fixed on the muscles of his arm. My eyes navigate to the tattoo of a camera.

"Nor am I," I say. He's standing there in his underwear now, and I suddenly feel really self-conscious. "How do you not look like you've eaten your body weight in food today?" I ask.

He shrugs. "Dramatic change of subject there, Vic."

"I'm just saying, you look like you've just come from the gym!" And then a thought flashes into my mind. "Oh, my God. You know I'm never watching our tape, don't you?"

"Why are you being so random? What's going on?"

"When are you going to the gym next?" I ask. My mind is whirling.

"Vic, you're making no sense. Start from the beginning." He slides into bed next to me and rolls over so he's looking at me.

"Don't look at me!"

"What the hell is going on?"

"I've definitely eaten too much today," I say.

"Everyone has, it's Christmas. But what are you getting at?"

"I've definitely put on a few pounds since college. And you look like a chiselled masterpiece."

"You have not!"

"I have, and now—"

He kisses me. "Calm down. You're beautiful, and I'm still just as attracted to you now as I was when I first saw you."

"You were attracted to me when you first saw me?" I blink at him.

"Why are you so surprised?"

"You avoided me for a long time."

"I was a teenage boy with a crush on his best friend's sister. What do you expect?"

"Hmm, I guess that makes sense."

"Now, take your panties off and spread your legs. I'm going to get a towel. I've been wondering if I can make you squirt again." I wasn't horny before, but the way he says it has my legs slightly wobbly with anticipation. "Actually, you should pee first, remember?"

I can feel the heat flooding my face. I do remember. I remember him reading up about it and learning about the dos and don'ts of it all. I thought it sounded disgusting at first, but the orgasm was something else. I get up and use the bathroom, trying to stop my legs from shaking. By the time I make it back to bed, he's laid a towel down, and he's grinning like the Cheshire Cat.

"On the bed, legs spread, baby girl," he says, grabbing my hips. But to my surprise, he pushes me onto my knees and shoves me forward so my ass is in the air. I position myself so I can peer at him, even if it's a little awkward.

I'm fully exposed. The previous conversation is now a distant memory as he runs his palms up and down the backs of my thighs. Slow and steady. Teasing. I can feel myself getting wetter.

"Fuck, Vic, you're soaking wet already."

A single lick is all it takes to make me quiver. I gasp as his tongue brushes over my ass too. Then I feel a finger slip into my pussy, and he hits my G-Spot straight away as if he's reaching for a light switch.

"Do you like it when I lick your ass?" he says, his voice deepening. He knows I do. I sigh as his tongue flicks across my ass again before he works his way to my clit. "Tell me."

"Yes. I love it."

"Do you? Are you sure?"

"Yes. I——" my breath catches as he licks again.

"You're a dirty girl, aren't you? Tell me what I should do next."

He knows what I want next. "I want you to show me you're in charge," I say. Then, he spanks me before rubbing his hand over the patch he just spanked.

"Do you want more?" He pushes his finger back inside me.

"Yes," I say, almost shamefully. But I have no shame, really. I love it and I want more. I push back on his hand, desperate for friction.

"Fuck, you're so keen. Do you love fucking my finger, Vic?"

"Yes," I say, and he spanks me again. I'd rather I was fucking something else, but right now he could do whatever the hell he wants.

His thumb finds my clit, and he rubs quick circles. Then another slap on my ass.

"You're doing so good, Vic. You've made my dick so fucking hard, you know that? I love seeing how much you want me to make you come. Just relax."

He pulls his finger out, and his tongue replaces it. I can see stars.

"I'm so close," I breathe. It's a beg for him to make me come, but he stops.

"Flip over."

And when I do, he's looming over me with his dick in his hand, stroking it ever so slowly. I want to ask him to fuck me; to satisfy the ache deep inside me. But I can't get the words out. He pulls me towards him slightly, throwing my legs back so I'm open to him. His finger slips back inside my pussy. He rubs that spot inside me, gently at first, then with more pressure.

"Rub your clit. Show me how much you want to come." And I do. Because I'll do anything he tells me to. "How much do you want to come, Vic? Because you need to relax, remember?"

Then, to my complete surprise, he pulls my hand away from my clit and sucks my fingers. "Are you still on the pill?"

"What?"

"You heard me. Answer the question."

I nod, too horny to care at this point. He leans down and takes my clit into his mouth, sucking on it at first, then flicking it with his tongue.

"I think I'm going to come," I say, trying to go with it, relaxing as much as I can. He sits back on his calves and pushes down on my public bone as he rubs at my G-Spot. When I come, I let out a moan that turns into a gasping breath that I don't care if anyone hears. And in a flash, Liam pulls his finger away, and there's a gush of something.

"I couldn't help myself," he says, and I prop myself up, seeing his come over my pussy.

"That's hot," I say, my eyes glued to the scene. His come mixed with mine.

He leans forward and kisses me, his tongue eager and demanding. I give him what he wants.

"Just so you know, I really want to fuck you," he says, pulling away from me. He goes into the bathroom. I hear the water running, then he returns with a washcloth. "I need to be honest with you. I'm just afraid. I'm terrified that if we're having full on sex again, then I'll get even more attached than

I am already, and then I'm opening myself up for a broken heart. I know we've been over it, but I can't help how I feel, or how I felt. It's stuck with me."

"I know. I'm sorry." I clean myself up and toss the towel and the washcloth into my laundry basket.

"I'll get over it, I'm sure."

I straddle him after he lies on the bed next to me, still naked but completely absorbed by him.

"Marry me?" I ask. Not even sure where it came from.

"What?" his eyebrows do that thing they do as he looks right into my eyes.

"Marry me ... I mean ... I'm sick of all this. I never want to break your heart again, and I'll spend every single moment of my life trying to make it up to you. I hate myself for it, Lee."

"Love yourself, please. As much as I do." He leans in and kisses me, wrapping his arms around my back and running circles over my skin. I fling my arms around his neck, and he moves my body in slightly closer. I can feel his dick between us. Hard again. "Just know that I appreciate you asking, and it's not a no—"

"But it's not a yes either?"

"It's a 'park it' for now."

It's nothing less than I deserve. I know I haven't been a good person—I've been a shit person, really. But he lifts my hips up and sinks me down onto him. And that feeling, which I felt like I'd forgotten about, comes flooding back and everything else disappears. I feel full and satisfied and loved and everything else. I throw my head back as he moves my hips on him, gently rocking me as he kisses my breasts and takes a nipple into his mouth. This isn't the hard fucking that we love so much, where I'm letting him take control. He's making love to me like we're in a Hallmark movie, and I love it. The rhythm builds, and it's like we didn't just climax moments before because I'm panting his name as I come undone at the same time as he does.

Whatever label we haven't put on this doesn't matter because there's only one thing in the world that we could ever be. Us. Together.

Chapter 30

Liam

"We're all done guys," Vicky says, moving away from her camera. She's set up a camera on a tripod, facing a white screen that's been erected in the conference room. We've been recording a few candid takes of 'Ask Us Anything'—questions which fans have sent in.

"Coach wants us in the media room in fifteen minutes," Johnny says, gathering his stuff. "We need to go over some plays, and I think he's delivering some news."

We chat amongst ourselves for a minute, but I'm struggling to concentrate. Vicky is busying herself with something on her computer, and she looks hot. Hotter than usual. Either that or I'm horny. She's got this white blouse on and a grey pencil skirt that hugs her hips and ass. I want to know what colour panties she's wearing.

The guys file out, and I follow Danny, leaving the room empty bar Vicky. As soon as the guys congregate at the coffee machine towards the end of the corridor, next to the media room, I excuse myself to use the bathroom.

I don't really need the bathroom, but it's an excuse I'm happy to use since what I have planned won't take long. I slip back into the boardroom. Vicky's standing at the whiteboard now, her handwriting looping across the surface as she moves the marker. She halts when she notices me.

Making sure the door is closed, I close the blinds, causing the room to dim slightly. I'm behind her in a few short movements. I sweep the hair away from her left shoulder and place my head directly next to hers. She smells familiar; back to her original shampoo and that, mixed with the Chanel, is a fucking treat.

"What colour panties are you wearing?" I whisper, pushing myself into her.

She trembles slightly, turns her head so her lips are level with my neck and murmurs, "Why do you want to know?"

"I've been thinking about them all afternoon. I wanna know."

"Does it matter?"

I spin her around and push her against the whiteboard and her marker drops to the floor.

"Someone could come in, Lee." The tone of her voice doesn't match her words.

"Yeah, they could." I pull at her skirt, hitching it up around her waist.

"I like black. I like anything, actually. Shimmy those fucking things down so I can see your pussy." I un-buckle my belt, not able to contain myself much longer.

I adjust our position, so if someone came in, they'd see the back of me. But Vicky tries to pretend she's worried.

"Lee, someone could come in!" she says, but she grips the side of her panties with her thumbs and tugs them just below the 'v' between her legs. My mouth waters at the sight of her; she's wet already.

"Touch yourself," I say, lifting her chin so she's looking directly into my eyes. "Then let me taste your fingers."

She's playing nice and does what's she's told, dipping her fingers between her legs. She moans before bringing her hand up towards my chin.

I make a grab for her, groaning as I suck her fingers into my mouth. Glancing back at the door, I make a split decision and free my dick from my pants, pushing it towards her panties that are still resting just below her pussy.

I thrust a few times, feeling how wet she is, but she grips me with both hands, rubbing the head of my dick over her clit as she strokes me. The heat and the wetness of her makes my breath catch in my throat.

"You're keen," I whisper.

"I just love how hard you get for me," she says, our eyes still locked.

"Make yourself come with my dick. Eyes on me the whole time. I want to see your face when you come."

I press my forehead against hers. Our breath mingles, her panting gets heavier.

"You're fucking perfect, you know that? Use me, baby girl, make yourself come."

We both know we don't have long, so it builds up quickly until we're both moaning. I know she's getting close because she's picking up speed. She risks a glance downward, and—I must admit—I also take a glimpse, watching how she works my dick.

"Eyes on me, Vic. I need to see that beautiful face of yours when you come."

A few more rubs set her off. She gasps as she thrusts forward. I grip her neck to stop her collapsing onto me as she comes. I can't help but let that look of pure bliss on her face push me over with her. I let out a grunt of approval, coming straight into the crotch of her panties.

"Fuck."

There are footsteps in the corridor, and Vicky's eyes widen. She acts quickly, pulling her soaked underwear back up and pushing her skirt down. I get my dick away just before the door flies open.

"There you are!" Bettsy chimes, grinning.

"Here I am!" I say, in a sing-song voice, not even recognising it.

He looks between us and then at the blinds, his eyes working overtime, taking in the scene.

"Betts—"

"Please don't tell Johnny!" Vicky blurts out.

Bettsy raises his eyebrows, having pieced it all together.

"We need you in the media room, Lee. Coach is waiting."

Shit. Fuck. Shit. Of all the people who could walk in on that, it's Bettsy. Although, seeing Johnny would be a hell of a lot worse; but we all know by now, Bettsy can't help himself. He's like a goddamn foghorn for any information he thinks someone else may be interested in.

Bettsy turns on his heels and follows the corridor back towards the media room, leaving the door wide open.

"Lee, that can't happen again!" Vicky's voice strains.

"Relax, I'll talk to him," I say, leaning down to take her mouth with mine, lingering for a moment before pulling away. "And I want those fucking panties, baby girl."

The thought of her having to make it home in that condition causes my excitement to elevate again.

She rolls her eyes. "Go."

I accelerate my usual walking pace and reach the media room just as Danny and Bettsy are grabbing their coffees from the machine.

"Betts—"

"Just keep me out of it," he flashes, grabbing Danny's attention.

"What's going on? Keep you out of what?"

"Nothing," Bettsy snaps. "It's not my business."

He takes his coffee into the media room, leaving Danny.

"Shit. He just walked in on a moment," I say under my breath.

"With you and—oh!"

"We still haven't told Johnny yet and I don't want him finding out from someone else," I say to Danny but I don't have time to dwell on it. Coach pokes his head around the door to the media room and uses a beckoning finger towards us.

Once we slip through the door, my eyes find Johnny who's sitting at the far end of the room with Ryan. He's got his notepad out, and he's tapping his pen against the paper.

"Boys. Tell me about that fucking shit-show you called a game last weekend," Coach says as he fiddles with the projector. I sit down next to Danny just as the screen springs to life. "I appreciate we will not win every game, but some of us are getting sloppy, and I need to know what's going on. Or is it a case of the January blues?"

I want to engage with Coach's session, but I can't help but shift my gaze between Johnny and Bettsy—wondering how I tell Johnny that Vicky and I are fooling around again.

"Are you fooling around with Vicky?" Coach says and my eyes dart forward in a flash.

"I'm sorry what?"

"I asked if you're finding leadership tricky?"

"Oh. No, but I'm happy to—"

"Right, so," Coach cuts over me, "Owens, please take some time to adopt a leadership style akin to Preston here," he points at me, "because I'm thinking we need to re-consider the roles going forward." Everyone looks around in confusion. "Danny, you're going to take on the role as captain, effective immediately, and Johnny will take the A."

Complete disbelief creeps upon everyone's faces, and Bettsy is the first to address Johnny, asking him what's going on.

"Coach's choice," Johnny shrugs, then glances in my direction. It's definitely not Coach's choice. There's a look on Johnny's face.

Coach nods. "Let's move on. Anyway ..." he muses, then taps something into his laptop. A video of us sitting on the bench shows on the screen.

"The problem I see here," Coach says after a few minutes of playback, "is obvious. Any ideas?"

He looks around the room, trying to tempt someone into talking, but no one does. I take a punt.

"Communication?"

He nods, and then presses play again. But it's clear that no one is really paying attention, myself included. Everyone is looking between Johnny and Danny, wondering what the hell is going on.

For forty minutes we sit and pretend to focus. Forty long minutes.

When Coach finally powers down the projector and unplugs his laptop, he tells us we're to be on the ice at eight o'clock tomorrow morning for an extra practice. No exceptions.

As soon as we're dismissed, Johnny pushes his way to the door and bolts away before anyone can stop him.

Liam

Can you come to the conference room?

Liam

It's urgent.

Vicky

If this is to do with my underwear.

Liam

I promise you, it's not. Seriously.

I stare at the messages for a split second before telling Jen I need to excuse myself. I've got no idea what he wants, but playing the urgency card is not a good sign.

The first thing I notice about the conference room is that the blinds are closed. I slip in through the door, finding Liam, Ryan, and Johnny sitting in a huddle towards the window.

"Is everything okay?"

"Kind of. Johnny wants to talk and he didn't want to have to repeat himself, so you should listen too."

Closing the door behind me, I walk over to the window and sit in the empty chair next to Liam but Johnny doesn't even realise I'm there. When he talks, he's addressing Liam directly.

"I've fucked up, Lee and I can't keep it going. I don't even remember the last time I slept longer than a few hours. I—" Johnny cries. Like actual tears. Silent sobs. His shoulders are shaking with the effort of attempting to keep it in, but he's crying. I haven't seen him cry since... never. Not even when our parents told us they were getting a divorce. He showed zero emotion then.

"What's going on, Johnny?" I ask, but he doesn't respond. He takes a gulp of air, and Ryan shoves a bottle of water into his hands.

"What's going on?" Liam and Ryan both say in union.

"Let's just say that I totally understand all the stuff between you and Jenna." He cocks his head to look at Ryan. "And why you stayed." Ryan stayed because of Jenna, even if he doesn't want to admit it. Which means—

"Who is it, John?" Ryan asks, leaning in.

"I've fucked up, bad," he says again.

"What? Is she pregnant?" Liam asks.

Johnny shakes his head.

"Married?" Ryan asks.

Again, he shakes his head.

"Are you doing anything illegal?" Liam asks.

Johnny shakes his head, and relief washes over me. "No, but she's young."

"How young?" Ryan and Liam say, their voices merged again. I just watch the exchange, afraid to break the flow in case Johnny decides he wants to keep quiet after all.

"Nineteen. Which is young. When you're pushing close to thirty."

"Who is she? Do we know her?"

And then Johnny drops his head into his hands. "Bettsy's sister."

"Kelly?" I yelp.

"Well, what's the issue?" Liam asks.

"I made such a fucking big deal about you and Vicky getting back together," he says to Liam. "And look at me. Doing exactly the same thing, really. I mean, at first it was just a cover story as—it doesn't matter. But I'm a fucking mess. This whole situation is a mess."

"I still don't understand what the issue is," Liam says.

"I think I love her."

"I still fail to see the problem." Liam leans back in his seat.

"Move aside, Lee," I say, scooting in to sit directly in front of my brother.

"Johnny, look at me. It's okay." I know exactly what the problem is. Johnny thinks he's unlovable and he's scared about whatever he's feeling.

"Is that why you wouldn't play with Bettsy? Why you switched pairs?" Ryan says. He turns to whisper something to Liam. "But why did you give up your captaincy?"

"You did what?" My mouth drops open. "What do you mean, you've given it up?"

"I had no choice. What kind of leader does this? I'm not a good role model. I'm not even a good person."

"That's not true. Johnny, look at me." He forces his head away from his hands. There's sorrow in his eyes. "You can't help who you fall in love with, and since she's not married and not underage, what's actually stopping you?"

"I—"

"You need time to think," I say. "Does Michael know?"

"You can't tell Bettsy!" Johnny protests, as if I've asked him to step in to goal.

"Well, if you want to be with Kelly, then you'll need to. There's literally no reason not to tell him. He'll be fine."

It crosses my mind if this is a good time to be telling Johnny about me and Liam, but it passes when there's a knock at the door.

The GM sticks his head in.

"Everything okay? We've got a meeting—"

"Yep, just leaving, sir," I say, shoving Johnny's cap back on his head.

We usher him out, trying to ignore the queue of people waiting to go into the conference room as we pass.

"Well, what now?" Ryan asks.

"Can you take Johnny home? Make sure he gets some sleep. He may feel exhausted enough now he's got it off his chest—"

"I'm sorry, Vic," Johnny says. "I mean, I'm really sorry."

"I get it, don't worry."

I may tell Johnny not to worry, but I'm doing the worrying for both of us.

A week following, Johnny still hasn't told Bettsy, by all accounts. When I call in to see him before my Saturday session with the rugby team, he looks paler than ever. He answers his door in sweatpants and an old t-shirt that desperately needs to be laundered. Uneven stubble covers his usually clean-shaven face, and his hair, desperate for a cut, is a ruffled mess.

"Oh, Johnny," I say, throwing my arms around him. It's only been two days since I've seen him, but it's clearly been two days of complete heartache for him. And he does not smell fresh.

"She doesn't want to see me anymore," he says, returning my hug. "She said she can't keep it a secret any longer, and she doesn't want to see me until we figure it out."

"Well, that's easily fixed," I say optimistically. But when I see the inside of his apartment, I want to take it back. Johnny, who's usually so neat and tidy is living in a pigsty. This will not be easy at all.

I glance around before making my way to the window to pull open the curtains. I open the window to get some fresh air circulating and turn back to the living room to assess the extent of the mess.

There's a Johnny-shaped imprint on the sofa, and he climbs back into his spot to resume his wallowing.

"Oh no, you don't. You've got a game today. Snap out of it and focus," I say. "You're going to morning skate."

"I'm going to call Coach and tell him I've got the flu. I really can't face it today." He pulls a blanket over himself and buries his head in a cushion. Who even is this guy?

"This is what you're going to do. You're going to go the barn, you're going to suit up, you're going to tell Bettsy you're in love with his sister … and then this evening, you're going to win your game."

I wander into his kitchen and grab and a trash bag, skimming around his apartment with it and grabbing all the empties I can find. Luckily, there's no alcohol, but there is Red Bull.

"Christ, it's no wonder why you can't sleep." I shake an empty can at him. "Take a shower. I'll clean up and then I'll drive you. Enough is enough."

Tough love works with Johnny. He peels himself off the sofa and does what he's told. And by the time we're in the car, he at least looks like Johnny again.

"How's your diet?" I ask.

"Crap," he says, and I make a mental note to get Ryan to triple up on his batch cooking to help Johnny.

As we come to a stop in the players' parking lot, Johnny turns towards me before getting out.

"Thanks for putting up with all my crap, Vic. I know I've been a nightmare. Evasive. I borrowed money to pay your rent so you wouldn't have to move in with me and I could keep sneaking around with Kelly. What kind of brother does that make me?"

"Would it help if I told you I understand? I mean, Liam and I—"

"I know. Finally, I understand. And I know you need to do whatever the hell you need to do."

"I asked him to marry me, you know," I say.

"Yeah, I rem—"

"Again. At Christmas. He told me to park it. I don't even know if we're officially back together," I say.

Johnny turns to me and looks me right in the eye. "I don't think you were ever truly apart, Vic. Thanks for the ride."

Chapter 31

Liam

Lugging the junior's gear from the storage room to the dressing room usually takes at least three trips when you're on your own, which is why I roped Danny in to help me. He's also going to help me with the training session except he doesn't know it yet. In fact, the entire afternoon was a last-minute bribe. I promised to take him through the drive-thru on the way home. Ryan and Jen have an appointment with their lawyer about the house they're buying, and I know Danny has a shit-tonne of free time now he's officially single.

"You never know," I tell him as we dump the bags down. "You may get lucky with a hot hockey mom."

Danny rolls his eyes. "You're as bad as Bettsy. Maybe you should have asked him to help. Give him a chance."

Ever since Bettsy found out about Johnny and his sister, he's been complaining about everyone coupling up. He said he needs to up his game.

The whole conversation was odd. We all knew how Bettsy would react, but Johnny was a mess.

"Rather you than me," Bettsy said.

"Rather you than me?" Hutch interjected.

"What I mean is, she's annoying as hell, and I wouldn't want to share a bed with her."

"She's your sister!"

"Which is why she's annoying, and I don't want to share a bed with her!"

After that, defensive pairing one was reunited. It was as if nothing had happened—at least that's what they've led us to believe. Johnny has insisted that Danny stay as captain for the time being, though—just for a few more weeks.

"I get where Bettsy is coming from. It seems like everyone is pairing up," Danny says. "And I'm dreading the party because I know Becca will be there."

I wondered how long it would take him to bring up the party that Ryan and Jen are having. It's a wedding celebration party in the coming weeks, and they've invited everyone, including Danny's ex who's also an old friend of Jen's.

"Invite a hot hockey mom as your date, Dan. Or ask Bettsy about his other sister." I wink at him, but it's clear that he doesn't find it funny. "Look, I get it. I know how lonely it can be."

I remember too well about the long and lonely times back in Toronto.

Danny gives a subtle nod and disappears into the small storage cupboard. He returns with a bucket of pucks and continues to gather everything we need for the session.

I grab my skates and head towards the bench to get ready. As I bend forward to lace them up, a familiar flash of blonde hair catches my eye from across the ice. Vicky is walking slowly, as if deep in conversation, with a guy about my height that I recognise straight away. He's dressed overly formal for the setting, and I don't like the way his face looks from where I'm sitting.

They stop at the boards, leaning on the edge to look at the ice. He nudges Vicky, leans in as if he's saying something directly into her ear, and she laughs. Her hair falls back over her shoulders as she tilts her head back in amusement. I find myself clenching my fists.

"Oh, my god. Is Vicky with Neil Jenkins?" Danny's standing behind me, craning his neck.

"It looks like it, doesn't it?" I say, standing up.

Danny quickly skates towards the glass where Vicky and Neil stand, comes to a stop and leans in. I can see his animated conversational style in full swing as he also laughs at something Neil says.

The kids have grouped behind me, and I can tell they're waiting for instruction, so I grab my clipboard and flick through the sheets of paper that Ryan has prepped for me. But only half of my attention is on the lesson plan because I'm stealing glances to where Danny stands, still laughing. To add to my growing annoyance, a few of the kids pipe up and start pointing and jumping at the scene across the ice.

"Aww, do you think he'll give me his autograph?" one kid says, bouncing up and down on his skates.

But then Danny turns and hurries back towards us, beaming like a tendy who's just had a shutout.

"He said he's going to get me tickets," Danny says, holding his arm out in invitation for the kids to step onto the ice.

"Tickets?" I ask.

"Yeah, tickets. Rugby tickets. Maybe even Six Nations tickets if I pray hard enough." He rubs his hands together with glee then reaches over to the bench to grab his gloves.

He talks and talks about what Neil has achieved during past seasons before switching to his career as an international rugby star. But I stop listening because I spot them walking away, and Neil's hand definitely hovers over

Vicky's lower back. If I had a stick in my hands, I'd be checking its flexibility right now. The jealousy I recall from 'Meet the Players' returns, making me reconsider taking that stupid quiz.

Watching them walk away, I feel possessive towards Vicky.

My heart ached in my chest when Vicky asked me to marry her because I was planning on asking her. It may seem completely ridiculous to everyone else, but we're all or nothing. We can grow together and help each other overcome our torments as a team. Or at least that was my plan, anyway.

I slip my hands into my gloves and grab my stick, my eyes drifting across the fresh tape job that Vicky did this morning. Then I remember the actual sex tape that Vicky thinks she has in her wardrobe, and I know it's time to take action.

Liam's sitting on the bench lacing his skates, and I can't take my eyes off him. If I remembered he would be here today for the junior session, I'd never have suggested giving Neil a quick tour. Not that I didn't want to introduce him to hockey, but I didn't want Neil or Liam getting the wrong idea.

I'm doing a good job at faking my amusement to Neil—or at least, I think I am. He's talking about a game he played last week, but my attention is still fixed on the bench where Danny is now standing next to Liam.

As soon as he spots Neil and me, he beams. I watch him skate over in a hurry, and he stops in front of the glass.

"This is Danny Owens. He's on the team with Johnny. I think he's helping with the junior session today," I say to Neil.

I've already filled Neil in on the team, and even though he hasn't officially met Johnny, he saw him when I first went to the rugby club to take photos.

"I love seeing the kids rising through the ranks," he says. "How's it going mate?" Neil greets Danny as best as he can through the gap in the glass, and they chat back and forth, laughing in intervals. I'm still fixed on Liam who's flicking through a clipboard, pretending to concentrate.

Neil says something that makes Danny break out in a raucous laughter, so I join in—just in case I missed the world's funniest joke.

"You're doing well this season," Danny shouts. "I need to come and watch soon. I haven't been to the rugby in ages."

"If you want tickets, I can sort you out with some," Neil says to Danny. "I'll put Vicky down for two. You can come with her and keep her company until after the game." He winks at Danny, who forces a laugh.

"Oh, you're being serious?" Danny says. "I'd love to, I mean, that'd be great, cheers!"

Danny's expression surprises me. At first, I think he's going to cry, but when he smiles, I feel a bead of dread sitting low in my stomach. I guess I'm going with Danny to a rugby match.

"Okay, we'll sort it out then. I've got to go, but it was great meeting you. Thanks for the tickets."

We wave to Danny as he skates back towards the bench.

"Ready?" I say.

We walk towards the double doors to the lobby and Neil makes another terrible joke, but I fake another laugh to be polite. People pleaser Vicky is coming in handy.

"Are you sure I can't tempt you to have dinner with me?" he asks, but I shake my head. "A drink then?"

I guess I'd give him a ten for effort, but even though I know Liam and I haven't put a label on us, I don't want to go out with anyone else. Neil's asked me every time I've seen him. I hoped that my saying no earlier would be the end but hearing him asking again now gives me a bigger 'ick' than I had before.

"I appreciate the offer, I really do, but I need to remain professional." I commend myself for pulling that one out of the bag.

We enter the lobby which is now quiet, despite it being just half an hour until public skate starts, and we head towards the public lockers. Neil fishes in his pocket for his key and slides it into the locker nearest the door.

"Well, thanks for the tour. Let me know if you change your mind," he says, pulling his bag out. "Oh, and I almost forgot. This is for you, a thank you for all your hard work." He unzips the top of his bag and reaches in, pulling out a rugby jersey. "It's from last year's 'Six Nations.' They don't usually put our surnames on the back, but they did last year." He holds it out to me. Where I come from, giving someone your jersey is more than just a thank-you. But I feel obliged to take it.

"If you ask at the desk here, they can set you up——"

Liam's showing someone to the front desk, and glances over to where Neil and I are standing, the jersey clutched in my hands. Looking down, I definitely notice Jenkins is proudly on display to any onlooker, Liam included. I feel a tug of embarrassment in my chest.

With a polite smile and nod, he greets us and leaves, the left door closing with a thud.

"Are you okay, Vicky?" Neil adjusts himself so he's standing right in front of me. "You've gone pale."

"I'm fine," I say, and I hand back the jersey to Neil, who accepts it reluctantly. "I'm sorry—I can't accept this. I appreciate the kind gesture, I really do ... but I can't." He nods and shoves the shirt back into his bag.

The atmosphere between us turns awkward, and I can't see him out quickly enough. I'm careful not to promise to see him soon, because I now feel like I have no choice but to call Dean, from the Echo, and withdraw from my agreement to help with the photography. While the money was helpful, I know I'm done photographing the rugby team.

As I watch Neil walk away, I wonder if things would have been different if I was attracted to him. Honestly, I can't remember when I last had feelings for someone other than Liam. Suddenly, I'm crying. Not full-on crying, but my eyes prickle with tears.

I make my way upstairs to the staff washroom and help myself to a tissue, trying to fix my mascara.

I smell his cologne first. Then his body fills the space behind me. Liam addresses me via the mirror. "I need to stop following you into the ladies' room." I stare back at him. He steps closer and puts his hands on the counter, one on each side of me. I'm boxed in. "The tattoo under your left breast.

What does it say?" He talks directly into my ear; my skin prickles.

"Forty-six," I say, still gazing back.

"And we both know you didn't get it as a birthday reminder."

I swallow. I know what he's alluding to, but I want to hear him say it. "Tell me I'm yours, and we'll quit the games."

Pushing my hair aside, his lips brush my neck. I roll my head to the side, giving him all the access he needs. Electricity flows between us as he nibbles at my skin. His arms wrap around me, and he cups my boobs in his hands. Squeezing and kneading, his kisses become demanding. He frees a hand and grabs my chin, thrusting my mouth towards his. Our lips meet as a growl escapes him.

"Why do you have jeans on today?" he complains but I pop my button and shimmy them down my legs, hoping we can make it work.

I hear him fumble with his belt before he unzips his pants, and in a swift movement, his dick is sitting between my ass cheeks.

"Bend forwards," he says, pushing me down. The mirror gives me the opportunity to watch his every move, and I'm living for it. The muscles in his arms twist as he positions himself to run his hands over my ass. "Your skin is so soft—do you want me to be gentle?"

I bite my lip and shake my head.

Spank.

"Do you?"

"No."

He pulls at my panties, pushing them to the side before rubbing the head of his dick up and down my pussy. I gasp and push back, almost desperately.

"Someone could come in, Lee, we don't—"

And he sinks into me. It takes me by surprise, even though I know it was his intention. Since my legs are pretty much closed, restricted by my jeans, he feels even bigger than usual.

"Fuck, you're tight. Do you enjoy watching yourself getting fucked, baby girl?"

"Yes!" As he thrusts into me, the air escapes my lungs, and I gasp to take in a fresh breath.

And then he says something that would probably be awkward to hear normally, but as he slams into me, it makes perfect sense. He asks me if I belong to him. He asks me whose number I should be wearing. But then I'm coming with a silent scream, my eyes rolling back in my head.

"You're fucking perfect, Vicky. You're such a good girl for me."

Then he pulls out and instructs me onto my knees. My jeans make it awkward, but I sink down anyway. He pushes the tip of his dick between my lips, and I let him fuck my throat. It's over in seconds as he holds my head still, groaning as he comes. Lifting me to my feet, he kisses me as he tucks himself away.

"Did you leave Danny in charge?" I ask, pulling my jeans up.

"Yeah, shit. I better go."

And as the door swings closed behind him, I thank the stars that no one caught us. But I'm wondering if that makes us officially back together.

Chapter 32

Ryan's Jeep comes to a stop in front of a large two-storey house nestled behind a gated driveway. There's a sejant stone lion on one side of the entrance, perched on a pillar, and the remnants of a similar statue on the opposite side—once a matching pair.

"It needs a bit of work, but I'm excited. You're still helping, right?" he says, his voice bubbling with excitement.

"Do I have a choice?"

Ryan hops out of the Jeep and unlocks the chain holding the gates closed. He rummages for a second, then pushes it open before getting back in the car.

"I want to get some electric gates installed," he says. "You can get some that open when they recognise your license plate."

He comes to a stop in the middle of the driveway and signals for me to follow him inside with a nod.

"It's a nice place from the outside," I say. "Are you going to resurface the parking area?"

"Yeah, once the inside is done. But how did the kids do yesterday? Did you follow the plan?"

"Yes. Danny was great with them, actually. I think he enjoyed it more than he cared to admit. That rugby guy was back, though," I say as he unlocks the front door.

"Oh yeah? What did he want?"

"Vicky was giving him a tour," I say as we step inside. There's an open entranceway with a staircase that runs up the middle. It looks very similar to the house Vicky lived in when we were growing up.

"Kitchen's this way," he says. I follow him into a sizable room, an island in the middle with a breakfast bar facing a sliding door which opens out on the garden. I walk to the window and look out.

"Looks good. Congratulations, bud. It's all happening for you, isn't it?"

"It's taken a fucking age. Jen said it would have been even slower with a mortgage.

I follow him into the living area, admiring the fireplace in the far corner. I can see how cosy it will look once Ryan's done the work he's planning.

"So, what about the rugby guy?" Ryan prompts.

"Oh, yeah. Well, they were talking and laughing, and then Danny went and joined in on the talking and the laughing—" I pause, wondering if I'm overreacting.

"What?"

"It's nothing," I say.

"Are you sure?"

"I went into the lobby to show one mom—anyway, it doesn't matter. He offered Vicky his rugby shirt."

Ryan sucks in a breath in through his teeth. "Competition?"

"Nah, she turned it down, but it's been bugging me. I keep replaying it in my mind. Why is it bothering me so much?" I leave out the bit about me following her to the washroom.

We go up and circle the landing.

"Probably because of what it signifies to you. I mean, I thought I didn't care about crap like that, but it bothered me to see Jen wearing Danny's jersey, and they were just friends."

"I guess so," I say, checking out the big-ass windows in the main bedroom.

"And you still don't know what you're doing, I guess? Are you back together?"

"She asked me to marry her. Christmas Day." Sharing that with my brother makes me feel like a weight has been lifted.

"Fuck. What did you say?"

"I suggested we park it because I want to be the one to ask her. It sounds ridiculous, doesn't it? Hey, this bathroom is huge."

"We can stick a corner bath-tub in. One with jets and shit. That's the selling point of this place."

"What, a bathtub?"

"A bathtub for two!"

We mosey through the rest of the house, mulling over the situation I'm finding myself in. I have no problem with Vicky being friends with a guy, but when said guy offers you his game-worn jersey, there's a different intention.

"I need to figure this out," I say to Ryan as we look out of the window of the third bedroom.

"Just give her your jersey," he says with a shrug.

"Nah, she's not like Jen. She hasn't worn one of my jerseys since college. It wouldn't match her shoes, would it?"

He sniggers. "It's more for the gesture. Even if it just hangs in her closet with the rest of them." He wiggles his eyebrows.

"Huh?" I pause for thought again, considering what to do next, but then I notice the dark brown wood everywhere. It's not Ryan at all. "On a completely different note, are you keeping the mahogany? Because it looks old-fashioned."

"Nah, we're ripping all that out. Which is where you come in. I think the walls and ceilings are good, but the base boards, architraves, doors... basically everything wooden is coming out and being replaced. We start on Monday."

"We?"

"Yeah, Johnny, and Bettsy are helping too. Jen is trying to persuade Danny. The more hands, the quicker we'll get it done. Then we can have a party."

"Are you still going ahead with that gym?"

"Yeah, but that's taking a lot longer because it's a commercial property."

We wander around the upstairs for a while longer, assessing what needs to be removed, and I check out the loft space—because I'm nosey. At the top of the stairs, a moment of realisation dawns upon me.

"I can't start on Monday," I say. "I need to do something. But if all goes well, I'll be here on Wednesday."

"What do you need to do?" Ryan asks.

"I'll tell you Wednesday, if it all goes to plan."

"If it doesn't go well, you're still telling me all about it."

Downstairs, Ryan opens the back door to the garden. The area is enormous, and I wouldn't be surprised if they were planning to get a dog or something next.

"So, what do you think?" he asks. "I mean, there's shit loads to do, and it feels a little overwhelming, but I'm sure you and Vicky need your own space."

We head back into the house, and Ryan locks the door behind him. Just as the doorbell rings.

"Any more thoughts on next season?" he says.

"I'll tell you Wednesday."

I head straight to the kitchen and pour myself the largest glass of wine I can muster. It's been a long week, and it's only Monday. Why does January seem endless?

I take a gulp from my glass and step out of my shoes before opening the fridge and peering inside. I close it, then open it again, hoping that something may have appeared in the interim. No such luck. Logging into my internet banking to check if I can afford a takeout, I spy an incoming transaction from Liam and make a mental note to send it back to him after I make myself some cereal. All I want to do is change into my loungewear, watch 'Grey's Anatomy' and block out the rest of the world.

I open my bedroom door and put my glass down on my desk, not bothering to turn on the light. But as I move towards my closet, I spot a dark object on my bed that definitely wasn't there earlier. I backtrack to the door and switch on the light.

A gasp escapes my throat and I look around as if I'm expecting someone to jump out on me, declaring that this is a prank, or that I'm still sleeping. A navy blue rectangular box, embossed with the Maple Leafs logo, sits there—unassuming, in the middle of my bed.

I stare at it for a moment, wondering what to do next. I mean, the answer is obvious, but I can't quite bring myself to step forward just yet. Grabbing my glass, I down another gulp of wine and take a breath before stepping forward.

There's a flap running across the long edge that faces me, magnetised down. It lifts with ease, and the lid flips back. I stare at it for a moment. The jersey, blue and white, stares back at me. My eyes flick towards the plaque on the inside of the lid that sits below another Maple Leaf logo with 'Toronto Maple Leafs Hockey Club' embossed below.

46

LIAM PRESTON

FIRST GAME PLAYED AS A MAPLE LEAF

TORONTO MAPLE LEAFS VS PITTSBURGH
PENGUINS

Over the date, there's a Post-it note, Liam's messy handwriting scrawled across the yellow paper. My heart thumps into next week.

A pair of arms engulf me from behind, and Liam's chin rests on my shoulder. "I'm done fucking this up, Vic," he says. I didn't hear him come in but the fact that he is in doesn't surprise me either. "If you don't want this, I'll understand. But that's the end. Neither of us can keep going like this."

I stand completely rooted to the spot, unable to move. He sweeps my hair to the side and plants a single kiss on my neck and then he spins me around and drops to one knee.

"Victoria Elizabeth Koenig, will you wear my jersey?"

I gape at him but when he breaks out into the smile, I can't help but giggle. "You're a doofus," I say, shoving his shoulder. "But I'll consider it."

The first time Liam gave me his sweater was after the first game when we were officially 'boyfriend and girlfriend.' I remember climbing out of my dad's car and spotting Liam leaning against the railing next to the rink entrance. He had his gear set down beside him, except for a jersey of his which was slung over his shoulder.

I remember thinking he looked so cool and how he even acknowledged my existence blew my mind. He could've had any girl he wanted, from school or hockey. But he was looking right at me. I walked towards him, leaving Johnny rummaging around in the trunk, looking for a rogue shin pad that had fallen out of his bag.

During that evening's game, he'd scored a goal. And I watched from the side of the ice as he dropped to one knee during his celebration lap before quickly skating back over to the net and seeking the puck out with his stick. He skated over to me, flicked it over the glass with a wink, then he skated away. It was another puck to add to my collection—all while I wore his road jersey.

Reflecting on those heart-pounding moments, I wonder why? Why did it take me so long to understand that being happy with him, even for a short time, is better than not being with him at all?

"We both know what I'm really asking here, Vic. Marry me? And I mean, actually marry me. Let's drive to Scotland and get married and forget about all the heartache and whatever."

I pull him up to his feet and cup his face in my hands, standing on my tiptoes. "Yes. A million times. Because I'm also sick of this back and forth."

"I love you."

"I love you."

After a moment of staring, Liam spins me around once more.

"I don't suppose you've looked in the box yet?" he says.

"At your jersey?"

"At what's under there."

"No …" Lifting the jersey up, feeling the weight of it. I slip it over my head and enjoy the heaviness of the material on my shoulders. It completely engulfs me, and I love it. But then I spot the disk that's sitting in the otherwise empty box.

"What's this?" I ask, picking it up. But I know full well what it is. "Is this the—?"

"Yes."

"Then what's the—"

"That's how I knew you didn't watch it because what you found before was my original proposal. Remember when I said I had it all planned out? Do you want me to put it on?"

"Wait. What is going on here?" I ask. "There're two disks?" I make a hurry for my closet, pulling out the box where I hid the sex tape. I fish it out, looking at it. There's a tiny 'V+L' written next to the hole in the middle. I look back at Liam who's standing next to the empty box, holding the second disk.

"This is the sex tape. That is my planned engagement tape. Or CD, I should say."

I step a couple of paces to my desk, reaching for my laptop and running my finger along the side of the computer.

"Does your laptop have a disk drive? Why is there no disk drive on this thing?" I panic.

He grabs his backpack from the hallway and pulls his computer out, setting it next to mine on my desk. He powers it on and we watch as Windows suggests now is a good time to finalise updates.

"Which one do you want to watch first?" he asks into my ear but I'm already fumbling with the button on the side which pops open the disk drive. I press the disk into the drive, push it closed and give Liam some space to make it play.

Finally, there on the screen, is a slide show of our entire lifetime together in photos, then a few home videos, then, to my complete surprise, Lois' beautiful face pops onto the screen.

"Hey sweetie, if you're watching this, I know he's finally gone and done it, but I just wanted you both to know, I'm proud of you, and I love you so much. Take care of each other, especially when times are tough. Remember why you came together in the first place. I know if you really want to, you'll make it work. I know neither of you are perfect, but you bring out the best in each other. Enjoy the time you have together because you really don't know how long you have. And make sure you separate your whites from your colours, or it'll ruin your clothes—"

"Christ, Mom, you can stop now—" Liam's voice cuts across Lois' at the end and then more pictures cycle through the screen.

But I'm laughing. And I'm crying. I don't even know the whole range of emotions I'm feeling now, but Liam's arm wraps around me again, and I feel completely elated and normal all the same time.

"Still keen?" he says.

"Yes," I nod, my eyes fixed on the screen as more pictures fly by.

My left hand is tugged away from my side, and he holds it out in front of us for a second before slipping a familiar ring onto my finger.

"She wanted you to have this. I can get you a new one if you want."

"No. It's perfect."

I spin around and kiss him as if it's the first time.

Epilogue

Liam

"I'm so glad Johnny is back to being captain," Danny says.

I unlock the door to our apartment, and we go inside. We have about ten minutes to get ready before we're off for what the guys are calling my 'Stag Do.' We both head straight to our rooms to change our clothes. The rest of the guys are meeting us downstairs for taxis.

As soon as I open my door, I can tell there's someone in my space, and the intoxicating perfume makes my dick twitch. The two things combined make me excited despite my inner battle to maintain sensible control: Vicky and my bedroom.

"How did you get in here?" I ask her. She's standing at the large window, looking out at the parking lot.

"I have my ways," she says, spinning around. She steps forward, her heels clicking on the hardwood floor, coming to stop right in front of me.

"I've missed you."

I drop my bag and stare at her, wondering what she's going to do next.

She leans up and positions her mouth directly near that spot on my neck that I love so much, my cock rock solid now, the anticipation driving me crazy.

"Let me help you relax before your night out," she whispers.

She opens her long coat to reveal what she's wearing underneath. She's standing there in my Leafs jersey, stockings, and a pair of heels. I can't move. I'm in awe, probably drooling a little, if I'm honest.

I can hardly contain myself as she wriggles out of her panties, tossing them towards me, forcing me to catch them. Then she pulls the jersey over her head and lays it down on my bed.

What a fucking sight. I can't resist giving her panties a small amount of attention before I step forward and cup her face in my hands, leaning down and meeting her lips with mine.

Electricity flows through us as our tongues meet. I run my hand through her hair, taking care not to lose the attention I'm giving her lips.

"Be a good girl for me, Vic, and stand at the window. Hands out in front of you on the glass," I say, breaking away.

She does as she's told, settling herself into position and looking back at me, lips full and pouty.

"Spread your legs," I say as I close the gap to stand behind her. "Good girl."

I give her ass a playful slap before leaning to kiss her again. She gasps when she hears the zipper of my dress pants. I pull my dick out and run the tip along her freshly waxed pussy, savouring a moment on the little bit of a landing strip she's left for me.

My middle finger presses into her and she groans, pushing herself back into me. She's fucking soaking, and I use her moisture to rub above her clit gently before thrusting my dick into her. I can't hold off. I need to be inside of her. Fuck, I always forget how good she feels—either that or she just keeps getting better.

"Does it turn you on, Vic? Knowing that anyone could be watching you getting fucked?" I rock myself into her before pulling out, slow and steady.

She doesn't answer, so I give her another prompt, refusing to resume the thrusts that I know she's aching for.

"Yes, love," she finally says, and I push into her, feeling her pussy grip around my dick.

"You're so fucking good, Vic, taking my dick like you do. You're so fucking horny for me, aren't you? Not caring who's watching you?" I thrust in and out. It's not a fast rhythm, but I need to pace myself.

"Give it to me, please," she begs.

I give her what I can, looking down slightly so I can watch my dick disappear inside her.

"Play with your clit. Make yourself come over my cock," I breathe into her ear.

She repositions herself slightly, and her right hand disappears. I keep pumping into her.

She comes undone in seconds, almost screaming, and I'm almost fucking done myself because she feels incredible, her pussy squeezing my dick as she comes.

"I'm close," I warn her.

"Where do you want to come?" she asks, and I never tire of it.

"I want to watch your reflection when I empty into your—" I can't even finish my sentence because my orgasm takes over as I pound into her one last time, spilling deep. Fuck me, she's incredible.

I pull out and she steadies herself, my come dripping out of her. What a beautiful fucking sight.

I head into the bathroom quickly and bring out a washcloth for her. "You did so well, baby," I say, kissing her forehead.

She nods and we embrace for a moment before she cleans up. I'm eyeing her breasts as she heads over to my closet and pulls out a t-shirt. I'm disappointed that I didn't get to play with her nipples.

"What?" she grins.

"You're incredible. And the sex is alright too," I laugh. "You're making me not want to go out tonight, that's for sure."

"Did you tell them we're already married?"

"Nah, Bettsy's so excited about planning a bachelor party that it'd kill him if I didn't go."

There's a knock on the door and Danny's voice chimes through. "Lee, you ready, mate?"

"I'll catch you up." I shout back. "Text me where you are, and I'll come and find you. I'm not done yet."

I'm definitely not done. And I don't think I'll ever be done.

Playlist

Special Thanks to Caroline Taylor and Amy Sykes

One More Time – Blink 182
Here to Forever – Death Cab for Cutie
Bad Habits – Ed Sheeran
Kiss Me Again – We Are The In Crowd
Want You Back – 5 Seconds of Summer
Amnesia – 5 Seconds of Summer
Ever Fallen in Love – Buzzcocks
Everytime We Touch – Electric Callboy
Remembering Sunday – All Time Low
I Can't Make You Love Me – Bon Iver
Want You Bad – The Offspring
If It Means A Lot To You – A Day To Remember
Mistakes We Knew We Were Making – Straylight Run
Breakeven – The Script

What's next?

Johnny's book is coming soon. It runs a similar timeline to this book. I hope you'll be looking forward to finding out what Johnny was up to.

Thanks for reading!

If you enjoyed this book, please consider leaving a review on Goodreads, Amazon, or sharing on your Social Media platforms.

About

Alys J. Clarke is the pen name of a British Author, who loves all things hockey. She lives in Wales with her husband and children and writes part-time.

To find out more, follow Alys on social media.
Instagram - @Alysjclarke
TikTok: @AlysJClarke
Facebook: Alys J. Clarke
www.alysjclarke.co.uk

Also by Alys J. Clarke

The Import Slot (2023)
The Tape Job (2024)
Johnny's book... (Title pending, coming soon)

Acknowledgements

The kindness of strangers has enabled the publication of this book; thank you to all who have helped and encouraged me.

My sincere thanks to my alpha readers, beta readers, volunteer editors, and ARC readers and a special mention to the following:

- Jess Potts and Amy Price—dealing with my 'READ THIS NOW' demands at random hours! Without you, The Tape Job wouldn't be where it is today.

- Caroline Taylor, for the art—and all my demands for art. And being a friend.

- Christina T for running the street team.

- Casey Garner for your help and support with all things ARC related and all the other bits!

- Lucy Lanceley, you are one of a kind and I cannot thank you enough for your help with my proofing. And the TikToks.

- Kel, for being my bookish bestie, the recommendations are always welcome!

- Members of #weloveBettsy—you guys <3

To every single reader who messages me with lovely comments. I am so grateful, and last but no means least, my husband—for everything.